BOOTS FOR THE GENTLEMAN

AUGUST LI AND EON DE BEAUMONT

Steamcraft and Sorcery Book One

Dreamspinner Press

Published by
DREAMSPINNER PRESS

5032 Capital Circle SW, Suite 2, PMB# 279, Tallahassee, FL 32305-7886 USA
http://www.dreamspinnerpress.com/

Cover Art
© 2011 Anne Cain.
annecain.art@gmail.com
Cover Design by Mara McKennen.

ISBN: 978-1-63216-633-3
Digital ISBN: 978-1-63216-634-0
Library of Congress Control Number: 2014947751
Second Edition August 2014
First Edition published by Dreamspinner Press, August 2011

Printed in the United States of America
∞
This paper meets the requirements of
ANSI/NISO Z39.48-1992 (Permanence of Paper).

This book is lovingly dedicated to the most important and inspirational person in my life, my dad, Ralph Paul. Thanks for teaching me to never give up and to always keep fighting, no matter what the odds.

Also for my cats, Merlin and Morgan, who keep me company faithfully while I work.

Gus

To Terry Gilliam for introducing me to the steampunk genre before I even knew it had a name. Thank you, sir.

Eon

CHAPTER 1

THE PERFECT summer evening practically insisted that a ball be thrown. Lord and Lady Merriwether found themselves unable to argue with the merry weather and organized the event. It looked like a lovely party. The many sets of doors stood open, allowing guests to float from the ballroom to the terrace overlooking the gardens. Soft music played inside, and bouquets of roses and topiaries decorated the entire space. Floral perfume and savory cooking smells rose into the night. Black-clad waiters moved among the gentlemen in top hats and fine suits and the ladies in dazzling gowns, offering champagne and hors d'oeuvres from silver trays. Polished silverware twinkled in the candlelight. Guests drifted like weather balloons, buoyant with good spirits, oblivious to strife, laughing and clinking their glasses together in the carefree manner of only the very wealthy. They greeted one another, conversed lightly, and even engaged in subtle flirtation.

Unfortunately for Querrilous Knotte, perched thirty feet above on a stone windowsill, his escape route lay at the other end of said terrace. Hours earlier, when he'd scaled the wall and made his way to the attic, only a few servants had moved within Merriwether Manor. It had taken him almost forever to secure the item his client had requested among the hundreds of trunks and crates, and, admittedly, he'd spent some time locating a few choice trinkets for himself. Holding the window frame for support, he leaned forward and swore.

There must have been a hundred people. A few times, one of the merrymakers strayed dangerously close to Querry's grapple. The forked end still stuck in the limestone next to his toe, and he could only hope none of the partygoers would notice something that resembled a complex metal crossbow hanging from the wall.

He looked back over his shoulder, into the musty dark. His stomach rumbled loudly, as if to remind him why he needed to succeed. He wound the little gear over his temple, changing the lens of his oversized goggles. Though Anglican law outlawed enchantment, one could still procure magical items, like the ensorceled glass, if one knew where to look. Blackness became grainy gray-greens as the disks clicked into place. Beyond the wardrobes, disembodied dresses, and hatboxes piled up like classical columns, Querry saw a small door, doubtfully locked. Maybe he could sneak back through the house. Likely, most everyone would be distracted by the party. He hated the idea, though. Among the city's twisting alleyways and across its rooftops, he could lose a pursuer. Inside, he could become trapped. There was nothing for it but to run. He preferred to take his chances in the open air.

Pivoting on the ledge, Querry gripped the stone and pushed with the ball of his foot. No one shouted; no one noticed his body drop down. His right hand let go of the thin rectangle of stone and groped for the rope. He pulled it to him and pinched it between his knees. Next came the scary second of releasing the ledge, swinging over, and hoping his hook held his weight. It did, and Querry inched down a few feet. A couple dozen people still milled about the terrace. Dressed for work as he was, in a reinforced leather waistcoat with four buckles up the front, matching knee-high boots and elbow-length gloves, his clunky mechanical goggles and a secondhand sea admiral's coat with long tails and rows of brass buttons, not even the nice-looking and charismatic young thief would be able to explain away his presence, not even if he stripped down to nothing but his trousers, white shirt, and striped cravat. These people would know he didn't belong. *There was something about the aristocracy*, Querry'd always thought. *They could smell their own.* He would never insinuate himself into their world; he might as well have been a different species.

Of course, there was also the presence of Querry's twin clockwork pistols, their holsters hanging from a belt, and his rapier, dangling from a thinner strip of leather. And there was the large canvas sack tied to a third belt.

Slowly Querry descended, until when the opportunity arose, he could make a safe drop and sprint for the rose trellis. From this proximity, he could hear the conversations of the partygoers. He rolled his eyes as they jabbered on and on about the latest fashions, new devices that would make their already-pampered lives even easier, and which slightly richer and more important people they counted among their friends. Men discussed hunting and the stock market while women talked of gloves and hats. On and on they prattled about the foreigners and their filthy customs, corrupting decent society. This was the latest fashionable topic. "Shouldn't they be driven out or at least sequestered to their own part of town?"

"But don't those girls from Xiana just make the best scullery maids?"

"My native staff absolutely refuses to work with them. It's too bad, really; they're quite cheap."

"We are truly blessed to live in such an era of peace and prosperity."

The thief scoffed at that remark before he remembered to be quiet. Querry's muscles started to tremble. He had a great deal more strength in his slender body than one might think to look at him, but he was only human, and he'd been clinging to the rope for probably an hour. If he succumbed to fatigue and fell, it would go badly indeed.

Didn't they have anything better to do than just stand around, picking at their food and throwing away more than he ate in a week? His shoulders and biceps really hurt, and a cramp threatened his left hamstring.

"Damn," he whispered. This silly job had sounded so easy. Maybe he'd been overconfident. He'd put less time into planning his excursion than he normally did. He'd been hoping for some quick money, and maybe he'd been too hasty. All he knew was that he couldn't hold on much longer. He didn't even know if he had enough stamina left to climb back to the attic window and hide until the party dispersed.

"Oh, look," said a woman. "It's Lord Thimbleroy. I think he's going to speak."

The rest of the guests looked in the direction she pointed, before trotting off like summoned dogs.

Wasting no time, Querry let go of the rope. Limestone met the thick soles of his boots. He straightened, took a small knife from a pocket on his vest, and cut free his firing mechanism from the grappling rope. He quickly pulled a release lever and folded the slender steel arms back. As he ran, he shoved it down the back of his snug black pants. He lunged for the terrace wall, vaulted over, and almost missed the rose-covered lattice. He climbed fast, ignoring the few thorns that scraped his face. His thick leather gear protected the rest of his body. He'd be damned if they'd take him in for this. If he was to be caught, it would be for something glamorous, something big. Just as his feet touched grass, Querry heard a man yelling down.

"I say! You there—"

Querry ran through the labyrinthine array of hedges, statues, and fountains until he reached the garden gate. He heard more men yelling to one another, doors opening and servants entering the darkened grounds with lanterns. Querry hid himself behind a sculpted shrub until the small team had checked around the gate. He struggled not to give himself away by panting until they'd wandered back toward the house. As soon as he thought it safe, he pushed against the iron gate, cleaving in half the large, sculpted M. It opened with a pained creak, drawing the attention of those fumbling about the grounds. The golden bubbles of their lamps moved closer, converging on the thief. With a strong oath, Querry bolted across the lane toward the back of the nearest mansion. As he ran he pulled his grapple free, extended the arms, and situated a hooked bolt. Once he made it within range, he fired and quickly climbed to the little roof over the servant's entrance.

Wasting no time, Querry freed his hook, positioned it, and shot it again. It caught about six feet above the ivy-covered balcony of the next house. Querry pushed off with his feet and swung through the thick night air, soaring over the lawn that divided the two homes. Despite the danger, he absolutely adored the feeling: free, almost like flying. He nearly laughed out loud. His feet met the carved stone as lightly as a cat's, and Querry took aim at the next residence. Gliding quietly through the dark, he soon put half a mile between himself and his pursuers. Finally he felt safe enough to descend to the ground.

He tried to look casual as he strolled onto the cobblestone streets. Still, he couldn't stay long in this part of town. It belonged to the wealthy. His presence wouldn't be tolerated (though a young woman passing by in a gilded carriage drawn by a jerky clockwork unicorn seemed to approve), and while the police might not arrest him just for breathing the same air as the privileged, they'd give him a good enough beating to send him back where he belonged. Hopefully they wouldn't check his pockets.

Luckily for Querry, the streets were relatively empty. *Probably some sort of holiday*, he thought. The rich got so many more holidays. A few coaches, both horse-drawn and steam-powered, passed him without incident as he made his way from the rich, residential district toward the expensive shops and eateries that lay a little ways to the south. He pushed his goggles down around his neck and walked with his eyes to the ground. The midnight-blue seamen's coat mostly hid his weaponry as he crossed Leopold's Folly Square. Halcyon's wealthy loved the massive clock tower that stood at its center, rising higher into the smoggy sky than the spire of any cathedral, or even the royal palace. At the top, an amazing clockwork menagerie of mythical creatures stood frozen. Something had gone wrong with the clock a century ago, and no one but the mad genius who'd built it held the knowledge to repair it, so the dozens of jeweled and gilded gryphons, mermaids, nymphs, and dragons, which could move as if alive when working, stood idle. Even now, Querry saw pulleys, scaffolding, and hot air balloons around the apex, as Lord Thimbleroy invested huge sums to repair the clock "as a point of patriotism and city pride." Every year some noble or another dedicated another statue, adding it to the ring surrounding the tower. A veritable army of bronze heroes and goddesses flanked the entire square.

Useless and expensive, Querry thought as he passed the empty benches. *That's why they love it so much.* He cut quickly through East Elysium Park and hurried past more closed shops: florists, confectioners, book sellers, and haberdashers. Stands and tables that sold meat, fish, and vegetables during the day stood covered in white cloth. The houses around Querry changed from cut stone to clay brick. They grew smaller and closer together. Soon the gaslight that spilled from behind beveled glass gave way to sputtering, smoking tallow and then darkness. Modest, middle-class homes stood vacant and untouched for three city blocks, shunned even by gypsies, beggars, and the mad. Nature slowly reclaimed them—moss spread over the roofs, and ivy infiltrated the mortar. The grass and rushes grew to Querry's knees. He smelled sewage and chemical waste, indicating his approach to the river that bisected the city of Halcyon. His client's home was not far now.

WHILE THE entrance to Neroche fluctuated, Querry always found it somewhere beyond the modest homes of the city's merchants and craftsmen, right before the shabby neighborhoods that hunched along the riverbank, home mostly to Rajallah and Xianese. He knew he was close, not only because the residents of the area had fled their homes, but because his teeth felt like they vibrated in his mouth, like he chewed on a thin sheet of aluminum. A dizzying perfume of rose and lavender replaced the industrial fumes and the reek of rotting garbage. Sure enough, Querry saw the gateway up ahead, two trees whose branches had twisted together to form an arch more elaborate and beautiful than the most skilled artisan could produce with iron. Golden leaves drifted down and piled around the trunks. A soft glow emanated from the silvery bark. As he passed beneath their boughs, Querry's hand went instinctively to the hilt of his sword. No guards would bother him in this part of town, but Neroche held plenty of dangers all its own.

Neroche resembled any other upper-class neighborhood. Elegant stone houses, surrounded by vast lawns and gardens, lined the cobblestone streets. But the stone here, instead of being gray, was ivory flecked with gold. Like the trees, it pulsed with its own subtle luminescence. Something other than gas, something bluish and flickering, glowed from the streetlights. Once in a while the lights fluttered from one lamp to another. Close inspection of the buildings revealed things that just couldn't be: towers jutting at impossible angles and whole upper stories stretching out, supported by nothing underneath. Also, the structures changed. Querry would never get used to the way they rearranged themselves the second he wasn't looking. Whole streets inexplicably switched direction, or simply disappeared. It didn't matter how hard he tried to concentrate, he could never keep track of his location. But that was another aspect of Neroche, the faerie quarter. Just entering made one feel fuzzy and giddy, almost intoxicated. Querry had learned to suppress the sensation, but he'd still be glad to conclude his business and be off.

Night in Neroche was never quiet. Querry pushed his way past residents in clothing so fine that the partygoers he'd left earlier would drool with envy. For the most part they looked human. But, as with their homes, there was always something amiss: indigo hair, crimson irises, skin and features too smooth, pointed ears, or gracefully curling horns. Groups of musicians picked lutes and blew strange pipes and horns, the music adding to Querry's distraction. More unsightly goblins scuttled down alleyways or peered out of dark recesses.

Querry heard commotion from the branches of the many trees. He passed humans too. Some came to Neroche to peddle their wares. The faeries adored jewelry and glass baubles. One never knew what they might fancy. Merchants had made their fortunes selling the twist-off caps from ale bottles. Others, wan and staring, had fallen under the thrall of the place or one of its denizens, and had simply forgotten every other aspect of their lives. An alarming number of them languished along the walkways or swayed in the streets. They were why Lord Thimbleroy railed against the faeries every day in the Hall of Ancient Nobility. They, like the foreigners who'd come to the city as Her Majesty's Empire expanded, corrupted good citizens with their loose morals and bizarre practices. Worse yet, if a fey took a liking to a human man, woman, or child, he'd see nothing wrong in plucking it like a wildflower. The papers reported strange disappearances daily.

Most of the other nobles agreed the faeries should be driven out. They just ignored the fact that they had no means of accomplishing it. Unlike the foreign humans, the fey had the power to fight back.

Finally Querrilous saw the home of his employer. It stood on top of a hillock, a classical-style mansion surrounded by so many sapphire roses that it appeared to float on a cloud of blossoms. The flowers also lined the stone walkway that led to the temple-like abode. As Querry passed the abundant foliage, a swarm of thumb-length sprites, naked and glowing every color, rose from the leaves. He swatted them away with his gloved hand. They bit.

Querry ascended the many white steps and walked beneath columns practically covered in vines. He could have sworn the porch they supported had curved the last time he'd been here. Now it was straight and square. It was hard to say, though. Whenever he left Neroche, Querry always felt like he'd just woken from a dream. The details departed just as quickly too. Sometimes, from the corner of his eye, Querry swore the grand house resembled nothing so much as a white mound perforated by irregular holes, like those dug by badgers or rabbits.

Querry knocked on the door, and a hunched man reaching only to the thief's belt buckle opened it. He had greenish skin, a bald head, huge, bat-like ears, and a long, hooked nose. He wore a butler's suit and white gloves.

"Good evening, sir," the servant said. "The gentleman is expecting you. You'll find him in his study."

"And what floor?" Querry asked. Like everything here, it fluctuated.

"The third floor, sir. At the end of the hall."

"Thank you," Querry said, heading through the eerie gloom for the staircase. The dusky light that let him find his way came from the walls themselves. Still, he managed to get to the study. Inside, he found his client sitting behind a desk of pale wood. Books lined the walls, reaching dozens of feet high. Between the shelves, silk curtains hung open, revealing windows of beveled glass. A lightning-blue fire crackled in the hearth. Perched on the end of a brocade chaise, a nude young man plucked a silver harp. His skin and hair were white and his eyes deep violet. Shimmering wings flickered in and out of existence behind him. Though he should have been shocked by such a scandalous display, Querry had learned to ignore his employer's eccentricities.

8

"Ah, Mr. Knotte," said the man behind the desk as Querry entered the room. On cue, the pale harpist stood, bowed, and left the room. Querry watched his willowy, white body as he departed. The door shut softly behind him. "Please sit down."

Querry took one of the chairs facing his client. The gentleman rested his elbows on the desk and stretched his long fingers into an arch, tapping the tips together. "A successful evening as always, I presume?"

"Um, of course," Querry answered, reaching to untie the sack from his belt. The gentleman made it hard for him to think. He was stunning—waves of golden hair spilling over the shoulders of his mint, velvet blazer, sparkling emerald eyes, and an angular face that looked both soft and devastatingly masculine—handsome, even by fey standards. Querry could see the svelte line of the gentleman's long neck stretching toward prominent collarbones and a smooth chest that finally disappeared behind a thin silk shirt and paisley waistcoat with pearl buttons. Trying not to make eye contact, Querry passed him the bag.

"Excellent!" the gentleman said, clapping twice. Why he was so excited with another gentleman's old boots, or why he'd pay Querry twenty pounds to steal them when he could buy them for a few shillings, the thief had stopped trying to figure out. A growing pile of things the gentleman had commissioned Querry to burgle sat in the corner: a broken phonograph, a wooden box of old pencils, a cart wheel missing a few spokes, a porcelain doll with only one eye, a matching ladle and fork, a tangled wig, and a set of lace curtains. While the thief suspected himself to be a piece in some unfathomable game, twenty pounds was still twenty pounds.

"My payment," Querry said, feeling vulnerable. He'd started not to trust himself—his reactions and responses—and needed to leave. The helpless sensation came quicker each time he visited this house.

"Indeed, indeed," the gentleman said, opening a drawer and sliding a bag of coins across the desk.

Querry snatched them greedily, and found himself embarrassed by his desperation. "Nice doing business," he said, standing and extending his hand.

The gentleman just stared at his proffered palm. Then, slowly, he got to his feet and came around the front of the desk. His steps, the twist of his waist, and the movement of his hair mesmerized Querry. Querry wondered at how such simple gestures could contain such perfection. How could something as simple as a fingernail be so sublime? The two stood very close now. The gentleman's chest grazed Querry's shoulder. He smelled like crushed grass.

"What a fascinating creature you are," he said in a whisper. He reached up and traced the line of Querry's brow. The thief felt powerless to resist leaning into the touch. Querry's eyes fluttered shut. His breath faltered.

Get a hold of yourself—

"You're far too beautiful for a common thief." He stretched his neck, so that his floral breath washed Querry's cheek and his lips rustled Querry's hair, turning Querry's muscles to quivering porridge.

"I'm an exceptional thief," Querry said, fighting for lucidity. He should step away.

A musical giggle escaped the other man. Querry felt it reverberate up his spine. His pores contracted and his cock skipped. "Exceptional, certainly. Even more so, I'm certain, beneath this cumbersome gear and all of these silly machines. What are you like under there?" His fingers moved down Querry's face and neck, over his heart and to the buckles of his padded vest. He tapped them one by one, as if he tickled the keys of a piano. Querry felt the faerie's erection against the side of his thigh, next to his pistol. He felt himself turning to face the other against his will.

"You deserve fine, soft clothing. The best food and wines. Nights of revelry and dance. A life free from toil of any kind." The gentleman's hands went to Querry's hips, pulling their bodies together. Querry curved against him and let his head fall backward so that the gentleman could pull his cravat aside and kiss up his neck. Fire bloomed in his cheeks, and a tingle spread across his pelvis. "You could stay here with me. Would you like that?"

Yes! In that moment, it was all Querry wanted. Nothing else mattered beyond the gentleman's lips, his hair, and his body. Those sparkling eyes that, in spite of the acceptable clothing, the outward trappings of civility, betrayed something wild. Querry wanted to strip slowly and stretch out naked across the desk. He wanted to lie complacent while the gentleman used his body any way he chose. But he also knew that the desire would fade when he left this place. He knew it just as he knew that if he gave in to this lust, in time he'd stop dressing at all. He'd wander the halls nude. He'd stare out the window at the flowers for days on end. He'd forget his name, stop eating—

"No, I can't." He pulled away. Predictably, the gentleman looked at him with even greater awe. "I'm afraid I've got to be going."

The fey lifted his chin and feigned indifference. "If you must, then you must. My offer stands. And if you find yourself short on money, there's a house on the corner of Tinkerton Street that you may want to visit. Tinkerton Street and Grace Lane."

"You have another job for me?"

"No," the gentleman said, turning his back to the thief and resting his hand on the surface of the desk. "I have all that I require, for now."

"Then what—"

"I said, I have what I require."

Querry stood staring at the golden sheet of hair flowing over the gentleman's back, fighting down the urge to touch it. He knew better than to ask why his client suggested the address. He could tell when he was being toyed with. Later, free from the dizzying effects of Neroche and the gentleman, he could try to work it out. Now, though, he needed to leave or he never would.

QUERRY TOOK a taxi across the bridge and to the easternmost outskirts of the city. The chill in the air and the acrid stink of coal cleared Querry's head as he made his way past the huge, dark factories. Day and night, their great pistons hammered up and down, and their smokestacks spewed soot and steam. Hordes of filthy men, women, and children trudged to and from their eighteen-hour shifts, between the foundries and mills and the row houses the companies provided. This part of town was like a city unto itself, and Querry hated it, hated it even more than Neroche. Each district within bore the name of the product it turned out: Loomston made textiles, Sparksfield munitions, Seagrave parts for ships, and so on. Querry hurried away from the resentful stares of the workers, toward home.

Between the massive manufacturing district and the river, on the very edge of Halcyon, almost to the docks, a little piece of heaven called Rushport stood in the perpetual shadow of the factories. At one time a port and some innocuous rushes occupied this space, and they'd left their names, though they'd long ago been replaced by shoddy houses, cheap motels patronized only by the poorest of sailors, unlicensed dance halls, brothels, and taverns. Querry passed several buildings hung with red paper lanterns. Perfumed smoke drifted from behind their curtained doors. A young Auriental man, his head shaved except for a long braid, wearing only loose, silk pants and slippers, motioned Querry over. He was attractive, smooth, and svelte, with a sensual droop to his eyelids. The flower resin his people introduced to the city promised an escape from hunger, fear, pain, and desperation. Some compared it to a religious experience. Many in this part of town had given up everything to seek its solace. Quite a few of the well-off had done the same. The smoking dens on the west side of the river resembled exotic palaces in some cases. Querry stopped walking long enough to admire the man. Most found coupling with foreigners distasteful and improper; though nearly all of them considered Querry's choice of companionship unnatural. Their opinions wouldn't stop him from having a smoke against the chest of the lovely young man. But it was an illusion of happiness, a glamour the same as that offered by the gentleman. Querry shook his head and kept walking. He waved away some men passing out handbills.

Most everyone knew Querry here. Few of the many whores propositioned him, and most of the beggars left him alone. He walked in silence, stepping over drunks and the homeless, his hands in his pockets and his fists clutching the jewels from the attic and the twenty pound coins. Gangs of thugs wouldn't hesitate to outnumber and mug the thief, especially if they thought he'd been at work. Along the way, he stopped in one of the better pubs and bought a kidney pie, a piece of fried fish, and a pint of ale, carefully bringing out only a few pence as payment, and making sure the others didn't jingle.

"Home sweet home," Querry muttered as he entered his building and made his way to his room on the third floor. Just like he did outside, he stepped over the prone bodies that littered the hall, and looked away from the prostitutes conducting business in the stairwells. He unlocked the intricate series of clockwork locks he'd attached to his door and lit the single candle on the table. Loud yowling greeted him, and he unwrapped the fish filet and broke it in half for Tosser and Toerag, two foreign cats he'd rescued from being stoned to death by kids. Sometimes he cursed himself for bringing them home when he could barely feed himself, but they had lovely, dark brown ears and feet, smooth, fawn-colored coats, and deep blue eyes that resembled Querry's own. Plus, they guarded his closet-sized room as well as any bulldog, and they were just as mean.

When Querry sat on the edge of his narrow mattress, his knee touched the table with the broken leg. Various tools and gears covered the surface, as Querry continuously experimented with tinkering and worked to repair and improve his weapons, so the thief ate his meal from his lap. Then he unbuckled his gloves and wriggled them off. He'd been too hungry to bother before. Carefully he placed his weapons, gear, and plunder in a wooden chest, the only other piece of furniture he owned. He draped his shirt and trousers over the headboard. He'd need to wash them, and his body, in the copper basin. But it could wait for morning. Going into Neroche always exhausted Querry. He stretched out on his back and folded his arms beneath his dark hair.

Tomorrow, he could pay his rent. He could sell the jewelry he'd taken and probably earn enough to buy food for the next few weeks. He needed another candle, bullets for his pistols, and some steel tubing. He sighed and listened to the contented purr of the cats.

It could be worse, he told himself. He didn't have much, but he had a roof over his head and enough to eat. He had his freedom. At least he could say that nobody owned him, not gin nor a drug, nor the factories, nor the gentleman. To be able to say that was priceless.

CHAPTER 2

GAINING ACCESS to the royal archives proved much simpler than one would think. Even though Royal Guards stood at the entrance in their archaic breeches, hose, and lacy ruffs, all Querry had needed was an open window. He found one, and in no time stood among the musty books, documents, and scrolls.

Head down, he slinked among the stacks. The monarchy required permits of those who wished to study here. Querry supposed there were plenty of secrets they'd prefer to leave buried among the mountains of paper. He found the stairs and descended all the way to the lowest level, home of the oldest and rarest documents. No sun reached here. Fancy gas lamps affixed to the walls provided light and their familiar scent. The place reminded Querry of a tomb, silent and still. He searched about and soon realized the floor was arranged like a wheel. Long hallways formed by tall, wooden shelves met in the center. There, beneath a chandelier hanging from a chain, a young man worked at a desk.

Smiling, Querry watched for a few minutes as the man, with thick, dirty blond hair and oval spectacles, wrote with a quill pen. His right hand reached for the ink well as his left thumb made its way to his mouth.

"Still biting your nails?"

The young man dropped his hand like it had been slapped. He scanned the darkened corridors around him. After letting him go for a bit, Querry stepped into the light and approached the desk. A little brass plaque read "Reginald Whitney, Chief Royal Archivist."

"You can't be here, Querry," said the young man.

"And yet here I am."

"How did you get past the guards?"

"Easy."

"And what do you want?" the archivist asked, sounding both exasperated and exhausted.

"It's nice to see you, too, Reg."

"So, you just dropped in for a visit?" Reg asked, raising one shapely eyebrow.

Querry bit his lower lip and looked guiltily at his shoe.

"As I suspected," Reg said.

"I just need the tiniest favor," Querry replied. "Do you think you can help me?"

Reg sighed. "I know I owe you, Querry. All those years that you looked out for me in that hell hole they called an orphanage, and later when they shipped us off to that factory."

Damn, that hurt. It hurt so much, and so unexpectedly, that Querry's words fell unplanned from his lips. "You think I did that so you'd owe me later, Reg? I came here because I thought we were friends. Back then, in the workhouse and in the factory, I looked out for you because you were the only thing I had to live for. I—"

Now Reg looked away, ashamed. His skin shone pale in the gaslight, the dark under his hazel eyes accentuated.

"Have you been sleeping?" Querry asked.

Reg brightened a little, even forcing a smile. He slid his glasses down his nose, folded them, and slipped them into the breast pocket of his coat. "Mother hen, just like when we were boys."

"Are they keeping you here late?" Querry persisted.

"No, it's Mum and Dad. They're on me night and day about marrying. Apparently a royal archivist is good enough to wed an ugly daughter of the aristocracy. They finally see their chance to make it into the nobility. They've been setting me up with a different lady, and I use that term in the loosest possible sense, Querry, every night."

The idea of Reg marrying stirred long-dormant feelings in Querry. To his surprise, he was jealous. "Can't you just tell them you're not ready?"

Reg's shoulders curled forward. He met Querry's eyes and shook his head. "Querry, the Whitneys adopted me. They took me away from that hellish factory, sent me to University. They gave me a future. All Mum has ever wanted is to be among the nobility, to go to their parties and have tea with them. It's the one thing she can't buy, no matter how many cans of fish their factory cranks out. I have to do this."

"But!"

"It's life for most of us. Work, marry, raise a family."

"You're really willing to be the trophy husband of some inbred hag?"

"Why are you so upset?" Reg asked. "This is what people do. What other alternative do I have? A man lives alone too long, and people start to talk."

"What about our plan?" Querry asked. He remembered finishing a dinner of stale bread after a day of shoveling coal into a furnace, and going with Reg to their straw-stuffed mats. Looking at Reg now, he saw the soot streaks clearly. He remembered whispering, staying up late even though they'd both been exhausted, planning. Probably because they rarely saw the sky, they'd decided to become traders. They'd get a ship and sail to the remote corners of the Empire, procuring all manner of exotic goods. Night after night they had lain in each other's arms and fantasized about the places they'd visit. Freedom and fresh air were all they'd wanted, and to be together.

"It was a child's dream," Reg said sadly. "I'm sorry, Querry. Not all of us can live by our own rules."

Watching Reg, Querry remembered the texture of his skin, the way he tasted. He remembered how they'd had to be quiet as they touched and fondled and explored, lest the other factory workers hear. During that horrible time, they'd been each other's only comfort. Now, maybe irrationally, Querry felt betrayed.

"What is it that you wanted?" Reg asked. Querry thought he heard regret in his friend's voice.

"Just some records. Anything you have on the house on the corner of Tinkerton and Grace Lane. A floor plan would be perfect."

"Why that house?" Reg said, shocked.

"What? Why do you ask?"

"Because! The Grande Chancellor requested records on that property this morning. I don't care for him, so I told him they'd take a few days to locate. And then a few hours ago, the Duchess of Lisine asked for the same records. I have them right here. What's so special about that house?"

"I have no idea," Querry said. "I walked by it on my way here today. It's not in a nice part of town, but it may have been a decent house at one time. It has one of those old stone chimneys in the front, and a big stained glass window. Broken now, though. The roof's caved in, and the thatch is gone, too, and the garden's completely overgrown with weeds. It's falling apart."

"What do you want with it?"

"Curiosity. One of my clients mentioned it. It was just so random of a thing for him to say." Querry didn't expound upon how he felt like a dog following a man with a bucket of innards. He didn't like being manipulated, but he'd reached the point where he had to know. What did those uppity aristocrats want with it? It could be a cute little place, if somebody fixed it up, but certainly not worthy of a duchess.

"What client?" Reg asked. "Not the faeries again?"

Querry said nothing, but Reg knew his expressions too well.

"Querry, how could you? They're dangerous! They aren't like us. They don't care who they hurt."

"They care," Querry said. "They just change their minds a lot. But don't worry. I know how to handle them. So, a faerie gentleman, the Duchess of Lisine, and Lord Thimbleroy. This just gets more intriguing."

"Well, if the Grande Chancellor wants the house, the duchess will try to stop him. She just doesn't like him. They argue in the Hall of Nobility every day about spending city taxes on the clock tower, and about foreigner's rights. I've heard that it gets pretty heated. Raised voices and personal insults."

"So she just wants to thwart Lord Thimbleroy," Querry mused. "But what about my gentleman?"

"*Your* gentleman might just want to thwart him too. Lord Thimbleroy is the leading voice in favor of faerie eradication."

"No," Querry said. "It isn't like that. They really don't care. If they did, they'd just kill him."

They sat thinking for a long time, until finally Querry said, "So tell me what you know about the place."

"That's just the thing," Reg said. "The place is nothing special, just like you said. It was built a little over a hundred years ago and belonged to a doll maker and his family. His wife and daughter died during the plague, and he died fifty years later. He bequeathed the property to an illegitimate son, who never showed up to claim it. It's been empty ever since."

"So it's been abandoned for half a century or so, and all of the sudden everyone's interested? Why?"

Reg shrugged. "It doesn't make any sense. The man made toys. Elaborate ones, with some of the first clockwork parts, but still just playthings for spoiled children."

"Floor plan?" Querry asked.

"Sorry," Reg said. "I guess nobody thought it was that important."

"But it must be," Querry said. "There must be something there. Something valuable."

"I don't see how there could be," Reg answered. "It would have been looted a long time ago."

"Something's going on."

"I have to admit, I'm curious now too," Reg said, brushing his fringe away from his forehead. "I'm sure you'll break in?"

"I don't know if you can call it breaking in," Querry said, feigning innocence. "But I'll have a look."

"I'll keep my ears open here." Reg looked up. When their eyes met, Querry noticed the old conspiratorial gleam. Reg hoped something would happen, an adventure like they'd fantasized about as boys, something that might save him from his predetermined future and dull occupation. Maybe he still carried hope for the two of them, but Querry didn't know for sure.

"We should get together," Querry said. He couldn't help it. For a minute, he'd seen his old Reg again, and that glimpse towed behind it a host of other images. Watching Reg's face in the low light, Querry could picture his cheeks darkening, his full lips falling open, and the little crease forming between his brows. He saw Reg throw his head back and bite his lower lip to stay quiet.

"Why are you looking at me like that?"

"I miss you," Querry admitted. "Could we go somewhere? I have a little money."

"Querry, we've talked about this. We can't."

"Why?"

"It just isn't done. I know that never stops you from anything, but if anyone found out the Whitneys would be ruined. Those few times we met in secret were dangerous enough. Consorting in public is out of the question."

"Don't want any of your rich friends to see you slumming?"

"You know that's not what I mean. I don't feel that way and never have!"

"In private then," Querry said. "Tell me where."

"I have an engagement tonight. The fair daughter of Baron Cackleberry."

Querry strode to the desk and grabbed Reg by the back of the neck, remembering all too well that his friend enjoyed a little force. He leaned in until their noses touched tip to tip. Sure enough, he saw a line of sweat sparkling above Reg's lip, heard the urgency of his breath. "You still want me, don't say you don't."

"Querry, I—"

"I know you're grateful to your family, but it's still your life, Reg."

"We can't. Please let me go, Querry. You're just making it worse."

Dejected, Querry let go. How amazing Reg's hair had felt against his knuckles. More than anything, he wanted to grab a handful of those wheat-colored locks and pull their faces together. He wanted to feel Reggie's bee-stung lips slide against his, then open slowly to his advances. He wanted to hold him by the back of the head and kiss him until his mouth swelled and he choked for air. And, looking across the desk, he saw that Reg wanted it too. Querry cursed at the world, the rigid social order that had stolen away the only thing he'd ever loved. They'd planned a future, no matter how fantastical, but life shattered it all.

"I can't accept this," Querry said.

Reg smiled a smile so full of understanding and lament that Querry had to turn away. "Of course you can't," he said, in the soft, slow voice he used after love. "It's your nature not to accept. You've never been any different. If you decide you want a sunny afternoon, you'll rail against the rain clouds."

"You make it sound so hopeless."

"After a while it's just too exhausting to fight against everything. We've got to take what we're given. If it rains, it's easier to put your umbrella up than to curse at the sky."

"We never believed that! We said we'd make our own way!"

"We were just boys. We didn't know any better."

The defeat in Reg's voice halted Querry's argument. He sounded like an old man, his life done and over. What had happened to the hope they'd been able to muster, even in the worst of times? Was this what they called good fortune?

"But you'll let me know if you hear anything about that house?" Querry said, trying to salvage the conversation.

"Sure, Querry," Reg said, without meeting his gaze. "But I don't think you should come back here anymore."

A MIX of light rain and mist blanketed Rushport, rising from the river and mingling with the industrial fumes. It stung Querry's eyes and bit his lungs when he inhaled. People only a block away looked ghostly, their feet lost to the fog. Querry's unruly, black hair glistened with acidic droplets. He'd been thinking too much: about Reg, society and class, luck and destiny. Why should it be that one person was born to wealth and comfort, while he and Reg had drawn a place in a workhouse that many never survived to leave? Some of the Rajallah in town believed that each person was reborn again and again, and that the deeds of his past life affected his lot in the next. Querry wished he could subscribe to it. If he thought he deserved this hardship, maybe he could accept it. But in his heart, he knew it came down to dumb luck.

If he'd wanted companionship, Querry knew of plenty of places to buy it. He could also find it for free not far from his neighborhood, in the public houses along the little cul-de-sac called Lickwhistle Circle. Men who shared his tastes frequented those taverns, and with his youth, looks, and charm, Querry could have his choice. Tonight, though, an accommodating body would not be enough.

He wanted a bottle of absinthe, and figured he could sell enough of the jewelry he'd stolen to afford one. An old, Gypsy woman at the Iron Vine Tavern would likely take it off his hands at a decent price.

Maybe it was because Reg, smaller and more timid, had it tougher in the workhouse and the factory than Querry. Or maybe tasting wealth and security made it more frightening to give up. Querry had nothing, and nothing to lose. But why the change? When he'd first gone to live at Whitney Manor, Reg sneaked away to see Querry every chance he got. They met in cheap inns, or on the street when Querry couldn't pickpocket enough for a room. Years in the factory, with the other workers slumbering drunkenly a few feet off, had taught them to touch discreetly. Did Reggie really believe in the course chosen for him, or had he just given up? Either way, Querry didn't want to think about it anymore, couldn't stand to think about it anymore. He wanted to seek the company of the Green Faerie and succumb to the pleasant apathy she would provide. Even Querry needed one night empty of struggle. He'd nearly made it to the pub; he could hear the raucous voices within and smell the greasy odor of questionable meat.

"You there. Pretty boy."

The fine hair stood up on the back of Querry's neck, and he turned slowly toward the alley and the voice.

"You'll be wanting to take your hand away from that sword."

There were five of them, all built like bulls and smelling just as pleasant. The speaker wore a much-mended top hat and an eye patch, and held one of the big, curved knives popular in the colonies. His tongue flicked out between his misaligned teeth and touched the tip of the blade. "What have we here?" he said.

"Looks to me like a cat burglar who ain't paid his monthly dues to the Cat Burglar's Union," said a big man in a leather helmet with spiked goggles over top.

"What?" Querry spat. They moved closer, circling him like vultures. He wished he'd had his guns, but until he sold the jewelry he didn't have the money to spare on bullets. He hadn't been expecting trouble.

"Ain't you heard?" said the man in the top hat, his dagger glinting. "To ensure safe and fair working conditions. Just like the Lady Duchess wants in them mills."

Querry's eyes darted everywhere, seeking escape. Grinning and chuckling, the thugs closed in on him. Running would be impossible.

"Ten pounds," snarled a bald man. His rancid breath struck Querry in the face like a fist, making him gag and turn away.

"How am I supposed to get that?" he asked through gritted teeth.

"Go and ask the faeries." All of them shared a laugh. Then the one in the top hat said, "We'll be needing a down payment. A show of good faith."

"I haven't got anything!"

"Ain't that too bad?"

"Terrible, ain't it?" They laughed again.

Querry cursed himself for letting Reg distract him to this degree. It wasn't like him to stumble into dark pockets. Normally his sharpened senses detected any hint of danger. But he'd been so wrapped up in his thoughts that he'd walked right into this. Now he had to figure a way out, and quickly.

"Let this serve as a reminder." The thug swung his knife at Querry's cheek, but the more agile thief stepped to the side and dodged. The man reeled forward, off balance, and his hat fell off. Seeing his chance, Querry shoved his doubled body to the side and bolted for the opening.

He only gained a few steps before a set of big, hairy arms caught each of his elbows, snapping him back. The two men held him as their leader pushed himself up from where he'd landed. Slowly and carefully, he replaced his headwear and picked up his weapon. Querry struggled, and his captors yanked his arms back hard, straining his shoulder sockets.

The man in the top hat grinned as he approached Querry. He drew back and punched Querry hard in the stomach, making the thief glad he hadn't yet eaten. Only a mouthful of bile splattered the cobblestone. Then his fist struck Querry's diaphragm, stopping his breath. The thug hit him again and again as he choked and sputtered, fighting through dizziness to stay on his feet.

Blows rained down on Querry's waist and torso. He couldn't protect himself or fight back, couldn't even crumple in half like his body told him he should. One after another, agonizing hits landed on his already screaming sides. He felt the sharp stab of a rib cracking, and he cried out. The stinking men who held him chortled.

Finally the assault ended. Elbows released, Querry fell to his knees, then on to his side. As he panted, trying to recover his wind, the dirty hands of the thugs searched his pockets.

"The little bugger was holding out," said one of them, his fingers digging into Querry's coat pocket and closing around the pound coins and jewelry within. Weakly Querry tried to grab his wrist. He needed that money. But the man struck him in the shoulder, flipping him to his back and making his head smack against the hard street. White fuzz erupted in his skull.

"Take that sword," instructed a garbled, far-off voice.

"No," he tried to whimper, but no sound came out. A knife severed the leather strap over his hip.

Blurry, dark masses looked down at him now. Querry couldn't even try to move, couldn't even focus his eyes.

"Ten pounds next time," said the leader. "Or I cut that pretty face. Filthy faerie-lover."

They ran off, laughing. A few minutes later a whore, reeking of sex and cheap perfume, knelt to scavenge Querry's pockets again.

Finding nothing, she cursed him and staggered away, holding the hem of her skirts up from the rubbish on the street.

Querry lay on the wet ground among the garbage until he could muster enough concentration and breath to haul himself up and limp back to his room.

CHAPTER 3

FOOTPRINTS THROUGH the thick dust on the floor told Querry a sizeable team had recently searched the dilapidated little house. They'd left a series of overlapping trails, as well as squares and circles where they'd likely placed equipment. If they'd found anything, they'd taken it with them. Only empty bottles and trash filled the main room now. Squatters had scrolled all manner of obscenities across the walls over the years. Barely a square foot had escaped without a badly spelled insult or explicit drawing.

Querry stepped into the huge, stone fireplace. Chicken bones, or maybe pigeon, crunched beneath his boots. Carefully, an inch at a time, he felt along the inside of the chimney for a latch or mechanism that might indicate a secret passageway or compartment of some kind. Soot darkened his gloves and sprinkled the lenses of his goggles. Through the special glass he scrutinized the surface of every stone until he felt certain he hadn't missed anything. Then he emerged from the hearth and sneezed.

Dusting himself off, Querry went up the rickety stairs to search the second floor a third time. Though he'd been all through the house, he knew he had to be overlooking something. Lord Thimbleroy and the duchess possessed teams of experts and expensive gauges and sensors, but they lacked the instincts of a thief. Querry could almost feel the presence of something valuable, a chest of money beneath the floorboards or hidden in the wall, maybe. He needed to find it. His assault two nights ago had left him depleted of funds. He hadn't eaten since, and the cats were left to hunt the plentiful rats of Rushport's alleys. Taking a shallow breath, mindful of his ribs, Querry entered the first of the three upper rooms.

It had probably been a bedchamber: small and square with a little window and recessed closet. Graffiti covered it now. Someone had relieved himself in the corner, and someone else left half a bottle of ale. The stump of a cigar floated within. Querry began the tedious process of tapping the walls. As he did, he held a curling, metal horn to his ear to amplify any irregularities. Once he thought he detected something and broke away the plaster, only to find the bricks worn away, exposing the timber supports.

Next he checked the floor, inspecting every plank. Even in the old place, none of them had come loose. Back then, craftsmen, rather than factories, made things, and they lasted. Finding nothing yet again, Querry checked the remainder of the second floor. Then he went back downstairs.

It was just a simple, middle-class home: bedrooms upstairs, sitting room, kitchen, and a storage room beneath. Normally Querry wouldn't waste his time plundering such a house. How could the faerie gentleman even care to know the place existed? What could Lord Thimbleroy or the duchess hope to find here?

"Damn," he hissed, frustrated. He'd spent most of the day searching. If he left empty-handed, it meant an empty stomach. He hated to ask Reg for a loan, after all those years in the orphanage, promising to take care of him. Spinning on his heel, Querry thrust his hands into his coat pockets and paced to the missing front door where he kicked the skeleton of an umbrella into the front yard. He pivoted again and strode all the way to the cold storage space beyond the kitchen, at the other end of the structure. Walking back and forth, he tried to think of anything he might have missed. He stopped in front of the blank, windowless stone wall. There was nothing here. Irritated, Querry pounded his fists against the stone. Immediately his bruised torso protested, and he winced and held his sides.

It occurred to him then that the room seemed too narrow. To test the theory, he hurried outside and around the side of the house. It definitely looked longer without than within. He felt certain that the storage room should be double its size. Ignoring the pain in his ribs and belly, he sprinted back inside and stood staring at the wall, made from the same gray stone as the chimney and then bricked over on the exterior. Something waited beyond it: another small, secret room. One by one, Querry pressed each of the stones. Nothing happened. He tried pressing them in different combinations. Again, nothing. Exasperated, Querry stepped back to look at the wall again. His eyes searched the surface for something, anything that might give him a clue to opening it. Just below the ceiling he finally picked out an irregularity: a tiny hole in one stone. Following the line of the ceiling he spotted another a few inches away. This had to be it. There were seven in all. Querry fished around in his jacket and found a ten penny nail. He fit it into the first hole and tried applying pressure at various angles. He pulled the nail toward the floor and heard an audible click.

A smile broke across Querry's face as he removed the nail and fit it into the next hole. Another click sounded. This lock operated on the same system as the one he'd built to protect his room: the pins had to be pushed into the tumblers in a specific order. Leaning closer, Querry listened and visualized the mechanisms within the stone. Subtleties of the sounds they made told him if the pins had clicked into place. He used the nail in each of the seven holes and stood back. Nothing happened. "What? Why?" Querry paced back and forth in front of the wall, fist balled against his mouth. This was it, the solution, but why didn't it open? He tried the locks in reverse. Nothing. "Some combination?" he asked the empty room. He tried every other lock and then the ones he skipped. Still nothing! This was maddening! Listening more carefully, Querry heard some of the pins slipping free as others snapped into place. For every one he managed to secure, another knocked loose, and no combination prevented it. Querry paced furiously, trying desperately to find the solution. He stopped abruptly as the thought occurred. "Oh! Of course!" He dashed outside and retrieved the decrepit umbrella. He quickly bent the spine into something that resembled a fork and placed one rib in each hole. Querry breathed deeply and then pulled the handle toward the floor. Simultaneously all seven locks clicked.

Querry stood amazed as the wall slid away. He heard gears and pulleys working somewhere out of sight to retract the heavy slab of stone. Slowly it sunk into the floor, revealing a thin corridor with a set of steps at the end. Beyond the first three, Querry saw only darkness. From an inside pocket, he took a small glass cylinder on a chain. Flammable oil filled the lower half. Querry unscrewed the metal lid and lit the wick with a wooden match. Then, carefully, his every muscle tensed and hurting, he descended into the black.

Far below the house, probably three or four stories down, Querry came to a metal door. He tried the handle and found it locked, of course, so he took out his picks and set to work. Some rust and damaged mechanisms impeded his progress, along with low visibility, but he'd always had a natural affinity for deciphering clockwork and had spent his childhood learning about it from anyone who would teach him, and in a quarter of an hour he heard the final gear click into place. He turned the handle, and the door creaked loudly as it swung open. Querry heard a loud snap from the ceiling followed by the rush of something heavy, and had only a moment to dodge the giant iron mallet that swooped through the space he'd occupied only seconds ago. The mallet dangled limply now and from the spot on the floor where he'd rolled, Querry could see the mechanism above the door that released it.

Interesting, Querry thought. *A locked door with a backup trap.* He smiled, reassured that something valuable lay ahead of him. No one went to this much trouble to protect nothing. He picked his way slowly along a short corridor, choosing his steps carefully. All the tiles along the floor looked identical but the thief wasn't taking any chances. He tried to detect any irregularity in the tile ahead when the one beneath his foot sank an inch into the floor with an ominous, grinding tick. He heard gears moving in the walls on either side. Querry looked at the walls and detected thin canals just below eye level. Without thinking he dropped to the floor and watched as two crescent-shaped blades slid from the ducts, slashing in opposite directions. Querry reached up and touched his neck without realizing he'd done it. Were he still standing his hand would not have found his head in the proper spot. He rose slowly, his situation growing much more serious. Someone thought something down here wasn't just worth protecting, but worth killing for.

Querry held his breath as he took another tentative step. His eye caught a gleam near the floor: a trip wire. The thief lay on his belly and cut the wire. Jets of flame burst from the ceiling and walls, focusing on the point where the target would have triggered the trap. Querry shook his head and crossed the remainder of the corridor to the opposite door without incident. The door was simple. Querry tried the handle, expecting resistance, and found none. It occurred to him that whoever designed these traps didn't expect anyone to make it this far so there was no need for this door to be locked. Slowly, suspiciously, Querry turned the knob until he heard the faintest of clicks. Nothing waited beyond except a small, empty room. Gently Querry released the knob and looked for an alternate means of entrance. He spotted it high on the wall: a tiny hole like the ones upstairs. He stuck his finger in and felt the familiar lever. Querry flipped the tumbler up and found himself slipping through a trap door and sliding down a chute.

The tube deposited him on the floor of a room just below the corridor. The chamber smelled of damp earth, oil, and metal. It was cold so far below the ground. By the light of the oil lamp, Querry saw several long tables, some affixed with drill presses and vice grips. Piles of gears and metal pieces sat stacked on top, covered in dust and cobwebs. He crept along the perimeter of the room, examining what he found. Most of it looked worthless: spools of tarnished wire, shapes cut from sheet metal, incomplete mechanisms of unknown purpose, something that looked like an eggbeater. A shelf held a variety of obscure liquids in glass vials. Scattered over the floor, clinking as Querry's feet waded through them, were more discarded gears and metal bits. In a corner lay a construct that too closely resembled a rib cage, and Querry shuddered.

On the wall Querry found the skeleton of a large fish, only forged in iron. He could see where, when wound, complex clockwork would enable it to move its tail and fins. If covered, it could make a marvelous toy, but Querry didn't think he'd be able to sell it unfinished. Beyond, dangling from pegs, were about two dozen tiny metal wings, each feather cast in incredible detail that made Querry's breath catch in his throat. Even so, they wouldn't put coins in his pockets, so he continued his trek through the darkness. He passed a half-finished dragon head, the left side covered in blue steel scales. Opening a wooden case, he found a dozen different eyeballs resting on a scrap of black velvet. A skinned human arm, the bones, tendons and sinew perfectly replicated by metal tubes and wiring made Querry clap a hand over his mouth. He squinted into the darkness, eager to find his prize and leave this place behind. A strange silhouette appeared a few feet ahead. It looked like a human form sitting on a bench, its hands folded in its lap and its head down. Cautiously, Querry approached.

Decades worth of dust coated the most magnificent doll Querry had ever seen. Nothing distinguished it from a beautiful young man, except that the face looked a little too perfect, in the way that some faeries appeared. But the full, bow-shaped lips looked soft, fleshy. Somehow each strand of hair had been produced and shaped into loose, ringlet curls. Leaning closer, fascinated, Querry saw that the doll maker had even formed each eyelash individually. The eyelids above them creased like real skin. The artist had dressed his creation in finery a century old: blue satin breeches and hose, a gauzy blouse with a high neck and ruffles surrounding the face like a blooming flower, little slippers topped with bows. At the ends of the fingers resting over a large, leather-bound book, clear nails caught the firelight.

It looked human, astoundingly so, a masterpiece. But what was Querry supposed to do with it? Finding a buyer would be a challenge, if he could even lift it. Could this really be what the gentleman meant? If he wanted it, why not just hire Querry to fetch the thing? If he wanted it, why not wave his pretty hand and make it appear beside him?

Holding the lamp-chain in his teeth, Querry picked apart the buckles of his right glove and pulled it off a finger at a time. With his thumb, he cleared a line of dust away from the doll's cheek. It even felt like real skin, and, under the accumulation of gray, blushed a subtle rose. The whole thing reminded Querry of a winged, adolescent love god painted by one of the old masters. He'd seen such subtly sensual portraits hanging in the houses of the wealthy while at work, and this doll held the same innocent appeal in its slender limbs and round face. Perplexed, Querry could only stare and marvel over the detail while he wondered how he might benefit from his discovery.

As he watched, the doll's eyelids fluttered. A soft hum came from within it, and its fingers began to move, not with the choppy motion of most clockwork, but with complete fluidity. Its eyes opened, revealing stunning golden irises that darted back and forth. The corners of the mouth curled up. It was smiling.

"Hello," it said, in a voice as idealized as the rest of it.

"Uh, hello...."

As the doll stood, nothing betrayed its mechanical nature. No one watching would have been able to distinguish it from a real boy as it tucked its book under its arm and looked expectantly at Querry. Every few seconds, it blinked.

"Do you have a name?" Querry asked. It occurred to him that he conversed with an inanimate object, but it felt like the right thing to say.

"Name?"

Touching his chest, he said, "My name is Querrilous Knotte, but that's kind of a mouthful, so most people just call me Querry."

"Keh-ree," the doll repeated.

"What are you called?"

It looked confused, brows knitting and lower lip jutting out. If it hadn't been a machine, Querry would have said it looked damned adorable.

"Well, that's all right," he said instead. "How long have you been here?"

"I've always been here."

"Do you know if there's money, or anything valuable, hidden down here?"

"What's money?"

"Coins? Jewelry?"

The doll shot him the cute, bewildered look again. The two of them regarded one another for many minutes as Querry decided the best course of action. Eventually he said, "I guess I'll be going."

He turned and started his way across the cluttered room. To his surprise, the doll followed him. Stopping, he faced it, ready to tell it to remain. But it looked so broken, so tragic, that Querry's words caught in his throat.

"I," it said, touching its chest as if aware, for the first time, of itself, "I feel—"

"Feel?" Querry stammered. This was just not possible. To mimic life, perhaps, but to create emotion—

"I feel—I am alone here."

"Lonely?" Querry asked, incredulous. "You're lonely?"

"I think—Yes."

"Well, you can't come with me."

"Why?"

"I—" Querry wanted to say that he had no use for a doll, but as he looked into its large, sad eyes, he couldn't bring himself to say it. "I need you to wait here, while I check that there's nobody upstairs."

The doll nodded, and Querry left it behind in the dark. When he'd made his way back to the storage room, he considered just escaping. But he told himself that the doll might be what Lord Thimbleroy wanted. It seemed absurd, but one never knew with aristocrats. Maybe Querry could still make a profit. And in the end, Querry just knew too well how it hurt to be cast aside. He checked the house and the street beyond. Satisfied that they wouldn't be seen leaving, he returned to the cellar workroom to fetch the doll and guide him past the traps meant to protect him.

IN THE orange light of sunset, Querry watched the doll walking beside him: silvery hair and skin coated in grime, except for a streak of peach-pink on its right cheek. Every tree stump, fence, and dumpster filled his gorgeous eyes with astonished delight. They'd kept to the back alleys, since the doll would certainly attract attention in his antique costume. Now that they'd made it to Rushport, Querry considered his predicament. He still had no money. The smells wafting from the taverns and stalls made him salivate. Since the doll was with him, he couldn't fall back on finding a crowd and cutting purses. Its beauty would be too much of a disturbance.

"Hello, darling," said a whore with bright red curls and a cheap, velvet frock to match. She stroked the doll's cheek and positioned her bulging chest at his chin.

"Hands off, Jane," Querry warned, stepping around and putting himself between the doll and the whore.

She held her lace-gloved hands up. "Sorry, Querry. I didn't see you there, and I'm just trying to put food in me mouth, ain't I?"

Querry guided his awe-struck companion away by his elbow. The first gaggle of Rushport beggars appeared on the corner, calling out, "I'm sick and I'm hungry. Anything, please. Take pity on us. I lost my eyes in the foundry."

"A crust of bread, please! An infection in Rajallah took my feet."

The doll stopped. "Querry," it said, touching his arm lightly. "Those people are hungry."

"So am I."

Eyes wide with surprise, the doll walked straight to the nearest kiosk and picked up a loaf of bread. Then he walked back toward Querry, with the attendant following.

"What the hell do you think you're doing?" the red-faced, chubby baker shouted. "You got to pay for that!"

On the street, people stopped walking and turned toward the commotion. Quickly Querry snatched the bread from the doll and returned it to the shopkeeper, saying, "Please forgive my cousin. He was born simple." Then he grasped the doll's hand and pulled him away from where he stood with that bemused expression on his dirty face.

Walking fast, Querry succeeded in getting away before the two of them attracted curiosity. They made it to his building without further incident, though the doll talked the entire time.

"If that man had food, why wouldn't he give it to people who are hungry?"

"You have to pay for it," Querry said. "You mustn't do that again. You can't take things. At least not when you'll get caught."

"But why?"

"It's just the way it is."

"Isn't it wrong?"

"In a way, I guess it is," Querry conceded. "But it can't be helped. Here, this is my room." He unlocked the door, went inside, and lit the candle on the table.

The doll looked around at Querry's meager possessions. When he saw Tosser and Toerag curled on the bed, he laughed out loud with enchantment and crouched down to stroke them. The big book he carried fell to the floor.

Querry stood with his palm resting on the table, watching the doll rub his head against the cats, as he'd seen them do. They purred loudly, and he nestled his cheek on the worn quilt next to them, eyes closed, smiling. Querry had never seen someone in such bliss.

Another stray, he chided himself. *You fool.*

"What do you say we get you cleaned up?"

The doll opened his eyes and smiled. He really was beautiful, Querry thought, with those harvest moon eyes and little blossom of a mouth. He'd like to meet a human man that looked like that—

"I need to be cleaned?"

"We both do. I need you to stay here, in this room, while I go get some water from the pump outside. Can you do that?"

"Yes, Querry."

Querry went to the pump and returned to find the doll sitting on his bed, both cats curled contentedly in his lap. The thief cleared enough space on the table for his wash basin, and filled it from the bucket. As the doll watched, Querry unbuckled his waistcoat and placed it in the chest. He draped his shirt over the back of a chair. In imitation, the doll stood and picked open the little white buttons of his blouse. When it fluttered down behind him, Querry saw that, protected from the dust, the skin of his chest shone smooth and fair. Again, nothing indicated he'd been formed from metal and gears. His creator had even given him small, pink nipples, complete with a few silver hairs surrounding them. How long would it take to construct such a thing? Twenty years? Fifty?

"Those clothes need a washing too," Querry said. He'd laundered his own the previous day; they were fresh enough.

Unabashedly, the doll toed off his delicate shoes and removed his shorts and hose. He stood waiting without the slightest embarrassment, rippling the surface of the water with his finger. Querry couldn't believe what he saw. The doll imitated a real boy in every way: from the trail of hair down his belly, to his flaccid cock and balls that huddled next to his body. Who would give a doll, presumably meant as a child's plaything, a cock? And why? The skin of his scrotum even possessed the proper texture, along with a few more silvery hairs. He looked so genuine that Querry felt things stir that shouldn't be stirring as he regarded a doll. Something occurred to him then, and Querry said, "You know, you mustn't just take off your clothes for anyone who asks."

"Why?"

Somehow, the doll maker had imbued his creation with basic knowledge: it knew about food and it could speak. But it had never seen a feline, never been taught shame over nudity. Carefully Querry said, "There are plenty of people in the world who would want to"—he considered—"hurt you. They might want to use you for... *things.*"

"Only when you ask, Querry?"

"That's right." Plunging a cake of yellow soap into the chilly water, Querry tried to banish the possibilities he imagined. He reminded himself that no matter how much it looked like a young man, a beautiful, young man complete with bands of lean musculature, accentuated by the candlelight, and the face of an angel, this doll didn't live. *But if it's not alive, I can't hurt or take advantage of it, can I? Can't take advantage of a fancy sewing machine or cookstove, right?*

But Querry knew it wasn't the same thing. Through some unimaginable means, this doll understood. It either felt or mimicked emotion. It needed delicate handling.

The thief splashed some cold water on his face to clear his head. The doll watched expectantly as he lathered up and shaved. Of all the luxuries he coveted, Querry desired a bathtub most of all. They'd even invented ways to pipe water, heated by a furnace, directly to the spout, removing the need to carry buckets. Soaking his injured body in hot, fragrant water sounded heavenly to Querry. He'd even heard of a self-emptying chamber pot. He rinsed his face and turned to the doll, who regarded him with fascination. "Your turn."

Querry immersed the cloth and wrung it out. Coming closer, he held the doll's curly fringe from its forehead and wiped its face. It inhaled sharply.

"You feel the cold?" Querry gasped.

"Yes," answered the doll. "Different temperatures can't damage me, except for the most extreme heat, but I can process the information."

"Can you feel this?" Querry placed his hand just above the doll's hipbone and squeezed the side of his waist. He felt amazing, satin skin over sinew—

"The pressure? Yes, I can perceive it."

"Amazing! It's just incredible."

"That means you like me?" it asked, beaming. "That we're friends?"

"I guess so," Querry said cautiously as he cleaned the doll's cheeks and round chin.

"I don't want to go back to that dark room," he whispered.

Querry rinsed his cloth. To wash the back of the doll's neck, he needed to lean forward. This caused their chests to bump, and Querry's cock to skip in his pants.

No, he scolded himself as he lifted the doll's too-soft hair, *you are not attracted to this thing!* Even so, he burrowed his fingers into the doll's ample tresses, squeezed a handful of the springy curls, and let his lips move near to the doll's forehead. He just wanted to know how his—no, its!— skin would feel, brushing against his lips. Close to his perfect, round ear, Querry said, "If you were aware of a world outside of that place, of buildings and people beyond that room, then why didn't you leave? Why stay if you were unhappy there?"

"I was meant to wait."

"Why?" Querry asked. "How do you know?"

The doll sighed. Indeed, air moved in and out of it in a semblance of breath. "I can't say. I only know I was meant to wait."

"But then," Querry continued, letting the tip of his nose burrow into the doll's locks, "how did you know you were meant to go with me?"

"I just knew," the doll said softly. The inflection in his voice changed, and his eyelids drooped languidly. If Querry hadn't known better, he'd have said the doll enjoyed the closeness between them. Querry enjoyed it, whether he could admit it or not. He still held the doll's hair, his face pressed into it, and his other hand, clutching the rag, draped over the doll's shoulder.

"Turn around, now," Querry said. "And I'll wash your back."

"Thank you."

Another surprise awaited the thief as the doll spun gracefully. Beneath his artificial skin, the knobs of his spine showed. He'd been constructed with ribs that grew more prominent when he drew in breath. He had a cute, relaxed way of standing, with his hips and belly thrust slightly out and his lower back curving forward. Querry stretched his palm over the little dip, drawing it down over a rounded crescent. His hand worked its way into the divot between the doll's lovely ass cheek and his thigh, and Querry squeezed, feeling a cushion of soft over the muscle beneath. The tip of his pinky touched the doll's balls, and again he pondered what purpose this anatomy meant to serve. Curiosity and a good amount of arousal compelled Querry to take the doll's other cheek in his hand. Slowly and gently he eased them apart.

"I'm not, um, hurting or upsetting you, am I?"

"No, Querry. I've never been cleaned before, and it does feel—I don't know the word. I'm in no distress, though."

Reassured, Querry spread the doll's cheeks wide enough to inspect his cleft. Again, no deviation from reality belayed his origins. Querry's finger brushed the wrinkled mound of his anus, and it even twitched at his touch. With his other hand on the doll's hip, he knelt down for a better view. He inhaled, but the doll didn't emit the masculine aroma he'd anticipated. He had no scent at all.

"Querry, that feels very strange."

"I'm sorry." Flushing and ashamed, Querry quickly moved away. What on earth had he been thinking? Ignoring his erection, he finished wiping the doll down in silence. Then he soaped up his underarms and rinsed. Normally he removed his pants to cleanse his lower body, but he felt awkward displaying his arousal to the doll. So instead, Querry replaced his white, button-up shirt and tied a blue ribbon around his neck to hold his collar shut.

"I'm going out for a bit," he said to the doll, who still stood naked, watching Querry's every move.

"I'll go with you," he replied brightly, clearly excited by the prospect.

"No," Querry said. "I have some work to do."

The doll's lower lip shot out and his brows curled down, his whole beautiful face a mask of the most sincere sorrow. Querry worried he might cry, if that was possible. Guided by instinct, he took the doll's hand and held it between both of his.

"Listen, it's dangerous out there. You don't understand yet. I want you to stay in this room, where you'll be safe. Don't open or unlock the door until I get back. I'm going to try to get some money, and I'll get you some new clothes, so you can blend in. And then tomorrow night, I'll take you out and show you around. How does that sound?"

"I don't want to be alone."

"Well, you won't," Querry said. "After all, you'll have these fellows." He indicated the cats, both of whom sniffed the doll's discarded garments intently. "Will you need food?"

"I don't require it."

"All right," Querry said, releasing the doll so he could sling his many belts across his hips. "Is there anything else, then? Before I'm off?"

"Yes."

"Well, what is it?"

Looking very seriously at the thief, the doll said, "I don't know why, Querry, but...."

"What?"

"I'd like to put my mouth on your mouth. I know it sounds an odd thing...."

Chuckling, Querry set his pistol aside and took hold of the doll's waist. As his hands snaked to the small of the doll's back, pulling them together, Querry said, "Not at all. It's called kissing."

Tilting his head, Querry smashed his lips against the doll's soft mouth, holding them there. Then, slowly, with the utmost relish, he opened his mouth and let his tongue slip between the doll's perfect teeth. He explored the ridges on the roof of the doll's mouth, the smoothness of its sides. Soon, learning quickly, the doll twisted his tongue around Querry's, poking playfully in and out of Querry's mouth. Too quickly the thief approached the point where the directions of his body drowned those of his conscience and mind, and he growled with satisfaction and desire, drawing the doll tighter into his arms and grinding his swollen cock against his naked thigh.

But then Querry broke away, panting and wiping his mouth with his knuckles. It wasn't right; it was a doll, a machine. It knew nothing of the world. To take it—no, *him*—like this would be selfish and sick.

But the doll reached up and touched the bow-shaped lips Querry had just tasted. He smiled and said, "That felt very pleasant."

"It's like taking your clothes off," Querry said, disgusted with the possessiveness he already couldn't deny.

"Only for you?"

"That's right. And while I'm gone, try to think of something I can call you."

With that, Querry secured the complex locks he'd designed and hurried out into the night. As he blended into the crowd, heading from Rushport toward the bridge to the more affluent neighborhoods across the river, he thought, in spite of himself, *Won't it be nice to come home to someone?*

QUERRY RETURNED midmorning to find the doll curled nude on his quilt, with his knees tucked up against his chest, his eyes closed and a serene smile on his face. Both of the cats slumbered between his back and the wall, the three of them monopolizing the narrow bed. Even so, the sight made Querry grin as he closed and locked the door.

The previous evening, a full moon had drawn many onto the streets. The night had been warm: one of those last summer nights that made the cold sting even crueler when it set in. Dew sparkled beneath the gaslight on the cobblestone. The wind came off the sea and almost vanquished the industrial stink. The well-off fell under the evening's cheerful spell. Faeries mingled with mortals within the bazaar held nightly near Leopold's Folly Square: fine ladies and gentlemen, equal to the human aristocracy in every aspect, as well as more peculiar creatures that kept to the tree branches and undersides of the hedges. As they moved about and conversed beneath the colored strings of lights, inspecting the latest mechanical novelties and listening to the loud voices of the men hawking them, Querry found it a simple thing to pick out those with the glaze in their eyes that wouldn't be able to recall exactly what they'd discussed after the fey departed. His nimble fingers relieved them of their worldly goods as they swooned. Tomorrow, they'd think they'd lost their coin on one of the elaborate, mechanical games, or squandered it on some foreign trinket.

Thankful for the luck, Querry placed the things he'd purchased next to the piles of gears and wire that occupied the table. He'd done well enough to afford a loaf of bread and a block of cheese, canned fish enough for himself and the cats, a pint of ale, and a tin of biscuits. He'd procured some second-hand clothing for the doll, the most unassuming he could find, since his striking beauty and unnatural coloration would undoubtedly draw enough curiosity. He bought a newspaper to see if there'd be any mention of the doll maker's house. And he'd paid too much for a pair of apples. Though the doll didn't require sustenance, Querry wanted him to have one, too, since they were so lovely: pale golden spheres flecked with green and blushing crimson around the tops. When he'd passed the stall, Querry envisioned the doll cupping the fruit in his hands with a bemused smile on his face.

He looked down at the bed. Last night, only work occupied the thief's thoughts. His every sense tuned to his surroundings and quarry, as they must for him to avoid detection. Now, watching the doll sleep, all of the uncomfortable questions returned. Querry recalled the doll's request for a kiss. He hadn't known the word, but somehow he'd desired intimacy. It was unfathomable. Though he hated to consider it, it seemed more and more to Querry that he'd been designed for pleasure with his soft, exquisite body. There were plenty of lecherous old nobles and clergymen who preferred young men of just his type, and paraded them around in the guise of apprentice or page. But to spend so much time and endow something like that with such artistry? This doll had been a labor of love to his creator, Querry felt sure. How else could one invest the decades he must've taken to complete?

Noticing the leather book on the floor, Querry bent down and opened it, hoping for a clue. Must rose from the crumbling pages. Nothing but gibberish was written within. Tiny, lowercase letters, with no space between and in no particular order filled every page from top to bottom. Shaking his head, Querry set it aside.

No matter how much he tried to convince himself that his reaction to the doll meant nothing more than that he was healthy and human and touching a naked man, a stunning, sensuous form that would tempt anyone with a heartbeat, Querry couldn't banish the warmth that filled his chest and belly as he watched the doll's long, white lashes flutter. Could he be dreaming? Whatever he'd been intended for, he belonged to Querry now, and Querry wouldn't let him be ill-used. Reaching down, he ran a finger from the doll's round shoulder to his elbow. As anyone might, the doll shifted slightly before falling still. Querry stroked the silver curls at the back of his head, then down his neck and between his shoulder blades, enjoying the texture of his skin, getting aroused again.

Maybe it was sick to feel this way, but Querry had been lonely too. He saw Reg less and less. Whores and men seeking easy thrills couldn't fill the void left by his first love. *Reg*, Querry thought. He and this doll were a little bit alike: delicate and vulnerable, but with strength running through like a vein of gold. Both inspired a strong protective instinct in Querry. Querry remembered the last time he'd watched Reg sleep this way, so long ago, when the leaves were still just tightly curled buds on the trees. They'd met for a drink and come back here. Too vividly, Querry recalled shutting the door, just before throwing Reg against it and pinning him, driving his tongue hard into Reg's mouth. He saw Reg's hands pushing against his chest, and his own closing around Reg's wrists and holding his arms at his sides. He could almost taste Reg's sweat, feel the skin of Reg's neck beneath his tongue, hear his halfhearted protests.

Querry's hand went to his groin, and he gave his aching cock a squeeze through his pants. He looked at the doll's idealized little feet, tucked up and almost hiding his balls and the dark line of his crack beneath. Querry unbuttoned his trousers and quietly let himself poke out. As his left fist squeezed hard at the base of his shaft, his right hand groped for an old rag on the table. Hand moving up his length, Querry felt a stir of guilt at the thought of pleasuring himself while the doll slept. But the tension in his body felt so unbearable, he brought his palm to his cock head and gave it a twist and a tug. He tugged again, churning himself with quick, short strokes, watching the doll's rosebud lips and remembering their softness.

He thought about how he'd practically torn away Reg's proper, gray suit and linen shirt, how Reg had almost tripped trying to get his feet out of his pants, and how Querry had caught him around the waist and thrown him, belly-down, on the rickety bed. A hard squeeze summoned the first droplets of come, and Querry used the heel of his hand to swirl it over himself and ease the friction. He picked up speed, desperate for release.

It was nearly there now. Querry drove his fist against himself hard and fast. His anus clenched and released as he watched the doll's graceful neck, blanketed in ringlets the color of a stormy sky. Biting down on his lip, Querry lifted the oil-stained scrap of cloth and prepared to finish.

But then the doll's eyes opened, and without the drowsiness of a human waking. His lids drew back like clouds parting to reveal a full, faerie-ringed moon, clear and alert. The shock dammed Querry's orgasm, and he knew that of course he should stop. But he'd reached the point where he didn't think it would be possible. Balls hurting, frustrated and embarrassed, he looked apologetically into the golden eyes, and the doll met his gaze without judgment. He didn't know to feel awkward, and within a few seconds Querry, too, felt at ease and began to slowly stroke himself. In no time he found himself ready to reach for the rag. Eyes locked with the doll's, Querry delivered the releasing jerk. He ground his teeth together and came with a single, stifled groan. Then he cleaned up and undressed, shooed the cats out of the bed, curled up behind the doll with his arm stretched protectively from his shoulder all the way to his ankle, and slept until late in the afternoon.

CHAPTER 4

"WHERE ARE we going, Querry?" the doll asked. He wore the clothes the thief had acquired: a coal-colored newsboy's cap, gray trousers, faded, cornflower shirt, and a checkered vest with a few patches on its satin back. Unfortunately, his springy curls poked from beneath the hat, almost touching his shoulders and eyebrows, and those few people who didn't look twice at his beauty stole second glances at his strangeness.

"We're going to see a friend of mine," Querry answered. Upon waking, he'd felt a little shamed about what he'd done, touching himself in front of the doll, but the doll hadn't mentioned it. It seemed unimportant now. "He works in that building, and he should be coming out soon. So, we'll just sit on this bench and read the newspaper while we wait for him."

They did so. Afternoon light gilded the royal and administrative buildings, and the pansies and primroses in their neat window boxes. Men in identical, dust-colored suits moved slowly from door to door, carrying books and papers. Now and then a carriage chugged by, spewing steam. Plenty of horse-drawn carriages clogged the streets at this time of day also. Two years ago, the University a few blocks up had begun to admit women, and a group of three such students walked past the men on their way back from class. They wore drab, simple dresses of olive and brown. One of them had even adopted the scandalous Colonial custom of wearing loose-fitting trousers beneath a too-short skirt. They spoke softly to each other, giggling and covering their mouths, stealing glances at Querry and the doll. The doll didn't know not to smile and wave. This caused the students to redden and hurry away.

Querry lifted his section of paper up, shielding his face. Beside him, the doll sat with a leaf spread over his lap. He hoped Reg would be along soon; they were attracting too much attention. One gentleman in particular, a strawberry blond with blue eyes several shades lighter than Querry's and clothing with a Continental flare, watched the pair intently from beneath a tree. Possibly his tastes ran similar to Querry's own, and he observed them only out of appreciation. Any man interested in another man had to rely on subtle looks and signals to convey his intent, at least beyond Lickwhistle Circle. Possibly, though, this well-dressed fellow found them out of place and waited to alert the authorities. If a Royal Guard or city policeman ushered Querry back where he belonged, so be it, but it wouldn't do for anyone to intuit the doll's peculiar nature.

"Have you decided on a name for yourself?"

"I haven't decided."

"Well, what about Jack?"

The doll curled his lip, as if tasting something sour, and shook his head.

"Patrick? George?"

"I don't care for either of those," the doll said. He was taking this matter very seriously.

Querry looked back at the paper. A large ad for a clothes-pressing machine took up most of the page. Also, a tailor in town would run a sale on ladies' hats. Perusing the articles, Querry hadn't yet seen mention of his exploits in the cellar of the doll maker's house. "Percival?" he said idly. "Percy, that's nice."

But the paper on his thighs held all of the doll's attention. He began to read aloud. "Early this morning, Lord Thimbleroy insisted upon an emergency assembly of the House. 'Good sirs,' he said, addressing his fellow nobles, 'the time has come and then some that we must act to rid our fair and wholesome city of that nest of deceit and vice which has come to be referred to as Neroche.'

"He uses so many words," the doll noted and then continued. "'The inhabitants thereof, whom I might note should in no way be considered citizens, and should not be assumed to possess the rights insured to Her Majesty's loyal subjects, are contributing quite rapidly to the dissolution of our virtuous women and the corruption and kidnap of our children. I call upon all of you now to ratify an act giving these inhabitants one month's time to vacate these premises and remove any evidence of their presence. If they are unwilling to comply, I call upon each of you to, as our noble ancestors have done so many times in the past, take up arms to defend this kingdom!'

"Debate continued past the noon hour regarding the feasibility of Lord Thimbleroy's proposal. Thimbleroy indicated some privately funded research that might be able to aid his worthy cause, while Duchess Lisine, who several years prior gained notoriety as the first woman to demand entrance to the house, but who remains a favorite of the queen mother, called for an alternative to violence, citing the Empire's already thinly spread military resources. Debate is expected to continue. The Grande Chancellor did, however, gain a small victory when House members agreed to the measure of having Royal and city guards remove any person not able to provide proof of citizenship to the area known as Neroche."

"I'm glad I'm not one of those guards," Querry said.

"What's this Neroche place?" the doll asked.

"It's nowhere you'd want to go."

"How long has it been there?"

"Nobody knows," Querry said. "Nobody remembers it not being there, not that it's ever in the same place. Some people will tell you it's not there at all. Maps still show Hawthorne Street continuing right down to the riverbank. Lord Thimbleroy's the worst sort of fool if he thinks he can do anything about it, either."

"I don't like this Lord Thimbleroy," the doll said decisively. "Look at his silly, curled-up moustache! And here's another article! 'Decadent fey frolic captured by daguerreotype in churchyard near the palace'."

Querry looked at the blurry image of gamboling sprites, faerie gentlemen, and girls in nightshirts. A long list of suspicious disappearances followed. Below it was an ad for a self-heating hair-curling iron.

"Frolic," the doll said, as if the word contained layers of mystery and meaning. "Do you think I can be called Frolic?"

Laughing, Querry said, "Really?" Others would have certainly tried to dissuade the doll from this improper choice, but the thief could see no harm. "'Frolic' it is."

The doll smiled, and his eyes returned to the paper. "What's this laundry powder?"

"Well, you—" Querry began, but just then he saw Reg emerge from the great double doors of the Archives in a hound's-tooth cape and bowler hat. He stood, tapped Frolic's shoulder, and went to meet his friend at the foot of the steps. The man who'd been watching them followed their progress. He observed the trio a few moments before melting into the crowd.

At first, Reg looked at Frolic with terror. Eyes darting back and forth, he hissed, "Querry! What are you doing? You can't bring a faerie out of Neroche; you'll be arrested! Haven't you heard the news?"

"This is Frolic," Querry said. "He's not a faerie. Frolic, Reginald Whitney."

"Hello."

"Querry, what—" Reg scowled, his intelligence insulted. Querry supposed Frolic did sound a little like a faerie name.

"Is there somewhere we can talk?" Querry asked.

"There's a pub around the corner where lots of us who work here like to stop. Or there's a little coffee shop where we go to play chess."

"That won't do," Querry said. "We need somewhere we can't possibly be heard."

Querry and Frolic followed Reg down a corridor between the Archives and the building next to it, across a desolate round courtyard, then finally through an iron gate. Beyond it, a concrete bench sat beneath a birch tree. The backs of the buildings enclosed a little triangle of high grass. Querry brushed the yellow leaves aside and sat down. Frolic sat next to him, the sun through the branches striping his face, but Reg just stood with his arms crossed. Wondering where he should begin, Querry said, "I went to the doll maker's house."

Reg threw up his hands. "I knew it was you! Lord Thimbleroy came into the Archives in a rage yesterday, demanding to know if anyone else had asked about the house. Then he requested dozens of records, everything to do with the doll maker and his family. He insisted that I scour everything written the year the clock tower was built, and personally deliver every mention of it straight to him. I heard he has teams of men, carting away everything that was found in a cellar there: tons of metal scraps. He doesn't seem satisfied, though."

Querry spent the next quarter of an hour relaying his adventure to Reg in as much detail as he could remember. When he came to the part where he'd found Frolic, though, he stopped.

"So," Reg said, "you broke in and saw some half-finished toys and clockworks. I don't understand. And who is he?"

"Reg, don't you get it? A *doll maker*—"

"You can't mean—He's a clockwork?" Reg eyed Frolic suspiciously.

"It's amazing, I know," Querry said, fondness insinuating into his words. "But the only explanation is that Frolic is what Lord Thimbleroy has been looking for."

"Me?" Frolic gasped.

"But what could the Grande Chancellor possibly want with a doll?" Reg said, tearing a sliver of his thumbnail away with his teeth. "I mean, his children are grown and married!"

"It can't be something as simple as wanting a toy," Querry mused. "Certainly he's exquisite, surely the only one of his kind in the world, but there must be something else." He turned to the doll. "Frolic, can you remember any important information your creator might have left with you?"

Looking forlorn, Frolic said, "All I can remember is that dark room."

"Can you remember the man who created you?"

"I'm sorry, Querry."

"His name was Archibald Lesh," Reggie offered. "Born 1714, died 1792."

"Impossible!" Querry said. "The mechanics to create something as complex as Frolic didn't exist back then! Nothing this advanced even exists now! There's nothing even close!"

"Maybe," Reg said. "But the clock tower was completed in 1791 and dedicated at the turn of the century."

"Built by a crazy genius and whole teams of wizards and craftsmen! And it stopped working five years later! Frolic is still functioning perfectly after almost a hundred years." Realizing what he'd just said, Querry held the doll's hand and said, "Oh God, Frolic."

"I slept most of the time," the doll said, forcing a smile.

Reg glared, envy rising from him like steam from the river. "What do you plan to do with it, Querry? Sell it?" he snapped.

"No! I'll keep him with me for now."

"For what?"

"To try to find out what's going on." Frolic looked shattered, betrayed, so Querry added, "And I like his company."

"It's a machine," Reg said.

"Reg, you can't deny what you're seeing with your own eyes. Frolic has perception, memory, and emotion."

"Not possible."

"A lot about this seems impossible," Querry conceded. "And yet here we are."

To this, Reg seemed unable to make a suitable reply. He spat the shard of fingernail into the grass. He wouldn't meet his friend's or Frolic's eyes, but stared off between the buildings, toward the sunset. Finally he said, "You know, if Lord Thimbleroy wants"—he paused, scowling as he said the word—"*Frolic*, he'll find a way to have him."

"I won't let that happen."

Exasperated, Reg raised his voice. "You have to accept that there are things you can't stand in the way of, Querry! He has resources you can't even imagine: investigators, soldiers, and thugs, even wizards!"

"Wizards are illegal," Querry stated calmly. "Driven off over fifty years ago."

"Why?" Frolic wondered.

"It was before our time," Reg explained curtly, "but I understand they got too powerful. With some of the innovations in industry, in weaponry, ordinary people finally stood a chance against them, and they took it. It was either magic or machines in their minds, but not both."

"Either way," Querry said, "the magic-users are gone from Anglica."

"That's just it," Reg said. "Thimbleroy is powerful enough to get around it. You don't think he'll find out that you were the one who beat him to that cellar? You don't think he'll find you, take the clockwork by force? He'll likely have you killed!"

"I can take care of it, Reg."

Clearly infuriated by Querry's confidence, Reg strode over and took hold of his shoulders. He shook Querry twice and said, "You have to be careful! You don't live among these people like I do. You don't understand them. I can't stand it if anything happens to you!"

"Reg," said Querry, softening and touching his friend's burning cheek. "I understand them better than you think. And I'll be careful. I've managed all these years. You don't need to worry over me. But if you find out anything more, you must let me know. If we could understand what connects Lord Thimbleroy and the faeries and the clock tower and Frolic, we'd be better able to protect ourselves."

"You think the clock tower has something to do with this?" Reg asked, curiosity replacing his frustration.

"I don't know," Querry admitted. "But it's his other obsession, along with being rid of Neroche. But how could Frolic help him with either of those things? It doesn't seem possible that Frolic could be what he's after, now that I think about it. Maybe the thing he wanted from that house is already gone or was never there in the first place."

The three of them sat in silence as the birch's lengthening shadow cast them further into darkness. The bells of the city's many cathedrals marked the hour. Querry's stomach growled, and he placed a hand over it and said, "Why don't we all go for some supper?"

"Speaking of the devil," Reg said, "I'm to accompany Lady Butterwell to a ball at Lord Thimbleroy's house tonight. He's raising funds for his little repair project."

"Maybe you'll find something out!" Querry cried, leaping up. Frolic, alarmed, also hurried to his feet. "Maybe you could get into his study, if you can sneak away from your lady friend!"

With a snort, Reg said, "I assure you, the buffet table will distract Lady Butterwell just fine. And the petit fours and custards and puddings. I bet I *could* sneak away."

"Now I'll tell *you* to be careful," Querry said.

"Not to worry. Thimbleroy thinks everyone of common birth is half-simple. I'll have no trouble convincing him I'm only lost."

"Then we'll meet tomorrow night?"

"You're putting yourself in danger coming here," Reg said. "And Frolic too. I doubt Lord Thimbleroy knows what he's looking for, but even so, Frolic is hard to miss. I'd better come to you."

Querry nodded, glad to see Reg concerned for Frolic. Try as he might, Reg's nature prevented his turning a hard heart against an innocent in trouble. "There's a pub called The Bell and Badger. It's just a block past the tanning plant. There's a badger on the sign with a hat just like yours." He winked, and Reg's eyes danced with mirth for a second. "Will you come around nine?"

"I'll have to tell the Whitneys that I'm not feeling well. Surely they've arranged another meeting for me. But I'll be there."

Querry and Reg stood facing each other, with Frolic a few feet behind. Reg looked over his shoulder, as if about to slip something that didn't belong to him beneath his cloak, then hugged Querry tightly around the waist. For a few seconds Querry was too shocked to respond, but then he let his arms close around Reg's shoulders. It felt so good to hold him, to feel the warmth of his body and breathe the scent of his hair. "Please be careful, Querry," he pleaded. "Keep your wits about you."

"Of course," he answered, and soon, too soon, Reg released him and went on his way.

Turning to Frolic, Querry said, "You'd better stay close to me. You could be in more danger than we first thought."

Smiling, the doll answered, "Of course, Querry. I always want to be close to you. Where will we go next?"

"Well, if you're going to be with me—"

There, I said it.

"—then I'm going to teach you how to earn your keep." They left the tidy little area where Reg worked and turned a corner. Droves of men and women were returning home from work or from the market, hurrying toward train stations or carriages, and soon the crowd, the twisting alleyways, and the increasing cover of night swallowed the thief and the clockwork boy.

A FEW weeks past, Querry had been eating his supper in a tavern. A few tables away, a very drunk, old man sat muttering to himself about a glorious event that would occur at the end of the month. The thief had listened closely as he ate his greasy sausage and mash, and when he'd finished he went to join the man.

"I can't help but overhear what a difficult woman your mistress is," Querry said to the man, who'd spoken of himself as a gardener by trade. "My sympathies."

"Harpy," the gardener slurred, finishing most of his gin and slopping the rest down the front of his soiled shirt. "Day can't come soon enough that she takes herself and those spoilt brats to the country house. Then the help will have some peace. Maybe even some time to get things done."

"Is it a very great house?" Querry wondered. "With many gardens?"

"'S practically a castle!" the gardener replied, clearly pleased and astonished to have the company of a person who both found his work interesting and bought gin. "Takes my boys six days to prune the hedges alone!"

"Amazing! There must be dozens of servants taking care of the house as well?"

The man snorted and slapped the empty air, as if words failed to describe it. "The Lady takes most of them to the country house, 'course."

"'Course. Where does the family go on holiday?"

"Somewhere up North," said the gardener. "Wouldn't know. All's I do know is: I won't have to listen to 'em soon now."

"How soon?"

"End of September."

"I'd like to have a look at this grand house," Querry said. "And of course its impressive and well-maintained grounds."

The gardener sat up a little straighter and told Querry the address. The thief spent another half an hour listening to scintillating tales of flower beds weeded and fruit trees trimmed. During that time, he presented the gardener, a man with the ironic name of Nathan Bloom, with enough gin to ensure he wouldn't be remembered. When Bloom's head slumped into his arm and he began singing a nursery rhyme to his elbow, Querry stood from the table and left unnoticed.

Since then, he'd strolled past the house, a Gothic-revival mansion that resembled a church more than a dwelling, complete with stained-glass windows, flying buttresses, gargoyles, and a bell tower, half a dozen times. Just as Bloom described, the huge staff always seemed to be rushing about: maids with laundry, governesses directing children, cooks hurrying to and from market with enough food for a fleet of sailors. Tonight, though, Querry and Frolic found the intricate corridors of rose bushes and sculpted hedges as quiet as a cemetery. The job would be an easy one. If any servants remained, they either slumbered below the stairs or took advantage of their employer's absence and found their way to a pub.

"Can you climb a rope?" Querry whispered to Frolic.

"I've never done it, but I'm sure I can."

"Good." The best way in looked like an arched door beyond a little half-moon balcony. The dark, arrow-shaped windows around it reflected the amber and black geometry formed by streetlights and leaves. Also, it stood around back, safe from the eyes of neighbors or people on the street. Querry squeezed the trigger of his bow-like grapple, and with a click of gears and a little puff of steam, the hook and the rope shot out with much more force than usual. Querry was nearly knocked backward into a pile of leaves.

"What on earth?"

"Oh," Frolic said. "I took it apart and recalibrated the clockwork while you were sleeping. I was able to eliminate a whole set of gears and make it more efficient. And more powerful. I hoped it would make you happy."

"Well, thanks," Querry said. He tugged the rope to make sure it caught, and then he started his way up, followed closely by Frolic. He could feel Frolic's weight straining the rope beneath him, but the doll made no sound, as he'd been instructed. When they reached the oak door, he stood quietly as Querry picked the lock. With a creak, the door opened, and they found themselves in a lady's sitting room. Portraits of matronly looking women hung on the rose-colored walls in gilded frames. Some velvet-upholstered chairs sat against the wall, round tables holding oil lamps or picture books between them. A writing desk stood in the corner.

"I don't see anything small and valuable," Frolic whispered.

With an approving chuckle, Querry said, "Right you are. Do you remember what we're trying to find?"

Frolic lifted his hand and counted the items out on his fingers. "Coins, bracelets, earrings, brooches, necklaces, watches, cufflinks."

"Let's go, then. Once you've had some practice, we'll split up and cover houses quicker. But tonight you'd better stay with me."

He nodded once, a determined expression on his face, and they crept into the hall. A mixture of gaslight and moonlight allowed Querry to see without his goggles. Frolic easily followed, causing Querry to wonder if he'd been given vision superior to a human. Perhaps it had something to do with his unusual eye color. Together they scoured the second and third story of the manor without disturbing so much as a mouse. A little over an hour after their arrival, they stood on the balcony again with their pockets full. Much to Querry's delight, the gentleman's study had been decorated with fine, antique weapons and armor. From the wall between the bookshelves, he'd selected a rapier to replace the one he'd lost. The blade felt sharp and springy, and gilt and small jewels adorned the hand-guard and ivory grip. For Frolic he'd chosen a similar weapon with a slightly shorter handle and a guard made to resemble twisting ivy. The intricately cast leaves meandered up the blade in a natural spiral. The sword produced a barely perceivable hum, and when Querry slashed the air he heard a single, echoing chime. Possibly the sword was faerie-made, or forged before practicing magic had been outlawed. Frolic looked delighted, and Querry looked forward to teaching him to handle the weapon.

They descended the rope and landed lightly in grass that sparkled with dew. The gardens were as extensive and lovely as Querry's informant had claimed. Hedgerows formed both paths and outdoor rooms, many with iron benches and fountains tinkling softly at their centers. Querry and Frolic passed flower beds bigger than their room, though most had blossomed months before. The sky above them was clear, save for the wavering columns of smoke rising from the factories in the distance.

"You did well tonight," Querry said as he opened a small gate that led from a secluded corner of the garden to an even more secluded alleyway.

"You're pleased?" Frolic asked, beaming.

"Yes. You know, I wish we could do something to celebrate. But you don't eat or drink. Is there something else you think you might enjoy?"

Looking down at the cobblestone, Frolic chewed his lip as they hurried from shadow to shadow. "I felt very happy when we sat on the bench earlier, in the warm sun, talking. I feel happy when the cats curl up in my lap. I like to walk and look at things. I like to see you smile. I like to kiss."

Impulsively, Querry reached over and squeezed Frolic's hand. He held onto it as they walked, passing other manor houses on their way toward the river. Only when they'd crossed the bridge and reached the factories did he let it go, and the two of them passed the workers with their eyes to the ground. Soon they arrived in Rushport, and were greeted by the familiar voices of the beggars, hawkers, and whores that clogged every corner. Imitating Querry, Frolic ignored them and followed the thief to a tavern. Once Querry had purchased some oysters, they headed home. In the small room on the third floor, Querry lit the candles, fed the cats, and finished his own supper. Frolic perched on the edge of the bed, watching and waiting.

"What is it?" Querry asked him.

"I've been thinking," said the doll. "About what you said earlier. Why was I made?"

"I don't know."

"Why were you made, Querry?"

Because a whore's luck ran out, and she couldn't afford the herbs that would fix the problem, he thought, though he said nothing and shook his head.

"Querry, what's your purpose?"

"My purpose? To relieve the wealthy of their worldly goods, I suppose."

"Then what's mine?"

"I'm sorry, Frolic. I just don't know. Why is this bothering you so much?"

"I want to know what I'm meant to do. I want to live out my purpose. The man who made me must've intended me for something, mustn't he? If I don't do that thing, won't I be meaningless? Useless?"

Again Querry picked up the leather-bound book and opened it to a random page in the center. He shook his head and pushed his fringe back, saying, "We won't find anything out here. It's nothing but a bunch of nonsense."

"May I see?"

Querry passed Frolic the crumbling tome. After looking at it intently for a moment, he said, "It has to be read every fourth letter."

Taking it back, Querry flipped to the beginning and covered the first three letters with his fingertip. The fourth letter was a lowercase I. The eighth was an N, and the twelfth a C. An arduous quarter of an hour later, Querry said, "'In constructing the skeleton, hollow tubing of solid gold is employed for flexibility, durability, and resistance to tarnish.' I think this book tells how you were made!"

"So it might tell what I'm for?"

"Maybe," Querry said, "but trying to figure it out like this will take me half my life. And I'll have to try to remember everything that's come before." He set the book aside, eyes and head hurting.

"But you'll try?" Frolic asked desperately. "Querry, please! I need to know!"

Balling up the paper wrapper that had held his food, Querry tossed it in the can and went to sit beside Frolic. He rested his hand lightly on the doll's knee and looked into his large eyes. Each of them reflected the single flame. Choosing his words carefully, he finally said, "Frolic. You're here. You're part of the world, experiencing life. Isn't there meaning enough in that?"

Frolic sighed heavily and didn't answer. Querry's hand moved up to give his thigh a squeeze. "You mean a great deal to me," he said softly.

"Why?"

"You said it yourself. We're mates. Friends, right?"

A smile stretched across Frolic's face, and it seemed to Querry that the dark room brightened. "I'm glad we're friends. But that can't be the only reason I'm here. I need to find out what I'm meant to do. Maybe your other friend, Reginald Whitney, will be able to help us."

Considering thoughtfully again, Querry finally asked, "Say you find out what your creator wanted you to do, and you don't want to do it. What then?" The thief's mind had returned to the possibility that Frolic had been constructed for another's pleasure, and it made his stomach churn with jealousy and outrage.

"I suppose I must do what I'm meant to do. Don't you think?"

Querry chuckled. "I don't. I do whatever I like, and to hell and the devil with what everyone else thinks. You've been given this life. Use it for your happiness."

"But—"

"No," Querry said firmly. Sitting with him now, Querry couldn't believe he'd ever considered selling Frolic. He couldn't bear the idea of Frolic being taken from him by Lord Thimbleroy or anyone else who might lay claim. They'd taken Reg; they would not take Frolic. "I found you. That means you're mine. And as long as you're mine, you are not a tool. I insist you live the way you want." He realized he'd dug his nails into Frolic's leg, and quickly let go.

"I've been thinking of something else, Querry."

"Hmm?"

"This morning, when you came into the room and took down your trousers—"

"Oh God," Querry groaned, burning with shame. He angled his body away from the doll, unable to face him.

Frolic's hand touched his shoulder, making Querry flinch. But the doll kneaded the muscles and explored the stretches and knobs of bone, and soon the thief relaxed. Slowly, he turned toward Frolic and mumbled, "Sorry."

"Sorry for what?"

"I shouldn't have done that, and I apologize."

"I don't understand," Frolic said. Again he looked cutely bemused, and Querry touched first the tip of his nose and then the apple of his cheek. The doll's hand covered Querry's own, holding it against his face. As Frolic pressed in, Querry's thumb and finger caught one of his curls, pulled it straight, and released it. Instantly it sprung back to its spiral shape. Frolic giggled and said, "I've thought often about what you did today. And whenever I think of it, I get a strange feeling." He touched his lower belly with his opposite hand. "I don't know what it's called, but I never felt it before. It's kind of a mix of happiness and, I don't know, impatience? The way you might feel if you really needed to figure out a problem, but couldn't find the answer? Not angry, but—"

"Frustrated?"

Squinting, Frolic considered. "Can we kiss again, Querry?"

"If you want to, then I'd like that very much." Querry took Frolic's other cheek and held his round face between his palms. For many minutes he just looked at him, studying the contours of his face and his lovely features. Frolic looked back at Querry, absolute trust and devotion spilling from his eyes. Once more the complexity and strangeness of the situation unnerved Querry, but he quickly decided he didn't care. He'd been lucky to find Frolic, was glad to have him. His heart beat faster and his skin warmed. He let his fingers snake into Frolic's hair, and he pulled their faces together.

Frolic opened his mouth and suckled Querry's lower lip. He drew it back and stretched it slightly before letting go. Then he leaned back in, planting teasing little nips and pecks over Querry's mouth. He pulled the corner of Querry's shirt free from his waistband, and his hand moved up the thief's side as he continued his erratic kisses. Lifting his leg, Frolic hooked his knee over Querry's and slid closer to him.

Unsatisfied with Frolic's innocent nibbling, finally able to admit he wanted more, Querry released his face and put one arm behind Frolic's back and the other beneath his knees, thinking to lift Frolic into his lap. He found Frolic much heavier than he'd expected, though, and he couldn't accomplish it. So Querry broke their kiss and said into Frolic's ear, "Come up here where I can get at you." Pressing between his shoulder blades, Querry guided Frolic to where he wanted him, and Frolic quickly complied. Now that he sat sideways across Querry's legs, Querry realized Frolic didn't weigh so much that he couldn't hold him. He did, however, outweigh Querry by almost a hundred pounds, even though he appeared much smaller and slighter.

"Now, then." Cradling the back of Frolic's neck, Querry brought their faces back together. Frolic's curls fell on either side of his face. Querry squeezed the doll tightly around his waist, drawing him in as close as he could, while he rubbed up and down Frolic's thigh with his other hand. The doll's soft lips parted, and the tips of their tongues bumped. With a groan, Querry opened wide, kissing Frolic deeply. They kissed hard, tongues wrestling and twisting like fighting serpents until Querry felt dizzy from the lack of air. Their lips separated with a loud pop and slurp, and both regarded each other breathlessly.

"Querry," Frolic panted, "could you touch me the way you touched yourself?"

As a test, Querry let his hand wander up Frolic's leg. Sure enough, his erection stretched the coarsely woven fabric of his pants. Querry found himself in no state to ponder the scientific or technical aspects of this occurrence. Instead he deftly unbuttoned Frolic's fly and freed his cock from its confines. He was about to seize it when he stopped and said, "There are all sorts of implications attached to this, and I don't know if you understand—"

"Querry, please touch me."

"I want you to be sure. To understand what—"

"Querry, please." Taking hold of the thief's wrist, Frolic guided Querry's hand to where he wanted it. His cock felt warm and solid against Querry's palm. He squeezed, felt it buck, and heard Frolic draw in a sharp and faltering breath. Frolic panted Querry's name as he directed Querry's strokes. When he felt sure Querry would take over, his small fist clutched Querry's shirt at the shoulder, holding on like he'd be swept away. The nails of his other hand scratched against the heating skin of Querry's back. Frolic turned his face toward the ceiling, gulping air through his parted lips. His spine curved so far forward that he would have surely fallen if not for his grip on Querry.

Watching Frolic's rapture made lust boil within Querry. He kept his strokes slow and steady, swiping from the base of Frolic's cock to the head, giving his corona a slight twist here and there. As he supported Frolic around the waist, he swiveled his hips, grinding his own erection against the other's slender hamstring. His tongue traversed the long, straight line from Frolic's collarbone to the tip of his chin, to which he gave a playful bite. In response Frolic let out a single, melodic moan and dug his nails into Querry's flesh. Nor could Querry stifle a frustrated groan. He smashed Frolic's body against his own and suckled his earlobe, all the time pressing against his lean leg with his cock.

Clamping his eyes shut, Querry could imagine standing with Frolic still in his arms. As erratically, desperately aroused as he felt, certainly his strength would equal Frolic's weight. He could hear the squeak of the mattress and supports as he threw Frolic down, could see Frolic looking up at him with his perfect faith. God he wanted to take Frolic, to tear his clothes away and rub his cock over the satiny skin of Frolic's belly. He wanted to see Frolic's full lips wrapped around it as he drove it into his throat. Then he wanted to wrench Frolic's legs apart and stab into him hard, wanted to see his neck twist and hear that cry of his that sounded almost like a note of music. But Querry had promised himself that he wouldn't take liberties with this sheltered and naïve person who trusted him so much. It was too soon.

Too soon to toss him on the bed and take him, but maybe—

"Frolic, stand up," Querry panted, letting go of the other's erection. "What do you say we get out of these clothes?"

After the few minutes it took for Frolic to return from the edge of ecstasy to some form of lucidity, he said, "Y-you and me?"

Caressing his cheek, Querry said, "Yes. I want to be able to see all of you. Feel your skin against mine."

Frolic took the initiative and kissed Querry hard before getting shakily to his feet. Querry really enjoyed Frolic's lack of shame: the way he undressed efficiently and quickly and stood displaying his beautiful form without a hint of modesty. He seemed to have come from some golden paradise of the ancient world, before the concepts of propriety and sin had been imagined. In opposition, Querry found his normally nimble fingers had become clumsy and thick. They couldn't remember how to pick apart a buckle or undo a button. After struggling with the laces of his boots and finally succeeding in getting naked, Querry sat back down on the edge of the bed.

"Come here," he said to Frolic, reaching out his hand. The doll obeyed and stood between Querry's knees, and Querry rested his hands on Frolic's hipbones. He kissed across Frolic's chest. Frolic's fingers burrowed into Querry's thick, dark hair.

"Querry, Querry," Frolic breathed. "Touch me again, Querry. It— it almost hurts when you stop!"

"I know, my beauty," Querry said, pressing against Frolic's heart, making him take a step backward so Querry could close his legs. Then he took both of Frolic's hands and pulled him to him. "Here, sit down."

Frolic dropped down and straddled Querry's knees, his balls squashed against Querry's legs and his calves hanging down.

"Closer," Querry urged, pressing his hand against the wonderful depression of Frolic's lower back. Frolic slid forward until his knees could rest on the bed and the tip of his cock poked against Querry's belly button, only an inch from the darkened and throbbing head of

Querry's own penis. The thief had begun to leak; a few droplets of his fluids gleamed like jewels in the firelight. These he spread across his palm, and then he seized both of their cocks at the base, jamming them together. Frolic looked down, his eyes wide with delighted amazement.

Moving his hand up, Querry began to churn their heads in his fist. Frolic thrust his hips up to match Querry's rhythm, his lips moving but bringing out no sound. He held tight to Querry's bare shoulders, swooping in now and then for a quick kiss. It felt fantastic: the crescents of Frolic's ass against Querry's thighs, their cocks rubbing together, tightly encased, their lips meeting, and their scrotums bouncing off of each other. Without thinking about it, Querry picked up speed. The slap of skin on skin filled the little room. Both men panted and moaned. Then Frolic's left hand darted from Querry's shoulder to their groins.

Momentarily confused, Querry stopped his motion. He looked into Frolic's eyes, and the doll smiled, as if their roles had suddenly switched and he was the wise one and Querry inexperienced. One by one, Frolic unfurled Querry's fingers. Then he wove his own into them, his thumb on top of Querry's thumb. He squeezed hard, producing a delicious pressure. In demonstration, Frolic thrust into the tight chute made from their interlaced hands. Querry looked down at their fingers and the heads of their cocks sprouting between. He thought it must've been the most beautiful, intimate sight he'd ever seen, and he stretched his neck out to kiss Frolic.

As their tongues jousted, they began to move together, hands coming down as hips pressed up. Soon they'd established a perfect rhythm, and again wet smacking resounded. Frolic reached orgasm first. Though he spilled no seed, Querry could tell he was coming when his whole body trembled, and he moaned as if sobbing. Holding Querry's hair for support, he threw himself back so hard his head almost smacked the nearby table. Querry quickly supported his back and took over with his hand while Frolic writhed helplessly, falling apart in his bliss. He didn't even notice when Querry's semen erupted, dribbling hot and white over their knuckles and into their laps. Querry wrapped his arms around Frolic and hugged him close, his face against Frolic's chest. At this proximity, Querry could hear the soft hum and click of the clockwork. Frolic's origins no longer mattered to Querry, though; he was no less human for them.

Touching Querry's hair lightly, as if it might be sharp, Frolic asked, "Is there a word for what we did, Querry?"

The vulgarities he heard on the street, words like rubbing off and fucking, came to Querry's mind, but he looked up at Frolic and said instead, "It's called love."

Then he wet a rag to wipe their hands and testicles, and he and Frolic lay facing each other, their limbs interlocked like the vines in a faerie's garden. They slept until late the next afternoon.

THE BELL and Badger served decent food and pints of ale brewed in its cellar, and so most evenings found it full of factory workers looking to drink away the day's woes. It was loud and smoky, and sawdust and mismatched furniture covered the floor. The smell was a mixture of grease, stale beer, and men and women who couldn't see the wisdom in washing when they'd be back in front of their machines in a few short hours. Some lower-end whores picked their way through the crowd, but it was much more a pub where people came to get drunk than to conduct criminal business.

Querry and Frolic sat at a table near the front door. The tallow candle in a jar sputtered low, deepening the shadows below their eyes, noses, and lips. The thief sipped idly at his brew, while Frolic watched the other patrons slurring out songs, brawling, or fondling each other with fascination. From a shadowy corner of the tavern, Querry noticed a familiar red-headed man watching with his hat almost covering his eyes. A drink sat untouched in front of him. Frolic detected him too, as he studied the Badger's other patrons. Once, a large, pock-marked man in suspenders asked the doll what he was looking at, compelling Querry to stand and push aside his greatcoat to reveal his sword. A lift of his brow sent the man on his way. Even in this part of town, many people knew the speed of Querry's sword by reputation.

The front door swung open to admit a man who looked decidedly out of place in his good-quality cape and hat. In his hand was a leather attaché case. Many of the pub's customers began to whisper right away, but in their various degrees of inebriation their whispers were more like shouts.

"Lost, is he?" Querry heard a woman say. "I'll give the poor dear a place to spend the night!" Her companions roared with laughter, and Querry grinned.

"Reginald Whitney!" Frolic shouted, springing to his feet and waving his arms as if a large field, instead of a few feet, separated Reg from their table.

Scowling at the attention the doll drew, Reg quickly took his seat. Soon the other patrons forgot about him and turned their backs. Querry slid a mug of ale that had been waiting to his friend. Reg sipped it and frowned. "How do you drink this piss, Querry?"

"Next time bring a bottle of wine," Querry said with a wink. "How was the party?"

Reg sighed heavily and set his case on the wobbly table. From within, he took a small journal, like an appointment book. "I had no trouble getting into His Lordship's study. With all of the influential people at the ball, nobody paid much attention to me. He had an inordinate number of foreign dignitaries as guests. I can't imagine what for, but they made for a fine distraction."

"Great!" Frolic exclaimed.

"Not really," Reg said. "His desk was strewn with notes and papers. Mostly things from the Archives: news articles about the tower, books written after it had been built, artist's depictions of the clockwork creatures at the top. There's an angel at each corner, which I didn't know. Really, why place all of that so high up that nobody can see it?"

"So, nothing?" Frolic said, his shoulders slumping.

"There was one thing. I didn't even know it existed, and I have no idea how Thimbleroy acquired it, but apparently the physician who'd attended Mad King Leopold had kept a journal."

"What's that to do with anything?" Querry asked.

Shrugging, Reg said, "Well, he was the one who commissioned the clock tower. Almost cleaned out the treasury. But I agree. The journal did little more than record the king's tendencies to wander around naked and hold court with pots and pans that he'd set up in his room. Thimbleroy clearly hadn't finished it, so I tore out the last page." He handed it to Querry.

"A royal archivist mutilating a rare book?" the thief teased, wagging his finger and earning a smile from Reg. He read aloud. "The king has been in a rage for days now. He will neither dress nor sleep, but storms about quarreling with paintings and chairs. The ladies of the court have been sent away for the sake of decency, and I fear His Majesty will need to be restrained. Oft times he has shouted at the sky, demanding the appearance of a Prince of Angels. Other times he calls for a key that he believes is being deliberately denied him. He seems to think these things will grant him immortality and sovereignty over the world, and threatens death and the most grisly torture upon whoever he believes withholds them. I am at my wits end as to how to help this poor man, and I fear for our fair kingdom. Still, my skills have failed me, and I can make no sense of His Majesty's condition."

They sat digesting the words, Frolic circling the rim of Querry's glass with his pinky. Finally he said, "It's all very sad, but, so what?"

"I agree," Querry said. "It's common knowledge now that the king was mad."

"Some say he was assassinated," Reg mused. "Before he could completely bankrupt the kingdom with his ludicrous projects."

"But what has this to do with anything?" Querry asked, frustrated. Something occurred to him then and he asked, "Reg, when is the first mention of faeries in a book?"

"Ancient times. They're a staple of our mythology. But the first actual account of a subject having discourse with a faerie was twenty-eight years ago. It's a queer little tale in a letter a visiting foreigner meant for his mother. Apparently he'd had too much to drink at a dinner party and decided a walk and some fresh air might make a cure. He made his way along streets he knew well enough, after having been in the city almost half a year. After a bit he came to a bridge he'd never seen before. He disliked it and the thick mist below it. He was of a mind to turn back when he saw a moth. He described it as big as a dinner plate, and more beautiful than anything he'd ever seen. Colored dust sprinkled down as it flapped its wings.

"And so this foreigner felt a strong compulsion to follow the moth. He went to the far end of the bridge, where there stood a single, square tower. He describes it in his letter as looking like a tombstone. A woman stood before the gate, wearing the most lavish gown, with a long train behind. As the man watched, the moth came to rest on her skirts, and he realized that her entire garment consisted of these insects, lying on their sides and forming layer after layer of what had first appeared as fine lace. The gentleman recounts dancing with this woman amidst a cloud of moths and the dust of their wings, which he said made him feel better and more confused than drink. And though the foreigner felt sure he'd indulged in only a single dance, he finally reached the home of his friends and found out he'd been away a week."

"What happened to him?" Frolic asked.

"He spent every night wandering the city in search of that bridge. Not long after he went mad and killed himself."

"Oh, how horrible! Poor man!"

Querry drummed his fingers. "They've been here twenty-eight years, yet nobody remembers them not being here. What a powerful enchantment. And Thimbleroy thinks he can get rid of them."

"But back to the point," Reg said, pulling his watch from his waistcoat pocket and flipping it open. "We're no further ahead than we were. We still have no idea why Frolic was made or what Thimbleroy wants with him."

"Don't forget, Reg, Thimbleroy doesn't know Frolic is what he's after. He doesn't know what he should've found in that cellar, does he?"

"No, I don't believe he does. Still, you must be careful. Could you, I don't know, do something about his hair? Tuck it up or flatten it out?"

Querry just laughed, and then he remembered something. "I say, Reg, would you happen to have some spare ink and a few sheets of writing paper?"

Reg produced them from his case, along with an expensive pen and blotter, and Querry put them in his coat pocket.

"What will we do now?" Frolic asked. "Could we go for a walk down by the water?"

"Join us?" Querry asked Reg.

"You know I can't."

"Why?" Frolic asked.

"It's very complex," he said, not unkindly, to Frolic. "I don't think you'd be able to understand it all yet." He stood, pushed his chair in, and lifted his hat to put it on.

Getting to his feet, Querry said, "Let's do what we said, Reg. Let's get a boat and leave this place. I'll be safe. Frolic will be safe. We won't have to worry over all this strange business ever again. We'll be able to live the way we want." He came closer, and said in a low voice, "You'd be able to kiss me whenever you felt like it and scream my name at the top of your voice when I made love to you."

"Querry!"

"Well, we have only to go."

Regaining his composure and taking an embroidered tissue from his pocket to dab at his sparkling forehead, Reg said, "Boats don't grow on trees, Querry. And none of us knows how to sail."

"I'll steal a boat. I'll learn to sail. How hard can it be?"

Frolic gave a little hop. "Oh, doesn't that sound lovely? Can't we go right away?" He reached out and took Reggie's hand, looking at him expectantly. Much to Querry's surprise, Reg didn't recoil. Holding Reg's fingers, Frolic bounced on the balls of his feet while he awaited Reg's reply.

But instead, the archivist addressed the thief. "It's not right to fill his head with this nonsense, Querry."

"Oh, come on, Reg! You can't still be considering marriage!"

"Of course. I have every intention of fulfilling my duties."

"They'll be expecting an heir. What will you do then?"

"I'll produce one."

Querry made an exasperated noise, lost for words. Beside him, Frolic's expression changed: his brows and mouth set into hard, straight lines. He dropped Reg's hand and set his own on his hip, chin lifted. "I, too, will find my duty and fulfill it, Reginald Whitney."

"Frolic!" Querry said. "I thought we'd cleared this matter."

The three of them stood in a triangle, each man's presence suddenly awkward to every other. Querry looked down at his boot, while Reg fidgeted with the clasps on his case. Frolic's eyes darted rapidly from the archivist to the thief. He seemed to sense the shift in mood, but didn't seem able to comprehend its cause nor correct it. Clearing his throat, Reg set his bowler on his head, mumbling that he needed to be off.

"You'll contact me if you learn anything more?" Querry asked.

When Reg didn't reply, but stood looking at Querry with a mixture of longing, exasperation, and possibly pity, Frolic once again took his hand, saying, "Please help me find out my purpose."

With a deep sigh, Reg said, "If I come across any pertinent information, I'll find a way to convey it to the two of you. Until then, I beg you, Querry, to be careful. Don't do anything foolish or flashy. Just keep your head down. Both of you."

"Reg—"

"I really need to be off. Mother will be asking questions."

Dissatisfied, Querry followed Reg and Frolic to the door. He looked over his shoulder and found the strawberry-blond man watching them intently. He smiled at Querry and raised his glass a fraction of an inch. Querry was just about to cross the room and speak with the man when some exiting patrons cursed him and his companions for blocking the door. Reg took Querry's wrist to hurry him along. Once outside, the three of them parted ways. Reg buttoned his high collar against the chill that had engraved the first frosty patterns on the Badger's dirty, little windows and headed up hill, toward the wealthy neighborhood that served as his home and prison. When he'd gone, Querry crammed his hands into his pockets, jabbed his thumb on the metal tip of the pen, and swore. His armored boot sent an empty bottle to shatter against the wall of the pub.

"Don't be sad, Querry," Frolic said. "Let's go for that stroll."

"I don't feel like going anymore. And it's cold."

"Let's kiss," Frolic suggested as he positioned himself in front of Querry. "That will raise your spirits, I daresay."

"We can't. Not here."

"Why? I saw plenty of people kissing inside."

"Men and women. Two men can't kiss where anyone might see."

"I don't understand the difference."

"You'll just have to take my word," Querry said. He thrust his shoulders up so more of his coat covered the back of his neck. Beneath his feet, the cobblestones looked sprinkled with confectioner's sugar. What had he expected, that the three of them would sail off that very night, and spend the rest of their days engaged in orgiastic bliss? Reg would never agree. Throughout the conversation, Querry had feared Frolic might say or do something and reveal to Reg that they'd been intimate. He found he didn't want Reg, or anyone else, to know. But, watching Frolic smile at the clouds of frozen air he exhaled, Querry couldn't deny his growing affection for the doll, either. But how would others judge a man who made love to a doll? The answer was simple: as a pervert, a deviant of the worst kind, on the same level as a man who took liberties with pigs and cattle, if not worse.

"I've never given a damn what anyone thinks, and I won't start now," Querry said aloud. "Come, Frolic. Let's go home. The cats will be hungry."

With a wide smile, Frolic skipped over and wound both of his arms around Querry's bicep. He nestled his cheek against Querry's shoulder as they began to walk, and Querry couldn't chastise him. The thief smiled in spite of himself. Before him, the frost had covered the grimy, dilapidated buildings. Everything sparkled: hedges, benches, trees, and even the blankets that covered the shoulders of beggars huddled in the alleys. Flurries fell in lazy spirals, even muffling the cacophony of drunkards and whores. Querry stole a kiss from Frolic before anyone could notice, and they made their way leisurely through fat, white flakes. Just as they entered their building, Querry caught sight of his strawberry-blond stalker, watching from underneath an awning across the street.

CHAPTER 5

OVER THE next few weeks, both Querry and Frolic gradually forgot about their problem. No one troubled them, and they had no more news from Reg, even though Querry made a point of inquiring every few days. Frolic proved almost as adept a cat burglar as Querry himself, and they lived rather well, with plenty to eat and some spare money for clothes and entertainment. Querry almost forgot Frolic's origins, as he felt so comfortable with him. Frolic proved the perfect partner in every way. With the money he'd stashed away, Querry even considered upgrading their lodgings. Before long, he'd probably be able to afford a small house in the merchants' district. Maybe one day, they might even move to the country.

But the presence of Frolic's leather book, and the work of translating it, always snapped Querry back to reality. Very slowly, he transcribed the weird code onto the paper Reg gave him. After he had a few pages, he read them before placing them in the back of the book. Soon he understood how Frolic had been constructed. His creator had put down, in meticulous detail, how his skeleton had been formed, and the complex clockwork at his joints that awarded him such natural movement. Querry discovered that Frolic drew in air so that it could fill sacks in his chest, where the vapor could condense and collect. His heart heated this water, and the small amount of steam produced traveled through a series of channels, turning gears that triggered other gears and powered tiny engines in the most intricate circuit Querry had ever seen. Thus, as long as he had access to air, Frolic had an endless supply of power.

His heart was made of magic. Though it was at times trying, Querry could comprehend the complex mechanics described by the doll maker. Some of the clockwork's gears were no larger or thicker than a fly's wing, but Querry understood the function of each, at least in theory. He couldn't, however, follow the arcane proceedings, and Frolic seemed made at least as much of enchantment as metal and gears. His skin, for example, consisted of fine silk, the clouds of a rosy sunrise, and the soft sighs of children during pleasant dreams, all woven together by an ensorcelled spider on May Eve. The book, at least, claimed so. Possibly it was another code. As for Frolic's heart, complex alchemy and rare enchantment kept it perpetually warm and able to turn water to vapor. The book explained how, inside a sphere of spell-protected glass, a mixture of dragon's breath, fire-flower petals, oaths spoken during love, and captive fever-dreams swirled together to produce mystic heat. The huge tome described Frolic's eyes, his perceptions, and his voice. Though fascinated, before long Querry set it aside. It no longer mattered to him how Frolic worked any more than it mattered exactly how Reg's stomach processed his dinner.

On the night of the first real snow, Querry and Frolic returned to find even Rushport white and pure as a maiden's chemise. Few boots had yet carved dirty furrows, and even fewer steam-carriages chugged through, leaving the snow mostly free from the grimy coating they left. The sky above them shone soft gray, similar to Frolic's curls. During their work, they'd found a fine bottle of port in a gentleman's library. It now waited within Querry's coat pocket, but he'd sampled enough to feel warm and giddy. His cheeks glowed with both drink and wind. Frolic looked happy, too, trying to focus on the snowflakes lodged in his long lashes.

"What shall we do?" Querry asked, squeezing his elbow. Though Frolic didn't need it, Querry had found him a scarlet soldier's greatcoat. It hadn't been easy to match his small size, but Querry didn't want to draw unnecessary questions. The color suited him, making his hair and skin look even more startlingly light.

Looking up at the sky, Frolic said, "Why don't we just walk? The night is so beautiful. I like it in the open air."

"Right then." In his high spirits, any proposal would have pleased the thief. He had to admit the chill air felt invigorating, and the white blanket muffled the din of the neighborhood and hid the grime beneath. He hooked his arm with Frolic's, and they set off in the direction of the water. If anyone commented, Querry could pretend to be drunk enough to require assistance. Just in case, he took another nip from the bottle.

Not a soul bothered the pair as they walked to the docks and back, feet wet and anticipating the warmth of the quilt and each other. They turned a corner, and Querry heard a familiar voice.

"Well, well, lads," said the thug in the patched top hat. "Ain't tonight our lucky night?"

His greasy cohorts laughed, and Querry stopped, his muscles wound tightly and his hand on his sword. The gang wouldn't get the advantage of surrounding him a second time. In the open they'd never match his speed. He heard the subtle creak of feet packing snow and spun on the ball of his foot, blade held out in front of him. Frolic also turned and drew, and his weight shifted to his back leg. He'd learned well.

"We've been looking fer ye," the leader said menacingly, though he kept a respectable distance. Behind him, the low light glinted off the knives and swords his men produced. Querry counted at least four or five more than last time, but he still didn't worry.

"It's a new month, pretty boy. Time to pay them dues. An' I regret to inform, the rates have gone up a bit. Fifty pounds."

Querry laughed out loud. This was a factory worker's yearly income and then some.

"Fifty pounds or an ear," said the man in the top hat, daring a step and holding the tip of his large knife just below his lip. "Or a nose. Or an eye. I ain't picky." Chortling, his gang began to close in. Querry and Frolic pressed their shoulders together, standing almost back to back, sword-arms parallel, their eyes never deviating from the large men.

When they got close enough to really see Frolic, though, all but the leader retreated a step. "Boss," said one, "he gots a faerie wif 'im."

"My arse!" the leader shouted.

"I once seen a faerie gentleman all in black, with a big, tall hat and two black cats on a leash," said another of the thugs. "Seen 'im walking up by the clock tower. Well, two constables came up, beating their sticks against their hands, and told him he had to leave. The gentleman just laughed, an' next thing I knew, where them two constables had stood was only a pile of turnips and a fat, pink pig eating to his heart's content. He didn't do nothin'. Only laughed."

"You bunch of whimpering girls," snarled the boss. "You collect my dues or you'll deal with me. Go on! I want his pretty blue eye for a cufflink."

They advanced slowly. Most of them were drunk. When a square-jawed brute, lower teeth jutting past his lip, swung a butcher knife at Querry's throat, the thief parried with a flick of his wrist, sending the weapon into a frozen pile of fish guts ten feet to the side. He similarly disarmed the next attacker, leaving the man without a button for his trousers. When two fat brothers rushed them from the left and right, brandishing clubs the size of small trees, Querry and Frolic each took a step back, leaving them to wallop each other unconscious.

The leader growled with rage, spittle freezing on his chin. From the corner of his eye, Querry saw a small, wiry man sneaking up behind Frolic. He was just about to warn Frolic when the doll turned and thrust deeply, just as he'd been taught. The man, who'd been holding a small knife over his head, had no time to block, and Frolic's blade sunk deep into his belly. Frolic's eyes darted to Querry, and he quickly pulled back on his weapon. A font of blood spurted from between the man's fingers, steaming in the snow.

"Querry," said Frolic, his voice trembling as he watched his victim sink to his knees and then fall facedown. The dark outline grew around him.

"You did well," Querry said quickly, remembering the first time he'd had to defend himself. "You did as you must. Keep your wits. There are more of them." He counted half a dozen, not including the man in the top hat, who showed himself more and more as the kind of man who only got his hands dirty when his victory could be assured: when his opponent had both arms pinned behind his back, for example.

The death of their comrade ignited the bloodlust of the gang, and they rushed Querry and Frolic screaming. Querry ducked to avoid a lead pipe swung at his temple, but caught a fist to the diaphragm as he rose. He landed hard on his tailbone, gulping for air. In desperation he reached for one of his guns, despite the attention a shot would draw. Rough, dirty hands grabbed the sides of his hair. A knee made contact with his lips, swelling them. Pain shot through his jaw and face and blood trickled down his chin. His hand went from his hip to protect his head. The leg in front of him drew back for another blow.

"Querry!" Frolic shouted. With his limited range of motion, Querry saw only a blur of grays and reds as Frolic dispatched two of the attackers with impossible speed. He heard the hum of the enchanted sword, two dull thuds and a sickly squish. Then the bodies fell, one on top of the other. The man holding him was thrown to the side with force well beyond even a strong human. He landed on his side, slid ten feet on the icy cobblestone, and didn't get up.

Shaking the haze from his head, Querry felt for his rapier and got to his feet. He licked the ferrous taste from his lips. Already Frolic ran toward the final three men, yelling and slicing arcs in the air before him. Querry hurried to follow. By the time he'd reached the group, Frolic had delivered a side-kick to the torso of the man in the leather helmet and goggles, sending him into the thug beside him. Both toppled like dominos, but before they could fall Frolic leapt into the air and hit each in the chest with one of his heels. The third man ran around the group and jumped to tackle Querry. Using the man's momentum against him, the thief crouched and flipped him over his shoulder. He landed badly on his head, jamming his neck into his shoulders and breaking it. To finish, Frolic went to each of the prone men he'd just defeated and plunged his sword into their throats with a cold sneer on his face. The flurries returned, melting on Frolic's cheeks.

Battle-lust coursing through him, Querry hacked with his sword and shouted, "Who else wants a go? Come on!"

The man in the top hat turned to run, but Frolic caught him by the coat, spun him, lifted him off his feet and slammed him against the nearest wall. He easily held him there, two feet from the ground, until Querry joined them.

Remembering what he'd suffered, Querry sheathed his blade and punched the man twice in the stomach. "It seems our positions are reversed this time. How does it feel?"

"What, what are you?" the man grunted at Frolic.

"Shut up," Querry said through his teeth as he hit the man with the back of his knuckles, making him spit out a rotting tooth. "If you ever come near us again, you'll wish that all I'd done is cut your other eye out. Do I make myself understood?"

He whimpered and nodded.

"Let's go home and wash the filth off our hands," Querry said, putting a hand on Frolic's shoulder. The doll tossed the gang leader far and effortlessly, as if he were a dirty rag instead of a large man.

"I knew you could handle yourself," Querry said as they turned their backs on bodies already disappearing beneath a blanket of white, "but that was amazing. Where in the world did you learn to do that?"

Frolic stopped in the street and looked down at his hands. Gashes and scabs covered Querry's knuckles, as he hadn't been wearing his gloves. The doll's fingers, while bloody and dirty, showed not a single scratch. "I don't know what came over me," he said softly. "When I saw them hurt you, I became so angry. I wanted to destroy them. To just tear them to pieces. I don't think I could have stopped myself."

"You have nothing to worry yourself about. If you hadn't, it would be us lying back there. I don't think they'll bother us again." They started off again, the snow building icy caps on the tops of their heads. Querry's blood still sang with victory and violence. He felt fantastic. Tonight, he decided, he would make love to Frolic. They'd proved quite a team, and the time to cement their union had come. Finally, guilt and uncertainty would be swept away. There would be only bodies writhing in pleasure, finally joined the way they both desired. In the dark, quiet street, Querry laughed out loud, caught Frolic's hand, and quickened his pace.

MUCH ABOUT the boarding house felt familiar to Querry: drunks and whores cluttering the stairwells, heated quarrels spilling from behind thin doors, and beggars crouched in the shadows, hoping to go unnoticed and avoid expulsion. But something felt wrong in the way the other tenants eyed the two men, looking quickly away if noticed. Fear hung in the air. Querry knew the other residents felt no loyalty toward him, so he didn't question them. He did stay near to Frolic, though, and urged him quickly through the shadows between the pools of candlelight from the wall sconces.

When they reached their room, Querry saw right away that the door had been pried loose with a bar. Deep gouges marred the frame. He held up his hand and Frolic stopped. In the dark houses of the wealthy, the two thieves had perfected non-verbal communication. Querry pressed his ear to the door and listened for many minutes to silence. Cautiously he opened it a crack. It creaked and bits of his clockwork lock pinged against the floor. A shaft of light from the window assured him the room was empty, and also that it had been thoroughly ransacked. The table lay on its side, gears spilled everywhere. The mattress had been ripped from the bed and slit open. Food and dishes had been flung about, chipping the plaster walls.

Frolic dug through the debris until he found and lit the candle. Holding it in his hand, he scanned around, making a clicking noise with his tongue. Beneath the shredded blanket, he found Toerag puffed up to twice his size. Frolic quickly scooped him up and put him inside his coat.

Querry heard movement in the hall: heavy boots failing to walk softly. "Frolic," he whispered. "We have to go. Now. The window."

"But Tosser!"

"She'll find us."

"No!"

"Frolic, now!"

Flinging up the mattress, Frolic retrieved the other cat from the corner of the bed frame. She yowled miserably as he tucked her away beside her brother and buttoned his coat. Meanwhile Querry secured his grapple to the sill and unlatched the window. "Go," he hissed at Frolic, who was trying to tuck his coat into the waistband of his trousers. After Frolic made it halfway, Querry swung his leg over and hurried down the rope. The questionable wood splintered, though, and they both fell the last six feet.

As he dusted himself off, Querry noticed a group of men stationed in front of the next building. Unlike the pack of thugs, they looked sober and well dressed. Already they approached Querry and Frolic, their hands disappearing inside their coats.

"Frolic, run!" Querry yelled.

They sped through the alleyways, slipping on the snow. Querry pushed Frolic in front of him, trying his best to shield Frolic's shoulders with his arm. He cursed the easily followed trails they left in the snow. No matter what a lead they gained, their pursuers quickly found them. Querry swore, his lungs burning, running as hard as he could. Their only hope would be to reach a crowded area, where many footprints would obscure their tracks. For once, though, Rushport was quiet, desolate. The few whores desperate enough to venture out huddled close to the warmth of the bricks, clutching their shawls.

Daring a glance over his shoulder, Querry counted four men, each holding a shiny new pistol in his hand. He couldn't imagine why they held their fire, unless they worried over damaging Frolic. No one would give a second thought to a back-shot cat burglar. Now and then Querry swore he saw someone else, a lone figure following at a distance, though he had no time to wonder or observe it.

Block after block of quiet houses stretched before them. Candles burned in a few windows, but most stood dark as tombs. The narrow alleys between them led only to dead ends. Querry pushed on, thighs burning and trembling. He almost envied Frolic, running beside him without so much as quickened breath. And in fact, Querry felt sure the doll could go much faster.

"Frolic," he panted. "Run on ahead. Find a place to hide and I'll—"

He waited for his coughing spell to pass, and continued. "I'll hold them off, catch up later."

"No, Querry!"

"Frolic, please!"

"You'll be killed!"

"I won't," Querry lied. Without the blessings of much luck, he'd be gunned down. He was worthless to these men. But he wouldn't let them take Frolic. "Go. Find Reg. Go to Reg."

Skidding to a halt, Frolic said, "I have no purpose, no reason to live! And without you, I won't belong to anyone. I'll be completely lost." He covered his face with his hands and started to sob, just as four dark shapes turned the corner.

Urging him forward, practically dragging him, Querry said, "We must keep going, Frolic."

"I can't go on alone. I was alone so long, Querry!"

"I won't leave you."

"Never?"

"Never. I swear it. But we must go. We can't engage in another fight. Especially not a gunfight. If those men don't get us, the police will! We've got to make it to the factories. Then we can blend in and lose them."

"Get on my back, Querry."

"What?"

"I can run faster than you. I can lose them."

"But, I'm almost twice your size!"

"Querry," Frolic pleaded. "I'm strong. You know that I am."

Though he hated the idea of being the saved rather than the savior, Querry's instinct for self-preservation couldn't argue, and he climbed onto Frolic's back, crossing his ankles over Frolic's belt and holding his shoulders. The doll began to run, and the lazily falling snowflakes changed to comet-like blurs. The rushing air hit Querry's face like a wall. His eyes streamed, and his lungs stung. Frolic ran at least as fast as a colt in the springtime, but so smoothly that Querry didn't bounce against his back. It felt like gliding, flying. Querry had always fantasized about flight. Not even the cats showed distress, but poked their smoke-colored noses out of Frolic's coat curiously.

Frolic sprinted tirelessly, block after block, mile after mile. The shouts of the curious were left far behind before Querry could process their words. In no time, throngs of factory workers appeared. Frolic slowed to a walk, and Querry checked behind them, seeing no sign of the strange men. He hopped down, and soon the mass of people absorbed them. As soon as he could, Querry ducked behind a cart heaped with scrap metal. It blocked the opening to a cinderblock corridor: a storage area for more refuse and also an excellent hiding place. Querry lowered his goggles over his eyes and switched to the night-vision lenses. He and Frolic navigated the junk piles until they reached the wall at the back, and then they leaned as Querry caught his breath.

"You know," he said when he'd recovered, "I truly thought they'd forgotten us. I thought they'd just let us be. Let us live. Those men were well trained and well equipped. Someone put up some money to find you."

"I still can't imagine why they'd want me."

Querry could. "Frolic," he said firmly. "No matter who gets a hold of you, no matter what they say, just remember that you're mine. I found you, and nothing can change that."

"Yes, Querry. I know. But what will they try to do with me?"

"They don't even know you're what they're after. I say we keep on letting everyone think you're a faerie. People are afraid of faeries. They let them be."

"I don't even know what a faerie is."

"Nobody really does."

"They destroyed our home," Frolic said, his back sliding down the wall until he crouched on the ground.

"It was just a rented room," Querry said, joining Frolic. "Nothing special."

"It was special to me. I've never had anywhere to be."

"Me neither. I'm sorry, Frolic. I'll find us another place."

"Where will we go until then?"

"I can only think of one option."

ROSEBERRY SQUARE was new and modern: a series of tall, thin, brick buildings circling a statuesque bronze goddess. Above her head she held an enormous glass orb. It glowed with gaslight to rival the moon, giving the square a striking semblance to a group of rakish men standing around a fire. All of the buildings looked identical, save for the different colors of their shutters and doors. Querry and Frolic crept quietly toward a house decorated with burgundy woodwork.

Since the work of the widow named Mrs. Spaulding was as much to report to Mrs. Whitney as to take Reg's suits to the laundry, prepare his bath, and cook his breakfast, Querry lead Frolic around the back of the building and picked the simple lock on the cellar door. They tiptoed past Reg's impressive wine collection, the generators that heated his water, and up the stairs, where Querry cracked the door to the kitchen. Mrs. Spaulding washed the china, tossed some wood into the potbelly stove, and set some dough to rise on the windowsill. Then the hunched old woman retired to her small room beside the pantry. The two thieves crossed the white tiles and ascended to the first floor.

The houses of the square had been designed specifically for wealthy bachelors, and contained everything such men would require in narrow rooms stacked high. This level housed a thin foyer, a gentleman's study, and a formal dining room in which Reg could host his obligatory small dinner parties. Querry and Frolic found him at the table, relaxing with his shirt untucked and leafing through the daily news as he picked at his food. Adept at sneaking as they were, he never noticed them standing in the doorway until Tosser mewled loudly. Jumping to his feet, Reg's silverware clanged on the marble floor.

"Querry!" he hissed. "What the hell are you doing here? You have to leave!"

"Relax," Querry said, coming forward. "Nobody knows we're here."

"I don't care! You know what kind of mess this could make! Mrs. Spaulding—"

"She's asleep. I made sure."

"You have to go, Querry!"

Putting both of his hands on Reg's shoulders, Querry said, "We're in trouble. We have nowhere else to turn."

Reg looked at Querry's battered knuckles. "Please don't drag me into this. I can't get involved. The Whitneys are a public family. You staying here is impossible."

"You'd really turn me out when I need you most? I mean that little to you?"

Shrugging off Querry's hands, Reg dropped dejectedly into his upholstered chair and leaned his forehead against his palm. With a swipe of his other hand, he indicated the leftovers. "Sit down. Help yourself to some dinner. That woman always cooks for a regiment."

Frolic tugged his coat from his waistband and the cats landed softly. They began to explore, sniffing and yowling. Reg's head crumpled even closer to his table linens. Querry removed his coat and sat down, his back to the cheery fire in the hearth. The food looked wonderful and smelled better: field peas in butter sauce, roasted parsnips speckled with herbs, two kinds of dinner rolls, cream soup in a silver tureen, a row of stuffed pigeons on a platter, some sardines and a rabbit. Safe now, he felt the loss of his dinner acutely and helped himself to a glass of sherry. As he ate, Frolic relayed to Reg the events of the evening in a dramatic way, using his hands to demonstrate how he'd vanquished the thugs. Querry grew less anxious as his belly filled, and his chapped skin warmed. Reg's presence soothed him, always had. After a quarter of an hour the three men conversed merrily as they enjoyed the wines with an apple tart.

"Mrs. Spaulding has been hinting about a visit to her daughters in the North," Reg said. "The youngest just had a son. I suppose I could send her off for a few weeks. You'll still have to make yourself scarce when the housemaids come 'round on Mondays and Thursdays."

"Thanks, Reg," Querry said. Content and a little tipsy, he already envisioned certain advantages to living in his friend's house. "We'll stay out of sight, and we won't be any trouble."

"You can't stay forever," Reg said. "And you can't go back to that boarding house. Thimbleroy or whoever searched your room will be looking for you. What will you do?"

The thief considered, though the matter didn't feel particularly pressing at the moment. For the next month or so, he had shelter, plenty of food, and the company of his lost love. "Hard to say. Save some money. Look for a new place eventually."

"You're infuriating! You two won't be safe in the city! They'll be looking for you and Frolic!"

"I'll have to make sure they don't find us, won't I?"

"Querry, when are you going to face reality and grow out of this bugger-the-world phase?" Reg said, slapping the table so hard that the dishes shook.

"When the world stops trying to bugger me!" Querry's voice rose with his anger. "What reality do you want me to face, Reg? The rest of my life in a factory? A dull wife and a brood of children I can't feed? No, thank you! I'll take a few years of freedom over thirty of misery."

"And you're so happy living in that little room, with the noose just a few steps ahead of you?"

"What choice do I have?"

"Well, you could apprentice yourself. Learn a trade."

"The trades are dying out, Reg. Nobody's going to wait a month for a hand-carved chair when a factory cranks out a hundred a day. And I won't take orders and sweep up at a blacksmith or a bakery. Why should I?"

"Has it occurred to you, Querry, that it's not just you any longer? You're putting Frolic in danger now too."

"Nonsense. Nobody knows what he is or where he came from. They think he's a faerie. How in the world will anyone ever find out—"

All of Querry's organs felt like they melted. Cold sweat sprang from his pores.

"What is it?" Frolic asked. "Querry?"

"The book," Querry panted. "It wasn't there. They got a hold of it, and my notes in the back. They'll break the code. Fuck me, they'll know everything!" He leapt to his feet, pacing and rubbing the back of his neck. "What am I going to do?"

"What book?" Reg asked, standing also. "What are you talking about?"

Coming around behind Frolic, Querry gripped his arms possessively. "Reg, I need you to help me. Help me, and I'll never ask you for anything again. I'll go away and leave you, if you want. I'll never bother you again."

"You're scaring me, Querry. Tell me what's going on. What is this book?"

"When I found Frolic, he had a book with him. It was all written in this weird code. That's why I asked you for the ink and paper, so I could try to translate it."

"And what's in this book?" Reg asked nervously.

"Everything!" Querry shouted. "Everything about how he was made, how he works. He wanted me to figure out what he was for. Except I never made it to the end, never found out. But Thimbleroy will! He'll have teams of people working on it!"

"And now he'll know that I'm what he's looking for," Frolic said.

Nuzzling his face into the top of Frolic's hair, Querry said, "I'll protect you. I'll find a way, I promise."

"I love you, Querry," the doll said in a shaky voice.

Querry looked up and met Reg's eyes. It was time he knew. "I love you, too, Frolic."

Eyes wide, Reg stammered, "You, you mean—"

"I'm not ashamed," Querry said. "He's no different than you or I, Reg. No different in any way."

"Oh, Querry. How could you?"

"We haven't done anything wrong. We make each other happy. What does it matter if we were made differently?"

"It matters, and you know it," Reg said.

"Not to me," Querry said. "And it hasn't changed the way I feel about you. I wanted you from the time we were boys, before I even knew what I was feeling. I love you, Reg, and I always will. And I need your help. Please."

"What can I possibly do?" Reg asked, his eyes glistening and his cheeks red.

"Just keep Frolic here. Keep him hidden. Send Mrs. Spaulding away."

"Where will you be, Querry?" Frolic asked.

"I'm going to get some answers."

"Where? From who?" Reg reached out for Querry, concern on his face. Querry clasped his hand and pulled him close, wrapping one arm around his waist and crossing the other over Frolic's chest. He squeezed hard, holding them, closing his eyes to enjoy the feel of their bodies, the sound of their breathing, their warmth and different scents. Then he took Reg's hand and placed it on Frolic's neck. The doll leaned toward Reg's chest.

"This is how I want it," Querry said. "Just like this." He inclined his face into Frolic's hair and Reg's shoulder, but Reg wriggled free of his embrace, and Querry cursed himself for pushing too far too soon.

"Will you help us?" he asked.

After a deep breath, Reg said, "I'll keep him here until you get back. I'll look after him and see that he's safe. But after that, you need to let me live my life. No more of this. No more coming here, reminding me what will never be, hurting me with your impossible schemes. I need your word."

"But we could still—"

"Querry, no!" Reg said firmly. "No, we couldn't. I need to put all of that behind me, content myself with a wife and family. And if you care for me at all, you'll let me, and stop ripping open these old wounds."

Nodding, Querry said, "If that's what you want, Reg, then so be it. You can forget all about me."

"You know I won't forget you," Reg said, his hand jerking like he wanted to touch Querry again. Instead, he shoved it into his trouser pocket. "But a memory's the only indulgence I can afford."

Querry turned to Reg, took his face in both hands, and kissed him gently, holding his lips to Reg's for a long time, swiping his tongue softly across Reg's teeth. Then he said, "Goodbye then, Reg. Thank you."

Reg spun away, his back to Querry and his knuckles to his mouth. Querry would let him have his private tears, deal with his choice in his own way. To Frolic, Querry said, "I'll be back for you soon. Trust Reg, and listen to him."

"Please be careful, Querry," Frolic said, standing. His hand curled around the back of Querry's neck, and they engaged in a much more passionate farewell. Then Querry donned his heavy coat, checked all of his gear, and took one last, long look at the two men he loved before braving the cold uncertainty of the night.

Chapter 6

THE SNOW deepened, drifting two feet up the sides of the buildings Querry passed. His boots carved furrows on the walks, and inside them his toes numbed. Many people had fallen back on the folkloric charms against the fey: red ribbon, rowan twigs, or iron nails decorated almost every door. Watching the smoke curl from the chimneys made Querry feel small and alone beneath the vast, white sky. That perfect moment, with his belly full, his body toasty, and both Reg and Frolic in his arms, felt months and years past. Querry put it out of his mind. He made his way past the abandoned homes, to the two glowing trees with the intertwined branches. Beneath them, the snow stopped. Even when a gust of wind sent flurries in their direction, they evaporated upon passing beneath the boughs. Not a droplet remained. The air, though, felt just as cold against Querry's exposed face. The chill couldn't dissuade the residents of Neroche from merriment. In front of Querry passed a cheerful procession of gauze-clad girls sprinkling flower petals and tapping hand-drums. Behind them came a huge white goat, and upon his back sat a chubby, rosy, young boy playing the flute.

Neroche looked wilder than Querry recalled, but his recollections felt more like distant dreams. Had the houses always been surrounded by little, gray woods, so that only their top floors and roofs were visible from the street? On the peaks of those roofs sat things neither human nor avian. Their glowing eyes followed the thief as he passed. Had the stone of the streets and walls been so pitted and crusted with moss and ivy? Lichen even covered the cobblestone beneath Querry's feet, and from the gutters grew tall, silvery rushes that swayed though he felt no wind. The rustling sounded too much like whispered promises, assurances that all of his desires would come true. Querry hurried past, and almost collided with a row of blue, glass bottles, hung on a rope like laundry. A hunched woman swore at him in her language and chased him off with a broom.

Querry wandered the narrow, twisting lanes for a long time. He couldn't find his way, couldn't even find a landmark to gauge his progress. A glimmering mist enveloped central Neroche, and though it parted now and then to reveal a star-lit pool or twisted sapling in perfect clarity, most of the time it hid from Querry objects only a few feet from his eyes. Above him, the balconies and gables of the manors looked as flat and translucent as if they'd been cut from tissue paper. Branches and clouds showed through some. In the distance Querry heard a lute being plucked. He went toward the sound, but found himself between two long benches, each of them full of hooded figures with their heads and shoulders cast down.

Querry reached for the comforting presence of his sword, and ignored the knowledge that it would do him little good. He was scared; he'd wandered deeper into Neroche than he'd known it extended. Neroche was a good-sized district, but Querry had been walking long enough to cross a small county. He had a distinct impression that he'd crossed into the Other World that many theorized overlapped with his own in Neroche. The fog was so deep now that he saw nothing but gray. Gray maidens flitted by him, taking corporeal form long enough to ruffle his hair, touch his cheek, or breathe propositions into his ears before dissolving back into the vapor. No plants or dwellings broke the monotony. Querry couldn't see his feet, so he didn't know what lay beneath them.

Loam-scented air gusted over Querry. Wet fingers fondled his earlobes, wriggled down his shirt-collar. He reached out with his hand, felt nothing, and ran. His soles made no sound against the walks. Desperately Querry pictured his golden-haired gentleman and ignored the sultry laughter off in the haze. So saturated was Neroche with magic that a thought alone might conjure one's wish, and Querry soon found himself looking up at the round palace, high atop the hill of blue roses. Ivory columns hundreds of feet high encircled the central structure. Amber light spilled invitingly from the windows.

Though it seemed miles away, Querry sprinted toward the house without looking back.

A party was going on. Guests arrived on the backs of white horses or in carriages drawn by red lizards, shining black lions, or overgrown albino rabbits. A handsome, young man with a tangle of fair hair and feathers sprouting from his head dismounted a barn owl and offered Querry his elbow with a smile. The thief saw his taloned feet beneath a white skirt that was his only garment, save for a necklace of hooked claws. His eyes, beneath his downy brows, were black orbs unbroken by any other color. A hint of blue tinged his lips, as if he'd been too long in the cold. Still, Querry let himself be escorted to the front door, where the bat-eared butler took his coat.

The hall inside stretched on for literal miles, impossibly immense. Hundreds of chandeliers hung from the ceiling, some so far in the distance that they struck Querry as mere pinpricks of light. He could see no end to the room, but along the sides he noticed an arched door every dozen feet or so. His companion patted his forearm, grinned, and pointed to the dance floor, where thousands of others whirled about in dizzying spirals of color and sparkle. Reeling, Querry let the other clasp his waist and spin him. He felt featherlight, carefree, dazzled by the beauty and opulence that surrounded him.

And yet, he felt small and lost in darkness, with horrible things flapping just above him.

How could two such sensations coexist? Querry's partner dipped him and held the back of his neck to guide him upright. The other man smiled, showing sharp teeth and a bruise-purple tongue. Querry knew he should be afraid, but the other man lowered his lips to Querry's neck, and to Querry that felt just fine.

His mouth was warm and sweet.

There was the tiniest prick.

"Mr. Knotte! To what do I owe this unexpected pleasure?" The gentleman had taken Querry's elbow and turned Querry to face him. Holding Querry's biceps, stepping to the side in something like a dance, he guided Querry toward the edge of the room. Hadn't someone else been with them a moment ago? Querry looked up and saw a small, white feather drifting down. He wondered where it had come from, since he hadn't seen any birds. But the ceiling was so high that darkness eventually obscured the chains that held the chandeliers.

"I wanted something from you," Querry said, watching the gentleman's gem-like eyes catch the light.

"I would say it's about time," came the answer. Querry twirled again. He felt the wall against his back, a chest against his chest.

"No."

"Surely you like to dance, Mr. Knotte?"

"Yes."

Querry felt himself whisked to the center of the hall. People backed away, giving the couple space to dance. A lively waltz began to play, but atonal and somewhat eerie. Querry could identify not a single instrument, nor could he locate the musicians. The gentleman held his lower back and left wrist as they spun back and forth. The thief found that he enjoyed himself immensely. How devastating the faerie looked, dressed in a copper suit with gold embroidery that only his hair outshone. He watched Querry with a hungry smile on his face as he twirled and dipped him. Querry felt the contented distraction that usually only came with half a bottle of absinthe. His feet somehow knew the steps, anticipated the tempo of the music.

Hadn't he come here for something? It had been important....

"I needed something—"

"Some wine, to be sure," the gentleman said, and released Querry's hand. A moment later he held a flute of pale liquid. "An excellent vintage. Made from the golden apples guarded by the Hesperides."

"What?" Querry took the glass. It was the oldest rule, not to eat or drink what they offered. But he felt so thirsty! Surely just a sip....

"I'm so glad you decided to come by," the gentleman was saying. "I was terribly bored. In fact, I was about to go out into the town and find some interesting people to keep me company. Alas, though, interesting people are so hard to come by."

"Are they?"

"Oh, not you, Mr. Knotte! I'm always captivated by you. I'm sure it's why we get along so well, us both being intelligent, adventurous, and cultured men. Beauty, I've always maintained, seeks out beauty as well." He stroked the side of Querry's hair, then his cheek, before taking hold of Querry's hand again to lead him in their dance.

"You are beautiful," Querry said, having given up on trying to control his actions and impressions. "Like nothing I've ever seen."

"Quite! But as I was saying, I'm more often than not bored and disappointed by the people of this age. I find they're nothing like I was led to believe. You see, for several centuries now I've had much to attend in my own lands, and little time to spare to explore yours. So I had my servants bring me records of your history. Such fascinating men! Such heroic exploits! That boy who traveled to the land of the giants and defeated their leader! The bastard child who became High King of your land and united all of the knights around his table!"

"Oh no. Those are just stories."

"And my favorite, about the thief-prince in the forest! Taking gold from the wealthy and giving it to the poor peasants. I could pass time with that fellow! These were the kind of men I came here hoping to meet. You can imagine my disappointment at finding a city populated by grocers and cart drivers. Scarcely a single person worth my attention! No one to engage in stimulating conversation. I'd almost given up hope when I met you."

"But... me?"

"Oh, indeed! I knew as soon as I set eyes upon you and your heroic bearing. What brilliant companions we'll make."

They continued to dance in wider and wider circles. It surprised Querry that they didn't collide with anyone else, at the speed they went. But the gentleman's other guests seemed insubstantial, more like shadows. The room seemed darker as well, and Querry had a distinct impression that the crystal chandeliers were really more like metal discs with fires lit on top. From his shadowed face, the gentleman's green eyes glowed. He smiled wide, teeth shining, and his hand slipped from Querry's back to cup his ass. They spun and spun, so fast that

Querry perceived only flashes of flame and darkness. He held tight to his partner, who smelled like a wood after the rain.

The blackness grew deeper. In front of Querry, the green eyes brightened until he could focus on nothing else. He stared into them without blinking, adoring them, his only anchor in the void. Hands snaked beneath his shirt. Their contact with his skin was the most sensuous, divine thing Querry had ever felt. They moved up his waist, and he was in paradise. His head lolled backward, and he groaned with sheer ecstasy. Seizing the opportunity, the gentleman kissed up Querry's neck and licked the ridge of his ear when he reached it.

He spoke softly into Querry's hair, in a voice saturated with lust and more beautiful than any symphony. "At first I took offense to your rejections of me. I thought to curse you, make you hideous so no one else would want you."

"Sorry," Querry panted. He couldn't think. He'd never stood in such a whirlwind of erratic need. As his hands darted from the gentleman's golden hair, to the angles of his back, to the soft globes of his ass, Querry felt like he'd be torn apart. Again he moaned.

"Not at all, Mr. Knotte. You see, it occurred to me that it was only a facet of your nobility of character. I realized that you were not the type of man to fall at anyone's feet. A man such as yourself would require expert seduction. Formal courtship of the most elegant kind. I soon found the challenge increased my fascination with you. How, I wondered, to get my hands on your willing flesh, my lips on your wonderful lips? And now you come to me."

They kissed then, mouths opening wide and tongues crashing together. Querry held tight to the shoulders of the other, whose fingernails cut Querry's scalp. He couldn't feel the floor beneath him as he ground his erection against his partner and tried to catch the gentleman's tongue with his own. They still spun, still danced, though Querry moved his body only to wriggle closer to the fey, claw at his brocade suit, grasp handfuls of his hair. His breath came in irregular puffs, and the sound of his pulse filled his head. The gentleman's finger skimmed the buckles of Querry's vest, and they fell open. Querry tore the garment from his body as if it were on fire, and followed with the rest of his clothes, ripping the buttonholes of his linen shirt in his enthusiasm. In the darkness he stood naked, flushed and sweaty, cock throbbing. The glowing eyes approached him, and silken, strong arms wrapped around him. The gentleman's body against his felt like a marble statue wrapped in exquisite satin. A patch of downy hair caressed Querry's belly, and a fine, long cock poked against it. Again lips touched his neck as fingers traced the contours of his legs. Querry circled his hips fitfully, barely clinging to sanity.

"How I've waited for this," the faerie said, swiping his burning tongue over Querry's Adam's apple. "To feel your skin. To know your scent." He inhaled deeply of Querry's hair. "And now." Grasping Querry firmly by the shoulders, he guided Querry to his knees.

"Yes!" Querry panted, burrowing his face into sparse hair as soft as pussy willow fuzz, smelling soil and wet mushroom. His tongue flicked out and found the seam between the faerie's balls. After a few moments of enthusiastic licking, Querry drew them both into his mouth and suckled them, rolling first one, then the other, across the top of his tongue.

The gentleman moaned softly and rubbed circles on the top of Querry's head. "You came to me, because you know, as I do, that there's no one else to make a worthy partner for you. These simpletons, butchers and records clerks—"

Withdrawing his mouth and mopping his chin, Querry asked, "What did you say?" Something stirred in his mind at the gentleman's words, but he couldn't connect with the thought. It swam out of his grasp like a minnow through a child's fingers. In only a few seconds, he decided it couldn't matter nearly as much as the slender fingers winding in his hair, pulling him close, or the velvety cock head pressing against his lips. He opened his mouth to taste the dew seeping from the slit, and purred with satisfaction. Patiently but insistently the gentleman pushed forward, and Querry relaxed his jaw as the wonderful delicacy slipped between his teeth and filled his mouth. He sucked hard, earning another drizzle of come. Querry's own penis, more painfully swollen than he could ever remember it being, responded in kind. He took hold of the other's calves, bracing himself to go to work, eager to feel the delightful texture of the gentleman's skin against his palate, the wonderful friction, the final, delectable explosion of seed.

Querry opened his throat and twisted his face slightly as he plunged toward the faerie's flat stomach. The other inhaled sharply, his fists closing around Querry's locks to guide Querry's motion. He pulled Querry's head back and then thrust in deep, tickling Querry's lips and chin with his gilded pubic hair. As they fell into a relaxed rhythm, Querry's mouth formed a tight vacuum around the gentleman's cock. His tongue twined around it, lapped at the sensitive underside and around the ledge of the head. Above his forehead, the faerie's ribs spread as he gulped quick, shallow breaths.

"Querrilous," he said, scratching the back of the thief's neck.

Motivated by the sound of his first name spilling from those divine lips, Querry picked up speed, desperate to taste the faerie's come, and eager to gain release for himself. But before he could accomplish either, he found lips, a tongue had replaced the dick in his mouth. The gentleman knelt facing Querry, his kisses soothing the pleasantly tender places in Querry's mouth. His soft hand felt out Querry's cock and squeezed it. Before Querry knew it had happened, he found himself on his back beneath the gentleman with his legs in the air.

The fey spoke sweetly to him, saying, "Here in the dark I can see your hopes and fears spilling out around your edges like light from under a door. I can almost see everything about you."

"I can only see your eyes."

The gentleman chuckled. "I see that you've had many lovers, Querrilous. Made love to many men. But I also see that you let very few have you. One, in fact, besides myself."

He continued to talk about Querry's high standards and his own worthiness, but Querry barely heard. He barely felt the other's weight on his chest or hands on his body. He was back in the factory, hid behind a triangle of oily canvas. Reg lay beneath him, his legs wrapped tightly around Querry's body, his pelvis moving in tight loops. Their dirty uniform shirts matched. Beyond their sanctuary Querry heard the chug and hiss of the machines, the drunken shouts of the other workers.

He spit into his palm, took hold of his shaft, and guided himself toward Reg's opening.

"Querry," Reg said in a trembling voice. "Please, Querry. Let me do it to you this time."

He'd kissed Reg hard and straddled him. As he lowered his body, wincing at the cleaving sensation, he'd said, through gritted teeth, "Only because I love you."

"Mr. Knotte, I refuse to make love to you whilst you think about another man." Querry was alone on the floor, which was cold stone. The gentleman had already stood. In a hazy light, like that which precedes a winter dawn, Querry saw him turn his back and walk away, his shining hair swishing back and forth. Querry was alone in the hall, which was round and lit by a chandelier of clinking crystals. Six arched doorways stood at equal intervals.

Querry went to one and turned the knob. Outside lay a hideous scarlet landscape. Noxious fumes rose from cracks in the parched ground and twisted black trees raised leafless branches toward a sunless sky. Filled with dread, Querry slammed the door.

Next he found a gray sea and sky. Waves lapped at a rocky outcrop many miles long. A single bird call complemented the rhythm of the tide. If the previous scene had filled Querry with terror, then this monochromatic world inspired deep loneliness and melancholy. Sighing, he turned away.

Trying the other doors, Querry found a path leading into a wood, an infinite sky, the stars beneath his feet, and a bubbling lagoon surrounded by brightly colored birds and flowers unlike any he'd ever seen. Finally he walked below the last arch and found himself in an alley, surrounded by the familiar smells of cheap booze, refuse and vomit. A few vagrants huddled together, drunk, snoring loudly, and dusted with snow. Bitter cold assaulted Querry's bare skin. His feet lost sensation instantly. He clapped a hand over his shrinking genitals and tried to remember why he was here. Where was here? Feeling disoriented and exhausted, Querry stumbled into the street, hoping to find his way home before someone caught him defenseless or he froze to death. He ducked behind a building and whisked a cloth from an empty newsstand to drape over his shoulders. Querry managed a few more steps before he fell to his knees. The world went dark and blurry. With the last of his energy Querry curled up behind a wooden barrel and covered as much of his exposed skin with the fabric as he could. He saw the silhouette of a person approaching and reached for his absent blade. He balled his fists to defend himself as the stranger drew nearer, but his head dropped to the side of the barrel and he saw no more.

A VIOLENT coughing spell woke Querry. He lay in a puddle of sweat, his head pounding and flesh on fire. He hacked until he nearly threw up, then choked down a few breaths to banish his vertigo. Darkness and flames blurred at the edges of his vision. He couldn't focus his eyes. He retched. Nothing came up.

He had another fever. They spread like wildfire through the workhouse in winter, due to the filthy conditions and lack of proper food. The many who succumbed would be wrapped in thin sheets and piled on a cart bound for pit-style mass graves. Querry hoped he wouldn't be among them, but he'd gone cold now. His hands trembled, and he couldn't feel his feet. Medicine, even a decent bowl of soup, were luxuries beyond the wildest dreams of the factory workers.

But someone had tucked a blanket around Querry and smoothed the damp fringe out of his face. Tepid water flowed into his mouth. He sputtered, but managed to get a teaspoonful past his swollen throat.

"You're going to be all right," said a gentle voice. Querry recognized it.

"Reg?" he croaked and tried to sit up. All of his muscles ached and shook, and he fell back against the ground before he could even lift his shoulders.

The cup came again to his lips. "Just rest," Reg said, petting Querry's forehead.

Thank the heavens for Reg, Querry thought. Without each other, neither of the young men would likely survive the horrors of the factory. Many times Querry had lifted a metal bar to prevent the older workers from sampling the delicate blond's favors by force. Reg talked Querry out of reckless fights and took care of him when he got sick. As Querry lay vulnerable, Reg guarded him against those who came seeking a distraction or revenge. But mostly they gave one another hope. Reg gave Querry a reason to try to get well, to keep fighting.

"Water?" he asked, trying again to raise his head. Though Querry's neck trembled, Reg supported him and propped him up on a doubled pillow.

Pillow? They'd never seen a pillow. They slept on scratchy mats filled with straw and bugs. The itchy lesions on their arms and legs provided proof. Everything still looked blurred, but it occurred to Querry that the ceiling above him was white, not gray block supported by riveted beams and coated in soot. He inhaled, detecting clean linen, coffee, and the must of books instead of the expected stink of the factory and its inhabitants. He tried to think, remember what he'd been doing, where, and with whom.

Again he sipped the liquid Reg provided. He realized he lay naked between impossibly smooth sheets and a thick, feather mattress.

"Frolic, won't you open the window just a bit?" Reg said. "I think his fever's finally broken, and some fresh air might be just the thing." Querry saw him in his crisp, celery shirt and paisley cravat, sitting in an upholstered chair and looking down with concern on his pretty face. The thief felt a breath of cool, snow-scented air, and another figure appeared behind Reg and put his hand on Reg's shoulder: a strangely beautiful, young man with silver hair and bright, yellow eyes.

"Querry's all right now?" the stranger asked.

Reg patted the other's knuckles. "I think so."

Something rubbed the ball of Querry's foot and began to purr. "What the hell is going on?" Querry croaked. "Reg?"

"Suppose you tell me," Reg answered, setting the fancy porcelain cup of water on a night table beside some red and white roses. He draped his fingers across Querry's forehead. "We found you in one of the worst parts of town."

"We?"

"Frolic and me. After you didn't come back for three days, we went out searching. We found you lying in an alley, almost covered with snow."

"You weren't wearing anything, Querry," said the silver-haired young man, Frolic. Slowly, the memory of their meeting returned to Querry's fever-scorched mind.

"The last thing I remember," he said, "is us having dinner. Rabbit."

"You said you knew where to get some answers," Frolic reminded him. "Where did you go?"

Querry thought hard. "I was planning to go into Neroche," he finally said in a surprised tone. "That's it. I was going to ask my gentleman—"

Reg's hand quickly left Querry's face.

"But I don't think I ever made it. I can't remember a thing after leaving this house. Damn, I've lost my gear, haven't I?"

"The fever lasted three weeks," Reg said. "I'm not surprised you can't remember. I can't imagine where you could have left your gear or your clothing."

"Three weeks?"

"We thought we'd lose you, Querry," Frolic said, and squeezed Reg's shoulder. "I've never been so afraid."

Even in his barely recuperated state, Querry could see something had formed between the two of them.

"You were delirious when we found you," Reg continued. "Burning up. Not unusual, I suppose, for spending three nights naked in the cold. Nothing I bought from the chemist did a lick of good, until, one day when I was coming home from work, a little sparrow landed on my shoulder. It held a little sprig in its claw, of flowers that looked made of blue glass."

"Roses?" Querry asked. It seemed significant, though he couldn't imagine why.

"Yes. The bird spoke to me. It told me to lay the flowers across your eyes, and to open up the curtains and let the light of the full moon fall on you. It said that after the blossoms absorbed all the madness, I should bury them in a church yard. It said I'd know when the flowers turned black."

"A faerie cure," Querry mused. Memories flitted and danced around the edges of his mind, just out of grasp.

"Yes. And Frolic and I had a great deal of debate as to whether we could trust it, I can tell you. He reasoned that it couldn't make things any worse. I disagreed, of course, but in the end I think it saved you."

"You said and did the strangest things," Frolic said. "You wanted to dance. We had to hold you down on the bed."

"I'm sorry I missed that," he replied. Both Frolic and Reg smiled at him, and then, looking at one another, they smiled more, their eyes crinkling shut.

"Just what's going on here?" Querry asked.

Reg cleared his throat. "The fever seems to have broken. You seem much more lucid now. How are you feeling?"

"Stiff. And hungry. Like the luckiest man in the world. Thank you. Both of you."

"Of course, Querry," said Frolic enthusiastically. "I love you."

Reg said nothing, but expressed volumes in his sad little smile. "You'll want a bath," he said. "You've been sweating buckets. Frolic, won't you take some cold chicken from the ice box and fry it up with some carrots and onions? It'll make a nice, healthy soup for Querry here."

"Of course!" Frolic spun on the ball of his foot and hurried out of the room.

"Quite the little cook," Reg said, looking fondly after him.

"You two seem to be getting on rather well," Querry said as he removed his blanket, swung his legs over the side of the bed, and tested his strength. He managed to stand, but had to grip the arm of Reg's chair for balance.

"He's completely devoted to you," Reg answered, standing up himself to offer Querry his arm. "He wouldn't let me rest until we found you, and then he never left your side. Poor fellow. I thought he'd fall apart when you were at your worst."

They made their way slowly down the hall. Querry, weak with lack of food, swooned several times and had to stop. Finally they reached the bathroom. It contained a huge, cast-iron tub with clawed feet, a porcelain sink beneath a gilt-framed mirror, and one of those fancy new latrines. Thick, brass pipes lined the walls. Everything was clean and white, spotted with royal blue drapery and linens. After lowering Querry to a brocade bench, Reg stopped the drain and turned the brass spigot. The plumbing pinged as it heated. Hot water splashed into the tub, and Reg added some citrus-scented salts. "I've never seen such a sensitive and compassionate soul," he said, still referring to Frolic. "Really, it's impossible not to want to protect him. It's impossible to dislike him, for he's nothing but goodness."

"I could have told you that," Querry said, getting to his feet. He caught a glimpse of his reflection: he'd lost about fifteen pounds, and his skin looked loose and gray. Beneath almost a month of whiskers, his cheeks appeared sunken. Puffy purple ringed his blue eyes. Holding Reg's shoulder, he stepped into the bath and lowered his body into the steaming, fragrant water. It felt just as heavenly as he'd always imagined it would, and he sighed with contentment and rested his head against the ledge. Reg removed his cufflinks and rolled up his sleeves. He dipped a cloth in the water, wrung it out, and wiped Querry's face.

"I comforted him, Querry," Reg said guiltily. "We comforted each other."

"How?"

"He wanted to be held. He was devastated and afraid. I couldn't say no. He didn't want to be alone at night. I let him sleep with me after we didn't feel we needed to sit up with you. And—"

"And?"

"I enjoyed it too. I was worried. I mean, it was you. The one person I suppose I never thought could come to any harm. I never thought anything could touch you. It terrified me, this proof that you're mortal."

Querry laughed, and it led to a brief spell of coughing. Reg soaped up his cloth and continued to wash Querry's neck and arms. The pressure felt good against Querry's muscles. It felt good to get the grime off his skin. "I was glad to have somebody to hold. To hold me back. And one night, he was in my arms, crying, and he wanted to kiss...."

"And?"

"It was lovely. He was enthusiastic yet innocent. I can't really describe it. There was nothing sordid. It felt so proper and good." He'd stopped washing Querry, and held the rag in front of Querry's heart.

"How far did this go, Reg?"

"We touched one another." Reg sank down and sat on his heels by the tub. He let go of the cloth, and his hand moved up Querry's wet neck and over his ear. Taking hold of Querry's hair, Reg brought Querry's face to his chest, where it darkened his pale green shirt. He wriggled his other arm beneath Querry's chin and drew him very close. Querry let his eyes close and savored the wonderful moment. Reg's nose burrowed into his locks, and Reg spoke into his hair. "Remember that first night in the workhouse, when our group had just been brought in? You offered to let me put my mat next to yours? Said we could look out for one another?"

"'Course I remember, Reg. I remember the first time I saw you." *Still dirty from the fields, eyes wide, hair askew, a combination of awkwardness and grace that made me want you right away.*

"Remember how we used to touch?"

"'Course, Reg." Querry would never forget those moments of discovery and delight: the first time he reached for Reg's hand in the dark, heart racing, terrified Reg would flinch, triumphant when he didn't, the first time he'd dared let his hand infiltrate Reg's shirt, his pants. The perfection of their first kiss returned to Querry as his eyes closed. They'd been lying in the dark, talking, fantasizing about freedom, when they'd rolled to face one another. Querry felt out Reg's face and explored his brow, lashes, cheeks, jaw line, and mouth. Then, holding his chin, trembling with nerves and anticipation, he'd moved closer. Their noses touched, and Reg didn't pull away. Still apprehensive, afraid to drive away his only friend but burning with desire, Querry closed the space. Their lips only just touched. Then Reg increased the pressure. His body curved against Querry, and his arm encircled Querry's waist. Of the many kisses Querry experienced over the following years, none approached that glorious moment. He'd felt victory and relief, his feelings vindicated and reciprocated when he'd feared their violent rejection. His dripping hand squeezed Reg's forearm.

Still clutching Querry's head tightly, Reg said, "I touched him like that. Like we touched, at first. Just with my hands. And he did the same to me. It was all very gentle and natural."

"Reg," Querry said, an unpleasant thought coming unbidden to his mind, "has there been anyone else?"

"What do you mean?"

"Besides me. Have you... have you let anyone—"

"No."

"All those ladies you see?"

"I kiss their fingertips when I tell them good night." Reg began to pet Querry's hair. "You know, after I left the factory I spent a lot of time thinking about what you and I did while we were there, and why we did it. I tried to figure out if it was just desperation that drove us into each other's arms. We were so young. We both still craved nurturing, care. Would all of that have happened under other circumstances? Did things progress as far as they did just because we were each other's only comfort?"

"I never even considered it!"

"Querry. Of course not. You're all passion and the moment. You let your heart take the reins while your brain runs along behind the cart."

"And what conclusions did you and your brain reach?"

"None. I can't say why I fell in love with you, or if I would have done at another place or time. But I can tell you that I didn't want to hurt Frolic. I didn't want to use him to comfort myself or assuage my worries. Before I could permit myself to enjoy him, I needed to know it wasn't just desperation."

"And?"

"I'm quite fond of him."

Elated, Querry bolted up, splashing water over the rim of the tub. He seized Reg's shocked face and smashed his lips against Reg's mouth. "Then, the three of us! We'll go somewhere!"

"Now I didn't say that."

"What? But—"

Just then Frolic flung open the dark, wooden door to announce that chicken soup, croissants from the bakery, and a kettle of strong tea waited in the dining room. With Mrs. Spaulding still away, Reg offered to help set out the dishes, and they left Querry alone. Hungry and eager to resume his conversation with Reg, Querry quickly shaved and washed. Seeing nothing else, he slipped into a red silk robe that hung on the back of the door and joined his friends at the table.

"Feeling better?" Frolic asked as he passed Querry a steaming bowl of golden broth.

The famished thief drank deeply, not bothering with the spoon. The soup warmed his insides and bolstered his strength right away. Frolic ladled him another helping, and he dipped a bit of bread before saying, "I think it's time a few things get resolved."

"Namely?" Reg asked.

"Namely our relationship. The three of us. We love each other. What are we going to do about it?"

"I think your current predicament needs discussing first," Reg said coolly. "Mrs. Spaulding will be back in three days."

"What happened while I was sick? Anything? Anything from Thimbleroy?"

"He actually seems in high spirits," Reg said. "It's perplexing. Apparently his restoration of the clock tower could be complete as early as spring. He's even let up a bit on the faeries."

"Haha!" Querry said, clapping his hands. "He's given up! Decided he doesn't need Frolic after all!"

"I'm not so sure. Constables emptied out the boarding house. Searched every room. Patrolmen and detectives have been questioning your neighbors in Rushport, and your, um, *friends* around Lickwhistle Circle."

"About what?" Querry asked, looking down guiltily. He'd never thought Reg knew of his occasional trysts in the public houses.

"I wondered too," Reg said. "So, I spread some coins around the place. Honestly, Querry, those taverns are ghastly! They asked about a young man who looked like a faerie. Who he'd been seen with and where. They know your name, Querry."

Querry swore. "What could they want with him?"

With a shrug, Reg said, "Not sure. Thimbleroy doesn't seem in a great hurry, though. He's much too involved in the renovation. Could be that he just wants Frolic because he's rare. Probably thinks only an aristocrat worthy of owning something like him."

"That's why Thimbleroy can't get him," Querry said angrily. "He'll think of him like chattel."

"I'm more worried about you," the doll said to Querry. "What will they do if they find you? The newspapers are saying you stole property from that cellar. They'll put you in prison. Maybe worse."

"Property?" Querry mused. "Unspecified property? Then Thimbleroy doesn't want the public to know about Frolic. Why?"

"Could someone else try to claim me?"

"What about the doll maker's mysterious son?"

"You're mine!" Querry said, hitting the tabletop with his fists, jiggling the flames of the candles. "Mine."

"But, Querry," Frolic said, "The doll maker's son might know why I was made!"

"I've told you it doesn't matter. None of this matters. It's time we put it all behind us."

"What do you mean?" Frolic asked.

"It's obvious that the time has come for us to say our farewells to this land. Time to set off. I have some gold hidden away just for a rainy day. Where will we go first? East to Prysia? Xiana? To the Spice Islands? The Caribique?"

"Querry—"

"You choose then, Reg! It doesn't matter to me."

"I'm not going anywhere."

"Come off it, Reg! You've admitted how you feel, finally. How else can we be together?"

"We can't."

"So getting at it with Frolic was just to pass the time?"

"It just happened," Reg said.

"The hell it did," Querry spat. "Reg, you enjoy the company of men. Do you deny it?"

"No, but I can't indulge it. I've chosen a wife, Querry. In six months time I'm to wed Emily Malvern, only daughter of Sir William Malvern, Earl of Ravenshire. It's better than Mum could've hoped. An Earl."

"I can't believe you're still on about this, Reg! When are you going to admit that it won't work?"

"It will work. The girl is plain, but not unpleasant to look at. She's quiet and well mannered. She visits the Archives regularly for Medieval Romances, and is apparently quite taken with me. Her father dotes on her, and that's why she's allowed to marry below her station. He's giving us a country house."

"But you and me and Frolic!"

"Damn it! This is fortune beyond my wildest dreams! Why can't you be happy for me?"

"Because you're supposed to be mine! You want to, and you know it."

"You promised me, Querry."

"You honestly expect me to just give up? Well I won't, Reg! I never will. You and me, the three of us, belong together, and the rest of the world can just go rot if they don't like it!"

"No!" Reg stood and balled his fists. "You made me a promise, and you'll honor it! You'll get dressed and you and Frolic will leave this house and go far, far away if you've got any sense. I'll give you something of mine to wear, and I'll give you some money if you need it. I'll even take care of your cats. But that's the most I can do."

"I'm going to miss you, Reg," Frolic said softly, causing the archivist to soften and sit back down. "There's a lot about this I don't understand, but I understand about purpose."

"Thank you," Reg said. "I wish things could be otherwise. But going to battle against the entire world can only fail. I'm sorry, but I think it would be best if the two of you left tonight. Excuse me." He got up and left the dining room, returning in a few minutes with clothes for Querry. He turned to leave again, reached the oak double doors that separated the room from the foyer and his stairs, and stopped. He stood in still silence for many moments. Only the crackle of the fireplace could be heard. Querry wished he could've seen Reg's face, intuited his thoughts. When he finally turned, tears sparkled on his cheeks. For the first time Querry felt ashamed; maybe he was hurting Reg. He also felt confused. Should he take Reg in his arms and comfort him, or would doing so cause the archivist more pain?

"I hope—" Reg began, but his voice broke, and he bit his knuckles, taking a few more minutes to compose himself. "I hope that one day you'll be able to understand, Querry. I hope you can calm your rage at everything. And I hope, truly hope, with all my heart, that everything will work out for you, both of you, one day. I wish you all the happiness in the world. Frolic, I'm glad to have met you. Take care of yourselves."

"So this is it," Querry said. "The last I'll ever see you."

Frolic held his sides and rocked in his chair, looking like he might be sick. "The world is...." He frowned, thinking. "So complex. So unnecessarily sad. Why?" He looked back and forth from Querry to Reg. "Why?"

"I'm sorry," seemed the only conclusion Reg could reach before disappearing through the double doors.

"Where will we go?" Frolic asked.

Querry went to the window but didn't move the velvet drape. He stood staring at the floral pattern embossed in the moss-green, staring at the thick gold cords hanging on either side, trying to digest the reality of Reg's loss, trying to stamp down that inner voice that screamed to go after him, make him understand. Frolic touched his back, his hand warm through the thin silk of the robe. Frolic needed him now; his pain would have to wait. He cleared his throat and said, "Well, I'm going to need new gear. Clothes that fit me. And then we can go wherever you want. What do you say, the Aurient? Bravelstein or Belvais? One of the colonies?"

"We have to get it back."

"Which?"

"The book that tells about me," Frolic said.

"We won't need it," Querry told him with a wave of his hand. "We'll go so far off that they'll never find us. They won't be able to use the information against you."

"That's not why I need it." Panic crept into Frolic's voice as he forced himself into the small space between Querry and the window. "I need to know why I was made. You say it doesn't matter, but it matters to me. I can't go the rest of my time wondering. I need to know. Please, Querry."

"It'll be dangerous, going right to the men who are trying to find us."

"But we'll manage, won't we? Won't we, Querry?"

"I can't tell you no," said the thief with a smile. "I'll squeeze into these clothes, then, and we'll be off. Go and fetch your sword. I'm afraid you might need it."

DINK'S SHOP was on the opposite end of the city, at the edge of the factory district, and getting there required the better part of the evening of dashing from one alley to the next, praying they wouldn't be spotted. As they crested a hill, Querry glanced over at his companion. Frolic's eyes grew wide. It was a common reaction; Dink's place was pretty impressive. The tiny storefront itself looked like any other junk shop, although it extended several stories below ground. The yard that stretched around it for several blocks on three sides drew the attention. It was like a city unto itself: paths wound among heaps of rubble that looked like exotic towers and turrets beneath the glow of sporadic lampposts.

"Oh my," Frolic breathed.

"Acres of raw materials," Querry answered. "I spent a lot of time here as a kid when I needed a break from picking pockets. And in between being carted back off to the workhouse. Dink employs an army of orphans and urchins to salvage parts from all over the city. Has what you might call a mansion below that shop, does old Dink. Enough room to house and feed at least twenty kids, plus workshops, a shooting range and a couple of floors no one but Dink knows for sure what's on them."

"And he'll help us?" Frolic wondered aloud.

"If anyone will help us, it's old Dink. I never had parents, but Dink was pretty close. He taught me to read and all about clockwork. He taught me to shoot and to handle a sword. Come on. He's going to love you."

"Me?"

"Of course," Querry said. "You're the ultimate clockwork. But don't let on. Let's see if he figures it out."

Frolic's face broke into a big smile. "A surprise? Sure, Querry! This will be fun!"

QUERRY OPENED the door slowly, listening for the tinkle and rattle of pipes and gears bouncing on the string that warned Dink if anyone entered the store. Frolic followed, eyes wandering over walls covered with every manner of salvaged material, just as the grounds outside had been. The difference being the things inside the shop gleamed like jewels.

"Dink only keeps the cream of the crop in here," Querry informed his companion. "You can make some fantastic finds out in the yard as well, but in here Dink's done the work for you." There was a clattering from the back of the store behind the small counter. Frolic looked toward the small door, curtained with tiny copper rings. A raspy voice drifted from beyond. A gnarled, shaky hand emerged from one side of the curtain and slowly pushed it aside. Then a stooped figure in huge spectacles with many lenses almost completely obscured by bushy, white eyebrows shuffled out into the room. The old man held a cane with tiny mechanical legs that propelled it and the man's hand forward. A sculpted tortoise head topped the cane. The man wore a smoking jacket over his humped back, giving him the impression of a large, paisley turtle. He pulled a number of gadgets on chains from various pockets of the smoking jacket.

"Eh?" The sound ruffled the fluffy, white mustache on the old fellow's upper lip. "*Vas*? What can I help you vith?" the old man managed to ask, through gasps of air.

"Dink!" Querry threw open his arms. "What have you been up to, you old sod?" The man looked at Querry, his eyes opening with surprise, then disappearing into deep creases as the mouth beneath the mustache broke into a huge grin.

"Querrilous Knotte!" Dink exclaimed, all traces of rasp and exertion gone. "I might ask you ze same thing! You've been stirring up a lot of trouble, ja?" In one deft movement the old man straightened up, slipped out of the smoking jacket, and to Frolic's surprise, the hump as well. He fairly leapt the space between him and Querry to embrace the younger, taller man, while his stick dutifully walked itself over next to the counter and out of the way, its necessity over.

Querry turned to Frolic, one arm still across the old man's shoulders. "Frolic, this is Terrapin Dinklundsmiter, one of the foremost authorities on everything clockwork and purveyor of junk." The old man walked toward Frolic with his hand out. When Frolic didn't offer his own hand, Dink took it and pumped twice, warmly but firmly.

"Dink, this is Frolic."

"Hello, Herr Dinklundsmiter. Pleased to make your acquaintance," Frolic said with a smile.

"Ja. But all mein friends just call me Dink, and any friend of Querry's is a friend of mine so I will expect you to do the same. None of this 'Herr Dinklundsmiter', ja?" Dink said, taking Frolic's measure over the top of his outlandish spectacles.

Frolic considered for a moment, and then a big, beaming smile lit his face, and he exuberantly exclaimed, "Ja!"

"*Zer gut*. Now, my boys." Dink clapped his hands together, "I will close up shop, and we'll go downstairs and get a bite to eat." With that he bounded to the door, locked a series of intricate locks similar to those in Querry's old apartment, flipped the sign, and dashed through the little room and behind the curtain. He slid open the door on a mechanized lift. "*Schnell!* Ve have much to discuss, I think!"

Querry followed Dink into the lift. Frolic looked at the interior apprehensively, but was forced quickly inside by a nudge from the walking stick, which had decided to join them. With the little group safely in the car, Dink pulled a chain, cranked a gleaming brass lever, and punched a button. The lift zipped below ground.

CHAPTER 7

QUERRY HELD his stomach as he shakily disembarked the lift. Dink strode out, unfazed and followed by his walking stick. Frolic leaned against the railing, before deciding it was safe to exit the lift. They found themselves on the cafeteria level: a large room filled with numerous mismatched tables, chairs and benches. The smell of freshly cooked food greeted their noses.

"Mmmm." Querry's eyes closed as he sniffed the air, "Dink, is that your root vegetable stew?"

"*Ja.*" Dink's voice came from the kitchen, where clanging and clicking could be heard. Frolic wandered over to see what Dink was up to. Querry knew the little clockwork would be fascinated; Dink's kitchen was almost completely automated. Gears and steam engines covered the walls, while mechanical arms chopped ingredients, stirred pots and washed dishes. Querry had seen it many times, therefore his attention was drawn to a small group of boys sitting in one corner of the room. He wandered over to assess Dink's newest batch of scavengers.

"Hello, lads," he said, approaching the table with a smile. The boys had laid waste to the meal before them and were making a plan of attack for their next outing. They paused to look at Querry. There were five boys, all dressed similarly in the garb of the standard street urchin: woolen breeches, suspenders and simple, button-up shirts. Their oversized outer coats draped the backs of their chairs. Two of the boys wore driving caps, and one a bowler pulled down over one eye. Who Querry assumed was the head boy wore a pair of driving goggles perched in his messy mane of blond hair and stood to greet him, a toothpick gnashed between his teeth.

"All right, mate," the boy said suspiciously. "And 'ow can we help you?"

"Name's Querrilous Knotte. Querry for short. Used to be a scavenger myself not so very long ago."

"That so?" The boy relaxed a little and offered his hand. "Pleased to meet'cher. I'm Lizard. This here's my crew: Sticky Pete, Tobias, Jimmy the Fingers, and Mike-Mike." Each boy nodded as he was introduced. "There's a thief what everyone seems keen to find by the name o' Knotte. Any relation?" Lizard narrowed his eyes slightly. It was Querry's turn to be suspicious.

"Who's everyone?" Querry asked, avoiding the question.

Lizard shrugged. "Ain't fer me t'know. Not our business, anyways. Our business is scavenging, ain't it? We don't stick our noses where they don't belong, do we boys?" The others muttered their agreement, and Querry walked back to where Dink had set two steaming bowls of stew.

"Interesting little group you've got there, Dink," Querry said, taking the seat across from the old man.

"They are very good at what they do. And they look out for each other. Eat, ja? It looks like you could use the nourishment." Dink indicated Querry's bowl with his own spoon. Smiling, Querry began to eat, the food just as good as he remembered. Dink took a bite of his own stew and then went on, quietly, "So. Zis Frolic." Querry looked up. "Ja. I am not so old just yet, *jungen*." He paused, looking toward the kitchen, where Frolic was adjusting the tension on one of the mechanical arms. "*Mein Gott*. He is a beautiful piece of work."

"I know." Querry kept his voice hushed as well.

"And he seems sentient. He has feelings, ja. Emotions."

"He does. He's incredible. And complete. He has everything, down to the finest detail."

"Amazing. And I am to assume you did not make him?"

"No." Querry tore a piece of bread and dipped it in the stew. "I found him. In a hidden chamber in a house that—" Querry paused to eat the sopping piece of bread and give himself time to think of what to say, because Dink, like everyone else, disapproved of his work with the faeries—"one of my clients gave me the address of."

Dink made a clucking noise with his tongue. "The faerie, ja?" Querry didn't answer. He couldn't lie to Dink, so he looked deep into his soup. "I won't lecture you. Although I wonder what he has to gain from this." Dink mulled it over for a moment. "No matter at this point. What do you need from me? Weapons I assume. And it looks like you have lost your work clothes also."

"I have a little money, and I can get more." Dink waved Querry's offer away.

"You don't worry about it. The opportunity to see this miracle of a clockwork is payment enough. Use whatever you need. But first, finish your stew. I have been working on something in my spare time that I want you to see." Dink's eyes sparkled at the prospect. "And I think Frolic will like it as well." Querry looked at the old man beaming across from him. "You found him in a secret chamber, you say?" Dink's countenance grew darker.

"That's right. Why?"

"Maybe nothing. Maybe"—his mind seemed to wander— "something." Dink shook himself. "Finish. Finish. I can't vait to show you!" The excitement returned to Dink's eyes, and Querry decided not to push him for the moment, though it was obvious that something about Frolic's discovery struck a chord with the old man, and Querry was determined to find out what that chord was.

AFTER ANOTHER unsettling ride in Dink's lift, the group exited on a floor Querry had never been on, and couldn't therefore be sure how deep beneath the shop it lay. Dink hopped out. Querry stood aside to let Frolic pass and noticed that the walking stick was now following the clockwork boy and even, it appeared, nuzzling his hand with its handle. Dink stood before a doorway that was ornately decorated with gilded wrought copper with intricate swirls, fleur-de-lis, and other strange design elements that Querry couldn't name. Above the doors, in a script that was barely readable with its many accents and flourishes, was the word Menagerie.

"You've got a zoo down here?" Querry asked, wondering why and how Dink had acquired animals to keep below ground.

"A zoo. That sounds delightful. What is it?" Frolic asked the old man.

"It's a bunch of animals in cages," Querry answered before Dink could respond.

"On second thought, that sounds dreadful." Frolic stuck his bottom lip out, looking at Dink.

"What you see before you represents decades of meticulous work. But I shall let the work speak for itself, ja?" Dink grabbed a lever, squeezed the handle and pulled. The shining double doors retreated into the wall, revealing a clockwork jungle: trees, plants, and animals all built entirely from spare parts and animated by clockwork and steam. Frolic squealed with glee and ran full tilt, followed closely by the tortoise-headed walking stick, into a clearing ten feet within the room, where a collection of clockwork animals meandered lazily in false sunlight created by a hydrogen lantern suspended high in the vaulted ceiling. A giant metal rhinoceros lumbered over to the pale boy, nudging him with its shiny horned nose until Frolic stroked the side of its enormous jaw. Querry's eyes widened with amazement and terror.

"Will they hurt him?" he breathed, unable to take in enough air to speak properly.

"*Nein*," Dink said, shaking his head. "They look like wild animals but they are as tame as puppies." Querry was relieved to hear that as a large, copper tiger stalked gracefully over to Frolic and rubbed its head on his thigh like a giant house cat. But even from the doorway, Querry saw the gleaming claws that peaked out from the wide paws. "It is mein greatest creation to date, but not half as impressive as our little friend there. They only approximate life, ja? But Frolic, he *is* life."

"You know something," Querry said, still staring into the jungle, not looking at Dink. A large, multicolored parrot glided down from a tree, using small propellers set into its wings to achieve flight. Dink didn't respond, so Querry said his name.

"Ja. Ja, I think I may know something. Just a story. But after seeing him," Dink indicated Frolic with a nod. "I cannot believe it is just coincidence." More animals emerged from the trees now. A raccoon, squirrels and a big black raven approached Frolic as if drawn to him. "He has an instinctual understanding of other clockworks. He can almost see how they vork." Dink's voice was dreamy.

"I noticed that too," Querry said, his eyes still on the animals and Frolic. "Dink. This is amazing. I'm astounded." He was growing impatient, though. "But the story?"

"Ze story." Dink sighed heavily. "Ja. Well, there vas a legend about a doll maker who managed to make a doll, a clockwork so perfect that it actually had life. It could think und feel und behave just like a human." Dink paused. "But better. The doll had none of the frailties that humans suffer. And it vas strong and fast."

Querry nodded. It all sounded too familiar.

Dink continued, "His dolls vere so beautiful and complex that someone got the idea he could make one a weapon. Twisting his vision. Then he saw how his beautiful, living creation might be misused. So he sealed it up in a hidden chamber and left the creation asleep. Waiting. For what? No one knows." Dink seemed to have finished his story. He and Querry watched what they both knew was the miraculous creation, petting and playing with Dink's clockwork menagerie. "There vas supposedly a book. The doll maker eventually was recruited to work on the clock tower, as were all the other clock workers and mechanists at that time. And they tortured the old man eventually, but they never got the book. If there ever vas a book."

"Oh, there was a book all right. I've seen it." Querry turned to Dink, fixing the old man's eyes with his own. "Thimbleroy knows the story. He searched the doll maker's house, before I got there and discovered Frolic. And now he has the book."

"*Mein Gott.*" Dink put a hand to his mouth. His worry strengthened his already thick accent. "Zhis is not good. You must get zhis boy avay from zhat man. He'll stop at nothing. It'll be your life, Querry." There was a trumpeting from the clearing and both men jumped at the sudden sound.

"Good Lord, Dink!" Querry exclaimed, "An elephant?"

"It's beautiful!" Frolic called from the clearing. "Well done, Dink!"

"*Danke*, my boy. But now you must leave mein little menagerie. You and Querry have much vork ahead of you." As Frolic trotted back to the doorway, Dink turned to Querry. "I still have some of your things. Clothes und such. Anything else you should be able to piece together, I trust?"

"Of course." Querry placed his hand on the old man's shoulder. "Thank you, old friend."

"*Nein*. No mention of it. You'll need a new sword also? I have been working on a vibrating blade that is marvelous at cutting through things." Dink continued to explain as the trio boarded the lift.

QUERRY MADE a list of supplies that Frolic had gathered while the thief slept, still recovering from the fever. After a huge breakfast and some lively conversation with Lizard and his crew, Querry and Frolic set to work replacing the arsenal Querry had lost. Frolic offered some ideas for improvements to Querry's designs and Dink's designs as well. Querry felt glad of the work, as it kept his mind from wandering into painful places.

They worked through lunch but took a break for dinner. Remembering how much he loved it and knowing it would help him regain his strength, Dink made Querry a batch of his roasted potato soup with warm pumpkin ale. Though Frolic didn't eat, he still sat with Querry and the old man and listened to stories of the time Querry spent as a scavenger, laughing heartily and thoroughly enjoying the company.

While Querry put the finishing touches on his weaponry, Dink fetched some of Querry's old gear from storage. He returned with a leather officer's jacket with brass buttons down the front, a metal-lined waistcoat with brass gearwheels for buckles, a pair of welder's gloves and his old Marten boots with the steel toes and spiked soles. Querry slipped into his old gear, which still fit perfectly, and added to it all his new weaponry, including the sword Dink created with the blade attached to a motor, causing it to vibrate for extra damage.

Dink stepped back and looked at the two young men. "Vell," he said, "I can't say I'm happy to see you go. I've missed you, and it was good having you around again." He hugged Querry and turned to Frolic with his hand extended. "It was vonderful to make your acquaintance also, young man." Frolic looked at Dink's hand and then threw his arms around the old man, hugging him tight.

"Thank you for all your help, Dink," he said into the mechanist's shoulder. "Your menagerie is delightful, and I hope I can visit it again." Dink returned the hug and then held the clockwork boy at arm's length, tears welling in his eyes.

"Anytime, *jungen*. Anytime at all."

"You sentimental old fool," Querry said playfully. "Don't worry. When the heat dies down, we'll be back as soon as we can."

Frolic petted the walking stick on its handle, and they turned to go. Querry turned back.

"Thank you again, Dink. You don't know how much you've helped us."

"Ja. Zhat's enough. Go! *Schnell*." And with that, they left the little shop and its owner behind.

FROM THE bell tower of a cathedral across the street, Querry and Frolic looked down on the sprawling Thimbleroy residence. Wind whipped the thief's black hair as he stood with his boot propped on a stone windowsill and his elbow on his knee. Doves cooed in the rafters above them.

"You're sure he has it here?" Frolic asked.

Querry nodded. This difficult job was just what he needed to distract him from Reg. Watching the Tudor-style manor through the telescopic lens of his new goggles, he felt focused, alive with excitement. In the last two hours, over a dozen men had entered or left the building. Some had the posture of hired muscle, while others displayed a sedate, scholarly manner. One man even appeared decidedly magical, with his dark cloak and long, white beard. Light poured from a window on the second floor, toward the eastern corner. Now and then Querry saw a silhouette dart quickly by. At the opposite end of the house, blue and orange flashed from behind a decorative iron screen covering a cellar window.

"There," Querry said, pointing. "In his study. That's where we'll find the book."

"How do you know?"

"From what Reg has told us about this Lord Thimbleroy, I think it's safe to assume he wouldn't trust anyone else to keep it. He'd think them too stupid or inept. Look, more of them are leaving!" Two large men came out the front door, struggling with an obviously heavy, coffin-sized box. Another half-dozen men followed, all of them lugging wooden crates or spools of wire. They waited at the foot of the stone steps, some of them lighting cigarettes, until an open cart drawn by a buckskin workhorse pulled into the drive. Then they loaded their packages and climbed aboard. The driver put his whip to use, and the animal's breath steamed as it took off at a trot.

"I haven't seen any light from below in a while," Frolic noted. They'd decided on a previous visit that the cellar window would provide the easiest method of entry. The iron shield had already begun to come loose from the stone, and Querry had pried it the rest of the way before replacing it. The area beyond was used for some kind of mechanical work, probably relating to the clock tower project. The other side of the lower level housed the servant's quarters. At this time of night, most of them would be in bed. Querry doubted they'd disturb anyone on their way to the study. No one would believe him bold enough to make such a brash attempt. The irony made him chuckle, but it led to a brief spell of coughing.

Patting Querry's back, Frolic said, "It'll never do if that starts up while we're inside. We should have asked Reg for some of those herbal lozenges."

"Well, we'll have to soldier on without them."

"Reg said it brought back memories, taking care of you when you had your fever. I asked him about it, but he wouldn't say anything else."

"It wasn't a good time for us, Frolic. There's plenty he probably wants to forget. It was harder on him than me."

"Why?"

"I was a city boy. Grew up on the streets, part of a gang of pickpockets. I knew how to take care of myself. And I was used to the grime and pollution. Reg was born on a farm. Fever took his parents, and he went to work for some relatives. Basically he got shuttled back and forth to wherever somebody needed an extra pair of hands. I think he was lonely and overworked, but at least he had the fresh air."

"Then what happened?"

Querry shrugged. "He ran out of people willing to feed him, I suppose. Got shipped off to the workhouse."

"Querry, why are people so cruel to each other?"

"I wish I knew, my beauty."

"I wish the world could be as beautiful as the clockwork menagerie."

"It isn't real," Querry said.

They stood in quiet contemplation for another hour while the study light burned steadily, waiting for the master of the house to depart to a masque or dinner party, as he did every evening. Then, finally, the room went dark, just as an elegant coach drawn by two black horses reached the front entrance. An aging butler opened the door, and Lord Thimbleroy appeared in a slate-blue suit and top hat, pulling on a pair of white gloves. A footman hurried to help him into the carriage.

"I think we're set to go," Querry said. Since rappelling down the side of the building could attract more attention than sneaking through, Querry and Frolic crept past the alcoves, statues and pews. They hurried across to the Thimbleroy property, and hid themselves behind a holly bush until the single guard made his rounds. Then Querry quickly displaced the screen, cut the glass around the window frame, and motioned for Frolic to go inside. After he joined Frolic, he reached up and replaced the screen so that nothing would look amiss.

They found themselves in a cavernous space with vaulted ceilings and stone columns holding them up. Switching to night vision, Querry jumped when he saw what looked like a dozen men standing in a line near the other end of the cellar. Quickly, though, he realized they kept too still and quiet to be living people.

"Who are they?" Frolic whispered.

Querry raised a hand to shush him and then motioned him to follow. Slowly, one hand resting on the grip of his new pistol, he slipped from one column to the next until he reached the cluster of bodies. Behind him, Frolic inhaled sharply. Querry felt for his hand and gave it a squeeze, hoping to steel him against the disturbing sight.

They were dolls, dolls like Frolic, but made without any attempt at aesthetic pleasance. Their metal skeletons were pitted steel, with holes drilled through to reduce the weight. Empty air sacs hung beyond their ribs. They possessed no hearts, but instead small gas burners fed from tanks welded to their backs. Their gears were large, clunky, and too few, according to what Querry had learned of Frolic's construction. They would move in an unnatural, jerky way. Large, greasy engines waited quietly on their backs. Worst of all, their faces bore no semblances of humanity. Large bolts held jaws filled with square, metal teeth. Milky orbs stared out from rusty sockets. Creeping closer, Querry reached out a trembling hand to touch one of the hideous abominations, but Frolic caught his wrist.

From nowhere, the air sacs inflated with a noise like gears needing oiled. With a creak the metal mouth opened and closed, chomping at the air in what Querry prayed wasn't an attempt at speech. The hands spasmed and shook like a sot in need of his gin, and the eyes rolled back. Then with a rush the lungs emptied, the air producing a sickly rattle as it passed the throat and teeth. Finally the thing went still, lowering its head. Frolic whimpered and slapped a hand over his mouth.

"Why?" he hissed through his fingers.

"I think I know," Querry said, recalling his companion's prowess in a fight, as well as Dink's account. "An army."

"But for what?" Frolic shook his head very fast, and his grip almost crushed Querry's fingers.

"To go against the faeries would be my first guess. But—" He stopped himself, not wanting to frighten Frolic. *But to bring these things to life, to imbue them with thought and feeling....*

He couldn't imagine the horror. So far, thankfully, the attempt appeared unsuccessful. In a corner nearby, a huge heap of scrap—failed prototypes—lay piled in a haphazard way. Querry walked over to the mound that looked for all its metal and gears like a pile of discarded corpses. The thief regarded the milky eyes in the metal skulls. Querry tipped one skull with a steel-toed boot. A rasping, rattling erupted from the pile and a metallic, skeletal hand flashed out and caught Querry's leg. Querry yelped and tried to back away, pulling the aborted construct with him. It looked up at the thief with a dull, sickly glow emanating from the weird ocular orbs, its mouth spasming and gasping, the metallic teeth gnashing together like some bizarre, clockwork zombie. The thing had no legs, just a spinal column trailing behind it as it climbed up Querry's retreating form. Querry pulled his pistol and realized he couldn't discharge the firearm. The horrible thing gurgled a strangled scream and one of the eyes burst, leaking a viscous, white liquid over the metal cheekbone. The thief spared a glance at his perfect clockwork companion frozen in a paroxysm of fear, his delicate fists pressed against his perfect lips, stifling a scream. Querry flipped the pistol so the grip emerged over his hand. He hauled back and smashed the butt of the gun into the metal skull with a dull thud. The clockwork abomination whined, and Querry hit it again and again.

Finally able to move, Frolic grabbed a large wrench from a workbench and swung it like a baseball bat at the mechanical corpse. The wrench connected with a sickly rending and the skull was ripped from the neck. It flew into a corner and bounced once before skidding across the floor. The metallic hands clawed at the thief, clenching and unclenching a few times before the entire frame stilled and dropped to the ground. Querry backed away from the thing, panting. The clockwork boy whimpered and dropped the wrench with a deep clang. Silence hung in the dusty room like death in a mausoleum.

"We can't let them," Frolic whispered desperately, having made the connection Querry had hoped to spare him from. "Querry, we have to stop this."

"We will. Let's find that book. Come on. The stairs should be around here somewhere." They made their way easily through the kitchens and the rooms beyond. Once they had to hide behind a sofa while a plump little maid helped herself to some of his Lordship's single malt, but they encountered no other obstacles before reaching the dark-paneled study. There, on the matching mahogany desk, as Querry had known it would be, sat Frolic's book. Notes lay scattered around, as well as various diagrams and schematics. These Frolic seized, tearing them to shreds with such fury that the scraps flew around him in a blizzard. In spite of the noise, Querry let him go, knowing that it helped him exorcize some of the revulsion of what he'd seen, until he reduced every piece of paper to a confetti-sized bit. Afterward Frolic stood panting, looking at the canvases and books lining the walls with confusion. Querry tugged his elbow, and he regained enough composure to follow Querry back through the house.

Worried over what Frolic might do when faced again with the machines below, Querry found a service entrance near the kitchen. It led them to a gravelly patch between the manor, carriage house, and stable. What snow hadn't been shoveled away had been fouled by the horses. Their footprints would easily disappear. Even in the dead of night, with the moon already set, the entire area glowed amber from the many lanterns hung on the buildings. Querry wanted to escape into the darkness, but Frolic stood looking up at the great house with his jaw set and his fists clenched.

"Come on," Querry said. "Time to go."

"Underneath, that's all I am," Frolic said, oblivious to Querry's insistent pulling on his arm.

"And I'm a pile of bones and guts. What does it matter?"

"Because!" he shouted, and Querry flinched. He went around behind Frolic and pushed him toward the little path that would take them to a driveway and, eventually, the street. The guard or a stableboy or groundskeeper, somebody, would have heard Frolic. Finally Frolic started to move on his own, though he kept talking. "There was no point to those things. Probably there's no point to me either."

"Is there any point to any of us?" Querry panted as he ran. "Life seems pretty damned pointless to me all around. You're born, you struggle to get enough to eat, and you die. The bloody world goes on just the same as it was before you were in it." A steam carriage came chugging up the street, and Querry pulled Frolic around the side of a brick sweet shop. "That's why you should do whatever makes you happy. Whatever you want. It's all there is." He checked the street before running half a block and disappearing down an alley. He took another few alleys, heading toward Hawthorne Street and the waterfront, before he slowed to a walk. They took a dubious-looking hansom to the industrial district before continuing on foot.

"I'm sorry, Querry," Frolic said, reaching for the tome tucked under the thief's arm. "I have to know."

"If you must, then you must. But first we need to find a safe place for this," he held the book up, "so that if they get one of us at least they won't get it back. And after we decide where we want to go, we can come back for it."

"And do you know of a safe place?"

Querry nodded, scowling. "Where I hide my money." He jutted his chin out to indicate a cinderblock shell, its entire front and most of its roof caved in. Approaching it felt like walking up Gallow's Hill, but he pressed on. Frolic followed him over piles of soot-covered rubble and into the vast, dark recesses. Above them, the stars twinkled beyond the metal beams that had once held the roof. Carefully Querry navigated more fallen metal and concrete, wrinkling his nose at the sulfuric stench.

"What is this place?" Frolic asked as they progressed deeper and deeper into the burned-out factory, passing melted and crumpled machines and disjointed assembly lines.

"It was a bottling plant," Querry said, unsure if he wanted Frolic to know the whole truth. He decided to tell him, though. Frolic was all he had left; he shouldn't keep anything from him. "This is where Reg and I grew up. When the workhouse got too full, they sold some of us off to the factories. They called us 'apprentice laborers', but Reggie and me were practically slaves. We were just cogs in a machine, and just as easy to replace. We stood right here—" He stopped in front of a furnace the size of a small house. The door was gone, and it had rusted and caved in, but a series of large pipes still spread from the top. "We shoveled coal from five in the morning until supper, then again from six to ten." His lip curled, remembering the cut of the strap on his bare back, the heat that made his skin and eyeballs feel like they'd melt, the choking fumes. They hadn't even bothered to light this part of the plant with the tallow lanterns that hung above the lines, and Querry and Reg labored among the hellish orange glow and frightening shadows.

Then he thought about Thimbleroy Manor and all the other houses his work had taken him inside. "Stupid," he spat. "Pointless."

"Querry?"

"I'm sorry," he said, forcing his tone to lighten. "Just some bad memories is all."

"I can't even imagine how horrible it must have been."

"No, you can't." Abandoned now, the factory looked eerie and forlorn, but to Querry it seemed peaceful in comparison to the sweltering, noisy place he remembered, where he fought for every scrap of food, and fought to protect himself and Reg. The two comely young men hadn't been safe a moment from the other workers. Even now, Querry looked deep into the shadows, sure he saw movement, men waiting with clubs or broken bottles.

"It's over now," he said, as much to allay himself as Frolic. Then he reached inside the boiler, felt around a metal shelf and brought out a steel box with a lid covered in gears. He set it on the ground, squatted, and pressed the thirteen levers protruding from the side in the proper order. The clockwork ground together, clinking and ticking, until the lid slowly opened. On top of the coins he'd been saving since recruiting Frolic as a partner, Querry placed the leather-bound book.

"You're sure it will be safe here?" Frolic asked, a little skeptically.

"Absolutely," Querry said, replacing the box on the shelf inside the furnace. "Not even beggars will come in here, after the fire. You see, Frolic, there was only one way in or out of this place: a tiny metal door at the front. They did it so we couldn't run away. Though I managed it, after Reg left. There were no windows. So when the place went up, almost everyone inside burned alive. Many of them were children. Hundreds of lives lost."

"I'd like to leave now," Frolic said. "And never come back here."

"We must decide where we'll go," Querry said, taking Frolic's hand to lead him away from the nightmarish factory. "Tonight and then forever."

Chapter 8

"ANOTHER OF my boyhood haunts," Querry said, indicating the notorious Slouch End Slum with a sweep of his hand. Unlike Rushport, no whores or beggars called out to the pair. No cooking smells spilled from taverns. The only drinking establishments here consisted of dank little rooms serving the dregs that other pubs threw out. Querry had been able to order a beer at eight. Fearful silence replaced lewd cacophony as they made their way up the street, Frolic gaping at the tumbledown row houses, most of which lacked windows and many of which lacked doors.

As they went, dirty children began to emerge from behind broken carriages and ruined walls. They approached slowly, circling like hungry wolves, with faces as wild and desperate. More small heads poked from the holes in the upper stories, and soon the whole neighborhood, a hundred or more orphans, became aware of Querry and Frolic. The thief, having spent much time here in his youth, knew they would cut his and Frolic's throat for a penny. He stopped in the center of the street and planted his feet in a wide stance. Theatrically he whipped open his coat to reveal his many weapons.

"Black Bethany," he said, his voice echoing through the hollowed-out shells of the buildings. Some of the urchins scuttled off, disappearing down the winding alleyways. The rest continued to gawk at them, waiting to be entertained in the way children will. Querry was little surprised at the appearance of heavy pipes, knives, boards wrapped with jagged wire, and all other manner of makeshift armaments. Frolic's training brought him to stand at Querry's back, ready to draw his sword.

"Wait," Querry instructed quietly, though Frolic's shoulders against his own felt reassuring.

The children began to chatter and inch closer, some of them fingering their weapons impatiently. Querry thumbed the hammer of his pistol.

Then the throng parted and a plump woman sauntered to where Querry and Frolic stood. She wore a garish tartan frock, tucked up in the front to reveal striped hose and armored, knee-high boots with sharp, silver tips. High on each thigh rode an assortment of blades in leather sheathes that matched the bodice pushing her freckled bosom almost to her collarbone. More plaid strips held red-orange ropes of hair, graying noticeably at the roots. Crisscrossing her ample body was a studded belt holding a clockwork rifle. The woman smiled, revealing teeth as black as the coal Querry used to shovel, and said, "Querrilous Knotte."

"Black Bethany." She took her name not from the color of her skin, hair, or even teeth, but from her rumored mastery of witchcraft. Querry couldn't be sure, though he had witnessed troublesome boys disappear just as new cats took up residence in the Slum.

As if unaware that her charms had long since departed, she put a hand on Querry's waist. "You've grown into a fine young man," she said with a wink, in her thick, booze-soaked brogue.

"Thanks," he mumbled.

"What is it ye be wantin' then, Querry?"

"Sanctuary, I suppose."

"Eh?"

"My companion and I just need a safe place to lay low for a couple of days," he said. "And if there's one part of this city law enforcement won't dare set foot—"

His words were cut off by cries of "Bugger those pigs!", "I'll slit their bags and make them eat my shite!", and many more colorful oaths from the assembled boys.

When the fervor died down, Querry continued. "All I ask is that you tell your people to let us be. We'll duck into one of these buildings and by the end of the week we'll be gone."

"An' who's he? A damned *sidhe fey*—"

"No," Querry said quickly. "A friend of mine."

"You won't bring no trouble down on me and mine?" she said suspiciously. "I heard about the work you been doin', Querry. And who for."

He took her rough, dirty hand and said, "Bethany. You know me. I always did what you asked and never tried to keep more than my share of the cut."

Swaying, she touched Querry's face. "Such a handsome lad you was. Quick little fingers too. Aye, you was always one of my favorites. Right then. Just this once."

"Thank you, Miss," Frolic said.

Black Bethany ignored him and addressed the throng. "Listen up, all of ye. These here are my guests, and if ye little shites don't want to end up catching rats for yer supper, you'll let them be."

Slowly the boys dispersed, mumbling, disappointed at the loss of participating in, or even watching, a good brawl. Black Bethany took a flask from somewhere in her skirts and enjoyed a long pull. She wiped her mouth on her dress sleeve and belched. "Ye remember your way around?" she asked Querry.

"Home sweet home," he answered, and she staggered away. He led Frolic up the steps of one of the long, rectangular buildings. Clothing, food, and bottles lay scattered about by boys who'd never been taught otherwise. Someone had ripped the door from the frame of each of the small rooms. Most of these contained groups of three or four boys, drinking beer, playing dice or cards, or resting on the mounds of discarded clothing that served as their beds. Plates and dishes of food, in various states of putrification, dotted the floor and scented the air.

"Fuck off someplace else," said a seven-year-old who sat cross-legged, gnawing on a chicken leg, in the first room Querry and Frolic entered, "'fore I cut your goods off and make ye eat 'em."

They encountered similar reactions until they reached a room at the end of the third-floor hallway. Though twice the size of the others, it held only two children: a flaxen-haired boy of about nine or ten and his younger sibling. The older boy reclined in the glassless window, while the younger, not more than two or three, arranged blocks of wood on the dirty floor. In the corner Querry saw a basket lined with scraps of cloth: a makeshift cradle.

"Suppose we could spend the night here?" Querry asked.

The older drew a long drag from his pipe and leisurely exhaled a stream of smoke. "Let me ask you somethin'," he said in a jaded tone. "You a faggot, mister?"

"Excuse me?"

"'S just some of the guys been talking. They say they heard about things you done. I gots to protect myself's all. And me little brother."

"You have nothing to worry about from me."

"What about him?" the boy pointed at Frolic with his pipe.

"He's a doll," Querry said with a wry grin.

"Fucking sick," the boy spat. "But as long as you keep it between the two of ye. And ye go fetch me two pints of ale and a quart of milk."

"What?"

"That's the rent, mister. Pay up or bugger off."

"We'll be back with them, then," Querry conceded. "What's your name?"

"They call me Tommy the Axe," he said, puffing with pride. "On account of her." He pointed to a heavy axe handle with a jagged, rusted blade. Her owner had driven heavy nails into the wood around the top, and Querry saw some dark brown stains. "Just remember that, if yer thinkin' of tryin' anything."

"YOU'D NEVER think it to look at the place," Querry said to Frolic, quietly, as the tow-headed toddler called Little Ricky had finally fallen asleep in his basket, "but this place was a paradise for a boy."

Outside, the winter wind howled, but Tommy had covered the window with a horse blanket and lit a fire in a pitted steel cauldron. He'd even been gracious enough to provide Querry and Frolic with a cloth sack full of rags for a pillow and a moth-eaten lady's coat to cover themselves. Within the fur and leather, Querry felt warm and secure, content with Frolic dozing on his chest. On his errand for ale and milk, he'd picked up a few links of bologna and a loaf of bread, so not even hunger troubled him.

"Total freedom," he said, watching Tommy in the corner, well on his way through the second bottle of ale. Frolic's face nestled closer to his chest, and he made a murmur of agreement. Querry tucked the collar of the jacket around his neck and stroked his curls. "But wouldn't a little privacy be nice?" he added, tracing Frolic's ear. "Feels like an eternity since we had some time together."

Frolic chuckled sleepily, and Querry kissed the part in his hair before letting himself drift off. Still weak from his ailment, sleep hit him like a wall.

IT FELT like he'd only been unconscious a few minutes when a loud crash woke Querry. Frolic stood over him, sword in hand. Forcing alertness, Querry analyzed the sounds coming from the hall and the street beyond: boys yelling and cursing, knocking on doors and rousing their allies. Droves of them ran down the building's halls and into the street. Feeling for his gun and then getting to his feet, Querry scanned the room. The fire had expired to coals; it was colder, and dark. Querry saw young Tommy tucking his brother's basket into a corner and heaping it high with garments. Next he made a barricade around the infant with a broken piece of a wooden sign and a three-legged chair.

"Be a good lad and stay right here," he said gently to Little Ricky. "Big Brother'll be back soon."

Then the boy's demeanor changed dramatically, and he bellowed, "Time to crack some fucking skulls!" He lifted his trademark axe over his head and let out a ferocious war cry.

As Tommy ran past, Querry caught his elbow and said, "What the hell is going on?"

"Barty Siddle's gang," he said, with a blood-crazed look that should never touch so young a face. "His boys been picking pockets on our turf. Now they got the stones to come here. Well, I'll cut them clean off!"

"Wait," Querry said, thinking. "Barty Siddle. With the eye patch and big hat?"

"You know that dirty cocksucker?"

"But Tommy, those are grown men!"

"We'll spill their fucking guts, mister. And piss in their faces, not to worry!" He broke free and tore off, yelling at the top of his lungs.

"I think we should get out of here," Querry told Frolic. "This little skirmish might attract attention that we don't need."

"Will they be all right?" Frolic asked, looking at the basket in the corner. "They're just children, Querry."

"They're young, but they can take care of themselves. I was the same at their age. Besides, us getting caught up in this won't change anything."

"Why is it always that way? Why does nothing we do ever make a difference?"

"No time for philosophy, beauty. We'll make our way to the docks and get on board a ship. Let fate decide where to take us."

Frolic didn't argue, though Querry could see the turmoil in his large eyes. They fought their way into the hall and onto the stairs as boys pushed past them on every side, yelling oaths that made even Querry blush and brandishing all kinds of weapons.

Outside was chaos. Piles of debris had already been set to burn. At least fifty youths blocked the street, standing shoulder to shoulder. Others poured from alleys and nearby buildings, shouting out their eagerness to join the fray. About a block and a half away, Querry saw the approach of more than twenty men. A young man of about fifteen noticed them, too, and he screamed, "Here those whoresons come! Let's tear their throats out!"

His troops bellowed a deafening response, and the group surged forward at a run. Querry grabbed Frolic's elbow, and they pressed their backs tight against the closest building. Not ten feet from where they stood, the two groups clashed. The din increased as metal met metal and flesh met flesh. Many of those who had been near the front of the group fell right away, only to be trampled by their enraged comrades as they tried to crawl to safety. Blood wet the cobblestone and screams pierced the night. Black Bethany's boys scored the first victory; one of them hurled a bottle of flaming oil into Barty's ranks. Four men caught fire and had to leave the melee to roll in the filthy snow. Others took their places, though, and the two factions crashed together again. More fell, and others rushed to claim their spots.

Inch by inch, trying to avoid wildly swinging boards or hurled bricks, Querry and Frolic made their way toward the back of the battle, past Barty Siddle's thugs. The street was a blur of flailing limbs, wrestling bodies, fire and blood. Endless reinforcements arrived to join Bethany's cause, and it looked like Barty's gang would be overwhelmed by the superior numbers. By now the boys surrounded the dozen or so men left standing, and pushed and clawed at one another to land a blow. Their adversaries held their arms in front of their faces, and succeeded a few times in pushing some of the boys back. But as soon as they did, another group closed the gap, and it seemed inevitable that the thugs would be crushed beneath a pile of angry young men.

Querry put his left arm around Frolic's shoulders, and wrapped his hand around his forehead to protect him as they prepared to sprint through the clusters of combatants fighting in smaller groups beyond the main battle. His right hand held the clockwork pistol ready. As soon as he saw an opening, he urged Frolic on. Small bodies lay in the street, and injured boys limped past them. Frolic let out a wail when they collided with a young man holding a blood-soaked rag over his eye.

"Don't look, don't look," Querry chanted, trying to soothe him. They'd nearly made it through, to a street corner that lead away from the slum. A boy sailed into his chest, knocking Querry on his ass and sending Frolic sprawling beside him. The clockwork pistols bounced against the street and landed a few feet off. It took a moment for Querry to recognize Tommy. The boy held his diaphragm and spat a mouthful of blood onto the cobblestone. He'd lost two of his front teeth. A big, bald man, his face so disfigured by scars that it barely registered as human, approached them with a meat cleaver. Tommy's signature axe was nowhere to be seen.

Querry crossed his arm over the boy's small shoulders and drew his sword. Being on the ground put him at a disadvantage. He needed to level the field, and fast. With a quick motion he sliced at the man's knees, severing the tendons and dropping him. As he fell, he swung the cleaver at Querry's hand. Querry tried to angle his blade to deflect the blow off the hand-guard, but he knew he wouldn't likely escape a deep wound.

Shouting Querry's name, Frolic tackled the big man and pummeled the side of his ugly face with his fists. The man's cries got the attention of three of his cohorts, and one of them struck Frolic hard in the ribs with a broken oar. Frolic flew threw the air and landed on his side.

Disoriented, Querry struggled to stand with Tommy still in his arms. He set the boy down, held his shoulder and looked seriously into his face. "Get home to your brother," he said, and Tommy obeyed without argument.

Instead of wasting time locating his gun, Querry ran to stand in front of Frolic, sword extended. He thrust at the thug with the oar, piercing his side and, from the rush of blood and air, his lung. The man staggered back, clutching the wound. Another member of the gang swung at Querry with a knife, but the thief kicked him in the groin and disarmed him as he doubled over. Behind him, Frolic had reached his knees and was using Querry's coat to pull himself up.

Pain erupted across the top of Querry's foot. Looking down, he saw the man with the cleaver had dragged himself through the street to attack. The blade still stuck in Querry's flesh, and blood darkened his leather boot and pooled around his foot.

"You son of a two-penny whore!" he yelled, and brought his sword down in an arc, hitting the man between the eyes with the hilt. His head hit the cobblestone, and Querry reached for the handle of the cleaver and extracted it with a scream. The momentary distraction cost him; the third of the thugs smacked him in the back of the head. He fell across the back of the man with the cleaver.

Everything blurred and bled together. Querry willed his eyes to focus, willed his muscles to get him up. Neither would cooperate. Nearby, Frolic fought furiously. Querry heard the hum of his blade. He had to get to his feet, get Frolic out of here. His foot throbbed and burned, shooting agony up his leg. Nothing but smudged rusts and grays met his vision. Frolic cried out. Querry heard a thud, ground his teeth and pushed with all his might.

Rough hands grabbed his hair, wrenching his head back painfully.

"Frolic?" he choked, but got no response.

"Shut it, pretty boy," said a familiar voice.

Querry twisted to escape. Something hit him between the shoulder blades, held him down.

"Frolic!"

He was dragged away from the man with the cleaver, onto the cement of the walk. Someone pulled his arms behind his back and restrained his wrists. They hauled him up, but his injured right foot couldn't support him, and he dropped to his knees. Through his haze, he scanned around desperately for his partner, but instead of growing clear, the world became fuzzier, darker—

Lost too much blood.

"I won't. Let you. Take. Him."

"An' I said shut up."

Something struck Querry's temple, and everything went black.

CHAPTER 9

THE FIRST thing Querry perceived was the smell. Even before he opened his eyes, it made him fight to keep from retching: human waste and moldy straw. A large cinderblock room slowly became clear. Indeed, straw covered the floor. Here and there sat a broken chair or a wooden crate made up as a table. Metal buckets lined the walls, and the swarms of flies above them told Querry their purpose. Across from him, a fat, naked man gnawed on a rat. The smears on his sagging chest proved he made it a habit. Tiny, semicircular barred windows let in the cold winter light. People huddled together for warmth: men, women, and children in filthy rags. The Halcyon penal system made no distinction between those who couldn't make their rent and the homicidally insane. Querry wondered which of the city's many prisons he could now call his home.

"What the—"

A boy of about twelve handed Querry a canning jar full of cloudy water, and Querry drank. Gradually he recalled the battle in Slouch End, though he couldn't envision how it had ended. Soon two other boys joined the first, crouching beside Querry with their elbows on their knees.

"We heard what you done," said one. "Back in the Slouch End."

"We wouldn't let them saw your foot off," said another proudly.

Remembering his injury, Querry curled and uncurled his toes. His foot felt cold, but the pain wasn't much, considering. Looking down, he saw a scabbed-over gash. It didn't look red or puffy, though: no infection.

"Got hold of some gin to pour over it," the boy continued.

"Thanks," Querry said. In a place like this, one didn't sacrifice gin lightly. "What happened?"

"Barty Siddle got hold of ye. Turned ye in for a hundred-pound reward."

"I had someone with me."

"Silver-haired bloke? The constables took him off somewhere else. I'll tell you what, he looked a little like a pansy, but he could fight like a demon. Took eight of 'em to get him in the wagon."

"Where did they take him?" Querry asked, even though he knew the answer.

The boys shrugged. The one who'd saved Querry's foot said, "It'll be off to the workhouses for us. Not that they'll keep us long."

"Better than the colonies," said the boy with the water jar.

"Why would they keep me alive?" Querry mused. Of course, they'd taken his gear and stripped him down to his shirt and trousers. One of his benefactors had wrapped a scratchy blanket around his shoulders. It didn't make any sense. Now that they had Frolic, why not just put a bullet in his head? Unless they wanted a hanging, a public spectacle.

Tearing a few strips from the blanket with his teeth, Querry wrapped his bare foot and stood. He could try to escape, but he had no great expectations. The windows with the iron bars were twelve feet above his head, and the walls were likely four feet thick. A huge metal door, green with oxidation, stood at the other end of the room. It had no handle on the inside. And while no guards patrolled the prison interior, Querry knew the yard beyond would be a different story. All he could do for now would be to wait and try to recover his strength.

A few hours later, just after sunset, the prison staff lit the candles that sat on the crate tables, and the residents lined up to receive a loaf of rock-hard bread and jar of water. Bullies immediately tried to take the rations from the weak, and several fights were broken up by the clubs of the guards. Querry found a secluded corner and finished his cheerless supper. Covering as much of his body as he could, he drew his knees up and leaned his head against the wall to try to sleep amidst the crying of babies, drunken altercations, and the babbling of the mad.

Off in the dark, he heard the too-familiar sounds of women and boys fighting off unwanted attention. He found it disgraceful not to even separate the women and children from the men.

Shivering and hungry, Querry thought about the Thimbleroy manor and the luxuries within: stuffed leather chairs beside cozy fires, trays of fruit, biscuits and fine cheeses to snack upon, tumblers of good whiskey and cigars, tubs of hot, bubbling water, soft towels, silk robes, satin sheets, and servants to turn down the beds. Was that where Frolic was at the moment? What would he be doing: sitting down to a dinner party or shooting billiards in the study? Did Querry have any right to deny Frolic a life of such pleasures, just because he wanted Frolic for himself? He'd introduced Frolic to a hard world, a world where survival meant struggle, and a world where innocents suffered. Thimbleroy could give him a life unlike Querry could ever dream of providing.

But Querry could picture the aging aristocrat closing a carved door and ordering Frolic to undress, to get on the bed. Querry could see Frolic's fair, slight form beneath the velvet canopy, waiting, wondering. Was it a good trade, comfort for freedom? If he believed that, Querry could just go and live with his gentleman and want for nothing. No, Frolic should be given the choice, and Querry would see, somehow, that he was.

Querry closed his eyes. He was tired after the fever and the fight. He thought about his gentleman. Maybe the faerie would come and rescue him, force the guards and prisoners to stare in dumb impotence as the two of them strolled leisurely away. He could imagine it: the gentleman talking animatedly about a play or party, completely oblivious to the danger and despair around them. He'd probably insist Querry accompany him to some sort of bizarre dance or symphony. Not for the first time, Querry had a sense of something significant that he couldn't grasp. But he was too exhausted to puzzle it out just now, and so he forgot it.

OVER THE next three days, little broke the bleak monotony of prison life. In the morning the prisoners got a metal dish of gruel and a cup of milk that had usually gone sour. Then the guards rounded up those people scheduled to be deported to the colonies and those to be executed. Orphans left for the factories. Querry spent the afternoons pacing, trying to examine the windows and walls for ways of escape without being obvious. So far it seemed his only chance would be to run past the guards when they opened the door to distribute food. He didn't like his odds of being shot in the back, though. Now and then the inmates got to spend a little time walking the desolate, gray yard.

On the fourth day of Querry's incarceration, four constables in their blue uniforms and silly hats came looking for him just after breakfast. They cuffed his hands with heavy, iron manacles and led him into a corridor beyond the entrance. They walked by more metal doors, until one of them stopped and unlocked one. Another pushed Querry inside the tiny cell, which contained a utilitarian desk and chair, and another chair facing it. At the desk sat a portly, middle-aged man in a brown suit and a salmon-colored kerchief that almost matched his complexion. His jowls drooped, and a ring of ruddy flesh squished out around his starched collar. He looked up at Querry without much interest, then back down at the papers he examined by a gas lamp. A guard dragged Querry to the unoccupied chair, slammed him down, and secured his ankles to the chains welded to its legs.

The man at the desk cleared his throat and began reading. "Name: Querrilous Knotte. Date of birth: unknown. Age: unknown, presumably between eighteen and twenty-two years. Current address and family are unknown. Charges include burglary, larceny, sodomy, treason— including faerie collaboration—inciting of a riot, assault and murder. The penalty for which shall be death by hanging."

"Aren't I supposed to stand trial?"

The man looked up at Querry and smirked, as if to say, *Who do you think you are?* He continued, "However by intervention on the part of Lord Pyramus Earnest Thimbleroy, Grande Chancellor, the sentence shall be reduced to permanent exile on the Gondwalla Island Colony, if the accused is willing to cooperate by answering fully all queries set forth by his Lordship."

Querry snorted. He knew if he answered the questions, the four burly constables would take him to a secluded alley and slit his throat.

"Skeptical, Mr. Knotte?" asked the pudgy attorney. He held up a page and pointed. "This is His Lordship's signature and seal. He's arranged for you to make the journey to Gondwalla Island in three days time. If you cooperate, that is. You'll be given lodging and respectable work."

"I've had a taste of your idea of respectable work," Querry said. "I don't care for a second helping."

A guard with a thick, red moustache hit Querry with the back of his hand. Querry's lips pulsed and swelled, and blood trickled down his chin. "No speaking out of turn," the guard warned.

Barely fazed, the barrister continued. "First question," he said, dipping his pen in anticipation of recording the answer, "Where and how did you acquire the clockwork mechanism that you refer to as Frolic?"

"I don't know what the hell you're talking about."

"Constable, if you please."

The guard backhanded Querry again, splitting his lip. Eyes watering, he spat the blood on the floor.

"Second question. Upon obtaining the aforementioned clockwork mechanism, did any other clockwork machines come into your possession? Or literature relating to the construction of clockwork mechanisms?"

"Clockwork mechanism," Querry said, shaking his head and making his chains rattle. "Fuck you."

The hairy fist struck him on the cheek, making him and the chair fly through the air. It landed on its side, and Querry smacked his head and scraped his shoulder. Two guards hauled him back up and positioned him in front of the desk. Blood dripped into his left eye from a cut on his brow, and a strand of his black hair stuck in the wound.

"Where is the book, Mr. Knotte?"

"Bugger it," Querry said, bracing himself for the next round of blows. The barrister asked the book's location three more times, and by the end both of Querry's eyes had nearly swollen shut, his mouth and nose bled, and a molar had come loose. But a little laugh escaped his blood-soaked lips, because he knew they couldn't kill him or they'd never find the book.

Finally the attorney stood and stashed his papers in a leather case. "Same time tomorrow, I presume," he said as he left the cell, leaving Querry alone with the guards. Querry knew well enough how it would go as he watched the metal door close and lock.

"Arrogant little faerie-loving queer," said one of the guards, knocking Querry back down on his side with a savage blow. "Like the taste of faerie cock, do ye? Like to steal babies?" They circled him, and Querry shielded his head with his bound hands as their boot-toes prodded his ribs and belly, feeling out the soft places to kick.

"Son of a mongrel bitch," they taunted as they drove their feet against Querry's back and sides. He sobbed dryly and began to cough, amusing the guards immensely. "Where's your faggot faerie friends now?" Querry curled into a tight ball and waited for the assault to end. Finally, panting with exertion, the guards dragged him back to the main room of the prison.

"We got this for ye every day, until you decide to talk. Miserable little cocksucker."

That night, Querry used half of his water ration to clean the dried blood from his face. The adolescent boys of the prison, to whom Querry had grown into an almost legendary figure, gave him a large bowl of some alcohol they made by fermenting bread crusts and the occasional potato peel. The stuff tasted like the Devil's piss, but it eased Querry's pain and helped him sleep.

True to their word, the four constables came to interrogate Querry every morning after breakfast. He gave up eating, as he'd almost certainly throw up the gruel during the inevitable beating. Through the questions, kicks and blows, Querry mustered the strength to stay silent by remembering the good times he'd shared with Frolic. No matter what they did to him, he wouldn't betray Frolic. By picturing Frolic's bemused smile, the trust in his eyes, and the way his lips trembled and fell open when he came, Querry could almost transcend the brutal assaults, almost step outside of himself until that attorney admitted another defeat.

Back in the cold, straw-strewn room, though, Querry's aches returned, and his growing sense of despair deepened. He'd been imprisoned over two weeks. Thimbleroy could have Frolic out of the country by now, and Querry was no closer to orchestrating his escape. His will was strong, but he was mortal after all, and he didn't know how much more his body could endure. How long before one of the guards ruptured an organ or broke a vital bone? His only hope seemed to be the faerie gentleman. Many nights, out of sheer desperation, he stared at the sky and called out to his gentleman with his mind. A few times he thought he caught a few bars of the atonal music he associated with the faerie, but still no one came. The beatings continued, and the lack of decent food sapped Querry's strength. Probably the fey had forgotten him in favor of whatever pretty thing had his eye at the moment. Querry couldn't blame him, either. His kind didn't measure relationships as humans did. Neither cruelty nor indifference caused the gentleman to ignore Querry's plight, or wonder about the thief's condition. It simply didn't occur to him.

The winter holiday granted Querry a two-day respite from questioning. Each of the prisoners received a salty scrap of ham, a roast potato and some mushy greens. Beyond the cinderblock walls, cathedral bells rang day and night. Sipping the foul-tasting, clear spirit brewed by the boys, Querry imagined Reg dancing around a lighted tree with plain Emily Malvern. He imagined Frolic in a red, sateen suit at the Thimbleroy Yule Ball, and he felt so lonely and forgotten that for the first time in his life he didn't know if he could go on, keep fighting. He missed the warm weight of his cats as he slept. Though he hadn't realized it at the time, he'd planned to settle down with Frolic. He'd been saving for a house. His neck crumpled, and his head came to rest against the cold, stone wall. He stared into the darkness, too depleted even to cry. Eventually, sheer exhaustion granted him a brief respite from his despair.

Querry was little surprised by the appearance of the quartet of constables the next morning.

"That's him there," bellowed one of the large men. "Querrilous Knotte."

But then, from behind the shoulders of two guards, appeared a smaller man in an understated, gray suit. He had a delicate, pretty face, thick, sand-colored hair, and the gentlest hazel eyes. He stared down at Querry with an unspoken plea, and Querry understood.

"You say this is the thief and murderer here."

"That's right, sir. He's an incorrigible one. No idea what his Lordship thinks you'll be able to get out of him. Begging your pardon, sir." It almost made Querry smile, the deference these brutes showed Reg.

"His Lordship merely wishes for an official account of this villain's career to be placed in the royal archives, for the sake of history. As Chief Archivist, the unhappy task of interviewing him falls to me. I don't suppose you could take him into another room? A gentleman in my position is unaccustomed to dealing with such a stink as fills this one."

"Right then, sir! On your feet, you rascal."

Heart racing and hope renewed, Querry followed Reg to the familiar cell at the end of the corridor. He didn't have any clue what Reg planned, but the fact that he'd come for Querry meant enough. He would trust Reg, and if he died attempting whatever Reg schemed, he'd die happy.

"You're sure it'll be safe, sir? Being alone in here with him?"

With a shrug, Reg said, "It will be as His Lordship wishes. He feels this criminal might be more candid about his activities."

"Well, we'll be right outside in the yard having a smoke," one of the guards said, pointing to a bleak patch beyond a wrought-iron door. "You just give a shout."

Reg thanked the men, and they left.

"My God," Reg said, seeing Querry's condition.

"Reg, what—"

Reg held up a hand. "Don't talk, Querry. Follow me. Run. Run as you've never run before."

He did, down a hallway opposite the yard and through the filthy, rat-infested little room they called the kitchen. Weak and injured, his bandaged foot numb with the cold, Querry sped after Reg around the side of the prison to a cart driven by a smoke-colored, Gypsy woman. Reg dove into the straw it held, and Querry followed. With a shout and a crack of her whip, the Gypsy urged her chestnut mare to a canter. Reg threw a piece of canvas over Querry and himself as the wagon made its bumpy, erratic way. When it came to a halt, Reg hurried Querry into the back of a milk truck, then to crouch among empty beer barrels on an ox-drawn flatbed. Finally they boarded an enclosed wagon driven by an old man in a wide-brimmed hat. Querry watched Reg pay the driver twenty times what the cart and both horses were worth, and then they climbed in back and sat among the sweet-smelling sacks of grain. Soon the vehicle disappeared among the many others that transported goods between the city and the farms beyond it.

"Reg, I don't know what to say," Querry panted. He held a stitch in his side. "You, you've thrown your life away!"

"They were planning to torture you, Querry. They've got this brain doctor who uses electricity and all sorts of ghastly devices. I couldn't let them. I've seen what this man leaves behind, rotting in the asylums. I'd have come some sooner, but I didn't even know they got you until a few nights ago, when the Head Barrister got drunk and started to complain about a stubborn prisoner. Didn't take me long to figure out he was talking about you." He smiled, and it was like a decade fell away. They were boys on an adventure again.

"I love you," was the only thing Querry could think of to say.

"Yes, and I love you. After you left, I thought about you and Frolic, off somewhere exotic, and me left behind. No amount of money is worth how miserable I felt, like the best part of my life was over. There was this one night. I was at dinner with Lady Malvern, and she was discussing the table service for the wedding. Two hours and two dozen different forks. Then she moved on to the napkins, and I realized this was the entirety of my future. She droned on and on, and all I could think about was you. And Frolic. Then, as soon as we left the restaurant and got into the carriage, she attacked me. I don't exaggerate when I say I had to fight her off. She said she wanted me to rip her bodice and have my way with her, just like a knight in one of those trashy, two-penny novels. Of course I couldn't do it. I almost became physically ill when she pulled my face against her chest. I don't know how I fooled myself as long as I did."

"No, neither do I." Lunging forward, Querry lowered Reg to the soft wheat sacks and held him around the waist. He kissed him, and Reg eagerly kissed back, digging his nails into Querry's ass cheeks, pulling Querry's groin against his own. Growing instantly erect, Querry ground his cock against Reg as he drove his tongue toward his throat. He tasted and felt amazing, even better than Querry's idealized memories of him. Querry ripped Reg's shirt free of his waistband to get his hands on his wonderful warm skin. Then he hooked his hands beneath Reg's knees and thrust them toward his shoulders. Beneath him, Reg looked up with that mix of vulnerability and anticipation that drove Querry mad. He pushed forward, against Reg's cleft in a preview of what was to come, and then he reached toward the buttons of Reg's trouser flap. He couldn't wait to get him out of those clothes, thrust into him hard and hear him cry out.

Reg caught his hand and kissed his knuckles. "Out of your mind, like always," he teased. "We can't do this here. Now."

"Why not? It's been forever."

"Because. We're in the back of an open cart, and, I don't mean to hurt your feelings, Querry, but you really smell."

"Thanks for that." Querry moved to the other side of the compartment and crossed his arms.

Tenderly Reg touched his cheek. "Don't worry. We'll have time. But we have work today. Our job's only two-thirds done. We can't abandon him."

"Never," Querry agreed.

"We need to find him and formulate a plan. They'll be looking for both of us now. What should we do first?"

Querry exhaled and pushed his filthy hair out of his face. "It's getting bloody expensive, always replacing my damn gear."

Before long, paved streets gave way to rocky, dirt roads and fresh air replaced the stench of the city. Looking out the back of the cart, Querry watched the dark fields dotted with snow, rolling gently, broken here and there by a copse of trees or crumbling stone wall. The color departed the world: everything was black or white beneath a uniform, gray sky. Reg filled Querry in on the details he'd missed over his weeks in the jail. There had been no mention of his or Frolic's capture. Work continued night and day on the clock tower. Lord Thimbleroy scoured the Archives for anything to do with clockwork construction, and he'd hired experts from all over the world. Querry told Reg about the theft of Frolic's book, and the ghastly dolls in the Thimbleroy cellar. They discussed the possible implications for an hour, and then the cart's driver stopped for lunch. Beneath a gnarled oak tree, the three men shared some savory liver and onion sandwiches provided by the driver's wife. They passed his flask a few times, to steel themselves against the cold, and continued on their way.

Back inside the cart, Querry made himself comfortable against the grain sacks. Lulled by the rhythmic sway and creak of the axles, he began to doze. When a rut in the track jostled and woke him, he bolted up defensively. But then he saw Reg reclining across from him, his hands folded serenely over his belt, and he let himself fall back to secure sleep.

CHAPTER 10

NIGHT HAD fallen when a touch on his shoulder roused Querry. He'd slept the better part of the day, and he felt stronger, as well as powerfully hungry. The cart had come to a stop in front of an old, stone barn full of bleating sheep. A harsh wind had dispersed the clouds, and beneath the nearly full moon the snowy fields glowed a ghostly bluish-white. Here in the country, away from the haze and artificial light, the stars twinkled brightly. Hopping down, Querry took a deep breath of the crisp air, and exhaled a frozen cloud.

"Put this on," Reg said, handing Querry a green rubber boot designed for mucking stables. "We'll have to walk this last bit."

"Where are we going?" Querry asked as he thrust his bandaged foot into the too-large boot. "We should be heading back to the city to look for Frolic. What are the chances that Thimbleroy has him stashed out here in the middle of nowhere?"

"Absolutely none," Reg said, hooking his elbow into Querry's and walking in the direction of a fallow field overgrown with frozen grass.

"Then what are we doing here? Besides wasting time?"

"We're safe here. I made sure to bring us here by such a roundabout route and by so many different drivers that it would be nearly impossible to retrace our steps. We need time to plan, and you need time to heal."

"But—"

"No," Reg said firmly. "This is a serious matter. Both of us are wanted criminals now. If we're caught, we'll be executed. And then what will become of Frolic, when the only two men in the world who truly know him are gone? You're going to need all your strength. We can't afford to rush into this unprepared. Agreed?"

"I see your point, but I still say—"

"Agreed, Querry?"

"All right then." They'd reached a strip of wood that separated the fields from a boulder-strewn hill. The bare trees were slim and stunted. Thick bracken snagged Querry's pant legs as he and Reg picked their way slowly around trunks and large rocks. Finally they reached a tiny, stone house nestled at the foot of the hill. It had only a door and two small windows to break its plain front, and one of the walls had begun to crumble inward, taking the back corner and a section of the thatch roof with it. Woodbine and ivy drove their persistent tendrils into the mortar, and had nearly covered the chimney in leaves. Querry and Reg took what had possibly once been a path, before the ferns and holly reclaimed it.

The rotting door opened with a groan, and Reg let loose of Querry's arm and disappeared into the darkness. Querry heard the scrape of a match, followed by a soft amber glow from an oil lamp on the hearth. Looking around, he couldn't believe how little the interior of the house matched its desolate exterior. Reg went to an upside-down half-barrel and lit a few more candles. Next to them sat several bottles of good wine and two crystal flutes. Near the fireplace, a single bed had been constructed from a feather mattress, half a dozen soft blankets, and a pile of down pillows and velvet and brocade cushions. A large sheet separated it all from the bare, earth floor. It all looked rather cozy, romantic even. Querry laughed out loud as Tosser and Toerag darted across the room, yowling loudly and winding their lithe bodies around his ankles. He knelt down and gave each of them a scratch behind the ears.

"I'll get a fire started," Reg said, ignoring Querry's surprise. "Fry us up some eggs and bacon. And some tea! I'm dying for a cup."

"When did you do all this?" Querry asked.

"I set it up a few days ago. As I said, I needed some place to bring you where you'd be safe. I knew what sort of shape you'd be in after over three weeks in that prison. And I wasn't wrong. What did they do to you?"

"They wanted me to tell them where I hid the book."

"By the look of your face, I'm going to wager you refused." Reg knelt down and lit the little pyramid of twigs in the hearth. It crackled and blazed, and Querry opened his fingers above the warmth. Soon, a healthy fire burned in the rough, stone enclosure, raising the temperature quickly and casting the room in a fuzzy orange light. Sensation began to return to Querry's extremities.

"It's all a big, fat lie," he said. "All their preaching about fairness and equality under the law. The right of every citizen to prove his innocence. The right of every person to decent living conditions. All of it's talk from people who've never had to experience any of it."

"You should wash," Reg said in the gentle but insistent voice he always used to calm Querry's fervor. "The pump out back still works. Take that big, copper kettle."

Querry did as he was told, walking around the small structure to a clear, leaf-strewn track around back. Some powdery snow sprinkled his hair from the shelf of rock above. It still hadn't quite settled in: his freedom and Reg relinquishing his life, walking away from money and power to be with Querry. He couldn't process the enormity of what happened, of what would happen, the dangers they would face. Frolic was out there somewhere, and they would have to find him and fight to get him back. All of their lives would be threatened every moment. But right now, it felt like he and Reg were on holiday. He looked up at the sky, at the silver orb and wispy clouds.

It felt like they were on a honeymoon.

Scanning around, Querry located the rusty pump. But then something else caught his eye: two rounded stones at the opposite end of the yard. He approached them and easily read their carvings by the bright moonlight. The first proclaimed "Mary and unborn baby," and the second read "Reginald, father." Querry felt irrationally angry at these people for abandoning Reg, leaving him to fend for himself in the indifferent world. The little, stone house may not have been a palace, but Querry could bet growing up within its walls beat the factory. Why hadn't they fought harder to stay by his side?

"Lost, Querry?"

"No, no," he answered, turning his back on the graves. "I'm on my way."

It took a bit of a struggle to get the rusted, old pump going, but it brought forth pure, clear water when Querry managed it. He filled the kettle and took it inside to hang above the fire and warm. Reg gave him a fluffy towel and washcloth, a box of little soaps made to look like seashells, and a porcelain basin. As Reg cooked, filling the room with the welcome fragrances of smoked bacon, fried bread and strong tea, Querry scrubbed himself from head to toe, dunking his hair in the warm water and lathering away the grime. Several times he caught Reg looking up from the frying pan to watch him, and Querry smiled. He shaved, cleaned his teeth with some minty powder and a silver brush, and sat down on a wooden bench, feeling better than he had in weeks. The fire had warmed the space enough that he wasn't uncomfortable in just his towel.

"I got you some things to wear," Reg said, indicating two large, paper bags. The words "Phillipe Fountainbleu and Son, Fine Tailors," were written across them in gold leaf. "I had to pretend to be on an errand for the Earl of Ravenshire, since the clothes aren't my size. So I apologize if they're a bit, well, not your style."

Querry looked at the pile of garments he'd just removed, fouled with blood and the worst kinds of filth and said, "I'm sure they'll do just fine. Thanks again, Reg."

Querry dressed in royal blue, pinstriped trousers and a matching waistcoat. He put on a pair of wing-tipped Oxfords, tied a silk scarf around his neck, and closed his cuffs with gold and lapis links. Then he and Reg sat down to their supper. The salt and grease satisfied Querry's cravings, and he ate until he was stuffed. Reg opened a bottle of Pinot Noir and then stretched out on the feather bed. The two cats finished their leftovers and curled at their feet.

Feeling a little guilty over the comforts he enjoyed and the time he spent idle, Querry said, "Where do you think he is, right now?"

"There can't be much doubt that Thimbleroy's got him. As for why, I haven't yet figured that out."

"Reg, there's something that worries me. Worries me sick."

"What is it?"

"Think about Frolic. Think about his looks, his eagerness for affection. He loves to kiss and touch; he seeks it out. With me, he instigated everything before he even knew what to call it. The first day I found him, he asked me to kiss him."

"He instigated with me too. Where are you going with this?"

"Do you think he may have been designed to seek affection? To provide affection?"

"Oh. God."

Querry nodded gravely and drained his glass before holding it out to Reg to refill. "It may have been written in that book. And if Thimbleroy convinces Frolic that his purpose, his whole reason for being, is to provide pleasure to others, Frolic might go along with it, whether he wants to or not."

"And if he doesn't, he'll likely be forced," Reg said in a shaky voice.

Bolting up, Querry said, "What are we doing here, Reg? We've got to go after him! Right now!" He trembled and panted with anger, and then he started to cough. Reg took the flute from his hand and set it aside. He rose up on his knees and wrapped Querry's head in his arms, smoothing his wavy, black hair.

"Please, just calm down, Querry," he said. "You can't hope to do anything in your condition. He wouldn't want anything to happen to you."

"If they—" Querry choked out the words between hacks. "I'll never forgive myself."

"We'll get him back," Reg said, his lips moving against Querry's hairline and his warm, wine-scented breath washing over Querry's forehead. "We'll get him, I promise. Please, just rest for tonight."

"Oh, Reg." A series of sobs wracked Querry's injured body, and angry tears stung his eyes. Reg held him tight, and he took Reg's small waist in his arms and balled Reg's shirt in his fists as he cried. In only two minutes, the spell passed, leaving Querry to feel a bit awkward and embarrassed, but cleansed and focused.

"Sorry," he said, sniffling. "I just feel so useless. I don't like to sit back and do nothing."

"You're only human," Reg reminded him. Then, slowly, he lowered himself down on his side, keeping Querry's face pressed tight against his heart. As he had so many times before, Querry closed his eyes and listened to its patter.

"Feels good to hold you again," Reg said. "Especially since I never thought I'd get another chance."

"Love you, Reggie."

"Love you, Querry." Reg placed a trio of long, hard kisses across Querry's brow. "I'm glad to have you back. Glad we're together. I'm sorry it took something like this for me to realize that's how we belong."

"Shh." Querry reached up and petted the blond hair out of Reg's face in two firm strokes. His fingertips skimmed down Reg's cheek and stopped to trace around the perimeter of his shapely lips. Stretching his neck, Querry closed the distance between his own lips and Reg's skin. He kissed and suckled just below his jaw as his adept fingers dropped to the bow he wore and worked the knot loose. Reg's shirt fell open, and Querry kissed along the muscle that stretched from his ear to his collarbone. His hand moved back up, over the delightful, soft hair on the back of Reg's neck and into his plentiful locks.

"Come here," Querry said, giving Reg's tresses a tug. "Give me your mouth."

"Yes, Querry," Reg breathed. He slid down until they faced one another, and their lips met. Querry took a second just to savor the contact of their faces pressed close, and then he angled his head and let his tongue venture into Reg's mouth. Reg's tongue met Querry's fervently, the tip swirling around Querry's tip as his hands clawed at Querry's shoulder blades. Wriggling his arm between their tightly pressed bodies, Querry began to pop the little ivory buttons of Reg's linen shirt one by one. As soon as he finished, he brushed it aside and took hold of Reg's waist, feeling the muscles twist and contract in his hand as Reg writhed with anticipation. Then he let his fingertips dance up Reg's spine and back down, to the downy hair just above his ass.

Reg groaned with need, the sound reverberating through Querry's body. Querry pried Reg's clutching hands away from his clothing and sat up on his heels. He tugged away his necktie and flung it off to the side. As he hurried out of the expensive waistcoat and shirt, he watched Reg stretched out on the blankets. He'd rolled to his back, and his white shirt hung open, almost off his shoulders, revealing a smooth, slender body that looked made of gold silk in the firelight. His heart beat so hard and fast that Querry could see it shake his entire torso. Across his lovely face came a look that mixed trepidation, desire, and compliance in an intoxicating way. With a trembling hand, he reached out to stroke Querry's bare chest.

"And just why did I bother dressing?" Querry teased.

"I- I don't know," Reg managed.

As Querry unbuckled his belt, Reg kicked off his plain, black shoes. Both pairs of hands seized Reg's waistband and tore his trousers and undershorts to his knees, then off. He sprawled back out, his head propped on one of the former sofa cushions, his dark erection pointing up and left and jumping with his pulse.

Querry stood, toed off his own shoes and slowly unbuttoned his fly. Taking his time, taunting his lover, he reached inside and took hold of his hardened cock, bringing it out through the opening but not removing his trousers. As Reg looked on with longing, Querry gave himself a squeeze, causing a pearl of pre-come to bud from his slit. Reg moaned again, and his hand jerked like he might touch himself. Instead, though, his fingers opened and closed around handfuls of blanket as his waist twisted. A shiny film of perspiration covered his body.

"Querry," he panted. "There's some hand lotion. In the box with the soap."

The thief got out of his clothes and dug among the fragrant shells until he found a little tin with a chemist's logo stamped into the lid. He turned back to face the bed, ready to scoop out some of the creamy, musk-scented balm, rub it over his length, dive on Reggie and take him hard.

But then he stopped. As much as he wanted Reg, wanted to be inside him, for once in their lives they had time. For once, they wouldn't need to rush to satisfy themselves before someone noticed them missing. They had all night, and Querry planned to put it to good use. He set the tin on the barrel table for later and crouched down by Reg's feet. Wrapping his hand around Reg's left sole, Querry lifted his leg into the air and kissed the dome of bone at his ankle. His other hand moved up Reg's opposite thigh slowly, leaving raised pores in its wake, until it reached Reg's balls and gave them a gentle squeeze. In response Reg's hips bucked up, and Querry chuckled.

Kneading Reg's sack, feeling the testicles inside it rolling over his fingers, Querry kissed up the inside of his leg. When it met his body, Querry let go of Reg's foot and stretched out over his chest, savoring the amazing feeling of skin against skin. He touched Reg's burning cheek and felt out his lips before kissing him long and hard, thrusting his tongue almost into Reg's throat. Reg's legs wrapped Querry's hips, his heels compelling Querry forward.

"Not yet," Querry said into Reg's ear.

"But, Querry—" Reg practically pleaded.

Sitting back up, Querry grinned mischievously and said, "Not until I kiss every inch of your beautiful body. Touch you everywhere. Just lay back, Reg."

He obeyed, and Querry's hands and mouth began their tour of his skin, beginning at his chin and taking a meandering path down his neck and across his chest and then down the gully between his stomach muscles. When he reached Reg's cock, he held it in his hand and licked from the base to the head, letting his tongue circle around the corona until it glistened with saliva. Then he kissed in an angled line over Reg's protruding hipbone, then up his waist. Taking Reg's wrist, he guided his arm over his head and ruffled the sparse hair beneath it with his nose before continuing across his bicep and forearm. Next Querry took hold of Reg's shoulders and rolled him to his belly.

Right away Reg started to draw his knees up and lift his ass into the air, but Querry held a hand to his lower back, halting him. He looked over his shoulder at Querry, confusion and need pouring from his soft eyes.

"I don't know how much more of this I can take," he said.

Running a hand up the long, vertical muscle of Reg's back, Querry said, "Just be still. Be still and let me admire you. I've never really had the chance."

With a deep sigh Reg dropped his head back into the nest of pillows, and Querry traced the lines of his calves and thighs. Reaching the soft crescents of his ass, he urged them apart and leaned in, breathing Reg's smell before letting his tongue swipe the length of his furnace-hot cleft.

"You taste so good," he breathed into Reg's crevice. He took another long, slow swipe with his tongue, this time stopping to let the tip breach Reg's tight opening. Reg cried out sharply with surprise, went rigid a moment and then relaxed again. Querry let his tongue slide in and out of Reg's hot, sweet hole. His semen trickled down his cock, and he knew his partner would be just as frustrated, if not more so.

Reg confirmed it, saying, "God, Querry. I know your strength is down, but could you—could you please...."

Lifting his head and bringing Reg to his knees, Querry breathed, "Say it."

"Fuck me, Querry!"

"Nice and hard? That's how you like it. Am I wrong?"

"No. No, please. Please, Querry."

"Get your hips up a little higher," Querry said, finding the tin of lotion and using it to make his cock shine. Reg scrambled to comply, and Querry wrenched his cheeks apart and circled his anus with the head of his penis. Then, holding tight to Reg's hips, he thrust in hard. Reg swallowed a squeal, turned his face to the side, and bit his lip. Querry drew himself out almost completely before stabbing back in again and again, hard and deep, just like Reg enjoyed. As he did, he listened to the muffled sounds of pain and passion his partner made.

"Scream," Querry said, driving in and out of Reg with all his might, drenching them both in sweat.

"Ugh. What?"

"Scream for me, Reggie. I want to hear you scream. We don't have to be quiet."

Querry gave him a few savage pumps, and each one elicited a low wail of ecstasy that turned Querry on more than he would have ever thought possible. Stamina renewed, he reached around Reg and grasped his quivering cock as he kept up his furious pace. Their skin smacked together, loud and wet.

"Scream my name," he said through gritted teeth, nearing the end of his endurance. He felt Reg's erection skip in his hand.

"Querry! Oh, Querry. God!"

Unable to hold off much longer, Querry plunged deep into Reg's body and fucked him with hard, short strokes while matching the rhythm with his hand. Reg cried out wantonly, Querry's name spilling from his lips again and again.

"God, I love you, Reg," Querry said. Then he threw his head back and released a shout of his own as he came hard inside the other, shooting spurt after spurt of come until his entire body felt drained. Just when Querry didn't think he had the energy to remain upright, he felt Reg's cock dancing against his palm. "I want to hear you come," he said.

"Querry, I'm coming! Oh my God! God, I love you." Reg beat fists against the blankets as he whimpered and shook, going to pieces with bliss. Hot, white come splattered Querry's palm. He slid his fist to Reg's head and squeezed and twisted. Reg's head thrashed from side to side, and his cries of pleasure were almost indistinguishable from pain. Finally both of them collapsed, Querry laying belly-down over Reg's back.

"I've never loved anyone like I love you," Querry said, raking his fingers through Reg's sweaty hair.

"Except maybe Frolic?"

"Maybe. Is that the way you feel about us?"

"I think," Reg admitted. "I don't think I'd like to have to choose between the two of you."

"We need to get him back," Querry said again.

"How?"

"The junk shop." Querry pushed himself up on his hands and knees and went to fetch the washcloth and basin. He wiped Reg clean, then himself, and poured them each another glass of wine. Both men propped the large cushions against the wall and leaned there. Reg covered their lower bodies with a satin sheet, as Querry explained. "I need to replace my gear again, and if there's any news about a clockwork, Dink will have heard it."

Reg nodded and said, "It's as good a place to start as any. We'd best get some rest." He kissed Querry on the cheek and then curled on his side. Querry spooned up behind him, feeling gratified and happy, but not quite complete.

CHAPTER 11

AFTER TAKING five different carts and a meandering set of country roads to the outskirts of the city, Querry and Reg arrived at the edge of the factory district just as night fell. It was bitter cold and still; nothing but the distant chug and clang of the plants broke the silence. The clouds hung low and pregnant with snow, but, as yet, none fell. Darting from shadow to shadow, hoping the hood of his fur-lined cape would hide his face, Querry led his companion toward Dink's shop, jumping at the slightest sound, unnerved even by the crunch of their feet on the filthy snow. Reg's gloved hand went again and again to the antique pistols with the mother-of-pearl grips that he wore across his hips or to the rapier beside them. Querry knew Reg could handle them. He'd been quick and adept when they'd played at swords as boys, and weapon proficiency remained part of a gentleman's education. Still, Querry hoped Reg's skills wouldn't be put to the test. Fortunately the brutal temperature gave them the streets to themselves, and soon Dink's scrap yard came into view. Taking Reg's hand, Querry sprinted the final block and turned onto the path that led to the small store.

The chimes announced their entry into the warm, well-lit space. Querry breathed into his hands to warm them as he looked at the treasures gleaming on the walls and lining the shelves and counter. Reg, who'd heard Querry talk about the shop but had never seen it himself, gazed around with almost as much amazement as Frolic had. Gingerly he touched a polished brass, telescopic monocle.

"Odd," Querry said, looking at the chain-mail curtain from which Dink should have already emerged. He called out his old friend's name, though, and heard a scuffling from the other room.

To his surprise, not Dink, but the blond leader of Dink's scavengers, the boy who called himself Lizard, appeared. Querry could see at once that something had badly shaken the boy; his face was pale and his eyes darted back and forth. In his hand Lizard held a heavy, metal wrench, and he didn't look like he planned to use it for tinkering. Seeing Querry, the boy relaxed only slightly.

"Lizard," Querry said, putting a hand on the boy's shoulder. "Where's Dink? Has something happened?"

"Yeah, you might say that," came the answer. "Couple of weeks back, half a dozen big blokes show up in the middle of the night. Me and the boys was asleep down below, and we woke up to hear all kinds of noise coming from the shop. We hear Dink arguing with someone, so we come up to investigate. Now, these blokes claim to be coming from that Lord Thimbleroy, but they sure don't look it."

"How so?" Querry pressed.

Lizard shook his head. "Just, don't. Too rough, like, street gang types."

Querry nodded. A boy like Lizard knew thugs when he saw them. "What happened?"

"They say they're recruiting artisans for work on that there tower. Old Dink tried to brush them off, when they tell him the job ain't optional. I come out from behind the curtain, tell them if they want to take Dink, well, they're gonna have to go through us first. But Old Dink calls us off. Told me to keep an eye on the place, and he'd be back as soon as the job was done. Wouldn't hear no arguments."

"He went with them?" Reg asked.

"Who the hell are you?" Lizard asked suspiciously, bringing the wrench to rest across his shoulder.

"This is Reg," Querry said. "We grew up together. Speaking of which, where are the other boys?"

"Ain't no more work or food here, mate," Lizard said. "Reckon they're off to find some someplace else."

"Why not you?"

A serious look fell over Lizard's face, adding years to his countenance. "I made Old Dink a promise. Said I'd look out for the place. If it weren't for Old Dink, don't know what would have become of me. Mum went off with a drunken gambler, see."

Querry spotted a three-legged stool in the corner and sat down. He dropped his elbows to his knees and kneaded his temples. His injured body still hurt, and he was tired. Reg came over and rubbed his back, saying, "What will we do now, Querry?"

"I don't know. Lizard, do you remember Frolic?"

The boy snorted. "Hard to forget, that one."

"He's missing. I think he might be in danger. Would you know anything about that?"

"Like I told ye, mate," Lizard said, "Ain't none of my business. Even if it was, I ain't heard nothing about him on the street. Dink would know better. You, now, that's different. Everybody been talking about Querrilous Knotte."

"But nothing about Frolic?" Reg urged. When Lizard shook his head, he said to Querry, "What next?"

"We have to get to Dink," Querry said. "They're likely holding him at Thimbleroy Manor or at the clock tower itself. He's sure to be well guarded, but I owe it to him to get him free. Trouble is, without him here it won't be easy to replace the weapons and gear I'm going to need. Sure, I can scrounge something up on my own, but I don't like the idea of facing the kind of fight we're likely to get into with second-rate equipment."

"That reminds me," Lizard said. "Package come for you the other day. Poor bloke what delivered it didn't seem like he knew his own name. He handed it off to me, looked all over like he didn't know how he got here, then just wandered off whistling to himself. I'll go and fetch it." With a musical jingle, he parted the chain drape and returned carrying a package almost as long as he was tall, wrapped in iridescent paper resembling wet leaves. Curly rushes fastened with intricate, decorative knots held the parcel shut.

"Querry," Reg said cautiously as the thief took the bundle from Lizard.

When he'd set the package down on the counter and opened it, Querry found, neatly folded inside, his snug black pants, striped cravat, shirt, and leather waistcoat. Beneath them he discovered his boots, pistols, and holsters, and even the ornate sword he'd obtained on his first outing with Frolic. It all smelled like a summer meadow sprinkled with clover. Staring down, Querry tried desperately to recall how he'd lost his things. The visions his mind conjured had nothing to do with the situation: dancing, swirling at impossible speed. A few bars of music played inside his head, and he began to tap his foot, but he couldn't recall anything specific. Querry swore under his breath, tired of trying to make sense of a world seen through a keyhole, with everything significant happening just outside the tunnel of his vision.

"Well," he said, shaking off the eerie feeling, "I suppose that's one problem solved."

"But we've got a bigger one," Reg said. "Namely, reaching the top of the clock tower."

"Climb the scaffolding," Querry suggested.

"Won't do," Reg said. "Even if it was physically possible, and it might be for you, were you in top shape. But in your current condition I'm not so sure. Neither am I sure I could make it at all. If we could, we'd be out in the open for much too long. Any number of people could spot us and pick us off with a rifle."

"You'd have made a good thief, Reg."

"And once we get there, we have to get Dink back down. I seriously doubt he could make the climb at his age."

"Might be I can help you out there too," Lizard said. "Since it's for Old Dink and all. Follow me."

He led them out of the shop and deep into the yard, past the heaps of sheet metal, engine parts, wheels, canisters, and pieces of machinery and clockwork in various stages of completion. The three of them came to a clearing, and Querry couldn't believe what he saw.

There, encircled by heaps of scrap, sat a car about the size of the average horse-drawn carriage. But the vehicle, which was made of brass panels along the lower half and sheets of clear glass on top, all held together with silver solder, had no wheels. Instead, a huge sack of pieced-together leather scraps hung over the opposite side. Half a dozen smaller balloons were tethered to the first with braided wire, and an expansive pair of bat-like wings, cut from aluminum and polished to a high shine, stretched beneath them. Copper tubing formed the spines on the wings and also extended from them to the base of the car. Querry could see, near the top, smaller tubes set within larger ones, as well as the gears that would allow them to extend or retract, moving the wings. A small propeller sat at the far tip of each wing, and a larger on at the back of the main compartment. Inside, brass levers and a wheel, just like that of a ship, gleamed in the gaslight.

"An airship," Querry breathed with longing.

"But will she fly?" Reg asked, eyeing the vehicle dubiously.

Lizard shrugged. "Old Dink said she was finished. Pretty proud of her, too, he was."

"But he never took her up," Reg said, his head and shoulders drooping.

"She'll fly," Querry said, taking a step closer, eager to get his hands on the beautiful marvel.

"Even if she will," Reg continued, "You've no idea how to operate her."

"How hard can it be? Reg, this is just the thing! We'll sail right over to the clock tower, rescue Dink, and be on our way. Then he'll tell us where to find Frolic."

"Oh, Querry," Reg began, but Querry cut him short.

"Lizard, could we go inside?"

"I don't see the harm." The boy opened a glass door, and Querry followed him into the airship's interior, trailed reluctantly by Reg. Like all of Dink's best work, the airship's hull, dash, instruments, and leather-cushioned benches had been adorned with swirling decoration cut from a contrasting metal and further enhanced with elaborate etching. It was truly a marvelous sight. Querry ran his bare hands reverently over the control panel. Lizard came to stand beside him.

"Beautiful, ain't she?"

"Amazing," Querry agreed.

"I helped Old Dink build her," the boy said proudly. He pointed to a button. "This here fires up the gas burner." He pointed to a metal disk in the center of the glass ceiling. "And this lever controls the flow.

More juice and you go higher. 'Course, you can drop the anchor round the other side here, and she'll hover in place just like a humming bird. You steer with that wheel, plainly. These two levers here control the angle of the wings. Pull up, and she'll dive. Flap 'em down hard, and she'll gain a little more altitude. Straighten 'em out to the sides to glide. Er, at least Old Dink says that's what'll happen."

"This is a bad idea," Reg said.

"No," Querry said, his voice soft with awe. "It's brilliant."

"Take her," Lizard said. "If it'll help Old Dink. But take care of her. We been working on 'er the better part of three years."

"Thank you," Querry said. "We won't let you down."

Reg groaned. "Is this really the best course of action, Querry? We could be killed in that thing. Both the government and several private companies have been trying to perfect air travel for many years. Surely you've seen the results in the news? Fiery explosions as often as not. Not a single prototype has been successful. I don't want to burn up or fall out of the sky."

Turning to face him, Querry took Reg's shoulders in his hands and looked deep into his eyes. "I wouldn't ask you to do this if I thought there'd be any danger. Do you really think I'd risk losing you now? You don't know Dink's work like I do, Reg. You haven't seen what he can do. This is going to work. I know it."

Convinced, but clearly not excited by the prospect, Reg nodded twice and patted Querry's knuckles.

"One more thing," Querry said to himself, as a solid plan took shape in his mind. "Lizard, I need a grapple and something to project it. I need one that can hold to stone."

"Right!" the boy said, saluting as he disappeared into the yard. Querry took the time to change back into his own clothing. It felt good to position his goggles above his forehead and strap his guns and sword around his hips. As he tugged his gloves into place and buckled them at the elbow, he caught Reg's reflection smiling from behind him.

"Yes?" Querry said, eyes narrowing.

"I was just thinking," Reg said, stepping forward and running his hands down the sides of Querry's leather-clad waist, "how much that gear becomes you."

Querry turned and took Reg's face in his hands, though he couldn't feel his skin through his armored gloves. He leaned in, about to kiss him, but was interrupted by Lizard's return. The two men stepped quickly apart as the boy opened the airship door. He handed Querry a device resembling a two-foot crossbow with a spool of heavy rope attached to the underside. A thick bolt topped with a serrated, three-pronged claw waited to be fired.

"We call her The Gripper," Lizard explained. "She'll hold to anything."

"Thank you," Querry said, stashing the device beneath one of the airship's benches.

"Just help Dink," the boy said, insecurity and concern cracking his tough exterior and showing him for the child that he was.

"I promise."

The boy nodded once, exited the ship and soon disappeared among the heaps of scrap. Querry went to stand at the helm, his finger trembling excitedly above the ignition button. When he pressed it, he heard a few clicks, then the gas lighting with a whoosh. A blue flame burned steadily above the glass ceiling. Slowly the balloons inflated with a steady hiss. When they stood full, Querry could practically feel the ship itching to take flight, tugging insistently toward the sky, like an excitable puppy on leash.

"Time to take her up," he said, his heart skipping. He grasped the cold, oily bronze of the lever, and pulled it a few inches toward the floor. The fire brightened, and a series of gears moved against each other rhythmically. The propellers began to spin, and the ship ascended, jerkily at first, rising a dozen feet, dropping two, and rising again. Querry gave her a little more gas, and soon he and Reg rose smoothly toward the sky. Gripping the other lever, Querry brought the wings down and they shot toward heaven with the speed of a bullet. Querry laughed out loud, and Reg staggered to a bench, holding its back with one hand and his forehead with the other.

The little glass airship entered the layer of cloud and smog hanging above the city. For a moment everything went white. Then they broke through, and Querry brought the wings horizontal, allowing them to glide smoothly.

"Oh, Reggie, look!" he said, stepping away from the controls. As far as his eyes could see, the snow clouds stretched beneath them, obscuring everything below. To Querry it looked like a tranquil ocean rippling with subtle waves of glowing lavender, turquoise, rose, and lemon-yellow. Here and there the mist rose up in wavering curlicues or translucent sheets that dispersed in their wake. Directly in front of them, the moon cut an ivory crescent in the rich cobalt of the sky, and the stars shone even brighter and purer than they had in the country. To Querry, it seemed the perfect picture of the paradise promised to the faithful in the cathedrals.

Reg regained his balance and came to stand beside Querry, saying, "It's like a whole other world up here. It's beautiful."

Querry stepped behind Reg, wrapped his arms around Reg's waist, and leaned the apple of his cheek against Reg's soft hair. For many minutes they stood in silence, the beauty and magnitude of the celestial view stealing their words. The airship continued to glide smoothly along, and Querry took the helm and guided her toward the only object piercing the clouds: the clock tower.

CHAPTER 12

WHEN THEY drew near, Querry could see artificial light burning just below them. Gradually he took the airship down, past the sharp peak of the massive roof that sheltered the mechanical creatures. Its copper shingles had long ago gone green. Clearly the work was being done on the fabled floor that housed the clockwork mermaids and dragons. As they passed only a few feet from it, obscured by the mist, Querry heard the ping of hammers against metal. Lights flickered and equipment hummed. Slowly he dropped lower, steering the ship toward a wide ledge just above the huge clock face.

"I'm going to drop anchor here," he told Reg, pointing. "And grapple up to the next level. I'll try to get to Dink without being spotted, and hopefully sneak him away without anyone being the wiser."

Reg's Adam's apple bobbed as he looked up at the distant lights. "Grapple," he said hoarsely, "all the way up there?"

"Don't worry, love," Querry said, giving Reg's wrist a squeeze. "I do this sort of thing all the time."

"Dink doesn't," Reg reminded him. "How on earth will he get down?"

"That's where I'll need you. Reg, do you think you could bring her up?"

"I don't know—"

"It'll be simple. Leave the anchor down, and just pull up on this lever here. Pull nice and slow, though. She's touchy."

"Querry, how will I know when? You'll give me some sort of signal?"

Querry shook his head. "Can't risk drawing the attention. Wait a half an hour, then bring her up. I'll be ready."

"Querry, I don't know. We're so high up—"

Giving Reg a hard peck, Querry stroked his cheek and said, "This is just an average bit of work for me."

It was a complete lie. Sure, Querry was accustomed to moving along rooftops, swinging from balcony to balcony and climbing up walls, but he'd never been so far from the ground that he couldn't see it. Up here, with a sharp wind whistling eerily and assailing him with cold, he could hardly convince himself that earth waited somewhere below the mist at all. A fall from this height didn't mean risking a broken collarbone or ankle; it would reduce him to a smear. Stamping down his fear, thinking of his old friend Dink and his dear Frolic, Querry pulled his goggles down in an attempt to keep his eyeballs from freezing. He switched to the telescopic lens and looked up. Directly above stood a massive archway supported by columns. A low stone wall stretched between them. Feeling like he'd be blown off his feet by the powerful gale any time, Querry braced the barrel of The Gripper against his shoulder and touched the trigger.

He hadn't been expecting the kick. The bolt shot up, driving the thief six feet back, almost over the edge. Querry teetered on the balls of his feet for a few seconds that felt like a nightmarish lifetime, then flung himself forward on his hands and knees. He crawled as quickly as possible to the stone wall and huddled against it, his whole body convulsing with fear. Trying to breathe in a slow, even way, Querry hoped Reg hadn't seen him almost fall.

I won't abandon you the way your parents did, he pledged. Then, conviction renewed, he stood, found the end of the rope, and gave it a tug.

The ten minutes it took to reach the next level were the longest and most terrifying of Querry's life. Even years later, he would wake now and then in a cold sweat, sure he'd been plummeting through a dark void. The wind battered his body so mercilessly that he swung back and forth like a pendulum. It threatened to tear the rope from his freezing hands. Finally, though, he reached the ledge and rolled his body over it. He spared a few minutes to will himself to stop trembling.

Then, well hidden in a shaft of shadow cast by the great column, he looked around.

Not even the most poetic descriptions Querry had read prepared him for the reality of bestiary atop the tower. Off to his left stood one of the angels Reg had mentioned: a ten-foot creature in a scarlet robe, holding an elaborate two-handed sword. It displayed some of Frolic's sort of beauty in its smooth face, but the face was clearly metal and shone subtly in the low light. The copper hair, while detailed, had been cast all in one piece, and the seams at the joints showed clearly. At its feet waited a red-scaled dragon and a phoenix, or at least Querry assumed. Scanning around, Querry saw a similar display at each corner. The angels and their mythical companions seemed to represent the directions and the elemental attributes associated with each. The fiery deity, Querry decided, likely stood at the south corner of the tower. To the east was a blue-robed angel, surrounded by a sapphire wyrm and gryphon. An angel in ochre vestments, between a unicorn and stag, and one in emerald with a mermaid and fantastic sea serpent, stood at the north and west, respectively. Between them, vines made of metal tubing, complete with individual leaves and a dozen kinds of flowers, formed arches beyond the stone arches of the structure. These also meandered toward the center, where they tangled together in a way too orderly and regular for nature, around a raised dais. Atop it sat a coffin-like object. The only thing Querry could compare it to were the ancient cases found in the desert recently by adventurers, which housed the remains of long-dead emperors and queens. It looked to be gold-plated and encrusted with clear jewels. Querry couldn't begin to guess its purpose, but for some unknown reason he didn't care for it.

All around, in little pools of light from hanging lanterns, craftsmen worked hunched over. Their hammers pinged musically as they adjusted intricate gears, some through huge lenses that clearly magnified the miniscule mechanisms. Armed guards stood at their backs. On silent feet and keeping to the shadows, Querry crept around until he located Dink, lying on his side and working with a wrench on the leg of the great stag. His overseer waited about six feet away, and didn't strike the thief as particularly attentive. Even so, he'd certainly notice if his charge disappeared completely. Querry considered. The best chance would probably be to wait until Reg had the airship ready, about another ten minutes in his estimation. Then he'd get Dink's attention, and do his best to make it to the ledge before the guard caught on. He realized they might well have to run for it. He'd get Dink in front of him and just hope his armored vest would slow, if not stop, a bullet.

Querry waited behind the robes of the angel until he heard the whir and patter of the airship ascending. Then, on his hands and knees, he crawled as close to Dink as he dared.

"Dink!" Querry hissed.

The old man sat and pretended to retrieve something from his tool box. He scanned the shadows and located Querry. A look of terror crossed Dink's face, followed by a look of confusion. He mouthed the words, "What are you doing here?"

"Rescuing you," Querry whispered with a grin. "We took your ship. She flies like a dream, Dink!" He stopped talking and waited for the guard to wander away from them again. "Reg will be bringing her up in a minute. We'll have to run."

"We can't do that, Querry."

"I'm sorry, Dink. I don't have a better plan. I think we can make it."

"You don't understand! It's Frolic. He's here."

"Where? Querry looked around, hope and desire welling up only to whither when he couldn't locate the clockwork boy.

"Oh, Querry," Dink said, shaking his head.

Scared by Dink's tragic tone, Querry grabbed his sleeve and shrugged his shoulders dramatically. "Where?"

Finger shaking, Dink pointed to the center of the dais, to the golden coffin. He had to grab Querry's elbow to keep the thief from leaping up and sprinting toward it.

"All right then," Querry said to himself. Four men guarded the tower. He was hidden; he could shoot at least two before being discovered. It didn't sit well with him, shooting men in their backs, but he couldn't see an alternative. Slowly, soundlessly, he freed his pistol from its holster. He got the guard closest to them in his sights, winced and looked away. He tried again, but he didn't think he could do it. Querry had never denied being a thief. He'd never hesitated to defend himself, but to murder a man in cold blood…?

But Frolic was here! Inside that—that thing. Querry lifted the pistol again. He pulled the trigger, and the guard fell. Standing, Querry aimed and shot the guard reclining next to the red dragon. Staggering back, the man toppled off the side of the tower. Querry ducked for cover behind the angel. Bullets pinged and ricocheted off of it as the other two guards retaliated.

"Who is it?" one of them yelled, reloading his rifle.

"How the hell did he get up here?"

Querry and Dink crouched with their backs to their angelic protector. Querry strained his ears, but heard only the wind whipping around the tower. The other workers had stopped their tinkering. No sound or speech came from the two guards, worrying Querry. He held his pistol parallel to his forehead and glanced around the angel's leg. He scanned about for the boots of the guards but couldn't find them. Just as Querry prepared to lean across Dink's chest and check around the other side, a guard stepped around each side of the metal statue, their rifles trained on Querry and Dink.

"Thimbleroy wants the old man," one said to the other. "Shoot the other one and throw his body over the edge.

The other guard nodded once and moved the barrel of his gun only a few inches from Querry's temple. A shot rang loud through the quiet night.

Almost to his surprise, Querry wasn't dead. He opened eyes he hadn't known he'd scrunched shut and felt his head. *No blood. No hole.* By the time Querry located the source of the sound, Reg had leapt from the airship to the stone floor of the tower, pulled his other pistol, and shot the remaining guard in the chest three times. He strode toward Querry and Dink, a gun in each hand. Querry exhaled with surprise and couldn't help smiling at how heroic Reg looked. Reg *was* a hero. He'd saved Querry's life yet again. The man who'd planned to shoot him lay crumpled on his side, a dark spot spreading across his middle.

"Dear God, Querry," Reg shouted over the wind. "What's keeping you? Let's go!"

Stumbling to his feet, Querry grabbed Reg's biceps and looked at him seriously. "Frolic is here. He's *here.*"

"Where?"

With a jerk of his head, Querry indicated the sarcophagus. "In there."

"Well, get him out," Reg said, his voice rising with excitement and joy. "Get him!"

Querry nodded, released Reg's arms, and started toward the dais. This time, Dink stopped him. "They've done things to him, Querry. He's different."

"Everything will be fine now, Dink. I'm going to get Frolic out of that thing, and we'll be off." He picked up a crowbar from a pile of tools and closed the space between himself and the dais. Stepping onto the stone lip, he looked through a rectangular slit and into the enclosure.

What he saw made the crowbar fall from his hand and cold sweat burst from his pores. Frolic stood within, his feet hidden beneath a piece of sheet metal. His clothes were ripped and dirty. Querry could see where each of the four sets of vines culminated in a column of gears, smaller than cufflinks and thousands thick. Frolic's fingers flitted among them with impossible speed, going from one set to another faster than Querry's eyes could follow. Heavy manacles made his wrists look even frailer. They clinked as he worked among the gears with his tiny fingers. His eyes looked glazed, the lids low over the golden irises. He didn't seem to need to look at what he was doing. An iron collar encircled his neck, and a metal rod poked from his sternum, shoved under the skin. Querry tried to follow the gears connected to this, but the darkness inside the container obscured them.

"Frolic!" Querry cried, pounding his fists against the metal. "I'll get you out of there!"

Frolic turned his head slowly and found Querry's face. He looked lethargic: drunk or drugged. "Querry," he said with a scratchy voice.

"Don't worry, beauty," Querry said, trying to quell the horror in his voice as he picked up the crowbar and searched for a seam in the gold casing. "I'll have you out of there in a moment."

Frolic interrupted him, saying, "Out? No, Querry. I can't come out."

"I'll break you out with my own hands if I need to!"

"But, I don't want to come out."

"What?" Querry gasped. Reg and Dink had come to stand behind him.

"I've finally found my purpose, Querry. Lord Thimbleroy explained everything. I was made to direct this tower. These creatures at the corners. I can feel them, just about ready to wake up. It will be my job to help them do as Lord Thimbleroy wants."

"Is this a joke?" Querry whimpered. "Frolic—"

"No. This is why I was made. I'm fulfilling the role I was built to do."

"No you're not! Thimbleroy has captured you and made you a slave!"

"I'm a machine. I'm a tool. A tool built for this purpose."

"Frolic," Querry hissed, as exasperated as he was when Reg planned to marry Emily Malvern, "you are not a machine. You have a heart and a mind, and as much right to be free and choose the course of your life as anyone. You are my friend and my lover. I love you. Reg loves you."

"This is what I choose," Frolic said numbly.

"Frolic, no!" Reg pushed Querry out of the way to look at the clockwork boy. "Thimbleroy is an evil man. He's using you."

"Only using me for the reason I'm meant to be used. He said only I can direct these creatures, make the clock tower work. The man who built me built me to stand right here. This is why he made me."

"*Nein*, my young friend," Dink said, shaking his head. "No man would make a tool with such beauty. No artist would spend the decades on something meant to stand inside that box. I have heard stories of your maker. He was forced to do this work against his will. I believe with all my heart that he fought back the only way he could: by giving you emotion, intelligence, and the free will to make your own decisions! He made you look human, so you could live among humans. If you want to do as your creator intended, you must use the gifts he gave you. You must choose the right thing."

"This is the right thing," Frolic said. "Thimbleroy explained everything. He said, he said Querry is a bad man. He said you tricked me, Querry."

"Do you believe that?" Querry asked.

"I- I don't know. Some of the things he said made sense. He said I hadn't been awake long enough to know you were bad."

"Did I make you feel bad, Frolic?" Querry asked.

"No. You made me happy."

"And how will you be happy standing in that box?"

"It's- it's my purpose. Lord Thimbleroy says I'm special, one of a kind. Remember the other clockworks we saw in his basement? None of them could do it. The Grande Chancellor tried dozens of different models and not one of them could make the tower work. This is my duty. My ankles fit just perfectly in these holes—"

"I thought I had a duty too," Reg said gently. "I realized that I couldn't let someone else tell me how to live. Though I was afraid, I walked away from my old life. I gave up everything to be with Querry. And with you. I fell in love with you, Frolic. I will not walk away and leave you here."

"If I leave here, my life will have no point," Frolic said miserably.

"What do you say we make our own purpose?" Reg said, laying his palm and forehead against the metal, "me, you, and Querry. Won't you come out, Frolic?"

He touched some of the gears, and a door opened in the box where Querry hadn't even seen a seam. Frolic held out his hands pitifully. Querry quickly took out his picks and went to work. As he did, Dink knelt with his screwdriver to loosen the metal plate. The manacles fell from Frolic's wrists and neck, leaving dirty gray stains to show where they'd been.

"Frolic, your chest," Reg breathed, barely audible.

Wincing and chewing his lip, Frolic pulled out the metal rod. Querry realized every muscle in his body had tensed to the point of tearing, and relaxed and exhaled deeply. Then, with a shout of pure relief and happiness, he grabbed Frolic and lifted him off his feet. Frolic shrieked with innocent delight and hugged Querry back. Then he hugged Reg. Then all three of them hugged, holding each other for long moments. Querry and Reg shed tears, and Frolic made a sound between a laugh and a cry.

Afterward, Querry and Reg herded the other men who'd been forced into labor to the airship. Their questions and compliments filled the cozy, glass compartment during the flight back to Dink's shop. When they reached it, the other men departed. Dink motioned for Querry, Reg, and Frolic to follow him.

"Where are we going?" Reg asked.

"Down," Dink said. "I will seal off the lower levels. If Thimbleroy's men come back, they will never know the underground chambers even exist. We will be safe. For now."

Chapter 13

THE FOUR men took the lift to the kitchen, where Lizard greeted them enthusiastically. "I knew you could do it," the boy said, pumping Querry's hand. Then Dink gave him instructions for locking down the underground passages, and the boy ran off to comply. Dink went to a table and dropped into a chair, looking older and more exhausted than Querry had thought him capable. He dropped his downy white head into his hands.

Looking concerned, Frolic offered to make tea. Reg offered to help, and the two of them disappeared into the kitchen.

Standing behind his old friend, Querry rubbed Dink's shoulder. Finally he mustered the courage to say, "It's bad."

"My dear boy, that is an understatement. I cannot quite comprehend the purpose of that tower, but after working on it, I can only deduce that it is some sort of a weapon. A powerful one."

"A big gun or something?" Querry asked. "I don't understand."

"Nor do I," Dink admitted, shaking his head. "Your friend may be able to provide more insight, though. He was built to be part of the tower, ja?"

"Fuck. Thimbleroy will never leave us alone now. He'll kill Reggie and me to get to Frolic."

"I have no doubt," the old tinkerer agreed. "His obsession is deepening into a mania. Several times he came to oversee our work and seemed quite mad."

"How so?"

"Talking to himself. Unwashed and unshaven. Shirt untucked. Sometimes his words barely made sense at all."

"Do you remember what he said specifically, Dink?"

"He rambled about unlimited power, power due to him. He called your Frolic his Prince of Angels."

"Because he thought Frolic could control the clockwork angels," Querry said. "But what did he think Frolic could make them do?"

"We will have to ask him."

On cue, Frolic appeared with a kettle and some cups on a tray. Reg carried another tray containing bread and butter, a canned ham, cheese, hard-boiled eggs and some preserved carrots. He set them down, saying, "Hardly a four-course meal, but I thought we could all use a little something. Dink, I hope you won't mind that we helped ourselves."

"Not at all, my boy," Dink said, forcing a smile. "I owe you and Querry my freedom."

Frolic and Reg sat down, and the three of them who needed to, refreshed themselves. Afterward, Reg sat with his cup held next to his chin, staring into the steam. "One of us has to say it. What the hell are we going to do now?"

Looking around sadly, Dink said, "It has taken me almost forty years to build this place. It is my life's work. With deep regret, I feel I can only leave it behind now, and go back to Bravelstein."

"Dink, I am so sorry," Querry said. "I brought this on you. And on you, Reg. God, I'm sorry."

"No, Querry," Reg said. "Because you found Frolic before Thimbleroy, we have a chance. You gave Frolic a chance to experience freedom before Thimbleroy could convince him he didn't deserve it." Reg squeezed Frolic's hand, and Frolic held tight to his fingers.

"I never would have found him if not for my gentleman," Querry mused.

Reg smacked the table with his other hand, startling them all. "Querry, I wish you wouldn't call him that!"

"Sorry. I won't. But he *knew*. Maybe I should go to him."

"Out of the question," Reggie snapped.

"We need answers," Querry pleaded, frustrated and tired of being in the dark.

"Ja, and we have one among us who might provide them," Dink gently suggested, looking at Frolic.

Querry looked at him too. Grimy bands still marred his wrists and neck where he'd been bound. His eyes looked dark beneath, if that was possible. Instead of the curious fascination and enchantment he'd shown before, Frolic now displayed confusion and sadness. Querry reached over and took Frolic's and Reg's hands into his. He met Frolic's golden eyes and asked, "Do you feel ready to talk about it?"

Frowning, Frolic nodded. "I thought I was doing the right thing," he said. Querry detected something in his voice he'd never heard before: shame. He'd tried to protect Frolic from learning these painful emotions, but again, he'd failed. His innocent Frolic was lost forever.

"He tricked you, Frolic," Reg said. "He took advantage of the little knowledge you had of the world."

"I was so sure," Frolic said. "I'm so sure I'm doing the right thing now. What if I'm wrong again?"

"We don't want to hurt anyone," Querry reassured him. "We aren't after power. We just want to live. How can that be wrong?"

Frolic nodded without looking convinced. "I felt like I belonged there. I understood instantly what every gear in that box did. My hands went to them almost on their own."

"And what is it they do?" Dink asked.

"Talk to the other clockworks. Tell them what to do. They'll only listen to me."

"Why?"

"Because my fingers know where to go," he said. "And because of my heart. It's all very beautiful. The other clockworks... I could almost feel their hearts with mine."

"They're not evil?" Querry asked.

"Oh no," Frolic said wistfully. "They aren't like me. They can't choose for themselves. They were almost ready to wake up."

"Wake up and do what?"

"I'm not exactly sure. They wanted something, craved after it like all of you do after food. I felt like when they woke up and found what they needed, we would be able to do anything. Anything."

"But even if you could," Querry pressed, "how much can you do from the top of that tower? How far would these creatures be able to fire or whatever they'd do?"

"Oh no," Frolic said, proudly as if he'd built the tower himself. "There are gears and propellers under the floor. When everything is fixed, the roof of the tower will transform."

"Fly?" Querry guessed.

"It's masterful," Frolic whispered with awe.

"Thimbleroy will be able to take his weapon anywhere," Querry despaired.

"No he won't," Frolic said. "Not without me. I'm the only one who can pilot it. I'm the only one who can talk to the other clockworks. As long as he doesn't get me back—"

"We'll make sure he doesn't," Querry swore.

"How?" Reg asked.

"Nothing for it," Querry said. "We'll have to do the same as Dink. Run fast and far. We'll board a ship tomorrow. A foreign one if we can."

"Where are Tosser and Toerag?" Frolic asked, brightening for a moment as he looked around the room. As soon as he saw Querry's face, though, his shoulders curled forward.

"They're in a good place," Reg told him. "They have shelter and a beautiful forest full of rabbits and moles to hunt. I'm afraid going back for them at this point is impossible. They'll be fine without us."

The four of them sat a few more minutes, finishing their tea and digesting all that they'd heard.

"We could all use some rest," Dink finally said.

"Dink," Frolic asked, "do you think we can sleep in the menagerie? I would love to see it one more time."

The old man laughed a genuine laugh and reached across the table to slap the shoulder of the clockwork boy. "I am too old for a campout, but if you want to spend the night there, I don't see the harm. Come, I'll let you in."

STRINGS OF tiny gaslights mimicked stars above Dink's mechanical jungle. Water tinkled from somewhere within, and nocturnal creatures called to one another softly. Querry made his way through the artificial foliage carrying a lantern. Reg and Frolic followed with cushions and blankets that Dink had provided for their beds. They passed several of the clockwork animals, bedded down in the grass or hanging from branches. Frolic stopped and knelt beside a tiger, petting her large, smooth head and earning a deep purr.

Querry finally located the water: a little fount that tumbled over some gray blocks and into a round pool surrounded by rushes. Metallic flowers of every color climbed up the sides of the fall. A monkey called to the trio from a nearby tree. Querry set his lamp on a large rock. The pool's surface reflected the golden light.

"Set up here, shall we?"

"This is a lovely spot," Frolic said, setting down his blankets.

"Are you sure Thimbleroy won't find us here?" Reg asked.

"Absolutely," Querry said. "We're several stories below ground. It's just as Dink said. If Thimbleroy's men come 'round they'll never know these levels exist." He reached out and found Reggie's hand, using it to pull Reggie to him. Querry petted his hair as he spoke. "Our lives aren't going to be easy. But tonight we can forget about that. We can forget that there's a world outside this forest at all." He kissed Reg softly, cursing the armloads of pillows that separated their bodies.

Reg nodded, and he and Frolic arranged the bedding in a circle around the lantern. Querry lit some candles to better watch the other two men, who sat side by side, holding hands. Smiling, Querry got out of his gloves and armored waistcoat before joining them. Before long, a small, spotted jungle cat crept from the undergrowth and curled in Frolic's lap. The cat lapped at his fingers with a rough little tongue.

Soon a badger and a hare rested at Frolic's side, and a family of small frogs watched the clockwork boy from a nearby branch.

"These creatures are so drawn to you," Querry marveled, reaching over to stroke the jungle cat, caressing Frolic's hand and fingers as he did. He looked up to find Reg watching, Reg's grip tight on Frolic's other hand. "What's wrong?" Querry asked him.

"This feels strange, Querry. I thought I wanted this, but, watching you two, I feel something. Jealousy? I'm not used to this idea. I suppose I've always believed that each person has his one true love, a partner to be faithful to."

Standing, Querry said, "I think I understand. I love you both, my Frolic and my Reg, and if it will make you more comfortable, I'll sit a ways off for a bit. If you want me to join you, just tell me so." He perched on a rock, not at all disappointed with the idea of watching, for now.

Reg scooted around so he faced Frolic. He smoothed Frolic's curls, stroked his cheek, and cupped his chin. "Frolic," he said, "I was so worried over you. I've missed you very much."

"I've missed you too," Frolic answered, pulling the end of Reg's necktie, letting his collar fall open. When it did, Frolic traced the line of Reg's neck with one finger. "Kiss me."

Reg leaned in and found Frolic's lips. His hand moved up Frolic's arm until he held Frolic's face between both his palms. Frolic held to Reg's neck and his wrist, moving closer and displacing the cat, who moved around to curl at his back.

Querry could see their cheeks ripple and churn, indicating the fury of their tongues within. He wet his own mouth with his tongue as he felt his pants grow tighter.

"Reg," Frolic breathed, breaking the kiss. He unbuttoned Reg's waistcoat and then started on his shirt. Reg followed his lead and started on Frolic's buttons. When he'd finished, he brushed the shirt from Frolic's slender shoulders, gasping with awe at Frolic's beauty. Then he removed his own shirt, and both of them rose up on their knees, letting their smooth chests join. Their hands roved over each other's lean arms, waists, and backs, the grasping and groping growing more urgent as they began to kiss again. Frolic circled his groin, grinding his body against Reg. Reg grabbed his butt and kneaded his cheek.

"Let's get out of these clothes," Reg suggested.

Frolic nodded eagerly and got to his feet, toeing off his boots and peeling his pants and underclothes away. His naked body looked soft and fuzzy in the firelight, and his erection stood out. Almost as soon as Reg undressed, the two men's mutual need pulled them together again. Bodies collided, and hands and lips resumed their fevered exploration. Reg bent his knees to suckle Frolic's small nipple. Frolic threw his head back and moaned, his fingertips digging into Reg's shoulders and his hard cock rubbing against Reg's own. Reg slowly kissed his way down Frolic's body, moistening the skin between his chest and belly muscles. Soon Reg dropped to his knees, his face pressed against Frolic's flat stomach and Frolic's hands in his hair.

Querry watched Frolic's chest heave as Reg's fist closed over his testicles. Reg planted little pecks up and down Frolic's shaft, making Frolic's legs tremble and his lips fall open.

"Oh, Reggie, please!" Frolic panted.

"All right then, my love," Reg said, parting his lips so the swollen tip of Frolic's penis could slip between them. Querry envied Reg the treat he now savored, the satin skin his fingers skimmed. He envied Frolic the skillful mouth he plunged into, the wheat-colored hair he held for balance. He unbuckled his belt and popped the buttons of his fly as he watched Reg's head bobbing, and Frolic crying out along with Reg's rhythm. He knew well that Frolic's body wasn't hindered by a normal man's limitations: he could come half a dozen times in an evening. Reg must've known, too, because he didn't take his time with Frolic, but drove hard and fast against him, sending Frolic deep into his throat.

Querry got out of his pants and walked over to them. He stood a few feet behind Frolic and watched Frolic's ass muscles clenching. His eyes were shut and his lips open. Over his shoulder, Reg's golden head moved back and forth.

"Please, tell me I can kiss him," Querry managed.

Reg paused in his work and met Querry's eyes. A tiny crease appeared between his brows as he considered, and then his eyes crinkled with a smile. He nodded, and Querry's arms snaked around Frolic's lithe waist. To Querry's surprise and delight, Reg's hand moved up the outside of his thigh. Frolic turned his head and found Querry's mouth. They kissed hard, Querry swallowing Frolic's moans and cries as Reg sucked and slurped at his cock.

Querry's hard dick left wet trails over Frolic's back. He moved against him while his fingers found Reg's hand on his leg and covered it. His other arm stayed around Frolic, holding him up as he quivered and swooned.

"This, this is perfect," Querry panted, his heart and mind soaring. He'd never been so aroused, so happy, or so in love. Frolic's inclusion hadn't diminished his devotion to Reg; it had multiplied it. Squeezing Frolic's ribs, Querry swiveled against him, sending him in and out of Reggie's mouth. A symphony of grunts, moans, and barely formed words escaped the three men. When Frolic came, he screamed Reg's and then Querry's name over and over again.

Querry let him recover a bit before he gently urged him to the side and took his place. Reg shot him a smug smile, but he opened his mouth and complied. Wet warmth enveloped Querry's cock, and his balls drew up tight to his body. "Oh my God, Reg," he panted, thrusting forward and delving into Reg's throat.

Frolic hurried to kneel behind Reggie and kiss back and forth across his shoulders. Reg purred with delight, the sound reverberating all through Querry's body. His cock skipped and his anus clenched. Frolic's arm wrapped around Reg, and his small hand found Reg's erection. He deftly used his thumb to swirl the leaking juices around and around the head. Reg's ample fluids eased the way as Frolic stroked him. Querry watched, enthralled. Soon Reg's movements became erratic, distracted. Querry grasped the back of his head and held it immobile as he thrust, taking over. Reg reeled forward, holding onto Querry's leg for support. Frolic's fist twisted, and white ribbons erupted from Reg's slit, covering his cock and Frolic's knuckles. Seeing Frolic's hand painted with Reg's seed was more than Querry could take. He felt his orgasm ripped out of him, his entire body drained and trembling. Reg didn't let a single drop go to waste.

"Reg," he panted, his erection bouncing against the roof of his lover's mouth. "F-Frolic. God. God, I love you both so much."

Weak, shaking, and satisfied, the three of them sunk down to the blanket. Querry lay on his back and drew Reg and Frolic onto his chest, draping an arm over each of them. They lay face to face, smiling, giggling, and stroking each other's hair. Querry looked up at the artificial stars, and a laugh escaped him. He squeezed his lovers tight, enjoying their warmth and weight. He was so happy, he worried he might cry. "I love you," he told them again. "That was, that was better than anything. You're both so wonderful."

They rested together for quite some time, saying little and listening to the song of an owl in the distance. Above Querry, Reg and Frolic felt liquid and relaxed. Querry, remembering from earlier, shook Reggie's shoulder gently and said, "Are you feeling better about everything? I don't want you to be uncomfortable."

In response, Reg pulled Frolic's face to his and kissed him, their lips joining right above Querry's heart. Querry watched their slick lips twisting together, seeing an occasional, tantalizing flicker of tongue. He felt his blood flowing south again as their fingers knit together and their thighs crossed over him, Reg's knee on top of Frolic's.

Querry pulled them up a few inches, so that they kissed right in front of his face. He pressed his mouth to the corners of theirs and thrust his tongue up. It slipped between two sets of lips. Two tongues licked up the sides of Querry's tongue. All of them opened their mouths wider, exploring this new sensation, tongues twisting together in a chaotic, wet knot. Hands curled into Querry's hand and fondled his nipples, penis, and balls. Reg's and Frolic's mouths moistened his cheeks and chin as they devoured his face with nips and kisses. Querry writhed, trapped deliciously beneath them. Each of his hands found the soft mound of an ass, and he guided Reg and Frolic closer together. Like their tongues, their three cocks rubbed against each other, Querry's squashed tight between the other two. He and Reg seeped fluid, allowing slippery flesh to glide over slippery flesh. It felt indescribable, like nothing Querry had ever experienced nor even imagined. His pelvic muscles tightened as a second orgasm built.

Throwing his head back, Querry broke away from the exquisite kiss. He gulped air until he could speak. "Frolic," he panted, trying to still the motion of their hips so he could form a coherent thought, "Frolic, would you like to try something new?"

Frolic's silver head rose from Querry's chest, his ringlet curls bouncing. He moved his arm so he could prop himself on his elbow as he regarded Querry. "Something new?" he asked.

"I've wanted, I want—" Querry shook his head to clear it as Reg sucked on his chin. "There's another way for us to be together. I want to be inside you. Do you think you'd like that?"

He contemplated Querry's words. Querry would never grow tired of his cute, confused expression. Frolic likely tried to picture how it would work. Finally, grinning, he said, "I think I'd like to try it."

"Frolic, you've never—?" Reg asked.

"I wanted to make sure he was ready," Querry said. "That the time was right."

"I think the time is perfect," Frolic said, absently twisting Reg's nipple.

"Let me up then," Querry said. They rolled off his chest, quickly coming back together to kiss and touch as Querry, his hands fluttering with excitement, searched his pockets. Finally he located the chemist's tin.

Reg disengaged from Frolic's limbs when Querry returned. Querry rolled Frolic on his back and grabbed a pillow for his head. Frolic looked up at him, the wonder returned to his magnificent eyes, as Querry gently parted his legs and sat between them. His eyes never left Frolic's as he guided his heels up next to his bottom and opened the lotion. He smeared some over Frolic's clenching opening, drawing a sharp gasp from the clockwork boy.

"Just relax, my beauty," Querry crooned as he circled Frolic's tiny hole. Frolic's pale lashes batted, and his breath hitched. With the utmost relish and care, Querry slipped his finger inside Frolic. Frolic's muscle tightened around it. "How is that?" Querry asked, pressing his cheek to Frolic's round knee.

"Odd," Frolic panted. "A good odd, though."

Laughing, Querry explored the geography of Frolic's erect cock as he plunged another finger into him. Frolic's body began to soften, became pliable and accommodating. Querry added a third finger and pushed deep. Frolic choked back a small squeal. Querry shushed him, petting his chest. He waited many moments for Frolic to adjust to the novel feeling, and then his hand moved back down Frolic's body to grasp his erection. Querry began to stroke him, moving his fingers in and out to match the slow pace. Frolic spread his legs wider, his waist twisting and his eyes falling closed.

"Are you ready?" Querry asked, his dick jumping with the anticipation of Frolic's tight, virgin body.

"I, ugh—"

Propping his hand next to Frolic's head, Querry leaned down and kissed each of his eyelids. "Do you want me, Frolic?"

"Want you. Want you, Querry."

Smashing his lips against Frolic's, Querry slowly drew his fingers out of Frolic's body. He touched the rim of Frolic's anus, and found it open and ready. Gripping himself, Querry guided his darkened, dripping cock into Frolic, burying it just past the head.

"Oh, Querry!" Frolic cried, his hands seizing Querry's shoulders. Querry pushed himself up so he could see Frolic's face. At first his beautiful features contorted with pain, but as Querry moved slowly, stroking Frolic as he pushed into him with the utmost gentleness, a look of pleasure spread across his face. Querry felt Frolic's muscles spasming, hugging his cock, and Frolic's penis skipping in his hand.

"Reg," Querry grunted, patting around beside them for the small tin. He found it and held it out to his side.

"Querry, what—"

"Reggie, please!" He thrust the balm toward the blond man. "Please. I need you."

"Oh, my dear love," Reg whispered, moving around behind Querry.

Querry circled his hips, continuing to stimulate Frolic, as Reg greased up his opening. He started to play with it with his fingers, but Querry stopped him, saying, "Please just do it. I don't want to wait. I want you in me now, Reg."

Reg spread Querry's cheeks and positioned himself. Querry winced at the tearing sensation, but he knew how to open himself up for his lover, and soon the discomfort ebbed and disappeared. Reg began to move against him. Querry let his momentum drive his body into Frolic, and soon they'd established the rhythm of a well-tuned engine.

Reg pried one of Frolic's hands from Querry's shoulder and brought it to his face. Querry could hear Reg kissing Frolic's hands, sucking on his fingers. Reg stopped now and then to nibble Querry's neck and ear. His hand reached around to pinch Querry's nipple, sending another jolt of sensation through his over-stimulated body. Sweat glistened over Querry's skin, and he felt Reg grow sticky behind him as they picked up speed. He couldn't take much more of this: being completely connected to both of the men he loved, feeling them pleasure every inch of his body with their eager hands and lips. Querry drew a shuddering breath and gripped Frolic's hipbones. Frolic's small foot came to rest on Querry's shoulder, and Reg grasped his ankle and kissed his toes.

"Querry, love," Reg breathed, "going to—"

"Give it to me," Querry begged.

"Ugh, yes! Frolic! Querry!" Reg cried, pumping Querry hard, driving Querry into Frolic.

Frolic's lower back bowed off the ground just as Querry felt the wet explosion inside him. "Querry, Querry, Querry," Frolic repeated in quick whispers. "Love you! Ah!"

Dropping his forehead to Frolic's chest, Querry felt the orgasm ready to explode like a barrel of powder. His anus squeezed tight to Reg's softening cock. He whimpered and thrashed, falling apart, coming harder than he ever had. He salvaged the presence of mind to pull out of Frolic just in time, and his seed splashed against Frolic's stomach.

They collapsed in a heap, one on top of the other, and lay panting, overwhelmed with bliss. Reg finally managed to stagger to his feet and wet his handkerchief at the pool. They cleaned themselves and retreated under the blanket, falling quickly into a deep sleep, their limbs wound together like tangled wires. Soon the clockwork creatures ventured out of the forest to cuddle next to Frolic. Opening his eyes once during the night, Querry smiled at them sleeping there, and then he surrendered to the deepest and most complete sense of peace he'd ever known.

CHAPTER 14

MORNING, AND the time for Querry, Reg, and Frolic to leave the warm shelter of their beds for the cold world outside, came too soon. They packed up their gear and checked their weapons in sad silence before going up to the kitchen. There they found Dink and Lizard sharing a cheerless breakfast of toast, preserves, sausage, and eggs. Querry sat down and poured himself some tea. Lizard solemnly presented Frolic with a simple sword and dagger, as well as an armored leather duster, skullcap, gloves, and a pair of goggles. Frolic thanked him and put the new gear over his ragged clothes.

"This is it," Querry said. "This is goodbye." The idea that he would never see the workshop again hurt much more than he'd expected. He reached across the table and squeezed Dink's hand. "Old friend, thank you for everything you've done for us. I'll never forget it, or you."

"It has been my pleasure to know you," Dink answered. "All of you. I won't forget you, either."

"Will the two of you be all right?" Reg asked.

Dink nodded. "We will fly north, above the clouds. What will the three of you do?"

"Make our way to the docks," Querry answered. "Board a ship and leave this island." He'd never been patriotic, but the idea of abandoning his home stabbed at Querry's heart. "We'll make a new life."

Standing, Dink said, "Be safe, my boy, and be happy." He hugged Querry long and hard before embracing Frolic, and even Reg.

Taking a last look at the magnificent shop, Querry, Reg, and Frolic ascended the lift for the final time.

Outside, as if to aid them, the clouds stretched low and thick above the quiet city. Black and white posters offering substantial rewards for Querry and Reg's capture stuck to buildings and lampposts everywhere they looked. In spite of the bad likenesses, Querry took one of each of the posters and put them in his coat pocket as a souvenir. As they made their circuitous way, keeping to alleys and backstreets, Querry realized that the city was *too quiet.* Even the great factories stood silent, their massive stacks free of smoke.

"Do you know what today is?" Reg said.

Querry and Frolic shrugged and shook their heads.

With a little smile, Reg explained, "It's New Year's Day. At this early hour, most people are probably still recovering from the cheer they had last night. They'll be off to dinners and parties later. This is in our favor. And it's poetic, don't you think?"

"How so?" Querry asked.

"The start of a New Year. The start of our new lives. I feel good about this, Querry. I think we're going to be all right."

"We will be all right," Frolic agreed. "We're going to be so happy."

Querry couldn't help but agree as their optimism and excitement spread. His nerves let up a little bit, and he actually enjoyed the walk to the waterfront.

AFTER ASKING about discreetly and spending a bit of coin, the three men located a ship willing to carry them. Querry stood near the quayside, talking to the captain, while Reg and Frolic stood a little ways off. This captain and his crew hailed from the states of Allied Libertannia, which Querry liked just fine. Libertannia had been a royal colony, but her people had rebelled and expelled their masters by force. The nation that had formed as a result maintained an amiable relationship with the crown, but the people were famous for being a bit belligerent, mistrustful of authority, and quick to take up arms. Querry felt he'd fit in just fine aboard the *Painted Lady*.

"All of you will be expected to work," said the tall, dark-skinned captain. While a white man like Querry, time at sea had darkened his complexion to a rich leather. He wore his brown hair in a long braid beneath a battered, tri-corn hat. "There may be times when you'll have to defend the *Lady*. Can you handle a sword and a pistol?"

"Practically born with them in my hands," Querry assured him. "Reg is a crack shot, and Frolic can fight like the devil. I've seen him take down a dozen men with just a rapier."

The captain's lip curled at the mention of Frolic's name, giving Querry a glimpse of his tarweed-stained teeth. "Call them over," he told Querry, who did. He introduced Reg to Captain Cassius Nelson.

"Captain," Querry said, "Reginald Whitney."

"You know how to use those pretty little guns, boy, or are they just for show?"

"I know how to use them just fine, sir," Reg said.

"Fine," Captain Nelson said, "You two men can go onboard. Not the faerie."

"Faerie?" Reg asked. "You don't mean Frolic?"

"No faeries on my ship," the captain repeated. "We don't have faeries in the A.L. and we'd rather keep it that way."

"Sir, he's not a faerie," Querry said quickly.

Captain Nelson answered him with an insulted chuckle.

"Sir, please!" Reg said. "Frolic just has a rare skin condition that has resulted in his strange coloring. Nothing contagious. His body doesn't produce the proper pigment. Look!" He pulled off the tight, leather cap and lifted Frolic's curls to show Captain Nelson a small, round ear. "Besides, why would a faerie spend weeks laboring aboard a ship, eating stale bread and sleeping in bilge water? They have their own means of travel."

Captain Nelson took hold of Frolic's chin, turned his head to the side, and regarded him closely. After staring many moments through squinted eyes, he nodded. "If I find out this is any kind of trick, I'll run you all through and dump you in the ocean."

"Thank you, sir," Reg said in a relieved voice.

By now the rest of the crew of the *Painted Lady* had come on deck to assess their new shipmates. They were a rough-looking lot, and Querry wondered if they were pirates. "What kind of cargo are you carrying?" he asked the captain.

"None of your goddamned business, son. Don't ask about it again, and I won't ask why you three are in such a hurry to get out of town. Hell, you never even asked where we were headed."

"Fair enough. Where are we headed?"

"South to the Caribique Islands to pick up a shipment. Back to Libertannia."

Querry wanted to inquire further about these places and determine which of them might be a good place for them to settle, but a disturbance a few docks down distracted them both. At first it looked like just another seaside brawl, but then Querry heard a gunshot, then another.

"Reg, Frolic," Querry called, "get on the ship!" All three of them hurried toward cover, but sailors pouring from ships and from the drinking dens and brothels pushed them further away. They stood little chance against the dozens of big men, so Querry grabbed Reg and Frolic and pulled them behind a small shack. He drew his pistol and watched around the corner.

"What's going on?" Frolic whispered.

"I don't know," Querry said. "It seems like more than drunken sailors, though." He strained to see something amidst the thrashing bodies. When he did, he wished he hadn't.

He recognized the men from the raid on his rented room. They weren't the same men, but they wore similar gear and walked with the same arrogance. Any seaman that attempted to avenge his crewmate got a bullet for his trouble. Still, the ten men wouldn't stand much chance against the hundred or so toughened sailors. Already the sailors surrounded them, brandishing large knives, swords, clubs, and oars.

"We have to get onboard the ship," Querry hissed. "Get below deck." He checked to make sure Thimbleroy's men remained distracted by their immediate threat. "Run for it!"

The three of them bolted for the ship, but just then a fresh wave of sailors, black-skinned men with big, curved swords, rushed from the left with blood-thirsty cries on their lips. They pushed Querry toward Thimbleroy's men, separating him from Reg and Frolic and knocking his pistol from his hand. Shielding his face with his forearms, Querry fought against the onslaught.

It took some time, considering the chaos, but Querry found Reg and Frolic crouching next to a barrel. He sighed with relief and hurried toward them. A hand closed around his elbow and spun him around. Two sailors, each a foot taller than the thief, stood smiling rotten-toothed smiles. The one who'd grabbed Querry held a serrated knife the size of his forearm, and his companion smacked his palm with an iron bar. They reeked of rum, fish, and poor hygiene.

"It's fifty pounds to him what turns you three over to them gents," said the sailor with the knife, indicating Thimbleroy's thugs with a jut of his chin. He pointed to another of those damned posters, nailed to a wooden post.

Querry wrenched his arm free, stepped backward, and drew his sword. "Your life worth fifty pounds?" he spat.

The sailors laughed. Wasting no time, Querry lunged forward and stabbed into one of their bellies. Blood bloomed across the big man's coarse shirt. He held his hand to the wound and swiped at Querry with his knife. Querry dodged, and his attacker lost his balance. When he stumbled forward, Querry smacked him hard in the back of the head with the hilt of his sword, driving him to his hands and knees. As he fell, the other sailor swung the iron bar. Acting on instinct, Querry shielded his head with his arm. Pain shot through his elbow, but his armored gloves saved him from a broken bone and allowed him to keep hold of his blade. The sailor raised his arm for another blow, exposing his midsection. Querry brought his sword down in an arc and buried it just above the sailor's hipbone.

He must have hit something vital, because blood sprayed from the sailor's mouth, and he crumpled. Using his foot for leverage, Querry dislodged his weapon. The other sailor groaned and crawled away, holding his gut. Querry turned around, only to see Reg and Frolic surrounded by three of his attackers' shipmates. Reg stood in front of

Frolic, his wrists crossed in front of his face and a pistol in each hand. The sailors stood cautiously back. When a forth tried to surprise the pair from the side, Reg flicked his wrist and put two bullets in his shoulder.

Querry crept up behind the group and stabbed one of the sailors in the back, drawing the attention of the others. Reg and Frolic hurried to his side, their weapons trained on the other two men.

"Leave us alone or die!" Querry said. He watched them closely as the three of them began to back away, their shoulders pressed together. Slowly, trying not to expose their backs, they made their way back toward the ship. They saw it, only about three hundred yards away, when one of the hired thugs stepped out in front of him. Unlike the sailors, this man held a fancy clockwork rifle the size of a cannon tight to his shoulder. The barrel waited a foot from Querry's forehead.

"Drop it," Reg said.

"I don't think so, boy," the man snarled. "There's no way you can shoot me with those little toys before I separate your friend here from his head."

"Don't be so sure," Reg answered.

The man stepped forward, and so did Reg. Querry felt cold steel against his skin as he watched Reg press the nose of his pistol into the man's greasy, black hair.

"I'll kill you," Reg hissed.

"I'm taking him with me," the man said of Querry.

Swallowing hard, Querry said, "Do it, Reg. They'll take Frolic and kill the two of us anyway."

"Querry—"

"Frolic!" the man said with contempt. "You named it?"

Reg's face contorted with rage. He shoved his gun hard against the man's head. "Son of a whore," he growled. "Shut your bloody mouth!"

"Reg, do it!"

"Go on, Reg," the thug mocked. "I'll blow your little friend's head to the colonies."

"Save Frolic," Querry whispered, closing his eyes and hoping it would be quick.

He heard a cough and a gurgle, and opened his eyes just in time to see the man drop his rifle, clutch his chest, and fall forward. Querry jumped out of the way. Captain Cassius Nelson spat on the man's body and wiped his blood from a large hunting knife. "Who do these whoresons think they are?" he chuckled. "We don't look kindly on being told what to do around here, much less threatened."

"Thank you, sir," Reg breathed.

"Let's get back to the ship." He turned and walked toward his vessel.

Querry heard another commotion behind him, looked over his shoulder and saw another group of hired guns: this one numbering fifty or more. One of the group spotted the three men, and he yelled and pointed. The rest of them took off at a run.

"Shit," Querry said. "Let's go. Hurry." They sprinted toward the *Lady* as guns were being drawn. Bodies on the ground and small brawls slowed their way, and the new attackers nearly closed the distance. A bullet hit a pile of netting two feet to Querry's left. "Faster!" he urged.

The crew of the *Lady* waited on deck, rifles and pistols of their own aimed at the new invaders. Querry could have sworn somebody, or several people, picked off his attackers from the roofs of the nearby buildings. A few times when they were nearly caught, the men closest to Querry and his friends fell to one of these mysterious bullets. At this point, Querry gladly accepted any aid offered. He had no time to consider the source; he needed to get himself and his companions on that ship. Querry, Reg, and Frolic would be safe when they made it behind that wall of armed and angry sailors. They had only a few feet to go.

A horrible scream spun Querry around. In slow motion, he saw a skeletal hand, the fingers made of metal and the joints built with gears, sprout from Frolic's chest amidst a shower of metal shards. Frolic's face contorted with pain and surprise. His knees buckled. Without thinking, Querry ran toward him, barely even aware of his own voice cursing and crying out. The clockwork hand drew back, taking Frolic's heart with it. Frolic fell facedown, and his cloaked and hooded assailant disappeared among the throng before Querry could reach him.

He got to Frolic and dropped to his knees, screaming his throat raw. He was vaguely aware of Reg coming toward them, of the bullets whizzing over his head as the thugs and sailors exchanged fire. Querry turned Frolic over and pulled him into his lap. His glorious eyes stared silently at the sky, and his lips hung open. The hole in his chest exposed the champagne alloy of his skeleton. Two of his ribs and his sternum had cracked, and his spine bowed to the side. The tubes and piping where his heart had been hung in tangled disarray. The millions of tiny gears were still.

"No!" Querry screamed, sobs wracking his body.

"Querry, the ship!" Reg urged, tugging on his elbow. "We'll be killed if we stay here."

Picking up Frolic, Querry ran, bent almost in half. They got aboard the deck of the *Painted Lady* and the sailors closed ranks around them. Querry collapsed, cradling his dead lover. He hardly noticed the battle raging around him as he touched Frolic's white eyelashes, his perfect lips and soft skin. He remembered finding Frolic, kissing him, showing him things, and touching him for the first time. Reg sat opposite him and held Frolic's knuckles against his mouth. Tears streamed down his face.

"I can't believe we've lost him," Reg choked. His other shaking hand closed around Querry's knee. "Frolic is gone."

Querry dropped his head to Frolic's decimated chest and wept until he had no more voice and no more tears to shed. Eventually Thimbleroy's hirelings retreated and the sailors, who'd suffered no more than a few minor injuries, tended to one another.

A hand on his shoulder made Querry lift his head. "I am truly sorry," Captain Nelson said, and by his face he meant it. He handed Querry a clean, white sheet. "We'll bury him at sea."

Querry looked at the crisp, white cloth, then at Frolic's face. He dried his tears on his sleeve, lifted his chin, and said, "No."

"Oh, Querry," Reg said. "It will be a good way to lay him to rest."

"We aren't laying him to rest," Querry said. He set Frolic's body gently on the deck and got to his feet. "I'm going to get him back."

"Querry—"

"No! I'm getting him back, Reg!"

"He's gone."

"I'll fix him!"

Reg took hold of Querry's shoulders and shook him hard. "You can't fight against this!" he yelled. "Frolic is dead, Querry! He can't come back."

"Yes he can!"

"He can't! You can't go against death itself!"

"I can! I will!"

"How?"

"I can get the book! I can fix him!"

"We're putting ourselves in great danger by staying in this city," Reg said. "Do you think Frolic would have wanted that? He's very complex; I don't know if you have the skill. And you'll need tools and supplies—"

"We'll take him back to Dink's!"

"Querry, love, please hear reason!"

"I am not leaving Frolic to die! Are you coming with me?"

"You know I am."

Querry took Reg's hand and squeezed it. "Trust me, Reg. I can do this. I'll bring him back to us."

"I hope you're right, Querry."

CHAPTER 15

"LAST OF the tea," Reg said forlornly as he set a steaming cup and a few stale biscuits next to Querry's elbow. Querry didn't lift his face, encased in bulky, cylindrical goggles that magnified his vision, from Frolic's chest. Tweezers, spools of fine wire, and screwdrivers as thin as needles lay scattered over the metal table where he worked. Gas lights hung low over Frolic's body, illuminating his still form as it lay among gears, tools, and stacks of paper.

After retrieving the book, Querry had spent more than a week analyzing it and drawing up diagrams. He'd mended the small tear in Frolic's lung sack, repaired and straightened his ribs and spine, and patched the steam conduits that twisted hundreds deep within his chest. He'd replaced and reset hundreds of gears, some no bigger than a drop of water. He'd checked and re-checked his work, comparing it to his schematics and the descriptions in the book.

Reg rubbed his shoulder and said, "Please have a break. You haven't slept nor left that table in almost three days."

Querry barely heard him and continued to work, staring at the delicate metal cage that had housed Frolic's heart. It was just about as big as his fist, and all the steam channels converged there.

"Querry, I insist you stop and have tea with me," Reg said, inviting no argument.

With a deep sigh, Querry slid the goggles off of his head and ran his fingers through his hair. He blinked as his eyes adjusted to the non-magnified world, and he leaned back in his metal chair. Reg sat on a stool next to him. He pressed the teacup into Querry's hand.

"You look awful," Reg told him. "You need to get some rest."

"I'm almost there."

Reg made an exasperated sound. "It's been over three weeks, love. I think it's time you face the facts. It's time we let him go."

"No," Querry said, shaking his head. "I'm close, Reg. Everything is repaired. All I need to do now is find a heat source to replace his heart and stitch him up. I'm afraid he's going to have quite a scar, but at least he'll be alive."

"If it's that simple, why is it taking so long?"

"Because there's nothing I know of that will burn at a constant heat without a great deal of fuel. There's nothing in his design that allows for fuel to be stored or fed into his heart. The best I can do would be to attach a hydrogen tank to the outside and install a burner. The tank would have to be changed regularly, though."

"Querry," Reg said gently, "do you suppose he'd want to live that way, with a tank attached to him and a big hole in his chest? From what you've said, he was horrified when he saw the clockwork soldiers in Thimbleroy's basement. It disturbed him to think he had anything in common with those things. I hate to say this to you, but you must decide why you're really doing this. Are you doing it for Frolic, or for yourself? You can't make him live as an abomination for selfish reasons. I'm sorry, Querry, but it would be wrong."

Querry bowed his head and bit his lip, tears stinging his eyes. "You're right," he whispered, sick with himself for not seeing what Reg couldn't miss. "Just give me a few more days. Let me try a few more things."

"I will. I guess you have the right to feel that you've done all you could, so you don't spend your life wondering." Reg reached out and smoothed the bouncy, silver curls away from Frolic's forehead. Tears ran down his cheeks. "When you're satisfied, I think I know what he would have liked. I found some panes of glass in a work room. We can use them to make him a casket, and lay him to rest in the menagerie. He loved that place. He'll sleep well there, among the trees and the animals. Then we can seal off these lower levels. Nobody will ever disturb him."

His chest heaving with suppressed sobs, Querry looked into Reg's red-rimmed eyes and forced a smile. "That's a lovely idea, Reg. Just give me a few more days."

"A few more days." He stood and left.

Querry strapped the goggles to his face and picked up a screwdriver.

CANDLELIGHT REFLECTED off the glass panes of the casket Querry had made. Inside, Frolic looked peaceful with his arms folded across his chest. Reg had found a clean, white shirt for him, and gathered some of Dink's metal flowers to place over his heart. The two young men stood at the foot of the coffin, holding hands.

"It's just not bloody fair," Querry said. "He had no time."

Reg cleared his throat. "Frolic was one of the finest people I've ever met. He had nothing within him but innocence and good. He made me see the world in a different light. He made me see hope. I'll miss him for the rest of my life, and the world is poorer without him. I can only pray that the universe will see the light within him, and reward him with a peaceful rest." He kissed his first two fingers and pressed them to the glass above Frolic's face. "Good journey, my love."

Querry looked down at Frolic's face, so pale and smooth in the low light, and tried to think of something eloquent to say. He looked around at the clockwork animals, still and lifeless now. He gazed up at the sheet metal tiling the ceiling, and he could think of no appropriate eulogy for this amazing person that he'd loved with all his heart. He couldn't accept the finality, the egregious waste. It wasn't fair and it wasn't right. Querry couldn't speak to Frolic's good when all he felt was anger.

"No," he said, balling his fists. "I won't let it end like this."

Squeezing his hand, Reg said, "It's over, Querry. Tell him goodbye."

Querry pulled his hand free of Reggie's fingers. "I can't." He flung open the lid of the glass sarcophagus and pushed the silver curls away from Frolic's face. "I failed you," he told his still lover, "but I'll fix it."

"You've tried to fix him," Reg said. "It can't be done. Give him his dignity and let him rest!"

"I'm going to give him the life he deserves!" Querry bent to lift Frolic, but Reg grabbed his elbow.

"You promised! You can't bring him back!"

"No," Querry conceded. "No, *I* can't bring him back. I've tried everything I know. We need magic to power his heart. I can get that magic, and I can save Frolic!"

"Good God, no," Reg breathed.

"Yes." Querry lifted Frolic into his arms, forcing his knees to straighten when they buckled beneath the weight. "I don't know why I didn't think of it before."

"Because it's dangerous!" Reg said frantically. "You can't seriously be considering this!"

"Considering, no," Querry said, his mind made up. "I will do this. I will get Frolic back, and the three of us will be together. As is meant." He walked slowly out of the menagerie and toward the lift, oblivious to Reg's protests.

CHAPTER 16

QUERRY WALKED with purpose through Neroche. As if sensing his unswaying determination and will, the denizens stepped out of his way as he carried Frolic's prone body up the slope of a hill. Reg followed, nervous and incredulous, but loyal. Deep down, Querry thought, Reg held out hope the same as himself. They passed several faerie manors, all but obscured by mystical flora, before finding themselves in a central square. Unlike human crossroads, this intersection had at its center an ancient and twisting tree, rather than a statue or fountain. Glowing eyes stared down at the young men. Querry looked left and right, trying to get his bearing.

"I don't like it here," Reg said.

"I know. I'll find him before long. Trust me."

"I will," Reg said, "and hope I'm not a fool."

In the distance, Querry saw mountains wreathed in mist. Halfway up one slope, an archway cut the stone. The dark corridor beckoned him, and he moved toward it, trusting to instinct. Reg followed. They picked their way carefully over the steep terrain, holding onto branches for support as they crossed the bluish shelves of rock. The thick forest, with its hanging ivy and dense vines, slowed their pace. A few times Querry nearly dropped Frolic when he slipped on loose gravel or lost his balance along a winding path. Eventually, though, they reached a door cut into the rock. Two rough-cut columns, little more than unworked rock, supported the entryway. Blue roses bloomed at their bases.

"I don't like this," Reg said again, looking back the way they'd come. "Querry, I'm afraid."

Querry turned to look down the hill. He saw nothing but a thick, gray forest. Mist obscured the tree trunks. Where he should have seen a collage of lights and rooftops, Querry found only disturbing, twisted branches reaching up out of the mist. The wood covered the ground as far as he could see, fading to blurry gray at the horizon. Neroche had vanished.

"We're in the Other World," he breathed, a tremor of fear shooting up his spine. Instinctively he hugged Frolic tighter to him.

"God help us," Reg said with a trembling voice. "How in the world will we get back?"

"There's no way back," Querry breathed, scanning the alien landscape. "Only forward." He took Reg's hand and led him into the tunnels beneath the mountain. The ground sloped gently downward, and the way grew narrower and the ceilings lower as they ventured further into the bowels of the earth. Querry could see where to go, though he had no idea how he saw it. It was bright as twilight, despite the absence of torches or lamps. He felt something drawing him forward, compelling him, and decided not to share this with Reg.

Reg showed enough distress, breathing heavily and drawing, then holstering his pistols at every flickering shadow. Querry worried he would fall apart, but he had no way to assuage his friend's worry. He remembered the first time he'd wandered into fey territory, lured by a cryptic message promising riches and glory. It had been more surreal than a dream, and every tiny detail had either distracted or terrified him. He recalled looking down at his gloved hands and trying to decide if they really existed, if his physical body really occupied space, or if it was just a projection of his mind. He knew many humans never recovered from the madness the Other World induced, and he wouldn't forgive himself if he lost Reg to it. What good would saving Frolic do if he lost Reg?

They'd reached a staircase carved into the stone. Though Querry could see little else, an inviting, orange glow waited at the base. "Reg," Querry urged, "feel your legs."

"What are you on about?" Reg said with a high-pitched giggle. He twirled on the ball of his foot and then went to press his face to the tunnel wall.

"Listen to me, goddamn it! Feel your legs. They're solid and real. Feel your toes inside your boots. Curl them around your socks. Feel it."

"I'm floating," Reg tittered.

"You're not." Querry turned, and, unable to slap Reg with Frolic in his arms, he kicked him in the shin. The glazed look departed Reg's eyes, replaced by annoyance.

"What the hell?"

"Does it hurt? Do you feel the hurt?"

"You bet your sweet ass it hurts," Reg said, bending down to rub his leg. "What was that for?"

"You were slipping," Querry said, explaining as best he could. "I need you completely alert." Reg merely looked at him with confusion. "Come on, we're almost there. It will be fine, Reg."

"All right." They descended the winding steps until they found themselves within a vast room flanked by stone walls. High above them, stalactites hung like banners. As soon as they walked into the space, dozens of translucent shapes departed for the darkened edges. One figure remained: Querry's golden-haired faerie gentleman reclined on a rocky bench covered in furs. His pointed ears jutted further from his head than Querry remembered, and his glorious mane looked uncharacteristically matted. Crumbling leaves and branches twisted among his shining tresses. He wore only a rough leather loincloth, and some dried vines wrapped his bare, slender ankles. When he noticed Querry and Reg, he sat upright, startled.

"Querrilous?" The gentleman's voice sounded odd: timid and surprised.

"Sir!" Querry said, happier to see the other man than he wanted Reg to realize. Even so, he hurried to kneel beside his bench, Frolic still cradled in his arms. The faerie tentatively touched Querry's hair, and, as always, Querry couldn't resist pressing back against his fingers. "I need you," Querry said softly. "Please help me."

"How are you here?" the faerie asked, still petting Querry's dark locks. "How could you make it to this place?"

"I need your help," Querry repeated. "Please." Querry looked into his gentleman's wild eyes and felt like he saw the other's true nature for the first time. He gasped in awe at both the power and the chaos radiating from the faerie's gaze. Like nature itself, he was unknowable and indifferent, as mighty as a storm or a season. Magic shimmered in the air around Querry, and he trembled with fear. He looked down at Frolic's face and resolved to remember his purpose, no matter what pleasant distractions the gentleman offered.

Absently toying with Querry's curls, the faerie regarded Reg. "So this is him," he said. "Come closer."

Querry nodded to his companion, and Reg walked slowly toward the bench. The faerie sat up straighter to assess his face, his eyes darting back and forth over Reg's features. Querry couldn't fathom what went on inside his head. Finally he turned to Querry and said, "Will you trade him for my assistance, then?"

"What?" Querry spat. "No!"

"What do you offer, then? Not this broken machine!"

"Sir," Querry breathed, trying to quelch his growing unease. The gentleman could easily keep Reg, Frolic, and himself inside the mountain. He could make them *want* to stay. Fortunately Reg hadn't rushed forward and announced his desire to be the faerie's prize. He wondered how he resisted it. Already pleasing possibilities insinuated themselves into Querry's intentions. He could stay here, in this stunning ballroom with its crystal chandeliers and polished stone floor. He could recline on a velvet chaise like the one his host rested upon. What could he possibly have to fear from this beautiful gentleman, in his fine, champagne-colored suit and silk shirt? The air rippled around him, and Querry saw another image superimposed upon the scene: rough stone, fur, hair matted with leaves.

The gentleman chuckled and leaned close to Querry's ear. "You have a little something of me inside you."

"No, I don't."

"You don't remember? I'm crushed. Nevertheless, you might as well have the rest of it." He kissed each of Querry's eyelids and the elaborate ballroom dissipated, leaving only the stone cavern. The faerie continued to kiss Querry's brows and the bridge of his nose, until Reg cleared his throat dramatically behind them. Looking annoyed, the gentleman lifted his hand and pointed his long fingers at Reg. Querry broke from his thrall just in time to grab the faerie's wrist.

"No, don't hurt him."

The faerie made an exasperated sound and dropped his arm. "I'm growing bored with this. If you want me to help you, then tell me what you offer in exchange."

"Anything I have to give," Querry said. "Name it."

"Intriguing," the faerie said. "I'm sure you think I'll ask you for your body. I am, however, above purchasing affection. Your body will not be enough. I can't think of anything just now that you could do for me, but I'll help you if you promise me a favor in the future."

"Querry, no," Reg said, coming to stand beside the kneeling thief. "You absolutely cannot agree to this."

"Reg, be quiet," Querry warned. He knew the gentleman's patience grew thin.

"I won't," Reg said. "I won't let you agree to this. This is a deal with the devil! He could ask you for anything. What if he asks you to kill someone or steal a baby?"

"Steal a baby!" the gentleman hissed.

"Sir," Reg said, facing the faerie and astonishing Querry with his bravery, "You must name the thing you want."

"But I haven't thought of it yet. How can I name it?"

"Querry needs to know what he's agreeing to!"

"No, I don't," Querry said. "I agree to this bargain. If you help me bring Frolic back, I'll do anything you ask, anytime."

"Then I'll do it," the faerie beamed. "We'll get to work straight away. Let me see what we're looking at here."

Querry lifted Frolic onto the bench and carefully unbuttoned his shirt. The faerie spread his fingers above the hole in Frolic's chest and cocked his head, as if he heard faraway music. "Human magic," he said, "but beautiful and delicate, like a woven bit of fine lace."

"Can you recreate it?" Querry asked.

"Oh, certainly! At least, mostly. I can weave together the spell components and perform the magic. The signature of the caster is always present, though. It can't be erased."

"What will that mean for Frolic?"

"Well, I cannot say. I've never done a spell like this. It will be great fun! What a wonderful adventure we'll have gathering the ingredients. We'll need a bit of glass, but that's just heated sand. And what else? I can smell the fire-flower; there aren't many of those left in the world."

"Will we be able to find one?"

"Certainly," the faerie said. "There are traces of dragon's breath." He furrowed his brow and considered. "It's not what I would have chosen. An elemental salamander's heat is steadier. And what's this? Strong human feeling? Dreams?"

"Fever dreams," Querry told him, "and oaths spoken during love."

"Ah! This human sorcerer was quite creative." The gentleman stood from his bench. "Shall we be off, Mr. Knotte?"

Querry set Frolic carefully on the floor and got to his feet. "Let's go."

"Wait," Reg said, causing the faerie gentleman to roll his eyes. "What about us?"

"Honestly," the faerie said, "I think we'll accomplish this faster on our own."

"I don't wish to go," Reg said, a shiver in his voice. "But I don't wish to stay here, either."

"Mr. Knotte, your companion is trying my patience," the gentleman warned.

"Please, sir, don't you know of somewhere Reg and Frolic will be safe?"

Sighing dramatically, he inclined his head toward a passage in the stone. "Follow me."

Querry picked Frolic up again with a grunt. He walked into darkness so complete that it seemed to have weight against his body. Reg's hand closed around his elbow, and they slowly picked their way down the tunnel. Far in the distance, miles off, Querry saw a faint gray sparkle. He walked toward it, though he never got any nearer. He couldn't locate his faerie host in front of him, and started to panic. "Sir?"

"Keep up," he heard, and moved toward the sound. Before long, he could hear the swish of the gentleman's clothing and smell the leafy scent of his hair. He tried his best to stay close to the faerie's oddly reassuring presence, and would have taken his hand if not for Frolic in his arms. Water dripped in the distance, and from the echo Querry assumed the dark space they walked was huge, cavernous. It grew colder as they went on, and it smelled damp and musty. It felt to Querry like they walked for hours, maybe for days. Many times he wanted to stop and curl up on the floor for a nap. He willed himself on, his arms trembling under Frolic's weight, and his legs feeling like porridge. Just to keep conscious, he turned toward Reg in the blackness. The other man moved like a sleepwalker, his hand barely clinging to Querry's sleeve. "I say, Reg, do you remember the first time I snuck into your room at Whitney Manor?"

With a subdued chuckle, Reg said, "How could I not? One minute I was sleeping in that huge bed, surrounded by things that felt foreign and so delicate that they'd break if I breathed on them, and then there you were, perched on the windowsill. I was so grateful to see something familiar."

"Were you? I never knew that. Because you cursed me out and demanded I leave."

"I seem to remember allowing you to stay," Reg said, his voice low and languid with the memory.

Querry chuckled. "I never knew they made sheets so soft until then. Your skin was better, though. Those fine soaps, I guess. You smelled so good, like lilies after a rain—"

"Enough," the faerie spat, interrupting them. "Will you both just quiet down? We're nearly there."

"Nearly where?" Querry asked, his eyes adjusting to the watery, pink light that spilled in through a cleft just ahead. Swirling eddies of dry snow blew through the same opening. In spite of the chill, Querry felt relief at the sensation: cold, light, real, concrete things. He could taste the cold, coniferous air beyond, and he longed for open space fiercely and quickened his step. The company emerged from the depths of the earth on a steep slope. Deep snow covered the rock-strewn trail to a small village. Smoke curlicued from the crooked chimneys jutting through the thatch roofs. "Where are we, sir?" Querry repeated. It looked similar to the countryside around the city of his birth, and yet felt alien. Querry knew he'd come a long way from home.

The gentleman continued down the hill, his back to the rest of them. He turned onto a narrow path to the left and into a thicket of old, gray trees. As he walked briskly, kicking up powder, he said, "This is the country of Magyary, far to the east of our island home. It is a wild place, populated by spirits unknown to your people. You'll want to take care after dark, *Reginald.*" He stopped in front of a cottage built of logs: quaint but spacious. The house had two stories, rows of windows, and a slate roof. "This home was the refuge of a wizard banned from your country. He crossed the sea and then most of the continent, to avoid persecution from your authorities. He was a great friend to my kind. Of course, this was decades ago. I can only assume he died or moved on. Still, this house has paths leading directly to my lands, and he protected it with powerful spells. No one will trouble your friends, Mr. Knotte. Provided they don't leave the shelter of its walls after sunset. If they are so foolish, I dare say the human's soft flesh and sweet blood will summon all manner of demons. During the day, the creatures' fear of my wrath will keep them off, but after dark their hunger will compel them." He opened the door to let Reg, Querry, and Frolic inside. The house smelled of dust and disuse. "Will this suffice?" the faerie asked without attempting to mask his impatience.

"Yes," Querry said quickly. "Thank you."

"I don't doubt your companion will enjoy the local cuisine. Some of the best food in the world: fresh pork and chicken, smothered in rich cream and paprika. Flaky pastries stuffed with apricot and poppy seed. The local wine is excellent as well. But enough. Querrilous, can we be off?"

Querry turned to Reg's face. His skin looked pale and his eyes tired. "I'll bring Frolic inside," he said. He didn't have to force his smile; he looked forward to his adventure with his faerie more than he'd ever want Reg to know. "Get some rest. This shouldn't take long."

"I just hope to God you know what you've done," Reg said. He kissed Querry's cheek, and they went together to a padded bench beside the kitchen window. Morning sun lit Frolic's smooth face.

Querry set him down, touched his full bottom lip and nodded with conviction.

"Do as my gentleman says," Querry said, reaching up to smooth Reg's hair. "Please be careful. I'll be back as soon as I can.

"I will," Reg said with a strained smile, "so long as you never call him that again."

"Sorry," Querry mumbled, looking down at his boots. "I'm going to make this all right, I swear."

"Querrilous!" the gentleman called from the small excuse for a yard beyond the cottage.

"I have to go," Querry said, kissing Reg softly. He hated the finality he felt even as he anticipated his journey. Why did it feel like he was leaving them forever?

"Come back soon, my love."

"I will. To both of you."

QUERRY HURRIED to follow the gentleman as he walked briskly down the trail, clearly eager to distance himself from Reg. To confirm, he said, "Truly, Mr. Knotte, I don't know how you can tolerate the presence of that dull, little man. I suppose you're just being charitable. Certainly you must be delighted at the company of someone more worthy of you."

"I am looking forward to it," Querry admitted. "Where must we go?"

"Back to my mansion. I'm having a party this evening. We both must wash and dress."

Querry stopped on the path as a horrible realization descended on him like night falling. "Do you mean to help me, as you said, sir? Or do you just want me away from Reg?" He feared he'd forget about Reg and Frolic as soon as the faerie music began to play and his body twirled in the arms of the gentleman. How would he resist it?

The faerie spun to face him, a dangerous look on his beautiful face. "I swore to help you and I will help you, so long as you continue to please me. You have no idea how much I indulge you, Querrilous. You truly have no idea."

Though he understood for the first time the danger he'd placed himself in, Querry hurried to keep up with the faerie. When they reached the edge of a cliff, the gentleman offered Querry his arm. Fractured light of every color swirled around him, and the next thing he knew he was on his hands and knees in the foyer of the gentleman's great house. As Querry gripped the carpet and tried not to retch, he saw the gentleman hand his coat to his trollish butler. "Draw a bath," he told the small creature, who hurried off to obey. "Ugh, I feel filthy."

Querry struggled to his feet, holding his head, and looked around. Everything in the house had been carved from light colored stone: the floor, walls, shelves, mantles, and stairs curving up. The décor seemed sparse and plain in comparison to Querry's jeweled and gilded memories of the place. The rugs and tapestries were ancient and threadbare. In several corners tangles of vines had worked their way in from the outer walls. Some of them stretched across the ceiling, dropping leaves in piles to the floor. As he followed his host up the steps, Querry noticed some of the large rooms held collections of odd junk like magpie nests: all manner of elaborate chairs filled one, and a pile of blue glass bottles reached the ceiling in another. On his way toward the bath chamber, Querry saw a room stacked with balls of yarn and spools of ribbon, with more bright strips hanging from the ceiling like banners. He saw an armory filled with weapons both familiar and bizarre. A rounded alcove collected baby shoes, from poor and tattered to ridiculously ornate, on a stone shelf. *But only the left shoes*, Querry noted with a shudder.

They finally reached the bath, a natural spring complete with curly rushes and water lilies on the top floor. Somehow, even three or four stories high, water trickled down a rocky ledge and into a round crater. It reminded Querry of the waterfall in Dink's menagerie, and the recollection triggered all his memories of the night he'd spent beside it. It had been the best night of his life, and he resolved to stay true to his mission, even as he watched the gentleman disrobe and ease his stunning body into the water. Querry joined him, delighted at the liquid's unexpected warmth. The water itself had a floral fragrance, so that they needed no soap. At the faerie's request, Querry helped him dress and comb his hair. He presented Querry with a night-blue suit with long tails and silver buttons, a waistcoat embroidered with stars, and a matching silk top hat adorned with a blue rose.

When they'd prepared, Querry took the gentleman's arm and walked back down the stairs, through the foyer and into the ballroom. They sat side by side at the head of a long, wooden table. Trays of fruit and berries swollen with juice tempted the thief, but he disciplined himself against their allure, even refusing a goblet of water. The feast stretched on for hours and hours. Though slightly fuzzy, Querry fought hard and retained enough of his lucidity to begin to grow bored. Many seated at the meal eyed him with unhidden envy. His host retired to a carved wooden chair, and Querry stood with his hand on the arm. A line of fey waited to offer gifts to the gentleman: string, polished spoons, bird skulls, mirrors, and lead pencils that the gentleman brought to his nose to smell. A few presented fair-haired, human children, which the bat-eared butler and his staff quickly herded down dark hallways. After each gift, the faerie turned to Querry and described in gory detail the way he'd razed the giver's lands to the ground or caused the earth to swallow up his entire clan.

"And for so grievous an insult as comparing her musicians to mine," he said of a pink-haired woman in a gown of rose petals, "I caused all the stones of the mountainside to fling themselves at her and her household, until she alone remained alive and crawled bloody to me, begging for mercy." He looked expectantly at Querry.

"Er, well done." The parade of supplicants thinned to a trickle of stragglers, and between them Querry said, "Sir, your power is so great and overwhelming that I have to wonder why you'd need to hire me to retrieve a pair of boots."

In lieu of an answer, he replied, "Those were such good times." The gentleman's hand draped over Querry's on the arm of the chair.

"I wonder," Querry pressed, "why, with all of the enemies you've defeated that you'd let someone like Lord Thimbleroy rail against your kind. Why in the world not just kill him?"

"Kill him?" the gentleman said. "Whatever for? He's done me the greatest service!"

"What do you mean? He'd see your kind destroyed!"

"Would he?" the gentleman mused. "Even after he opened the way for us to come into your world?"

"He—What?" Querry gasped. "Are you certain?"

"Oh, quite! I remember watching him trying to tear through. Very entertaining, if a little pitiful. He brought one wizard after another to attempt it. Most of them were laughably inept, though. Your people have forgotten nearly everything they learned from mine." He shook his head with feigned regret.

Querry couldn't understand. He didn't know which of the many questions flitting through his brain needed asking first. "He hates faeries," he muttered, shaking his head.

"He spared no expense to open the gateway to our realm."

"But, if you wanted to come here, why not just come? Why would you need Thimbleroy to clear the way for you?"

The gentleman's lips curled into a sour expression. "An ancient contract forbids us from coming to this realm unless *summoned*." He spat out the last word like tainted wine. "We could not breach the barrier, until he found a magician able to blow it open."

"When was this?" Querry asked.

"Just now. Two or three decades past."

"I can't imagine," Querry said, rubbing his temples. "Why would he bring you here, open the door to your lands, only to demand that you be driven off?"

"How should I know?" the gentleman said, thrusting his palms toward the ceiling theatrically. Some golden cider splashed out of his stone cup. "I can't see a reason to trouble myself over his motives. I have nothing to fear from the likes of him or anyone in his employ."

"Sir, I must ask why you originally sent me to the house on Tinkerton and Grace!"

"Ah," the faerie said, smiling languidly. "I sensed a very strong magic concealed within that place. I was curious. I felt, I'm not sure how to express this, but I knew that the house was integral to our story. Important."

"Do you have any idea what you set in motion? Did you mean to do it?"

"Well, I meant to do something! I wasn't sure at the time what it was. I knew only that the secret within those walls would be pivotal to our adventures together. And here is Lady Anteres, leader of the wanderers of the Forlorn Waste."

"Magnificent Lord," said a woman draped head to toe in gauzy, red cloth. Querry could see the shape of her head and body beneath the fabric, and her spectral black wings and glowing coal eyes. The sheath-like garment trailed in tattered layers behind her. "Will you let my people rest from their drifting? Will you lift your curse on us, and free us from the Red Sands? I offer these, for your pleasure." She knelt, bowed her head, and presented him a bouquet of poppy-like blooms that smelled of cinnamon and sulfur. In the silent seconds that followed, Querry heard them crackling.

"Be off," the gentleman said with a wave of his hand. The red-clad woman backed away and went scurrying. The fey stood and turned to Querry, a wide grin lighting his face. With one hand he held the proffered blooms, and with the other he squeezed Querry's waist and drew their bellies close. His brilliant, green eyes locked with Querry's confused, blue ones, and he offered the arrangement. "For you, Mr. Knotte. Fire-flowers."

CHAPTER 17

QUERRY WOKE, though he didn't remember falling asleep, in a pile of leaves that felt as though cut from velvet. He rolled to his side and swiped his hand over his face, brushing the top hat away. He pawed at his waist and felt relieved to find his night-sky clothing intact. Gradually he sat up and looked blearily around the stone hall. As soon as he stood, a light breeze whisked away his verdant bed, and it disappeared. In its place a little round stand materialized, and on top sat a silver platter of berries, cakes, tarts, cheeses and a pot of tea. Even though he knew better, Querry's stomach, empty for two days now, compelled him to eat. Afterward he wandered through the house, looking for his host. He found his original clothing and gear on the top floor where they'd bathed and changed into it. The faerie and his serving staff remained elusive. Querry wandered about the abode. Did it connect with the modern mansion and the underground cavern? Were they one in the same somehow? He couldn't find any way to reach beyond the foyer, bath, ballroom, and the cells where the gentleman stored his bizarre treasure. Feeling woozy and light, as if he'd breakfasted on several bottles of Reg's good merlot instead of fruit and bread, he browsed the strange items. Some of them he couldn't even identify. One room held dozens of mirrors. Some of them returned Querry's reflection; he looked better than he had in ages, with smooth, glowing skin, rosy cheeks, and clear sapphire eyes. It didn't surprise him, seeing himself thus, that the faerie gentleman lavished him with attention.

Some of the mirrors showed Querry distant paths leading up mountains or along rocky beaches. One, he felt sure, showed the road that led to the little house where Reg and Frolic waited. Querry touched the surface, and it jiggled like gelatin. He managed, with some effort, to press his fingers through the skin on the surface and feel the cold wind of the eastern climate. Doing so sapped his strength, so he quickly withdrew his hand and went to inspect the other glasses. Within one blackened frame Querry found a vast universe of fire: flame as far as his eye could see in every direction. He stared into it, mesmerized by the flickering lights and shadows. His breath caught when he noticed a tiny sliver of gold that he'd mistaken for just another tongue of flame. Squinting, he recognized the faerie gentleman far in the distance, struggling unarmed with a huge lizard made of orange light. The two of them wrestled and fought, one gaining the advantage and then the other. At one point the creature pinned the fey beneath it, and opened its mouth to strike at his head. Just in time, the gentleman spread his fingers in front of his face and shielded himself with golden light. When the lizard made contact, it fell to the side, stunned. Wasting no time, the faerie wrapped his elbow around its throat, trapping it in a headlock. Its clawed feet flailed, and its elongated body twisted for a few minutes before it fell still.

The gentleman got to his feet, swooned, and fell to his knees, head hanging. Acting on instinct, Querry pushed through the barrier to aid him. The hot air, incomparable to even the factory, scorched his skin and dried his eyes and mouth. He smelled his hair burning and felt the soles of his feet blistering, though there was nothing solid beneath them. His frantic journey to help his gentleman felt more like wading through molten wax than running. He finally reached the other man and crouched beside him.

"Querrilous," the fey panted. "What are you doing here? Get out!"

"You're hurt," Querry said. Tears fell from his eyes and instantly evaporated from his cheeks. "Let me help you!"

"I am fine. Just, tired. Must finish. You, ugh—You must go back."

"Not without you. I need you."

"Very well. Help me up."

Querry put his arm around the gentleman's waist, and they staggered to their feet. The gentleman took a small bottle from somewhere within the hide loincloth he wore, uncorked it and held the open end out to the unconscious lizard. His body convulsed in Querry's arms, and he stumbled back with a grunt. "Can't trap it. Too weak."

"Can I help?" Querry asked.

"Concentrate on drawing it in," the faerie said.

Querry tried as hard as he could. Soon his whole body shook, and he couldn't keep his footing, let alone support the faerie. Both of them crumpled, but the faerie's arm remained extended. He cried out, and his bottle sucked the creature inside. He replaced the cork and promptly went limp in Querry's arms. Querry tried to lift the gentleman but found himself too depleted. Instead he draped his body over his back like a shawl and held his forearms in front of his chest. Slowly he made his way toward the silver rectangle so far in the distance. When he reached it, though, he hadn't the strength to push through.

"Sir!" Querry hissed. "We need to get through. I can't do it. Please wake up."

The gentleman didn't respond. Sparkles danced at the edges of Querry's vision; he knew he wouldn't survive much longer.

"Sir!" He reached over his shoulder and swatted the side of the faerie's head. Finally he jolted awake, grumbling. "Get us out of here," Querry urged.

He waved his hand and said a word like soft rain against the surface of a lake, and the two of them somersaulted through the portal. They landed on their backs in the stone room, and Querry didn't even have the energy to lift his head. His skin still felt on fire. Even his innards burned. His charred throat choked on a sob of pain. His eyes closed on their own, and he didn't know if they'd open again. With his last scrap of strength, he turned toward the gentleman and said, "If I don't make it, please promise me you'll fix Frolic anyway."

"Don't, make it?" the fey croaked with a dry chuckle. "Ridiculous." He said another word in his tongue. To Querry it resembled gentle thunder. He could smell the storm, and soon felt refreshing rain on his face. When he could open his eyes again, he saw dark clouds covering the ceiling. Healing water fell over his singed body and pooled inches thick on the floor. Querry opened his mouth and let it trickle down his throat. For a long time he just lay in the cool dampness. Soon he felt as good as new. He looked at his exposed fingertips, expecting blisters, and found none.

The gentleman sat up beside him, his wet hair dripping down his svelte torso. He looked at Querry with unmasked awe and admiration. "I wasn't wrong about you," he said, touching Querry's cheekbone. "You were brilliant. I never would have imagined one of your kind could accomplish something like that. We two shall do great things. We'll be legends."

"What was that thing?" Querry asked.

The fey held the bottle out to Querry, who took it. He studied the tiny lizard twisting and turning through the ether within.

"Elemental salamander," the gentleman said. "The very spirit of fire."

"Two out of four, yes?"

"Indeed! And the worst is over. If you feel well enough to continue on, we can collect the rest of what we need with ease. What do you say?"

"Actually, I feel incredible," Querry said.

"Jolly good!" The faerie got to his feet and extended his hand, helping Querry to stand. "You and I, then. What an excellent match we've made!"

"DON'T FIDGET, Querrilous," the gentleman scolded. "I've assured you we're perfectly safe. They cannot see us nor hear us. Calm down before I take offense at your lack of faith in me."

"No, sir," Querry said. "You've been perfect, and I thank you. This place is just so mournful. I can feel the sickness and despair."

"Yes, now that I've given you my sight, you'll sense such things much more acutely. For what it's worth, it is worse for me."

"Sorry." Querry reached out and took his hand, squeezing the delicate bones as they moved between the closely packed, narrow cots.

The faerie squeezed back with his smooth, cool hand. Querry wondered if it was wrong to love him, to want him. He wondered if his feelings were authentic, if he could trust himself. He decided to concentrate on the task at hand. He looked at the sick and dying around him. The religious order of women who cared for them had retired for the night. A few hanging lanterns lit the faces of the factory workers, orphans, and vagrants who'd come here because they had nowhere else to go. Querry knew most of them would never leave; the sisters would feed them and dress their wounds, but they could do little more than keep them comfortable until the end came. In the shadowed corners of the long, narrow room, Querry could almost feel Death waiting to claim his due.

Eager to leave, he approached the foot of one of the beds. A middle-aged man lay upon it, his left leg missing from the knee down and a foul smell wafting from the dressing. Querry knew the wound was likely infected, and caused the man to thrash and perspire in his sleep. "What about this fellow?" Querry asked, drawing his gentleman closer by the hand. "Looks like a fever dream to me."

The faerie smiled coldly as he watched the injured man's glistening face. "Yes, he is dreaming of hell. He left his wife and young daughter in the countryside, and promised to return for them as soon as he'd found work in the city. Instead, he squandered his meager wages on gambling, whores, and gin. His family starved to death. They're pointing at him with their bony fingers while demons gnaw on his leg."

"Won't you gather it up so we can be off?" Querry said, sweating himself now.

"This will never do," the gentleman told Querry. "The structure of the dream I choose to weave into the spell will have a profound effect on your companion. A horrible thing like this could turn him quite dark. Let's check some of these others. This little girl is dreaming of the night her father beat her mother to death, and this poor bastard is being chased by circus bears." He chuckled. "Many of them are dreaming about sex. Or eating."

His statement raised a question in Querry's mind. "If the dream we choose is so important, I can only assume the love oaths are just as significant. I mean, the squeals of back alley whores probably won't do."

217

"You're correct," the fey said as he continued to inspect the sleepers, bending close to some of their faces as if doing so gave him a better view inside their heads. "The words themselves are not important. It's the passion behind them that the spell requires. We'll need to find lovers with a strong desire for one another. But first, the dream! We may need to look elsewhere. There is nothing but misery within these walls."

Querry passed baskets holding babies covered in the sores that resulted from diseases that went best unmentioned. He saw a poor woman with lumps deforming her face, and some lepers mummy-wrapped in filthy rags. "What about this one?" he asked, motioning his companion toward an elderly woman who'd probably once been quite handsome. Though she sweated and writhed, a smile twisted her lips and now and then she giggled like a girl.

"She's very sick," the gentleman said gravely. "The fever will take her soon. Tonight or tomorrow. Let's see." He held his long fingers above the gray, creased brow. "Ah! She's dreaming of her childhood tending sheep in the northern mountains. Her dogs are licking her face and the lambs are frolicking about her feet. What's this? Memories of my people? It seems she had some of my kind as friends and playmates, and she's recalling fondly their games of hide and seek among the heather fields and forests. She's lifting her skirts to run across a small stream—" He rubbed his thumbs against the tips of his fingers and his tongue worked against his upper lip as he concentrated. Querry noticed a round, glowing patch form at the center of the woman's forehead. The gentleman snatched the end between his thumb and finger and slowly brought forth a long strand of shimmering greens and golds. It twisted in his grasp like a garden snake caught by the tail. He uncorked another of his bottles and stowed it away in his jacket pocket.

Just as the two of them turned to leave, the woman opened her eyes. A wide grin broke across her ancient face when she saw the faerie gentleman. "It's you! You've come for me at last!" Then confusion stole her joy, and she shook her head despondently. "No, I'm mistaken, aren't I? I thought you were somebody else."

"I am sorry, Madam," he said with no real compassion.

"Could you help me?" she pleaded, reaching for him with an age-stiffened hand. He stepped back to avoid being touched.

"I don't know what I could possibly do for you," he said, "or what you could offer me in exchange."

"Oh, sir!" Querry said, but a dangerous glare silenced him.

"Aye," she said bitterly. "You've already taken the only good thing I had left."

Sighing with impatience, the gentleman made a quick, complex gesture in the air. When his hand stilled, it held a sprig of mountain heather. He placed it beside the old woman's head. She nestled closer to it, breathed deeply of its fragrance and fell back to sleep. "I simply didn't want her resentment tainting the dream," he explained. Querry lowered his head to hide his smile. "Now if we could please take our leave of this ghastly place!"

"Thank you, sir," Querry said, hurrying to keep up with him.

CHAPTER 18

"UGH, THE stench," the gentleman hissed, pulling a lace-trimmed handkerchief from his pocket to cover his nose. "Why have you brought me here, Querrilous?"

"For the oath," Querry said gingerly, looking around the abandoned factory.

"In this desolate place?"

"This is the place where Reg and I... where we first—Could that energy still be here? Here in the stones and supports?"

Though the faerie looked violently annoyed, he closed his eyes and reached his hands out in front of him. A quarter of an hour passed before he finally said, "Yes, I can feel great love here, but it's all buried beneath and tangled up with scores of other things. Hopelessness, fear, and death. It's going to take me forever to unwind all of this mess and isolate it. Is there nowhere else we can look? Couldn't we simply go back to them, and you could have him again?"

Querry chuckled. "What, while you watch with your jar at the ready? I don't think he'd be able to, um, accomplish it. Besides, even though I still love him, I've never felt anything like that first time. Both of us were so overcome that we wept. It would mean a great deal to me if we could make that night part of Frolic too."

"I could make you hate the sight of him," the fey said, raising his voice. "I could make you to be sick whenever you touched his skin. Why, I could turn him into a toad with the head of a jackass! Why shouldn't I? Why should I continue to suffer this insult?"

"I mean no offense to you," Querry said, "but you could never make me feel that way."

"I could kill him!"

Squaring his shoulders, Querry looked deep into the gentleman's eyes and said, "I would never forgive you. For all of your power, you could never make me forget him."

"And that is the only reason I spare him," the faerie sighed, "because I value our friendship so highly. I couldn't bear for your love of me to diminish over such a triviality. Honestly, it's not as though I could feel threatened by such a person. I suppose I must get to work."

Querry took a seat on a pile of rubble and watched as the gentleman searched around with his hands in much the same way Frolic's quick fingers had moved among the gears in the clock tower. But the things the faerie sifted and sorted remained invisible to Querry. He closed his eyes and reached out with his newly found faerie sight, trying to locate some remnant of the passion he'd shared with Reg. After a few moments of hard concentration, he detected faint screams, the pop and hiss of fire, and the thick, suffocating stench of smoke. His eyes sprung open, and he saw shadowy figures at the corners of his vision, running for the single exit, trampling one another to save themselves. He shook his head, but the vision remained, the tragic events playing out over and over again as Querry shook and whimpered. He was about to collapse when a graceful hand wiped the scene from his eyes, the way one might wipe dust from a tabletop.

"Do you see?" the gentleman asked. "The psychic energy left by those who died in the fire is burying everything else. I cannot untangle anything from it, and besides, I—" He slumped down and took a seat beside the thief on the heap of scrap. He put his elbows on his knees and rubbed his palms together in such an inelegant way that it frightened Querry. He'd never seen the other man lose his regal bearing.

"Sir, what is it?"

"I feel very weak. This place feels desolate with the lack of magic. Dead."

The horrible memories the factory contained had exhausted Querry; he couldn't imagine the toll they'd taken on the gentleman with his finer perception. It was no wonder he felt strained. With a great effort, Querry got to his feet and took the other's man's elbow, urging him to stand. "Let's get out of here, sir. I'm sorry I ever asked you to come. Some fresh air will fix us right up." He escorted the faerie out of the factory and into the night, troubled by the sluggish way he dragged his feet. Querry thought it wise to put some distance between them and the ghosts of the burned-out bottling plant, so he urged his companion through the alleys until they reached the great, rusted pipe that had once spewed the factory's waste into the river. They continued to walk beside the water, away from the factory district and toward Neroche.

"This is wrong," the gentleman said in a frightened whisper. "The stars are so dull."

"Pollution, I'd wager," Querry said.

"No. Where are the voices of the trees? The song of the ocean and the wind? What has happened here?"

"I don't know," Querry admitted. He couldn't name the change he sensed in the world. He supposed everything felt washed-out, muted. He moved as fast as he could toward the nearest bridge, toward the west side of Halcyon. "Let's get home."

"Home," the gentleman moaned. "This place is... sucking... the life... out of me. I don't understand how this can be."

"My people are poisoning the sea and sky," Querry said. "I'm sure that's what you're feeling." The faerie had slowed and taken hold of the bridge railing. They inched their way over the great expanse of fetid river water as Querry tried to reassure his companion.

"No," the gentleman began, but a loud voice interrupted him.

"You there! Stop where you are."

Querry looked to his left and saw three patrolmen headed their way. He swore under his breath. Then he forced a laughed, indicated the gentleman with his chin and said, "He's had a few too many."

"Bring out your papers," one of them said, "both of you. Now!"

"This is a misunderstanding," Querry began.

"Nonsense," the gentleman said, reaching into his pocket. "The papers you require are right here." He handed the burly officer a stack of yellow leaves.

"You think you're funny, you faerie son of a bitch?" He unbuckled the club from his belt and lifted his arm to strike the gentleman.

The fey laughed and pointed his fingers toward the cudgel. Querry would never know his intention, because the thick wood smacked the side of his head with a hollow thud, and he sprawled on the ground. The other two officers joined their comrade, encircling the faerie, vicious grins beneath their moustaches.

Querry had no time to ponder what had just happened. He had to act. He pulled his pistol, took a few steps back, and fired three times, striking each of the constables once in the leg. As they crumpled, he holstered his gun and drew his sword, holding it to each of their throats as he removed their firearms and flung them into the water.

"You'll hang for this," one of them said.

"Treason!"

The third man reached for a whistle around his neck and gave it a deafening blow. Ears ringing, Querry knelt beside his gentleman and tried desperately to rouse him. When he failed, he scooped him into his arms. They had to escape before the rest of the city guards arrived. Luckily the gentleman was surprisingly light despite his stature. Querry couldn't exactly run, but he made his way briskly toward Hawthorne Street. He heard shouts and more whistles behind him. They had to reach Neroche; Querry couldn't hope to overcome the dozen or so men he heard gathering. He needed the gentleman's magic, but his stamina waned with each step he took. Finally he resolved to rest in a sewer pipe down an embankment from the street.

Querry lay the gentleman against the semicircular wall of stone and crouched in the trickle of cold water, rubbing his biceps and thighs. He heard a groan and the gentleman's eyes opened, glowing like a cat's.

"Oh thank God," Querry breathed. "Get us out of here. We're in heaps of trouble."

"I- I can't," the fey whimpered.

"What? Do what you did on the cliff! Swirl us back to your manor house, or we're dead!" He could hear the guards shouting to one another as they searched for "the faerie-loving little bastard and the goddamned sprite." They were maybe half a block away. Querry and the gentleman wouldn't be able to emerge from the sewer pipe, or they'd be shot on sight. Querry wouldn't have thought a bullet would harm the fey, but now he wasn't so sure.

"Sir, please," Querry said, taking his hand.

"My head," he grumbled. "What a strange sensation...."

"Sir, we've got to go!"

"I've told you there's nothing I can do," he snarled, growing irritated.

"Then we crawl for it," Querry said, pointing into the dark depths of the pipe. He expected strong protests from his companion, but none came, and Querry began to lead the way through the fetid tunnel. They made their way slowly. Querry's knees cracked and bled under the combination of frigid water and coarse cement. Even through his armored gloves, his palms scraped raw and broke open. The gentleman would be hurting worse in nothing but his fancy suit, but he didn't complain. Querry heard his labored breathing. He looked over his shoulders and found the chartreuse eyes markedly dimmed.

They reached a grate and Querry tried to estimate how far they'd come and in what direction. He felt fairly certain they'd come out only a block or two from Neroche. Unfortunately, if the guards had any sense, Neroche would be the first place they'd look. Querry cocked his head but didn't hear anything. He turned to the faerie. "How are you feeling? Will you be able to run?"

"I'm going to make these plebeians pay for what they've done to me," he hissed. "I'll curse their families for seven generations!"

"Yes, sir," Querry said. "Just as soon as we make it out of here. Is there anything you can do to help me?"

"Give me that sword. I know how to use it."

"All right then." Querry unsheathed his blade and handed it over. With a few kicks he dislodged the rusty grate from the stone, and he pushed it aside so that they could crawl out. He offered his hand to the gentleman as he scanned around. Ivy and moss covered the empty houses, a good sign. "We shouldn't have far to go."

"I don't know," the faerie said, a shiver in his voice. "I can't feel it."

"It's just through here." Querry held his wrist, and they sprinted down the street, turning left at the end. The two trees marking the entrance appeared, but leafless and dead. The gentleman said a word in his language that expressed so much anger and fear that Querry's stomach clenched at the sound of it.

"We thought you rascals might come this way," said a voice. Before Querry could even turn toward it, a shot rang out. The gentleman yelled as the bullet grazed his upper thigh, drawing a font of blood. Querry pulled his pistol and spun on his heel, firing indiscriminately at the source of the shot.

"Run!" he told the faerie.

"I'm bleeding," he said, more taken by the peculiarity than the pain.

"Sir, just go!" Querry reloaded his weapon as he backed toward the trees and carpeted the area in front of him with bullets. He heard the faerie's boots on the cobblestone as he frantically fed bullets into his gun, resolving to find some way to increase its ammunition capacity in the future. "Get behind something!" he instructed. "Get back to the Other World!"

"Querrilous—"

"Go!" A bullet whizzed by Querry's waist, but he tucked and rolled to the side to avoid it. With another leap he made it to the shelter of one of the desiccated faerie trees. He crouched behind the trunk and yelled, "Come and get me, you sons of whores!" Predictably, the guards' fear of Neroche held them at bay. Querry emptied his gun in the direction of the incoming shots, and looked at the handful of bullets he had remaining before reloading for the last time. Instead of firing haphazardly, he squinted into the darkness. He noticed a fleeting gleam of metal around the side of a crumbling wall and took the shot. He grinned when he heard a hollered curse, but he only had another four bullets. He looked over his shoulder, hoping to retreat deeper into Neroche, scanning around for something to cover his escape. Neroche was not only abandoned, though, it was *gone*. Where the streetlights and manor houses had once stood, only piles of dust and rubble remained, as if the quarter had been deserted for a thousand years. Winding between the piles of debris, Querry discerned a narrow path. It led up a hill and into an eerily familiar, gray wood. At the point where the trail disappeared into the trees, he saw a bright, white, circular gateway. If he could make it there, he knew he'd cross the veil, but it meant almost half a mile of running out in the open. Querry swore with uncertainty. While glad his dear gentleman had made it to safety, he missed the faerie's reassuring presence.

A bullet struck the tree, showering Querry's face with shards of bark. He shielded his head with his arms and looked again at the path. He fired at a movement in the shadows, though his shot bounced off the snowy ground. Three bullets left. Querry took a deep breath, sprinted a few paces, and knelt behind a pile of square stones. The guards shot, but their bullets pinged off the blocks. He ran to the next pile of rubble and made it unscathed. The way before him offered no shelter, but he decided to chance it. The patrolmen had been so liberal with their ammunition that he doubted they could have much left. He stood up and ran and for it. The lack of fire told him his guess had been spot on.

Nothing lined the rest of the trail but some brittle, frost-gilded grass. It sparkled in the moonlight as Querry pushed himself hard toward the shelter of the wood. To his shock, he heard heavy footsteps behind him.

"Come on, lads," one of the guards called. "There ain't no faeries here! Let's make this son of a bitch pay!" The others, probably six or eight of them, yelled their agreement.

Energy fading, Querry summoned a last burst of speed, but it wasn't enough. A large hand caught his shoulder and yanked him back. His heel slipped on a patch of ice as he tried to pull away, and his tailbone smacked the hard ground. The guard who'd caught him raised his baton and swung for Querry's head, but the thief rolled to the side and avoided the blow. Scrambling to his feet, Querry reached for his sword and swore out loud when he remembered he'd given it to his gentleman. Without it, with only his bare hands, he'd have little chance against the six hulking figures that approached him, slapping their sticks against their palms and chuckling with anticipation. The one who'd grabbed him struck out again, toward Querry's ribs. He dodged, but he wouldn't be able to keep dodging once all seven of them surrounded him. Already they closed the circle. Querry looked for something to back up against, but there was nothing but shadow and cold air.

"You're gonna answer for what you did to our mates, faerie-lover," one of them snarled.

"Time to take your medicine, boy." A club struck him between the shoulder blades. By the time he turned to try to defend himself, another hit his lower back and sent him down on his elbows. Blows rained down, and the best Querry could do was try to cover his head. When he attempted to crawl away, a boot blocked his way. He felt a rib crack, and he swore. After everything they'd done, after as close as they'd come, it was going to end like this. Querry couldn't see any way to save himself.

But he had to try. Ignoring the pain, he punched at the kneecap nearest him. The man didn't fall, and Querry brought his wrist up between his legs. This time he crumpled and collapsed. Querry grabbed the baton that fell from his hand and swung his arm out to the right, dropping another of his attackers. That gave him time to stagger to his feet, and at least now he had a weapon. Stumbling backward, almost tripping over the groaning patrolman, he widened his stance and prepared to fight. He was bruised and bloody, hurting all over, and he still faced five men. They approached Querry cautiously, and he raised his stick.

"Well, this will be a bit of sport," said a voice to Querry's left, that managed a derisive giggle in spite of the pain that tightened it.

"Sir?"

The faerie bounced the hilt of the sword in his hand, testing the weight. "This is a good blade," he remarked. Without another word, he lunged forward, spun, and vanquished two of the guards with much more elaborate flourish and showmanship than necessary. The remaining man stood with his mouth hanging open before he turned and ran.

Catching his breath and holding his side, Querry took a second to look at his savior, now that he was safe. The faerie's skin was pale and waxy, and his blood darkened his pant leg to the cuff. Still, a curious smile tugged at the corners of his lips. He offered Querry his arm, and they locked elbows before limping toward the portal and disappearing into it.

EVERYTHING WENT black and then exploded into blinding white. Querry pitched forward and would have somersaulted down the steep, snowy path if his gentleman hadn't caught his arm. For many minutes he perceived only blurs of ivory and brown, accompanied by an intense pounding and humming between his ears. His stomach cartwheeled; his legs wouldn't hold him. Querry reached across his chest and clung desperately to his gentleman's lapel until his eyes started to focus and his nausea settled. When it did, he recognized the Eastern hillside that led to the wizard's lodge. His spirits rose as soon as he realized Reg waited just down the path.

Querry felt a pang of guilt when he looked over and noticed the faerie's pallor and the blood that streamed onto the snow with every step he took. "Let me help you," Querry offered. He expected resistance, pride, but the other smiled weakly and offered his elbow. Together they carefully picked their way down the rocky trail to the little cabin. By the time they reached the front door, Querry's gentleman put most of his weight on Querry. Querry knocked on the door as the fey slipped his arm over Querry's shoulders and let his knees bend. His head drooped forward and his breath grew jagged and irregular. For the first time since the shooting, Querry worried. Certain metals did great harm to the Fair Folk. How much blood could one of them stand to lose? The gentleman's skin and sinew felt the same under Querry's hands as any other man. Maybe he wasn't as omnipotent as the thief had always assumed. What if he died?

Querry pounded harder against the thick wood. "Reg, please! Open the door!"

The door opened not long after. Reg, in a cinnamon colored shirt and wool-lined vest like the natives wore, smiled at first. The bracing climate, physical work, and rich cuisine suited him: he'd filled out, gained muscle and a rosy glow to his cheeks. When he saw the state of Querry and the gentleman, his lips dropped with concern. "What's happened?"

"Met with some resistance," Querry said as he guided the faerie into the sparse, utilitarian kitchen. Frolic still lay on the bench beside the bay window, so Querry helped the fey to a wood-framed sofa covered in threadbare cushions. The gentleman lay down with a groan. Reg hurried to retrieve the kettle from the hearth and dump the water into a clay basin. He returned with it and a clean rag, his dislike of the faerie overshadowed by his innate compassion. Querry tore the fine fabric away from the gentleman's wound. His blood poured out in a sheet. His color flowed out of him along with it. Reg wiped it away, but it continued to gush. Soon the water in the basin became thick and red.

"Querry, who did this?" Reg asked. "What, what if he dies? Can he die?"

"I'll explain it later, Reg."

"What do we do?"

"I don't know," Querry admitted, sweat breaking from his brow.

Reg took a deep breath and rubbed his forehead with the back of his hand, leaving a bloody streak on his fair skin. "This needs to be stitched," he said matter-of-factly. "I'll stitch it."

The gentleman's head bolted up from the cushion. "You'll do no such thing!" He swatted weakly at Reg's hand.

"Sir," Querry said, taking his hand and squeezing his knuckles, "please, let us help you."

"I can help myself," he snarled. "There is plenty of magic here." He opened and closed his fist a few times over his injury. He drew a breath and held it in as he drew a symbol over his leg with his fingers. The blood stopped flowing, and the skin knitted together as good as new. He let his head fall back and his eyes flutter shut. He stretched his fingers toward Reg and said, "Bring me some wine. The local varietal that they call Bull's Blood."

Reg hurried off and returned with a dusty bottle and a wooden mug. He served the gentleman the wine. The faerie drained the cup and held it out again. By the time he'd finished, his color and vigor had returned. He propped himself up on his elbows and looked down at his newly healed flesh. "Ugh, my trousers," he said with a shake of his head. He closed his eyes for another quarter of an hour. Eventually he opened them again, and they shined as green as morning sun on new grass. He addressed Querry and Reg with the elegant formality Querry recognized, saying, "Gentlemen, I believe we have work to do."

CHAPTER 19

QUERRY AND Reg stood facing one another in front of the bay window. The setting sun lit their left sides with rosy light, and the crackling fire in the hearth washed their right sides in soft orange. Candles sputtered on the utilitarian stands beside the couch, and the savory aroma of the goulash Reg had made for supper hung in the warm, moist air. Reg looked down at his toes, wiggling them against the coarse wood of the floor. Querry caught his chin and forced Reg to meet his eyes. He smiled at Reg and pushed his overlong fringe off of his forehead. Reg forced himself to return the smile, and Querry let his hand skim down Reg's neck and back to cup his hipbone and pull their bodies closer. Their bellies met, and Querry moved his face toward Reg's parted lips. Reg accepted a few playful pecks, but when Querry tried for more Reg pressed his lips tightly together and turned his face away.

"Can we get on with this?" the gentleman asked from the sofa where he sat with the stem of a wine glass between his thumb and finger. "I have urgent problems of my own to deal with."

"You're not helping," Reg snapped.

Leaning forward, resting an elbow on his knee, the faerie asked, "Would you like me to?"

"No!"

"Sir," Querry interjected quickly, before the gentleman could take offense, "You must understand how difficult this is for us. We aren't used to an audience."

"I don't think I can do this," Reg said, pulling away and going to stare out the window at the darkening trees.

Querry rubbed his shoulder and buried his face in his thick hair, speaking close to Reg's ear. "We have to do this for Frolic," he explained. "We've gathered all of the other ingredients. We need an oath spoken during love. Once we have it, my... the gentleman can do the magic and bring Frolic back." He held Reg by the waist and turned him slowly, kissing his cheek when he could. "We love each other. All we need to do is express it, and everything will be fine."

"All right." Reg let his eyes fall closed and his lips fall open. Querry kissed him, and he kissed back, but without any real intimacy or passion. Not giving up, Querry scratched lightly down his spine and kneaded his cheek. He suckled Reg's neck and reached around him. He found Reg completely flaccid.

Querry knew how to turn his lover on. He grabbed Reg's elbow, spun him around, and pushed hard between his shoulder blades. Reg stumbled forward, toward the table. Querry hurried up behind him and slammed his chest down on the wood, making the simple dinner plates rattle. Reg looked over his shoulder, his eyes wide with surprise, and tried to stand back up. Querry seized the back of his neck and held him down, smacking his inner thigh to encourage him to spread his legs. He heard Reg's breath catch, and he smiled. As he ground his erection against Reg's cleft, he maneuvered his hand toward Reg's groin and found much more to fill it. He leaned down and bit into the muscle stretching from Reg's neck to his shoulder. Reg groaned, and his cock skipped in Querry's fist. "Oh, Querry, yes," he breathed.

"Good show," the gentleman said. "Carry on."

"No," Reg said, twisting and throwing Querry off. He walked to the far end of the simple room, rubbing his upper arms with his hands as if they were covered in filth and needed a scrubbing. "I simply can't do this! Even if I can complete physically, it won't be authentic. This, this is just sick, and I can't."

Cursing, Querry pulled on his pants and threw his coat over his shoulders. He stomped to the porch and slammed the door behind him. His breath and feet froze almost instantly. Dry snow blew against him and clung to his hair. Why was Reg being so unreasonable? Querry couldn't imagine what the big deal could be. They only needed to make love, and they could get their Frolic back. How could Reg be so selfish? Querry swore again and kicked the logs Reg had chopped for the fire. The neat pyramid collapsed and wood rolled everywhere. Pain shot through Querry's foot and up his ankle and calf, bringing unwelcome tears.

The door opened with a creak and a rectangle of light. Querry turned, ready to tell Reg off. Instead he saw his gentleman, and an idea occurred to him. He took a few steps toward the faerie as the other quietly latched the door. Querry caught a long strip of flaxen hair and let his hand slide to the end, enjoying the silken texture. "Sir," he said softly, his tongue mopping his swollen bottom lip, "I think it's time. For us."

With a wicked smile, the fey leaned toward Querry and sucked his lip and tongue into his mouth, trapping them between his teeth. He bit just hard enough for the pain to be pleasant and arousing, and then he let go. "No, Querrilous," he said. "Not for this spell. I am not a fool. You feel desire for me but not love. Honestly, I can't understand why, but neither can I deny what I see. I have another idea."

"I don't understand."

"You will." The faerie took his hand and led him back into the cabin. They crossed the sitting room and went up the steps to the tiny sleeping rooms. The gentleman stopped in front of one of the doors and laid his palm against it. His eyes closed and a sad little smile crossed his face. "Look at this."

He turned the knob slowly, and Querry marveled at the scene he saw inside the small room. Everything looked blurred and distorted, as if he watched it through old, rippled glass, but a healthy blaze in the hearth and half a hundred candles illuminated it all perfectly. The room contained little but a bulky armoire, a bookshelf, and a narrow bed. Upon this last Querry saw two bodies: one white-gold and the other a flushed, healthy peach. The gentleman, his gentleman in the vision sat with his back to the headboard and his legs folded beneath him like a foreign yogi. The other man, a small, lithe creature with long, auburn hair crouched above him, his heels beside the gentleman's hips. His delicate fingers gripped the faerie's shoulders as he rocked against him. When he threw his head back, the faerie's lips found his Adam's apple and the muscles of his neck. Querry had seen true love, passion, and desire, and he had seen people satisfying their baser instincts in the arms of whores. He knew the difference, and he knew he witnessed love. He felt a knot low in his body.

"Who is this man?" he asked. Despite his best effort not to be, Querry was jealous. He continued to observe as the two men made love, clinging to one another and staring deep into each other's eyes. Now and then they spoke to each other in breathless exhalations, and though Querry couldn't understand the words, he understood the sentiment perfectly: devotion, delight, and need. "He speaks your language," Querry noted as he watched. When the faerie in the vision touched his lover's cheek, Querry's gentleman reached his long fingers into the room as if he could do the same. He realized he couldn't, balled his fist and pressed it against his mouth, watching his former partner with misty eyes.

The faerie cleared his throat. "Yes, he had much discourse with my people and learned our tongue. Usually it is hard for humans, but he picked it up easily. He was so brilliant—"

Without thinking, Querry wound his arms around the gentleman's waist and rested his chin on his shoulder. The other tilted his golden head and propped it against Querry's temple. "He was one of the most gifted human magicians I'd seen," he whispered. "I loved him. He loved me back, in my true form and without glamour."

"What happened?" Querry asked.

"It broke his heart to be banished from his homeland. I offered him the world, but all he wanted was to set foot again on that little island. He went to wander the roads beyond the veil, in the hope that when he returned your countrymen will have lifted the ban on wizardry. I can't imagine how it will affect him to learn that the magic is being sucked out of the place somehow. If he even lives. But that's a problem for later. Go now, Querrilous. These next words are for him and me alone. I'll collect them and be along in a bit."

Querry nodded and kissed his cheek, but the gentleman's eyes never left the writhing bodies in the room.

Downstairs, Reg sat on a stool, poking at the fire and nursing a large brandy. Without looking away from the coals, he said, "I know you're cross with me, Querry. I'm sorry, but as much as I love you and Frolic, I just couldn't perform with him watching and offering commentary. We'll have to find another way, even if you have to—I mean, I see how you look at him."

"I don't love him." Querry felt guilty for being angry with Reg and overreacting. He understood how difficult all of this new liberation was for his more traditional friend.

"What will we do, then?" Reg asked.

"He," Querry indicated the steps with a flick of his chin, "he knew the wizard who lived in this house. They were close."

"Lovers?"

Querry nodded. "It seems that among the fey, friendships like ours are more permissible."

Reg took a long pull from his drink and raked his fingers through his hair. He set his cup beside the fire and stood, pacing back and forth in front of the inglenook. Finally he said, "I don't pretend to understand any of this, Querry. But that wizard hasn't lived here in decades. How on earth are they going to, going to collect the words?"

"Strong emotion can leave echoes behind," Querry explained. Since his gentleman had kissed his eyes, he understood such things intrinsically, even if he'd never considered them before. "What's really bothering you?"

"I don't like him," Reg hissed, stopping in front of Querry. "He's dangerous and insane. I worry about the effect it will have on Frolic. I don't want him to be a part of Frolic. This is going to mean he'll never be out of our lives!"

"Frolic will be Frolic. This isn't going to change him."

"Do you really believe that, Querry?"

"You don't know him like I do, Reggie. He isn't so bad. I think you're just jealous. You don't have any reason to be. I promise you."

"I am jealous! I see him fawning over you, hear you calling him yours! He's beautiful and powerful, and I can't compete. I don't know if I can spend the rest of my life watching you make love to Frolic and wondering if you're seeing a piece of that, that thing!"

"If I'd wanted to be with him I could have done so a hundred times!"

"I'm supposed to believe you haven't? Not ever?"

"No! What's wrong with you?"

"I've been stuck out here in the middle of nowhere for over a month, not even knowing if you were coming back, or if you'd just run away with him. Then you stroll in and ask me to sleep with you and let him watch."

"For the spell! For Frolic!"

"Oh, but not because you would have enjoyed it! Maybe you could have asked him to join us after a bit?"

"That's not fair," Querry said defensively, getting angrier and more confused each second.

Reg took a deep breath and said, "No, it isn't. I'm sorry I said that, but I don't want any of him to be part of our Frolic. We have to find some other way. You said yourself it needs to express true love. You can't possibly believe him capable of feeling love as we do. Maybe none of them can. I absolutely won't budge on this point, Querry. We'll have to think of something else. I've already compromised more than I would have liked." He lifted his hand toward his mouth and considered his fingernails.

"Is there a problem?" the faerie asked from the bottom of the steps. He held a little jar that pulsed with warm, red light.

"Sir...." Querry had no idea where to begin. How could he tell his gentleman that he planned to refuse his intimate and beautiful gift?

"Shall I do the magic now?" the faerie asked, striding confidently toward Frolic. "It should not take me long."

"Actually—" Reg began, but stopped when Querry shook his head. He chewed on his thumbnail as he scowled.

"We're all very tired," Querry said. "If it's all the same to you, sir, Reg and I would prefer to wait until morning."

The gentleman's eyes glowed from the shadowy corner of the room, scrutinizing Querry until he felt the gaze scraping against his soul. He had to look away. It suddenly felt cold. Shivering, Querry piled a few more logs on the fire and jabbed at the coals with the poker.

He felt the faerie's eyes on his back, like icy water running down his spine. The wind picked up, howling down the mountainside and shaking the walls of the little house. When the gentleman spoke, his voice sounded just as frigid and terrifying.

"Have I not done everything you asked of me, Querrilous? You should be falling at my feet with gratitude, but you insult me instead?"

"Sir, no!"

An icy gust swept down the chimney, extinguishing not only the fire but all of the candles. In the blackness that followed, Querry saw nothing but the faerie's eyes, smoldering with anger and offense. Reg's breath faltered somewhere off to the left. Querry pawed at the darkness until he found his arm. He pulled Reg close and shielded him in his arms, though he had no idea how he'd be able to save them. He felt enchantment crackling in the air like electricity before a storm. It moved over his skin, making the fine hair stand up.

Instead of any of the perverse violence Querry expected, the magic fluttered around the room, igniting the fire in the hearth and the candles on the stands. The faerie looked around bewildered, telling Querry he hadn't cast the spell. The kettle that they'd emptied earlier that evening filled itself and began to whistle and steam. A coarse wool blanket unfolded itself and spread itself across the back of the sofa. The closet door creaked open, and a well-worn pair of suede slippers padded across the floor and waited beside the ottoman. Querry jumped when a cork popped out of a wine bottle on the counter. A full pipe with a brass bowl materialized beside it.

"What on earth?" Reg said.

In answer, the doorknob turned and the door swung open, admitting a gust of wind and snow, and a man in an old-fashioned traveling cloak. Ice lay thick on the shoulders and the hood that obscured the stranger's face. Querry broke away from Reg and retrieved his sword from the corner, his mind swarming with the gentleman's tales of the bloodthirsty demons living in this part of the world.

"Who and what are you?" Querry asked, extending his blade toward the dark, cloaked figure.

The man pushed the hood back and shook the sparkling crystals from his long, auburn hair. He couldn't have been a day older than Querry or Reg. "I'm Kristof," he said with a gentle smile. "What are you doing in my house?"

Querry lowered his arm, almost too amazed to speak. "Your house?"

"Yes," the young man said, hanging his cloak on a hook near the door. He removed his gloves and went to pick up the wine that had opened itself in anticipation of his return. "I expected a bit more dust," he said with a chuckle. He looked around and noticed the faerie gentleman, standing over Frolic near the window. The bottle slipped from his hand and shattered on the floor, but he didn't seem aware of it. Kristof said a word like cherry blossoms on a spring breeze as he threw himself into the other man's arms. The faerie stared at his face and touched his brow as if to prove to himself Kristof existed. A tear ran down his cheek, and Kristof caught it on his finger. They exchanged a few whispered words in fey before they started to kiss. The reunion grew so heated that Querry and Reg had to look away.

"Still going to tell me that's not love?" Querry said softly to his companion.

Reg only snickered, shook his head, and squeezed Querry's hand.

AFTER SEVERAL glasses of wine and half an hour relaxing in front of the fire, everyone calmed down and put the earlier altercation to the backs of their minds. Kristof and the faerie gentleman sat on the couch stroking each other's fingers and cuffs as if it hurt them not to touch. Querry and Reg sat cross-legged on the floor, their backs to the hearth. They snacked on cold sausage, pickled beets, boiled eggs, and sharp cheese. Kristof regaled them with fantastic tales of his travels in the Other World and the vast knowledge he'd gained there. He proved an engaging and entertaining storyteller. To Querry's great relief, Reg appeared to enjoy the anecdotes as much as any of them.

"Tell us how you learned magic, Kristof," he urged with authentic interest.

"Ah, well." The young man looked embarrassed and played with his cufflink. His clothing seemed antique and his long hair anachronistic. Even the cadence of his speech dated him a bit. "I don't remember a time in my life when magic wasn't present. My father was a simple man, and happy to be so. He worked as a veterinarian around the countryside where we lived. His arcane knowledge assisted him in his profession."

"You learned magic from your father?" Reg asked.

"Yes, he taught me. Though I must admit I'd mastered the dozen spells he knew by the time I was five. You see, he cared only for that magic that helped with the lambing in the spring or healed a horse's wounded foot."

"That's not the extent of your schooling, though," Querry inferred.

"No, certainly not," the wizard confirmed. "My mother's father was a respected and learned Wizard in the College of the Arcane Hand, in Bravelstein. He'd been retired many years by the time I was born, but I spent my summers at his estate. He taught me everything he knew about the Mystic Arts, the Arcane and the Noble Magics. All the things my father scoffed at. And yet—" the gentleman's lover trailed off.

"And yet?" Reg prodded, eager to hear the rest. The magician chuckled.

"I learned more from the land around me than anything: the tidal pools that pitted the beach, the shadows the trees cast at twilight, the rocky crags that disappeared into the clouds."

"The soft places," the gentleman said.

"Yes," Kristof agreed, nodding enthusiastically. "The places that were neither water nor soil, light nor dark, sky nor earth. That is where I first heard the voices of the *Sidhe*." He looked at his faerie lover with unabashed adoration. "Beings who knew magic like we humans know breath. Magic is their flesh and blood, their language. I learned to speak those words, learned so much, and then—"

"The Crown gathered the wizards and drove them out," Reg said softly.

"Let us talk of other things," Kristof said, looking at Reg and trying to smile, though it looked like he'd drunk sour milk.

"Of course. What brings you back from the Outer Lands?"

"Do you not know?" Kristof's tone grew frantic. "Someone has, has—" he couldn't articulate his theory, so he demonstrated by punching the air in front of him. "There's a hole in the veil between the realms. And through that hole, the energy, the life, the *magic*, is being siphoned from the Other Lands. As I've said, magic is their sky, their rain, their everything. The signs are subtle, but the Old Places are dying. If this keeps up, they'll collapse. And the human world will follow. I came back to find out how and why this is happening, and to put a stop to it."

"You must help him, Querrilous," the gentleman said. "That is the boon I ask of you."

Querry quickly said, "Of course!"

Reg said, "Why?"

"Why?" Kristof gasped. "This is disastrous! Your world can no more exist without the Other than it can without the sky above it or the rock beneath!"

"But first Frolic," Reg firmly insisted. "That was our deal, was it not?"

Querry sat up straighter, swelling with both shock and pride at his partner's audacity and courage. "Yes, Frolic," he agreed.

Kristof stood and walked slowly toward the still body on the bench. "He had life. True life. What must we do to return it to him? He, he feels worthy, deserving—"

"It's a simple bit of magic," the faerie stated. He rose and stood a few feet behind the young wizard. "I have all of the spell components. We need only to weave them together and encase them in a glass shell. Then we can restore this young man to life and the three of them can help us close the rift."

"Glass?" Kristof mused, examining Frolic's injuries, "no, glass is not strong enough. My love, let us cast together a hard gem of these elements. A white-hot ruby invulnerable to destruction."

"Yes!" The gentleman clapped his hands. "A marvelous idea. Let us get to creating it right away!"

Kristof looked to Querry and Reg for permission. Querry waited, his eyes on his companion. Reg took Kristof's hand and held it, saying "Please help him. He's very dear to me. I can see you understand what that means."

"Yes." The young wizard smiled sincerely. "This will be a brilliant enchantment. Wonderful, I promise."

"I trust you," Reg said, squeezing and then releasing Kristof's fingers.

"Let us do the magic," Kristof said.

FROLIC'S HEAD rested in Reg's lap, and Querry sat behind him with his knees pressed against Reg's forearms and his hands on Frolic's neck. On either side of Frolic's waist, the gentleman and Kristof sat with their eyes closed and their fingertips drawing delicate symbols upon one another's palms. Their lips mouthed the mystic fey words, though Querry heard nothing. He ignored it and concentrated on the memories of his lost love. Doing so, he felt a warmth in his palms that spread into Frolic's body. He felt his energy draining into Frolic, and he was happy to give it.

I want you back. I love you, need you, Querry thought. He opened his eyes just in time to see Kristof and the faerie knit their fingers together. A scarlet orb formed between their palms, and soon it contracted and solidified into a ball, then a brilliant jewel that glowed so brightly that it hurt Querry's eyes even when he closed them again, the vermillion glow searing through his lids.

"Place it there," he heard Reg instruct.

"It's done," the gentleman said.

Querry expected to see Frolic spring to life, blink his eyes with confusion, maybe, and then sit up. Instead, Frolic lay still with his dulled eyes on the ceiling. The faceted jewel the faerie and the magician had conjured pulsed within his chest, illuminating the faces of the men who now leaned over him. His gears remained motionless.

"What's wrong?" Reg asked quietly. "Why isn't it working?"

"I have done the magic as you asked," the gentleman said. "Don't expect me to understand the workings of an inelegant machine. The enchantment is flawless, as powerful a spell as I've ever seen."

"He's hardly an inelegant machine," Kristof argued gently, touching Frolic's round chin, "but you're right. Our work is perfectly wrought. I'm afraid all of these gears and wires are beyond my realm of expertise as well."

"Querry?" Reg asked, turning to look over his shoulder.

Querry considered. He'd practically memorized the book, and felt certain none of his own work had been improperly done. He couldn't imagine why Frolic still slept. A quarter of an hour passed as he retraced his steps, checking and rechecking the repairs. Despair loomed over him as he stared into Frolic's chest, watching his new heart burn within its golden casings. "I don't know what I could have missed," he said to himself. "He should be alive. Moving and breathing—

"That's it!"

"What?" Reg asked, crouching down beside Querry.

"Steam," Querry said. "Steam travels through all of these conduits," he showed Reg by pointing, "and causes his gears to turn. Each gear then turns several other gears, and so on. He needs steam to get his engines started. Steam needs two things: heat, which we have, and water to be evaporated."

"Water?" Reg asked.

"Yes. He has sacks in his lungs which collect the water vapor from the air and channel it to his heart. We need to fill his lungs. Open his mouth and breathe into them, Reg."

Reg looked surprised for a second, but then he tilted Frolic's head back and did as Querry said. Querry heard him inhale deeply and watched Frolic's lungs expand. Reg did this three times before he had to sit up and regain his own breath. Frolic still didn't move.

"Again," Querry said.

Reg looked ready to argue, but he leaned back down to Frolic's mouth. He inflated Frolic's lungs five more times before stopping to rest. Then he bent in for another three breathes. Just when Querry was about to give up hope, he heard an almost imperceptible hiss. Slowly Frolic's gears began to turn, triggering the chain reaction that Querry had described to Reg. Miniscule wheels turned, and tiny pistons thrummed up and down. Frolic gasped like he'd been drowned, and his chest heaved off of the floor. Kristof and the faerie gentleman, who'd been talking in the kitchen, hurried over to observe. Frolic's body convulsed. His limbs flailed and smacked against the wood. Reg tried to shush him and stroked his face, looking worried. Frolic's head turned from side to side. Reg's hands over his ears could barely hold him still.

"Querry?" Reg said.

"I- I don't know what to do!"

"Please, don't worry," Kristof said, kneeling down next to Reg. He touched Frolic's forehead with his first two fingers, looked into his eyes, and said a soothing word. Frolic's seizures subsided, but he still panted, looking at the hole in his body with horror. Kristof noticed his distress, smiled, and waved his hand over the wound. Both the metal plate over his heart and the skin beyond it knit back together seamlessly. It was a bit paler than the skin surrounding it, and the scar reminded Querry of a child's drawing of a five-petaled flower. Gradually Frolic's breathing became slower and more regular, and Querry and Reg petted his hair and spoke to him softly. At first he didn't recognize them and looked at them with fear and confusion.

"You're safe, my love," Reg said, happy tears spilling down his cheeks.

"R-Reg?" he croaked in response.

Reg could only laugh out loud with joy and kiss him hard on the brow. His laughter mingled with his sobs as he hugged Frolic around the neck. "I thought I'd lost you, my dear, dear Frolic. Oh, thank God."

"Querry?" Frolic asked weakly.

"I'm here, beauty." He squeezed Frolic's hand. "I've missed you."

"Kristof, is that you?" Frolic asked.

"Yes," the magician said, confused.

"How do I know you?" Frolic wondered aloud. "I feel strange. How do I know…? I know—"

Frolic sat bolt upright and said a word that was clearly a fey profanity. "I know! I know how the clock tower works!"

CHAPTER 20

QUERRY OPENED his stateroom door and crossed the dark and empty saloon, emerging on the deck of the passenger steamship *Unicorn.* Reg claimed the constant rocking of the large vessel helped him sleep, and he rested soundly in his bunk. The motion made Querry sick, and the weeks he'd spent cooped up made him restless. Worst of all, he'd woken in the night to find Frolic gone again. Needing fresh air and hoping to find his companion, Querry walked around the first of a pair of huge metal smokestacks. He saw a figure leaning against the railing on the port side of the ship, and he headed in that direction.

When he got closer, Querry discovered not Frolic but Kristof with his elbows on the metal bar. The young man stood looking out to sea with his hood up. The water lapped calmly against the boat's metal hull as Querry joined the magician. He gazed out in the direction Kristof looked, but beyond the caps of sea foam closest to them, he saw only darkness. At least it was warmer; Querry's hands felt fine without his gloves.

"Trouble sleeping?" Kristof asked. He offered Querry the pipe he'd been smoking.

"I suppose," Querry answered. Though he didn't smoke often, Querry accepted Kristof's pipe and took a few pulls. It calmed his nerves a little. "Have you seen Frolic around?"

"No. Is he missing?"

Querry nodded and passed the pipe back. "He slips away during the night. Says he likes to be under the moon and stars. Last night I found him over by the masthead, singing a song. He told me he was talking to the ocean."

"I think he's reacting to the fey in him. The effect is more profound than I would have thought. Without it, though, I doubt he'd have had the knowledge to understand the magical workings of your clock tower. You mentioned he couldn't figure it out before?"

"No, he couldn't."

Kristof nodded, almost apologetically. "Because we used fey words and emotion in the spell, and possibly because of those parts of myself that we used, Frolic understands magic now."

The explanation ignited the bitter feelings Querry had been trying to douse since meeting Kristof. He couldn't help his envy. He didn't want the faerie gentleman as his partner or permanent companion, but the idea that he preferred Kristof, found Kristof worthier and more interesting, burned at the edges of Querry's ego. Being the favorite of such a powerful person had defined his sense of worth more than he'd realized. But Kristof was not to blame. He was a humble and gentle sort, especially for a magician. Querry wondered if it hurt him to know his lover would never be exclusively his. "How is he doing?" Querry asked.

"Sleeping," Kristof said, shaking his head. "He's weak with the lack of magic already. I begged him to stay behind, but he's as stubborn as ever. I told him he wouldn't be able to help us, with that awful tower siphoning all the enchantment out of the world. He refused to leave me, though."

"Because he loves you," Querry said, trying to comfort the worried, young man.

"Believe me, I understand the magnitude of what he's done, choosing my company over his own comfort. It's contrary to his nature in every way. I just, I'm afraid for him. I—"

Querry put his arm around Kristof's shoulders and squeezed him. He tried to think of words that might assuage Kristof's concern, but he couldn't summon them when he felt just as afraid himself. "What the hell are we going to do?" he whispered.

"I don't know. I've never felt so helpless. We're still a day away from home, but I can already sense the effects Frolic described. By the time I set foot on my native shore, I'll be powerless."

"I still don't understand it," Querry said.

"From your friend's explanation, I assume that each of the guardians at the corners of the tower is designed to filter elemental magic: fire, air, earth, or water. When these powers are combined in the center of the structure, they'll form a limitless power, pure possibility. A person controlling that power could do almost anything he wanted: create or destroy. He'd be godlike."

"Frolic was meant to be that person," Querry said.

"Not quite," Kristof amended, "he was meant to be a tool by which another controlled that power. Only because his creator granted him free will could he resist. Luckily for all of us."

"What will we do?" Querry asked.

"As I see it, we have only one option: destroy the mechanisms atop the tower. It will be difficult enough if they haven't found a way to replace Frolic in directing the power, and if they have—" He shuddered. "I'm afraid I'm not going to be much help without my magic."

"We'll need weapons," Querry said. He wondered where they'd get what they needed now that Dink had left the country. "God help us, what we need is an army."

The two of them stood in silence, the weight of the situation crushing down on them. Before long they heard light steps approaching them. Frolic stopped a few feet away and greeted them. "I've been looking for you," Querry told him. "How come you're not in the bed with Reggie?"

Frolic looked haunted as he turned his face toward the first sliver of rose stretching across the horizon. "My dreams have been strange. I see and hear things that weren't there before. I understand things that I never even knew existed. It's unsettling to feel so unlike myself."

"I'm sorry," Kristof said. "If it's any consolation, some of the things I saw in the Other Places disturbed me, until I grew accustomed to them. I think you'll eventually get used to your new perceptions, Frolic."

Frolic nodded sadly and thanked him. Querry stroked the curls on the back of his head and felt Frolic press back against his hand. Querry cupped the back of his neck and drew him into his arms. Frolic rested his head against Querry's chest and said, "I *am* tired, Querry. Maybe we can try to get some rest. Hold me?"

"Of course." He kissed the top of Frolic's head. "Let's try to sleep for a few hours before morning. Kristof, will you be all right?"

The young wizard looked back toward the sea, his features guarded and unreadable. He tapped his pipe against the metal railing, emptying the ashes into the water. "I will be fine. I wish to stay here and think for a bit. Good night to you."

QUERRY, REG, and Kristof stood in line holding the false documents they'd procured before leaving the East. Querry resisted the urge to look over his shoulder and hoped none of the *Unicorn's* other passengers would ask the whereabouts of their other companions. They'd tried to keep to themselves during the long voyage, and they'd decided even before departing that there would be no way to get Frolic or the faerie gentleman past the heightened security in their home country. Querry was nervous. The fake papers were good, but he and Reg were wanted criminals and Kristof attracted attention in his outdated clothes.

Finally their turn came and the few minutes the guards took looking over their paperwork felt like hours. Querry felt himself starting to sweat as the portly, balding man looked from his documents to his face and back again.

"You all right, mate?" he asked, furrowing his brows.

"Seasick," Querry said quickly.

"Right, well, on your way."

Querry struggled not to sigh with relief.

"Wait," Kristof said. "Where do we pick up our cargo?"

"Cargo?" the guard asked suspiciously. "What kind of cargo?"

Querry froze. They hadn't planned how they'd answer that question. Kristof was clever and quick, though. "I purchased a set of antique leather chairs for my study. The workmanship is quite exquisite. If you have a crowbar, we can open the crates and admire them."

The guard, clearly bored, said, "No time for that. Off you go. You can pick up your things right over there." He pointed to a gangplank stretching from a barge to a gravel circle where several horse-drawn carts and taxis, as well as a few steam carriages, waited to be hired by travelers. A few crewmen hauled two wooden boxes that looked just the right size to hold leather armchairs. Kristof hurried over and directed them to be loaded onto a flatbed cart pulled by a shaggy, gray gelding. He climbed in beside and pressed his cheek to one of the boxes, stroking it with his hand.

Querry cleared his throat. "I know those chairs mean a lot to you, but everything will be all right. Let's not cause a stir." He climbed into the cart beside Kristof and sat down in the straw. Reg took a seat next to the driver and handed him some money. The driver slapped the reins against the animal's haunches, and the old beast grunted before starting slowly on his way. A long procession of carriages slowed their progress and caused them lengthy and frequent pauses. Querry longed to escape the crowds and scrutiny, and he wondered where Reg thought they might be safe. Finally the pony broke into a slow trot. Querry allowed himself the relieved breath he'd been holding. The thick snow that had been pushed to the sides of the streets had started to melt, and icicles dripped from the eaves. Querry smelled new grass forcing its way up through the piles of garbage and horse manure that littered the walks. He saw a few snowdrops blooming between the tree trunks and the fences that surrounded them. It surprised Querry not to see more people out strolling or visiting the shops and booths. Normally after such a brutal winter, every person in the city made his or her way outdoors as soon as the temperature reached above freezing. The streets should have been crowded and the air heavy with the new hope that spring always inspired. The few people Querry saw walked with their heads down, their eyes darting from side to side as they hurried to their destinations. The thief had seen enough fear and anxiety to recognize it, and he wondered as to the cause. Even so, Querry relaxed a little and smiled at Kristof. "It's going to be fine," he told the harried-looking wizard.

"Where are we going?" Kristof said. "When will we be there? Soon?"

"I'm sure it won't be long."

"Does this not seem odd to you?" the magician continued, looking at the empty walks.

"A bit," Querry admitted. "But please don't worry yourself."

"How can I not? Imagine yourself stripped of your sword and pistol, without even your fists to protect the ones you love. I cannot remember ever being without this power; it has been my companion since childhood. Never could I have imagined anything to rival magic, let alone a machine! Can you understand how this feels to me?"

"I won't let anything happen to you," Querry promised, and, looking at the crates, added, "any of us."

"Thank you. I just wish I knew where we were going. This does not feel at all like the country I left behind."

"No, it doesn't," Querry agreed. "But we're going to put it right."

The pony stopped at an intersection and waited while some pedestrians crossed the street. A blond young man pushed his way past the skittish stragglers and, to Querry's surprise, jumped onto the cart and sat down beside Reg. It took a few minutes for Querry to recognize Lizard, as the boy had grown several inches in the months he'd been away. Lizard looked seriously at Reg and leaned in to whisper in his ear. Reg nodded gravely, spoke to the driver, and handed the man more money. The cart made a sharp left, shifting Querry, Kristof, and the two crates to the side. Querry crawled around the wooden boxes and tapped Reg on the shoulder. "What's going on?"

"Lizard says the city is in trouble," Reg explained. "He says there are people who will want to speak with us. That we'll be safe there."

"We need your help, mate," the boy said. "At least hear us out."

"I thought you were leaving with Dink!"

"Things happened," Lizard said. "I'll explain more in a bit. Ain't safe to talk out here."

"Why?"

The young man looked about nervously, curled his shoulders forward and pulled his hat down over his eyes, inviting no further questioning. "Just wait, and hear what we have to say."

"We didn't have any better idea anyway," Querry conceded. He shared the news with Kristof, who looked impatiently at the crates. The elderly pony slowly ascended a hillock, and the litter grew sparser and homes and grounds larger and finer. The two of them settled back in for a quarter-of-an-hour ride to a quiet, residential neighborhood. They stopped in front of a three-story, brick building surrounded by an iron fence and old trees covered in ivy. Querry and Reg unloaded the crates while Lizard went to the front door and spoke to someone when it opened the tiniest crack. He looked over his shoulder and motioned to the others.

"Inside," the boy said. "Hurry."

"Not without—" Kristof began.

Querry put a hand on his shoulder to calm him. "I say, Lizard, can you find us a hammer or a crowbar?"

Lizard went inside and returned with an iron bar. Querry pried the first carton open and Kristof hurried to help the faerie gentleman out, embracing him and whispering to him in fey. He brushed away the sawdust that clung to the faerie's fine clothes. Querry freed Frolic and took his weapons back from his companion, who'd been keeping them safe in his hiding place. It felt good to have his gun and sword back by his side. He handed Reg his pistols, and the five of them followed Lizard inside and through the house to an expansive cellar. Some oil lamps set on the mismatched tables lit the faces of about forty men and women, many of them foreigners from Rajallah and Xiana. Querry noticed right away that all of them were well armed, and that their hands went to their weapons as they eyed the newcomers suspiciously. If he'd sensed nervousness on the city streets, in here, Querry felt outright panic and paranoia.

"Stop right there," said an older man with thick muttonchops. He wore pieced-together bits of military and naval uniforms and had a rifle strapped to his back. "We were told to expect three men."

From the darkened corner of the basement, another man spoke. Querry smiled when he recognized the accent. "These men can be trusted. They saved me from the clock tower and recovered the book about its operation. They are the kind of fighters we need." Dink made his way to where they stood and patted Querry on the shoulder. "Hello, mein old friend. We are very glad to have you back."

"Glad to be back," Querry said, embracing Dink.

The smile dropped from Dink's face when he saw Kristof and the faerie gentleman standing behind Reg. He broke away from Querry and pointed. "How could you bring him here?"

Kristof stepped in front of his companion protectively. "Just what's going on?" he asked. "Who are all of you?"

"Concerned citizens," the man with the rifle said. "We need all the help we can get, but we don't need help from the likes of him." He pointed at the faerie.

"Kristof, let's go," the gentleman said weakly. "We certainly don't need anything from these ignorant peasants."

His statement drew angry retorts from the people assembled. Some of them stood up, and Kristof reached inside his cloak. Querry's hand went to the hilt of his sword before he knew what he was doing. He stepped backward and stood beside Kristof. "We don't want any trouble," he said in warning.

"You got trouble," said a portly woman with a rolling pin in her hand. "You're a traitor. Faerie lovers! You come to the wrong place!" Most of the room agreed with her enthusiastically.

"I wouldn't," Kristof said, his voice low and threatening in a way Querry would never have thought it capable. Frolic balled his fists and took his place behind Querry's right shoulder. Even Reg, despite his animosity toward the faerie, brought his hands to the pistols on his hips. A few more people stood up and produced weapons of their own.

"Wait!" Lizard said. "I told them they'd be safe here! They came to help!"

The crowd grumbled angrily. Querry could pick out just a few curses and slurs. It would be a fight after all, and a hard one.

"All of us need to settle down," Dink said above the din. Eventually everyone sat down, muttering to themselves. "If Querry trusts this- this man, then so will I. If you trust me, value me as one of you, then I beg you to give them a chance. They are the hope we have prayed for these past months. If we have any chance of saving this land, then we must work together."

"Is that it?" a young man asked, coming closer to inspect Frolic. "Is that the clockwork that can control the tower?"

"His name is Frolic," Reg snapped. Once again the people in the room began talking in excited and nervous whispers. "Enough," Reg finally shouted. "Tell us exactly what is going on here or we're leaving."

Dink showed them to a wooden bench beside the wall and all of them sat, except the faerie gentleman, who stood sneering with his arms crossed. Chair legs screeched against stone as the people assembled gave him a wide berth. "Many of us have noticed a change in the city over the past few months," Dink explained. "The people have fallen into despair. They have no joy in their lives. They're confused and afraid. I can't say what is happening, but somehow he is sucking all of the life out of this place."

"Who?" Querry asked. "Thimbleroy?"

"Fools," the faerie said with a sardonic chuckle. "You're missing the magic you claim to despise so much."

"It is not just that," Dink continued. "He has taken control of the tower and is using its power to destroy anyone who stands in his way. He's purchased several factories and is building those horrible clockwork men by the dozens. We have sabotaged them several times, but they are repaired again in days. Some of the stories I have heard— the stuff of nightmares!"

"How?" Querry dared.

"The way the clockworks are built, I have heard, is from things beside metal and gears. Living things, some say. We are among those citizens who know he must be stopped."

"So he's managed to harness the power," Kristof said, shaking his head. "And now he's using the knowledge to build an army."

"Who's in charge here?" Querry asked.

"I am," said a female voice. The woman, her face hidden by a hood like Kristof's, stood up and approached the bench. "I was one of the first people he came after. My home was destroyed, and most of my staff and family killed. I only live because that monster thinks I perished."

"And who are you?" Querry asked.

"Elaina, Duchess of Lisine."

"My Lady," Reg said, reaching for her hand. She pulled away before he could take it.

"What exactly happened?" Kristof asked. "What sort of magic did he use to attack you?"

With a trembling hand, she pushed her hood back. Querry and the others gasped. The entire left side of her face had been burned. The skin had healed in ghastly bumps and whorls. Missing flesh revealed her teeth, gums, and the entire orb of her eye. The hair on that side was gone, and on the opposite side it hung in white tangles. A stunted antler, like a young deer's, protruded from her forehead. She opened her cloak and stretched out what had once been her left arm. It had been shortened by half, and ended in two long, black claws. A spine extended from her elbow and loose skin hung down in a horrifying suggestion of a wing. "At first I thought it was a storm. I saw flashes of light outside my bedroom window, heard the wind battering the house. Then the roof above me was torn away. Streaks of energy circled me, and strange things began to happen: plants growing from the walls, the furniture moving about as if alive. When that energy hit my body—" She pointed to her horrible deformities and looked away from the men.

"May I?" Kristof asked gently and stood. He carefully examined the duchess's condition and then looked meaningfully at the gentleman. "He has no control over the magic. He can gather it and fling it about, but he has no means of directing or shaping it. This is evidence of magic gone haywire."

"You're a wizard?" the duchess asked, clutching Kristof's lapel. "Can you put me back the way I was?"

"I don't know," he said sadly. "Unfortunately, I'm unable to even try until we can stop this man from draining all of the magic away and using it to do things like this."

"I could do it," Frolic said softly. "I could tell the angels to put you right. I could tell them to create beautiful things. We could make a paradise of this city." He looked at Dink. "As lovely and peaceful and perfect as your menagerie."

"Ah, *kinder*...," the old man said.

"Have you gone to the queen?" Reg asked the duchess. "She's always valued you as an advisor. What about the rest of the nobility? Certainly Thimbleroy is powerful, but he couldn't possibly stand against all of them."

"The nobility are of three minds," the duchess explained. "I am ashamed to say that most of them have cast their lots on Thimbleroy's side. They are cowards, too afraid to be his enemies if he should prevail. He's succeeded in eliminating our kingdom's greatest threat. Who could possibly defeat him as Grande Chancellor? The rest are even worse: doing nothing until they know for sure who will triumph. A few are standing with us, though not publicly."

"I regret to inform that no one here is addressing the larger issue," said a man with a slight accent. He pushed his way through the throng to stand beside the duchess. Querry's breath caught in his throat when he recognized the strawberry-blond hair and pale eyes.

"You—" the thief sputtered, pointing.

"I'm afraid so," the man said, removing his hat and pressing it to his chest in a theatrical bow. "As I was saying, I fear all of the fine ladies and gentlemen assembled here are missing the larger picture."

"Such as?" Querry asked. "But wait. Who *are* you exactly?"

With a smile and a wink, the man bowed again. "Jean-Andre," he said, offering Querry his hand.

"Jean-Andre what?"

"Jean-Andre will have to do for now, Mr. Knotte."

"You've been following me," Querry said, ignoring the Belvaisian's hand. "Why?"

Jean-Andre sighed dramatically. "I was trying to keep you alive, sir. Not that you made it the least bit easy."

"Why?"

"Because you possess the knowledge to operate the clock tower. That knowledge is very valuable, to many, many people."

"Like who?"

"Who wouldn't want the ultimate weapon? Who wouldn't pay for it? Your Lord Thimbleroy knew its value. From the time he understood even the most rudimentary functions of that tower, he began taking offers from foreign sovereigns and wealthy mercenaries alike."

"He planned to sell the knowledge?" Reg gasped.

Jean-Andre nodded. "During my time posing as a representative of the Belvaisian government, I witnessed many bids upon this information, from over a dozen different buyers. Money, it seems, remains the great motivator."

"But, but that's treason!" Reg continued. "He should be arrested! Do you have proof of this?"

"But of course," Jean-Andre said.

"Just who are you working for?" Querry demanded.

"I am currently in the employ of your fair duchess," Jean-Andre said. "She hired me to keep her informed of your Lord Thimbleroy's activities. As I have been trying to tell you all along, the issue we face with the current clock tower is only the smallest sliver of the problem. Your Grande Chancellor sold plans to duplicate both the clockwork and the magic to at least a dozen different people. Before long, there will be another twenty towers here on your own soil, as well as those that are constructed in foreign lands. One man, and one tower, and one clockwork army we might defeat, but the knowledge of their construction will spread. I cannot imagine how many nations will have standing clockwork armies in the next decade."

Dink shook his head and chuckled. "They will only get so far, for they cannot copy our Frolic, *nein*?"

"Well, not yet," Jean-Andre said.

"I don't understand what the problem is here," the gentleman said, irritated. "Why doesn't someone go to this tower, find this inept usurper and kill him? Querrilous, you must do it. Kill this man and bring me back his heart and his eyes so that I can crush them under my boot heel. As soon as you do, I'll raze that silly tower to ash and scatter it on the wind. And anyone who's aided in this blasphemy shall—"

"Destroy the angels?" Frolic gasped. "No!"

"I agree with him," Querry said. "I'll kill Thimbleroy. I'll need weapons. Dink? I'll need a way to reach the top of the tower and—"

"I am sorry to say that the government confiscated mein beautiful airship," Dink lamented. "I can help you with the rest, though."

"You're going to need a lot more than weapons, mate," said the man with the rifle, whom the others called Captain Saul. "Nobody can get anywhere near that place, on account of the storms."

"Storms?"

"Aye, it storms almost constantly for a half a mile around that tower. Buildings have been destroyed and anybody who stays too long in the area, well—"

"They're likely to end up like me," the duchess said. "If not worse. Even those who escape physical injury are driven completely mad."

"Most people cannot handle magical energy," Kristof agreed. "I can scarcely imagine the impact it's had on this Thimbleroy himself. He must be 'round the bend by now."

"Aye," said a Rajallah woman with a red scarf over her hair. "You wouldn't believe the things he's done! To others and even to himself."

"The statues around the tower move on their own sometimes," another man said. "They're twisted, awful things now."

Frolic, who'd been looking at his shoes with his elbows on his knees, lifted his head and said, "The magic is overflowing. The angels are drawing it in as they're supposed to, but there isn't anyone to tell them how or what to shape it into, so it's just boiling up. Doing whatever it wants."

"Uncontrolled magic is the most dangerous," Kristof offered. "But it's also magic. I may be able to do something with it if I can get close enough."

"We're going to need a solid plan," Reg said. "And a lot of luck."

"I can get you the equipment you'll need," Dink offered. "Lizard and I have been working hard to supply these good people. We have quite a store built up, and I've invented some useful new things." His thick moustache fell with his face. "I hope one day I'll not need to make weapons any longer. I long for a day when ingenuity and industry can be used for beauty instead of slaughter."

Querry doubted such a day would ever arrive, but he had no time for philosophy. "Let's sit down and share what we know," he suggested. The duchess, Jean-Andre, and Captain Saul found chairs, and some of the other people, presumably the leaders, formed a circle around the bench. "Frolic has told us that the top of the tower can detach," Querry said.

An older woman nodded. "True," she said, biting on the stem of a pipe. "I don't know how he fuels it, but it can fly."

"The magic," Frolic explained.

"Magic as fuel," Kristof mused.

"Kristof," Reg said, "how long would a person be able to survive inside that magical storm without being changed?"

The wizard considered. "Given the high concentration of power and the chaotic nature of it, I'd say not more than a few hours. Maybe less. It's impossible to say what the magic would do or how long it would take."

"Then we must lure him away," Reggie concluded. "We must find a way to force him to fly away from the tower. We could lay a trap for him: create a distraction and draw him into a place where he'll be confined."

Saul nodded, looking at Reg with surprised respect. "And then what?"

"Well, he's still a mortal man. He should die like one."

"He won't come alone," the duchess said. "He'll have human guards as well as those ghastly clockwork ones he's been building. And he'll have the power. It's more devastating than I can impart to you. The trees, the ground, the buildings and even the sky will be altered when he uses it."

"All the more reason for stealth," Reg said. "What we need is a place where men can remain hidden until the last possible moment. Then one of us can take the shot."

"I know the place," Querry said. "His home. If we attack Thimbleroy Manor, he'll be sure to hurry to its defense. He's building the clockwork soldiers in his basement. I've seen them. And there's a large cathedral right across the street. It has a tower of its own where we can station men. I'd say we could hide at least a dozen of our best marksman up there."

"And what about the rest of us?" asked a freckled young man with an overbite. "What happens to those of us on the ground? The guards will rip us to pieces!"

"Maybe we won't need men on the ground to attack," Querry said. "What about an explosion? Is there any way we could get access to powder, or to dynamite?"

"Only if we break into the plant that makes the stuff," someone muttered incredulously.

Querry laughed. "Is that all? Well, I'll get the dynamite!"

"With a lengthened fuse we can detonate it from a distance," Dink offered.

"Then I volunteer to do that too," Querry said quickly. "Reg, I think you should be up on the cathedral tower. You're a fantastic shot."

Reg looked pleased and nodded. "I'll knock his monocle off!"

"I'll hide in the church," Kristof offered. "As soon as I sense magic, I'll try to put a shield up around anyone on the ground. Possibly I can negate some of the tower's effects as well, but I can't make any promises."

"I'll come and watch out for you," the fey said, "though not inside the *church*. We'll have to find another place to take shelter. I have much desire to spend a few moments with this man before he dies." Kristof looked dark, but he reached up and stroked the outside of the faerie's arm.

"There is still the power," the duchess said. "Even a small burst could dash this entire plan to nothing."

259

They all sat in silence, their optimism evaporated. Finally Dink said, "I may be able to replicate some of the tower's magic-absorbing ability. I learned more than Thimbleroy knows during my time in captivity there. Probably not enough, unless I had some help. Frolic understands the workings of the mechanisms better than any of us, and we finally have a wizard as an ally. The three of us might be able to come up with something, build a sort of magical lightning rod of our own." He looked expectantly at his two would-be assistants.

Kristof rubbed his smooth chin. "There are certain elements that attract enchantment," he said tentatively, "though I know nothing of clockwork."

"I do," Frolic said so quietly that only those closest to him heard.

"I was hoping to take Frolic with me to the munitions factory," Querry said. "Though this seems a bit more pressing. I don't suppose there's another experienced thief in our company?"

Lizard cleared this throat and raised his brows when Querry looked at him. Querry slapped his thigh, chuckled, and said, "I thought maybe. The two of us should be able to manage just fine. We'll go in between shifts, and we shouldn't need much. It's just a diversion, after all."

"Thanks, mate," the boy said with a bright smile. "I'll enjoy a few pointers from the best."

Querry laughed, oddly satisfied. "We'll start tomorrow morning. First we'll need to observe, find out where they store the stuff and if it's guarded."

"We will also start in the morning," Kristof said.

"It will take us at least a few days," Frolic said. "We can't hope to make anything as sophisticated as the angels, but I already have some ideas."

"Nothing left tonight but to get some rest then," Reggie said, stretching his arms above his head. "Do any of you know of a safe place where we could stay? I think it's in all of our best interests if the authorities remain unaware of our return."

"You can spend the night here," the duchess offered. "We have little space, but this location hasn't been compromised and I have my people watching and patrolling the area. I can offer you a small room in the former servants' quarters in the attic."

"Unacceptable!" the faerie gentleman said. "I'll not sleep on a cot reeking of filthy human scullery maids, old onions, and shoe polish!"

Kristof looked up at him and said a pleading word, and the sharp, defensive angle of his shoulders softened a little. The wizard grasped the faerie's hand and stroked it with his thumb. "Beloved, you do too much for my sake. I wish you'd stayed where you could be safe and provided for in the manner that you deserve."

"I shall be satisfied to sleep next to you," the faerie said with more gentleness than Querry had ever heard him express. "However, I will add this slight to my growing list of offenses this city and its people have committed against me. They try even my good and merciful nature." His eyes narrowed as he looked around the room. Every man and woman dropped his or her gaze from his vengeful face.

"Thank you," Kristof said. All of them stood up and followed their hostess toward the tiny cell on the fourth floor.

Jean-Andre stopped Querry with a hand on his elbow. "Might I have a word?"

Querry, his mind full of questions, nodded once as the rest of his party ascended the stairs out of the cellar. The two men stood quietly, waiting until they were alone.

"You are quite the thief," Jean-Andre said, folding his arms across his chest and leaning back against the stone wall. "I was quite impressed with your skills."

"What do you want me to say?"

"I want you to say nothing until you've heard me out. And then, hopefully, you will agree to what I propose."

"Go on."

"As I said, you are good at what you do. You fail, however, to see the bigger picture. Coins and jewelry hold value only so long. In our world, sir, the most valuable commodity is information. Information such as the book in your possession. I wonder if you have any idea what that book is worth? No, of course you don't. But I do. I also have the connections necessary to find you the highest bidder. For a modest share of the profits, of course."

"Not interested," Querry said. "That book belongs to Frolic."

"The sale of it could provide for him the rest of his life. I'm not talking about dealing with back-alley fences, Mr. Knotte. The people who would be interested in that book would be willing and able to provide you with lands, properties, money beyond your wildest dreams. And that brings me to my second proposition."

"I doubt I'm going to like this, but go on."

"I would like to offer you a business partnership."

"What exactly is it that you do?" Querry asked.

The other man considered. "I make friends with wealthy and important people. I listen and learn useful things. Then I decide who else might want to know these useful things. And who will pay me to know them."

"Does the duchess know about all of this?"

"I'm sure she suspects," Jean-Andre said, waving the matter away with a flick of his fingers. "She's not a fool. I am in her employ at the moment, but without the stipulation that I can't keep any knowledge I glean from this situation for future use. The knowledge of either magic or industry, possibly both, will determine the course of the future, Mr. Knotte. He who controls that knowledge will control the world. We have turned an important corner in our history. One way or another, clockwork automatons will be produced. I'm offering you a chance to work with me and be a—I don't know—a guardian after a fashion, of that knowledge."

"By doing what, exactly?"

"By learning how to dress properly and speak well. Your ability to avoid detection will be quite helpful, as sometimes the useful knowledge I seek is not freely offered. You are also very beautiful," the Belvaisian said, lowering his head and looking up at Querry through his peach-colored lashes. "I have been told I'm not altogether hideous myself, and let me assure you, that beauty can open many doors for you. I can teach you how."

Sweat ran down Querry's spine as he noticed how hot the cellar had become. He noticed the loose waves in Jean-Andre's hair. The other man stood so close that Querry could smell his expensive cologne, could practically count the freckles that peppered his nose. He took a large step backward and said, "I- I don't know about this. What about Reggie and Frolic?"

"What about them?"

"I have to think," Querry said, mopping his moist brow with his shirtsleeve. "I have to go, or the others will wonder what's kept me."

Jean-Andre laughed. "You see, you knew without me saying a word to keep this between the two of us! You're a natural."

Querry turned away and hurried up the stairs to the servants' quarters. There was scarcely room for the three narrow beds contained within, and the slope of the ceiling prevented them from standing upright. Reg had lit the oil lantern on the night table and sat down to clean his guns. Kristof took the bed opposite him and held out his hand to his partner. The faerie, though he grumbled incessantly about the conditions, nestled between Kristof's parted legs with his head on the magician's chest. Kristof stroked his hair, and in mere moments he fell asleep. Frolic looked from the pair to Reg, as if trying to decide where he belonged. He gave up on sorting his memories and pulled a three-legged stool to the tiny window. With a deep sigh he sat down with his back to all of them and brushed the plain curtain aside. It wounded Querry to see him hurting and confused, and Querry wondered what he might have done differently. Maybe he really was too impetuous sometimes. Somehow he knew not to rub Frolic's back but to leave him alone. He stretched out on the third bed and folded his arms beneath his head. The guilt he felt over his clandestine meeting with Jean-Andre didn't help him to relax, either. After thinking over his plan for half an hour, he removed his armored vest, gloves, boots and weapons and got under the coarse sheet. He heard Reg doing the same and let his eyes close. He'd been resting for some time and was almost unconscious when Frolic lifted the bedclothes and curled up beside him. Querry rolled over to embrace him and kiss his forehead before surrendering to a much-needed sleep.

CHAPTER 21

THE THREE days Querry and the others took to make their preparations passed in the blink of an eye. Querry found little time to consider Jean-Andre's words, and since he didn't see the man again, he put them to the back of his mind. The temperature rose enough that the five men sat in the small room on the fourth floor with the window wide open. The evening air was warm as tears, and an aroma of fresh green and rising sap drifted on the wind. All of them perched on the edges of the beds, looking at one another. Finally, to break the tension, Querry said, "Here we are, then. Tomorrow morning this all ends, one way or the other."

"We're as ready as we can possibly be," Reg assured him. "It's a good plan, and it's going to work."

Querry nodded, smiled at him, and tried to believe his words. True, they'd done everything to make their scheme work flawlessly, but Querry knew from experience how many things could still go wrong. He looked at the four men: his beloved Reg with his reserved exterior hiding burning passion and brilliant bravery; his sweet Frolic with his innocence and enthusiasm buried beneath disorder and doubt; the faerie who played at being a gentleman but was more a force of nature; and the great magician, Kristof, who had the demeanor of the most unassuming servant. Querry loved all of them more than he ever had, and he decided then and there that he'd die before he saw them come to harm. He memorized the details of each of their faces, hands, and bodies, right down to their eyelashes and fingernails. Each of them was so perfect in his own way. He'd been lucky to know them for the time that he had.

"Querry, what's wrong?" Frolic asked, wiping a tear from Querry's cheek that Querry hadn't felt escape.

"All of you mean so much to me," he said. "I just wish you'd all find someplace safe, and wait until this is over."

"We're in this together," Reg said, taking Querry's hand. Frolic took his other hand, forced a confident smile, and nodded. Kristof reached across to cup Querry's knee. The faerie looked a little bewildered by the exchange, but he finally patted Reg icily on the shoulder.

"We should try to get some sleep," Kristof urged, "we have an early start, and we're in for quite a day tomorrow." From the way he gazed at his companion, Querry knew Kristof felt the same thing he did—that he'd like a night with his lover, just in case it was the last.

Instead, though, Querry, Reg, and Frolic pushed two of the beds together, while Kristof and his fey lover lay face to face in the third. Reg put out the light, and Querry heard the magician and the faerie whispering in their secret language. He heard their lips meeting, their hands in each other's hair. From their breathing, he knew neither Reg nor Frolic slept. He doubted he'd get any rest either, but all of them lay in silence, their worries and regrets left unspoken.

At some point, Querry fell into a fitful sleep, because the next thing he perceived was a muffled knocking. He opened his eyes and took a second to recognize his surroundings. A weak, gray light seeped through the curtains. Frolic already stood dressed and armed at the foot of the bed, and Kristof sat cross-legged with his partner's head in his lap. Querry's left arm tingled, numbed beneath Reg's weight. While it gave him a curious comfort, he gently pulled it from beneath the other man's ribs and whispered, "Reggie, it's time." He looked a long time into Reg's hazel eyes when they opened.

Lizard came into the room and informed them that everyone would meet downstairs. After washing up a bit and dressing, the five men made their way to the dining room where they found almost a hundred people packed in. They parted to allow Querry and his companions to approach a large, rectangular table where Dink, the duchess, and a few more important men and women waited. Querry,

Reg, Frolic, and Kristof took seats, and the faerie stood with his hands on the back of Kristof's chair. Querry reached for the kettle and helped himself to strong tea while Dink passed him a diagram. He pointed out the various places around Thimbleroy Manor where fighters would take position on the ground, as well as the bell tower where the marksman would hide. He showed Querry where he and Kristof would set up the device they'd built to gather stray magic, and where Querry would need to place the three sticks of dynamite he'd acquired with Lizard. Dink handed Querry a canvas sack and Querry took out the wires and devices within. Though he'd done so before, Dink explained again to Querry how he'd need to set them up.

"Does everyone understand what he needs to do?" asked Captain Saul. Everyone grumbled in assent. "We're only going to have one chance at this." He stood and pushed his chair in. "Riflemen, with me. We're going to spread out our arrival times to the area so we don't arouse any suspicion. Let's go. The church Father is expecting us." Six men and four women queued up behind him.

"I guess that's me as well," Reg said, squeezing Querry's knee underneath the table. He told Querry he loved him in the only acceptable way: with his eyes. Querry hoped Reg knew he felt the same, since he couldn't say it out loud. "I'll see you soon, Querry. Frolic."

There were so many things Querry wanted to say, but he only managed to croak out, "Yeah." Then Reggie was gone, and the heavily armed men and women who'd volunteered to stay on the ground departed next. After a few more silent cups of tea, Dink stood.

"I have the device waiting in a cart a few blocks away. We must go now while most of the city still sleeps." Kristof reluctantly joined him. Querry felt his heart plummet another half a mile when Frolic left the table. It was all he could do not to grab his arm and stop him. It wasn't right; they belonged together. How had he not seen it before?

"Wait," he said, getting to his feet. "Frolic—"

"Querry?" He looked at the thief with his bemused smile, the one he'd always worn before they'd replaced his heart.

Querry pulled him into his arms and squeezed him tightly, holding him for a long time despite the whispers in the room. He dug his chin into the curls on top of Frolic's head and blinked back his tears. Then he put his palms against Frolic's cheeks and pulled his head back so he could look into his glorious, golden eyes. "Frolic, I—" The people around them stared in dumb shock. Querry cleared his throat. "I want you to be careful, Frolic."

Frolic's lips curled with a wise, world-weary smile that contrasted with the sadness in his eyes. "I understand, Querry," he said.

Querry hoped he did.

Before long, Querry was alone in the room, alone in the house. He was to wait an hour in order to give everyone time to get into position. He stared down at his gloved hands, inspecting the places where the leather had worn thin above his knuckles. He open and closed his fists, remembering everything he'd done in that old pair of gloves. Outside, a single dove cooed from the branches of the dogwood tree near the window. The sound cut through Querry. He'd never felt more lost, not even when he'd been imprisoned and tortured. Again and again he told himself that splitting up had been a mistake. *We belong together. Why didn't I insist? I'm not there to protect them now.* Maybe it was his new faerie sight, or maybe just nerves, but Querry had an evil feeling about their undertaking.

Even so, people depended on him. He owed a debt, and he would pay it. He picked up the satchel and started off just as steady thunder began to rumble in the distance.

AN UNBROKEN sheet of dark clouds held the dawn at bay as Querry looked at Thimbleroy Manor, still a block away. He'd taken his time reaching it, both to stay out of sight and to avoid jostling the explosives. He approached slowly, his every nerve acute and aware of the slightest sound or movement. Soon, he discerned that six groups of two men each patrolled the perimeter. Querry crept closer and knelt down behind a manicured hedge. A pair of guards passed only a dozen feet in front of him. About ten minutes later, another pair made their rounds, with a third following another ten minutes after that. The regular interval of their patrol made it easier for Querry, and ten minutes would be more than enough time for him to climb the ornamental iron fence and sprint across the lawn to the elaborate gazebo that was his target. The dynamite he carried would decimate the large structure, set its remains on fire, then blast the neoclassical statuary and fountains around it to bits with minimal risk of injuring any innocent servants.

The next pair of guards strolled leisurely through the damp grass, passing a cigarette back and forth and debating the merits of the manor's serving girls. Querry let them get about twelve feet from where he stood before he vaulted over the fence and landed silently on the other side. Keeping low, he hurried to the gazebo. It was ten times the size of the room he'd rented, and fresh lilacs decorated the round tables within. Shaking his head at the excess, Querry planted the dynamite under a chair and tied the fuses together as Dink had instructed. To these he attached a cotton cord so that he could light the explosives from a safe distance. They'd soaked it in kerosene so the flame could travel quickly. He hid beneath a tablecloth until the next patrol passed by, and then he began to unroll the spool of cord as he backed toward the fence. He made it over well before the next round of guards entered the area and, trailing the rope behind him, he crossed the street to the cathedral.

Querry took a deep breath. The first phase of the plan had fallen into place beautifully. Maybe he'd just been paranoid and morose before. He looked up at the bell tower. Reg and the others would be there, waiting to fire. The knowledge of their presence let him relax a bit, and he hurried around the side of the old building. He saw Dink, Frolic, Kristof, and the faerie waiting within a sprawling cemetery. An ornate mausoleum concealed a clockwork device on a wheeled platform. Querry's eyes followed the crank to a pyramid of interlocking gears, and up to four curved, metal arms that formed a bowl-shaped enclosure. Here and there a gem sparkled among the dull steel, and odd symbols and runes were scratched into the frame. He didn't really understand the machine; he just hoped it would work.

"The dynamite is ready to go," Querry informed the others, severing the end of the cord from the spool with his dagger.

"Hurry and light it," Kristof urged as he knelt and began to wind the crank on the device. "There's no time to lose."

Querry fished in his pockets for his matches as the gears began to click and hum. A crackling, metallic-blue ball took shape between the tines of the metal arms. The faerie gentleman inhaled it like he'd been denied breath to the point of suffocation. Querry lit the end of the rope and dropped it on the ground, watching with satisfaction as a tiny flame skipped along its length. If everything went according to plan, the ensuing explosion would lure Thimbleroy away from the clock tower and the marksmen would finish him before he ever rounded the cathedral's corner. A peel of thunder broke his concentration, and a light rain began to fall. Luckily the flammable liquid they'd used kept the fuse burning. They all watched with held breath as the fire disappeared behind one of the church's buttressed walls.

The rain fell harder, soaking through Querry's armored garments and dampening his shirt. A drizzle became a downpour. The five men huddled together as it drenched them. A quarter of an hour passed and not one of them would give voice to his worry. Finally Querry said, "It should have gone off by now. It's gone out, hasn't it?"

Dink nodded twice, and Frolic looked miserable. "What are we going to do now?" the young man asked, his silver curls dripping.

"There's nothing for it," Querry said. "I'm going to have to go back and light it off by hand."

"Isn't there another way?" Frolic asked, touching Querry's gloved hand.

"I'm afraid not, beauty."

"Once it's lit, you must get away quickly," Dink warned.

"Be careful, Querrilous," Kristof said.

Querry smiled at him and sprinted back across the street. Instead of dealing with the fence again, he ran for the manor's main entrance and took cover behind a jutting chimney. He crept slowly toward the grounds around back, hoping the sudden storm had driven the guards to seek shelter. Soon he saw the gazebo. A silver mist surrounded it as water droplets bounced off of the roof. Querry looked left and right and, seeing no one, dashed for the structure. He found the explosives he'd placed within and took a box of wooden matches from his coat. First one and then another fizzled and failed to light in the moist air. Querry swore to himself and grasped the finger of his glove between his teeth. A finger at a time, he tugged the wet leather off his hand. The third match lit, but Querry's shivering quickly extinguished the flame. "Damn," he said, striking another and willing his hand to be still. Shielding the burning match with his other hand, he touched it to the place where the three fuses converged. With a hiss and a pop they caught fire. Querry spared a few seconds to make sure it would hold, and then he turned, jumped the gazebo steps and ran hard across the lawn. He had no time to bother with stealth; Dink had been quite adamant that he wouldn't survive the explosion.

Slipping on the wet grass, Querry rounded the corner and pushed for the street and the cathedral across it. He'd nearly made it to the house's front entrance when two men stepped in front of him.

"What do you think you're doing here?" one of them asked.

Querry looked behind himself and made a decision. Dropping his shoulders, he pushed his way between the guards, knocking one to the ground. He feared the dynamite more than the remaining man, whose fumbling fingers struggled to load his single-shot rifle. He also knew he couldn't retreat to the church or he'd risk leading the guard to his friends, so Querry ran back the way he'd come. He didn't get far before a deafening boom tore open the quiet morning. It lifted Querry off of his feet and flung him forward. He landed hard on his chest, the breath knocked from his body and his ears ringing. Wood, stone, and earth showered him. Pieces of debris cut and bruised his body as he pulled himself forward with his elbows, his rattled mind desperately seeking shelter. An agonizing few minutes passed before he noticed a narrow alleyway between two stone houses. Forcing his body up, he staggered toward the blessed shadows and found himself in a little cobbled lane. Apparently the two houses' kitchens disposed of their waste here. Querry could smell bad food even over the acrid smoke drifting up the street. A mangy dog growled to defend his garbage heap. Querry sat down on the ground, holding his ribs.

Gradually the high-pitched whine in Querry's head lessened enough that he could hear the aftermath of the explosion. Thimbleroy's personal guards shouted to one another. Querry took stock of his condition and found that while his body was scraped up and sore, no major damage had been done and nothing was broken. On his hands and knees, he crawled to the corner and peered around. Most of the patrolmen ran toward the gazebo to investigate the commotion, but half a dozen more astute guards spread out to canvas the area and search for the culprit. They headed toward the alley where Querry hid, diligently checking every nook and cranny. Querry saw that a stone wall blocked the opposite end of the alley. He wouldn't be able to escape that way, and he couldn't risk running into the street. Aching, he didn't want to engage the armed men. He had nowhere to go but up.

Querry freed The Gripper from his belt and braced his back against the stone wall. He aimed for a stone ledge beneath a window on the third floor of the opposite house and fired. The barrel of the device kicked his shoulder like a mule, but the grapple held to the limestone. Querry tested the line and began climbing, using his feet to push himself up the wall as he pulled himself up the rope. The exertion exacerbated his minor injuries, but he soldiered on until he reached the sill. He released the metal claw in case he needed it again. On his left, the exposed blocks of the chimney formed a sort of staircase just wide enough for Querry's toes. He fastened the grapple to his belt and carefully stepped onto the first of the narrow stones. He got his balance, and his fingers found places to hold between the blocks of the wall. His entire body tensed as he slowly stepped up. One tiny slip and he'd fall backward into the street. Gradually he ascended, his calves trembling from standing on his tiptoes and his fingers stiffening up. Finally he reached the rain gutter and used it to hoist himself onto the slate roof. From there he could see what was happening in the streets below.

Thimbleroy's men, dozens of them, had discovered some of the duchess's fighters hiding around the area. The rebels fought valiantly, but quicker than Querry would have thought possible, reinforcements arrived: Royal Guards, city constables, mercenaries, and the lurching, clockwork soldiers Querry and Frolic had seen in the basement. They arrived at the manor from every direction and quickly outnumbered and surrounded the resistance. Thimbleroy himself had yet to appear. Before long the bodies of the brave men and women who stood against the mad tyrant littered the street. The metal claws of the mechanized army had a predictable result on soft flesh. Bullets bounced harmlessly off the steel shells. A few models had been built so large as to be able to trample the resistance fighters beneath their huge, heavy feet. Querry knew he had to help them if he could. He looked across the alley at the other house's roof and wondered if he could make the jump. He didn't think too long about it before trying.

Querry pushed off hard with his feet, propelling himself across the alley. He closed the distance, but his fingers couldn't get purchase on the slippery slate, and he slid down. At the last moment he got hold of the drain pipe and held to it for dear life. It buckled and bowed under his weight, but eventually held. Using every ounce of strength he still possessed, Querry pulled himself onto the roof and made his way across, his muscles screaming in protest. He could see Thimbleroy's fenced-in lawn just below him. He crouched down and took his pistol from his belt, but in the chaos he could barely isolate his allies from his enemies. Every time he got a guard within his sights, the man either moved or a group of rebels converged around him. He could do no damage to the steel monstrosities that lumbered up the street, exhaling steam, leaking grimy oil, and delivering death to anyone who stood in their way. Querry moved closer to the corner of the roof above the street and tried frantically to see the cathedral through the smoke and rain. He definitely detected movement in front and around the side. He had to get to Frolic and the others, had to defend them. Desperately he searched for a way to the ground that wouldn't leave him completely open.

He'd just resolved to jump when he heard a loud whir approaching. He looked back the way he'd come and saw a large disk atop a conical series of gears and propellers. As it came closer, he noticed the roof was missing; it must've opened up to allow the dais to detach. In the center stood the gold coffin that Querry remembered only too well, though its walls had been cut down and now reached only to the knees of the man standing in the center. Tendrils of sparkling mist snaked around him and moved to and from the angels at the corners by way of the metal vines. A dense ball of power hovered over the pilot's head. The disk moved fast, its propellers kicking up eddies of debris as it went. In no time it hovered only ten feet below Querry. He could see the few strands of black hair brushed across Thimbleroy's bald head. The Lord held a claw-like mechanism that looked vaguely familiar, using it to manipulate the exposed gears around him imperfectly. Querry held his breath. Thimbleroy had done the marksmen across the street a tremendous favor by removing the walls of the sarcophagus and leaving himself unguarded.

Before long, one of them took the shot. The bullet hit the device Thimbleroy held, and while it didn't knock it from his grasp it did drive it away from the controls. The disk tilted sharply, turned almost sideways, and nearly collided with the house on which Querry stood. The angels flapped their great, metal wings in an attempt to right the machine, and Thimbleroy got the long fingers of his claw back in among the gears. He'd only just straightened out the disk when another bullet struck his shoulder, drawing a spray of blood. This time the angels spread their wide wings until they touched tip to tip and formed a barrier around the aristocrat. As bullets pinged uselessly off their engraved feathers, Querry saw a fresh supply of troops moving down the street in formation. They'd already outnumbered the resistance, but now it would be a wholesale slaughter, and Querry could see no way to help. The sharpshooters tried their best, but none of them could penetrate the barrier. Querry wished he'd saved one of the sticks of dynamite, but since he hadn't, he aimed his clockwork pistol at Thimbleroy's balding crown. Hopefully he could make his way to the shelter of one of the dormers after he took the shot, because he'd be giving away his position.

Querry felt calm and alert as he prepared to squeeze the trigger. Soon it would all be over. He braced himself and prepared to fire, but the disk suddenly spun and he lost the shot. The red-robed angel extended his long arm choppily, displaying none of Frolic's grace, and pointed toward the cathedral tower. Magical energy pulsed through the conduits until his entire form glowed. Frantic, Querry fired on his hand, but the bullets bounced off the thick metal. He emptied his gun and before he could reload, the sentinel sent a burst of power straight for the top of the structure where Reg and the others hid. Instinctively Querry knew that a full blast of the magic would tear the top off the tower and kill everyone inside, but the sparkling beam bent at the last moment and curled around the edge of the church. Querry exhaled with relief; Dink's device was working. Even so, some residual magic struck the cathedral tower about halfway from the base to the summit. It buckled and pitched forward, the top part almost parallel with the ground. Querry saw three bodies plummet over the railing. At the bend where the magic struck, the gray stone bubbled and turned black and shiny like glass. The transformation slowly spread in every direction.

Querry tried to reload his gun, but a tremor shook the earth and the bullets fell from his hand. He dug in his pocket for more. In the meantime, the disk spun again and the ochre angel attacked. Again Dink's lightning rod caught the majority of the energy. The rest hit the worship hall nestled to the right of the tower. Great, black shards of glass-like material tore through the ground like the claws of an enormous beast through soft flesh. They splintered the church's rafters and decimated its stone walls. A confetti of colored glass flew in every direction. A short, fat clergyman ran screaming from the doomed building, and a black, stone spear broke through the cobblestone to impale him. He twitched a bit and then went still.

The disk rotated, the green-robed angel facing the cathedral. Clockwork troopers crushed the few remaining rebels, while guards easily picked off those that attempted to flee. Blood wet the street and the sharp, black bones continued to break through. Enchantment crept over the bell tower, causing it to darken and mutate. Querry knew if he didn't act soon everything would be lost. He gave up trying to load his pistol, moved to the edge of the roof, and jumped.

He landed lightly inside the ring of angels, behind the mad aristocrat. Querry quickly unsheathed his sword, ready to sink it into the base of Thimbleroy's skull. The Grande Chancellor turned toward the thief, and the horror Querry saw almost made him drop his weapon. The claw he'd assumed Thimbleroy held was in fact fused to his body, replacing his arm from the elbow down. A thick bolt held it to the bone of his upper arm. Sinew stretched in moist, red clumps down the metal, and dried blood stained the armature. Querry gagged when he saw Frolic's stolen heart within the aristocrat's open shirt. Wire and metal tubing disappeared into Thimbleroy's skin, holding it against his ribs.

A strong stench of decay wafted off the madman. Driving down his disgust, Querry lunged forward with his blade and shattered the enchanted glass. The red mist within dissipated in a burst of heat. Thimbleroy roared and moved his unnatural limb among the gears.

The red dragon lifted its feet clumsily as it approached the thief. It opened its mouth, bearing rows of ivory teeth like daggers. "Finish him," Thimbleroy ordered. "Burn him to a crisp."

Querry braced himself, but the flame never materialized. The crimson creature waited, flicking its tail from side to side. Querry laughed triumphantly and advanced on his adversary. "You damn fool," he yelled over the din of the battle below them, "you can't control them! You're a pretender!"

"Wait and see, scum," Thimbleroy snarled. "I've studied them all of my life." He adjusted the gears.

"Why?" Querry couldn't help asking.

"To protect this kingdom," Thimbleroy said. "To stop it being overrun by dissolute foreigners and filthy fey. To insure it keeps to the traditions that have made it great! To insure that its fate is decided by *men*."

"But you opened the gate to the faerie realm," Querry said, slicing at Thimbleroy's neck. The aristocrat's mechanical arm parried the blow, and he laughed maniacally.

"Ingenious, wasn't that? There's power enough in the magic here, but by siphoning it from their world I can make myself a god!"

"You're a sick son of a bitch," Querry said, feigning with his sword and then punching Thimbleroy in the face. Two of his teeth and a mouthful of blood flew from the corner of his mouth. "You sold the plans to our country's enemies for money! You're a bloody traitor!"

"You're street trash, Querrilous Knotte," he said, licking the blood from his lip. "You're the son of a whore and a criminal piece of garbage. I wouldn't expect you to understand. These things are far beyond your station. Much of what I've done has been to keep people like you in their proper place, and stop them from infringing on their betters. Really, the peasants are happier when the nobles make the decisions for them."

"I'll kill you," Querry shouted, enraged. He lunged for the aristocrat, but the clockwork stag lowered its head and rammed him. His armor prevented the horns from piercing his lungs, but the momentum knocked him over the side of the disk. Querry grabbed the rim at the last second and pulled himself back up. He'd lost his sword, but anger and outrage compelled him, and he prepared to attack Thimbleroy with his bare hands. He ran for the platform, but the unicorn joined the stag and the two creatures drove him back toward the edge.

"Please stop," Querry said, thinking of Frolic and trying to reason with them. It did no good. The unicorn struck out with his front hooves and the stag prepared to butt Querry. The thief crouched and rolled, avoiding the assault. He got back to his feet and saw the yellow-garbed angel had joined her minions. Before Querry knew what was happening, she backhanded him in the face and sent him flying from the disk. He flailed his arms as he fell through the open air, Thimbleroy's laughter echoing all around him. He felt his body hit the ground, saw blurry, dark shapes moving around him. Then everything went black. Querry's last conscious thought was that they'd failed. He'd failed.

CHAPTER 22

QUERRY HADN'T expected to open his eyes again, and when he did he thought he was surely in hell. Thick smoke that stung his eyes and bit his lungs obscured the sky. Jagged black buildings and grotesque, twisting obelisks surrounded him. The air reeked of blood and machine oil. Even the rain that fell against his face stunk of sulphur. Through the pounding in his head, Querry heard gunshots, explosions, and screams. He tried to push himself up from the wet ground where he lay, and every fiber of his being exploded in agony. He fell back down with a groan.

"Easy there, mate," said a familiar voice. A blurry form moved toward Querry and crouched down. It took a few more minutes for Querry's eyes to focus and for his rattled brain to recognize Lizard. The boy took a flask from his pocket and poured brandy into Querry's mouth. The thief swallowed the rich liquid, feeling the warm bubble travel down his body to his belly. He closed his eyes and rubbed his face with a gloved hand as he tried to recall and make sense of the things that had happened.

"Lizard," Querry finally managed to croak, "what the hell is going on?"

"Hell is about the size of it," Lizard said, shaking his head. "Our people are all dead, or soon will be. Thimbleroy's got an army out there, and they're shooting on sight, wiping out everyone they see. They don't stand a chance against those damned machines. And that horrible tower is spewing magic, changing everything, warping it."

"What about Reg?" Querry asked, pushing past the pain to sit up. "What happened to the shooters on the cathedral tower?"

"I'm afraid there ain't no tower."

"Frolic?" Querry asked, starting to panic. "Kristof? What happened to the device that was supposed to stop the magic?"

"I can't say, only that it don't work," the boy informed him. "Much as I hate to say it, likely they're all dead, and old Dink too."

"No," Querry said. "This can't be happening." From nearby, he heard shots fired and looked at his surroundings more carefully. They were in a narrow corridor. Maybe it had been an alley, or maybe it had formed when house walls collapsed. The darkness and smoke made it hard for him to tell for certain. High piles of stone surrounded them on three sides, and at the small opening three men stood defending their position with rifles. The shots Querry had heard had stopped a pair of Royal Guards. It was a good place to hide, but they wouldn't be able to hold it forever. Querry felt around his waist. In his fight with Thimbleroy and the fall afterward, he'd lost both his gun and sword. Even The Gripper was gone. He turned to Lizard and said, "What's the plan, then?"

"Plan?" The boy laughed without any trace of amusement. "No plan, mate. Best we can hope for is to stay alive until this massacre is over. Maybe then we can get away. Not that we'll have anything to go back to. They're... they're all gone." Lizard looked ready to cry, but he stamped it down and put on a brave face. Querry reached up and squeezed his shoulder, and he smiled with gratitude at the comfort.

"Listen, thanks for saving me," Querry told him. "But I'm not ready to give up on the others. Stay here. I'm going after them. We're getting out of here together."

Lizard shocked Querry by grabbing his arm and holding tightly to it. "Don't go," he said in a young and fearful voice. "You're the only friend I have left."

It broke Querry's heart to pull away from the frightened boy, but neither would he abandon Reg and Frolic, if there was any chance they might still live. "I've seen what you can do, Lizard. You can take care of yourself. Stay here where it's safe while I go look for our friends. Then I'll be back. I promise you."

"I understand," Lizard said, trying to appear unaffected.

"Can you spare me any sort of weapon?"

"All I got is this." Lizard reached inside the soiled suit coat he wore and handed Querry a small dagger. It looked more ceremonial than functional with its engraved ivory handle and etched blade, but Querry took it gladly. He gave the boy what he hoped was a reassuring nod and crept to the corridor's entrance. Peering around the corner, he determined that their hiding spot lay three or four houses down from the cathedral and on the opposite side of the street. Directly opposite them he saw the smoldering ruins of what had been another house, and decided his best chance would be to run and take cover there.

One of the men guarding the entrance turned to him and said, "You're off your bleeding rocker if you go out there, mate."

Querry knew he spoke the truth, but he saw no other choice. "Best of luck to you," he told the guards. "I hope we'll see each other again."

"Right then," said another of the men. "Good luck."

Querry crouched low and tossed the knife from hand to hand. He scanned around for movement and then sprinted across the street. He was injured, but his fear for his friends overshadowed his discomfort, and he ran hard, reached the husk of the mansion, and dove behind a collapsing wall. He allowed himself a second to clutch his bruised ribs and catch his breath. Then, crawling carefully over heaps of rubble and beneath dubious doorways, he reached the grounds behind the house. The neighboring manor had crumpled against the stone wall dividing the two properties, and Querry was able to climb it and gain access to the next door second story. As quickly as he could go without falling through a hole in the floor, he crossed through the second house. He exited through a broken window and leapt to where a fallen chimney made a bridge to the next residence. It led him directly onto the sagging roof.

From here Querry could see the cathedral. The decorative apple and cherry trees surrounding the old building had grown and twisted, their mutated branches curling around each other to form a kind of net around the church. They stretched and spiraled as Querry watched. Behind them, blood-red windows dotted the worship hall's slick-looking black walls. Querry looked up, and the sight of the tower tore a scream from his throat. The top half had fallen and the belfry had smashed into the street. Ebony tines rose from the top of the tower, stretching toward the sky and giving the structure a horrid resemblance to a gigantic spinal column. The spikes grew larger by the second, and the lower portion of the tower buckled under their weight. Some stray shards broke from the belly of the tower and then disappeared, leaving gaping holes and crumbling rock where they'd been. Colored lights flashed within the decimated walls.

The idea of Reg trapped inside that awful place banished any thought of his own safety from Querry's mind. He ran along the roof, following its downward slope until he found the place where it had caved in. He had no way to reach the rubble-filled rooms below, so he opted to jump the ten feet to the street. Though he landed more lightly than most would have been able, the impact sent a jolt of pain through his knees. Ignoring it, he ran for the misshapen grove of trees and the tower beyond. He reached the base without attracting attention, but he soon realized he had a much bigger problem.

The bottom ten feet of the tower had fallen in on itself. Blocks lay around it like a pool of wax around a cheap candle. The wall where the tower met the worship hall was nothing more than a heap of stones. Querry had no way in. Swearing, close to panic, he circled around three times, hoping for any kind of an opening but finding none. He walked out beneath the leaning structure and looked up. It swayed and groaned precariously, showering him with rock and threatening to collapse and bury him at any moment. He continued on toward the street, hiding if he saw any sign of Thimbleroy's men. The belfry hadn't fared any better than the base, though; its impact with the ground had shattered everything. Querry hoped with everything he had that Reg had made it down. Even if he had, where would he be now? Somewhere in the belly of the bent and mutilated tower? He had to find a way inside, get to him, save him. He had to be alive!

Hurrying back toward the church, Querry looked up and saw a hole left by one of the spines. It was only about a dozen feet above his head. Hope renewed, he reached to his belt for his grapple, only to remember that he'd lost it. *Bugger it, I'll climb,* he thought, searching desperately for anything he might hold on to. He tucked Lizard's dagger into his belt and prepared to begin. But the surface of the stone was smooth and shiny. In some places it melted and dripped, though Querry felt no heat. The way leading up to the opening was a sharp angle, almost parallel with the ground. Short of flying, Querry had no way to reach it. He balled his fists and beat the sides of his thighs with frustration. Then an idea occurred to him, and he sprinted back to the worship hall.

He began climbing the ruined wall, planning to travel up the tower and then swing down into the hole. It would be difficult if not impossible, but he saw no other choice. Ascending the hill of stone proved easy enough, but when Querry reached the wall of the tower itself he found the black substance even slicker than it looked. His feet slid like he stood on ice, and he dropped to his hands and knees and tried to crawl. After almost sliding off of the edge, he finally sunk to his belly and shimmied along slowly. Now and then he managed to grip one of the spikes and move a little more securely, though once one of them erupted at his left side and tore through his vest and the skin beneath. It hurt and bled, but the wound was minor. Querry shuddered to think what might have happened had it emerged another few inches from where it did. He inched arduously on, his limbs aching and trembling from holding tight to the stone. His hope of finding Reggie unharmed waned with every second that passed, but he couldn't move any faster.

Finally he reached the place opposite the hole. He found a little good fortune in that a row of spikes stretched down the side of the tower, almost like stairs. While he knew they could disappear at any moment, Querry wasted no time. He slid over the side of the tower until his foot caught on the black rock. He crouched down, bending almost in half, and wrapped his arms around it before swinging his legs down toward the next. Though he could barely trust his muscles, the opening soon came into view. It was much further away than Querry had estimated. Carefully he clutched the outcropping and let his lower body drop into the open air. His hands started to slip almost instantly. Hysterical, he reached out with his leg and found that it missed the opening by at least three feet. He looked at the ground as his hands lost another inch. The fall might not kill him, but it would render his already injured body useless and steal his chances of getting to Reggie and Frolic.

He pressed his thighs together and began swinging his body back and forth like a pendulum, trying to build enough momentum to propel himself into the hole three feet away and two feet below him. The motion pulled his hands down the side of the spike quickly. When he could hold on no longer, he closed his eyes and aimed his body as best he could.

Querry's back met stone, and he laughed out loud with relief. Opening his eyes, he saw disarray to rival what had happened outside. He wondered whether to make his way up or down. Everything looked the same: wrecked blocks dotted with puddles of bubbling black ooze. Magic sparked and crackled unchecked. Querry felt it in his teeth. He hoped he wouldn't find Reggie changed by the energy coursing through the tower.

"Reggie?" Querry shouted. "Anybody?" Only silence and the crash of the emerging tines answered him.

As Querry carefully navigated the remains, he saw grisly evidence of the toll Thimbleroy's attack had taken: arms and legs sticking out from beneath massive heaps of stone, rusty smears on the walls and floor, wet chunks of what had once been human bodies. The increase of these sights as he moved lower told Querry the marksmen had been trying to get down, to get out. They also told him few, if any, had succeeded.

He saw a glowing, white shape ahead in the shadows and moved toward it. His heart leapt. *Reggie was alive!*

"No," Reg said, shaking his head, "I'm not. I'm dead. Dead because of you. You sent me here to die."

"No. I sent you here because I thought you'd be safer here than on the ground. Reggie—"

"You selfish bastard. You always put your own desires before my happiness. Always mucking up my life. Now you've destroyed it. I wish I'd never met you. I'd have been better off on my own in the factory. Why couldn't you let me go? Why did you have to drag me into this when I had a decent life? Querry, why did you let me die?"

Querry shivered and sobbed as he looked at Reg's pale face, his hazel eyes hidden within the shadowed sockets. He tried to respond, to defend himself, but he couldn't because he knew Reg was right. "I- I'm sorry."

"It's too late for that now."

"No, it can't be! It can't!"

"What will you do, Querry? Repair me like Frolic so you don't have to feel guilty? Ruin my life all over again?"

Querry dropped down on his knees and reached out for Reg's pant leg, but the shade stepped back out of his reach.

"You ruined Frolic as well," the specter continued, "with that evil damned faerie's heart. But you had to have him for yourself, in spite of what was best for him. You never think about the consequences of your actions. Look at the trouble you caused us by going to that faerie ball, then expecting us to tend to you while you had your fever."

Tears streamed down Querry's face; he felt like he'd be sick. He thought about the dagger in his belt and considered turning it on himself. He deserved no better. Reg, gone. Frolic, irreparably damaged. He deserved to die and go to hell for the life he'd led. He fell forward, his forehead on his knees, as cries and gags wracked his body. Then something clicked in his memory. Images flooded his mind. *Faerie ball. Dancing. Making love with his gentleman.* He'd never told Reg about that. He hadn't remembered it himself until just then. He sat up and faced the sneering, ghostly Reg. He felt for his faerie sight and let it snap into place, just like one of the lenses of his goggles. Looking through this new glass, he saw not Reg, but himself standing in the shadows. He stood up and lifted his chin. "Go away," he commanded, and the transparent figure dissolved.

Querry heard someone muttering in a language he didn't understand, and he moved cautiously toward the sound. Behind a section of fallen stairs, he saw a young, Xianese woman lying on her back.

"Hello?" he asked. "Are you hurt?"

In response she lifted a pistol with a speed that impressed Querry and aimed at his head. He held up his empty hands and said, "I'm a friend."

Groaning, she dropped her arm to her side as if the pistol weighed a ton. "Yes, I remember you. You were with the clockwork and the *shen.*"

"Shen?"

Her eyes squinted shut in thought. "Is a- a spirit being? Nature spirit?"

"Oh, right," Querry said, understanding. "Are you all right? What can I do?"

She grabbed her calf and pulled on it. "My foot is trapped."

Querry knelt down to investigate. He shifted a few pieces of stone and soon released the woman. Her ankle was swollen and bruised. Querry ran his fingers over it gently and guessed nothing was broken. "Is that better?" he asked. "Do you think you can walk?"

She nodded. "Do you know a way out of here?"

"I'll get us out. I need to find somebody first. Check for other survivors."

"I'll go with you." She pulled herself up and tested her weight on her injured foot before following Querry deeper into the tower. She gasped and clapped her hands over her mouth when she saw the carnage, which only grew worse as they got lower. She whispered nervously in her native tongue. Querry wondered if he should hold her hand, but he decided against it. Every few feet he called out to his Reggie. He heard nothing for so long that he started to slip into despair.

Then, near the base of the tower, he detected a low groan, barely discernible above the gunfire outside and the crumbling stone within. Looking around, Querry saw an arm sticking out from beneath a slab of flat stone. The fingers were moving. He didn't know if it was Reg underneath that rock, but it was a person needing help. "Come on," he told the young woman. They both knelt down and grasped the edges of the stone sheet. The piece of rock turned out to be long and awkward, though not very heavy. Querry guessed it had been a section of veneer that had covered the tower's block foundation. After a few minutes of work they removed the stone. Querry couldn't help his disappointment when he saw the freckled, young man with the overbite. He grasped his hand and helped him to his feet. The fellow seemed disoriented, but not so much that he couldn't manage a charming smile for the Xianese woman.

Querry cleared his throat, and the two of them looked away from each other at last. The freckled man rubbed the back of his neck and said, "Reginald! Reginald was right beside me! He must be close."

Querry began tearing away at the stones. He felt his knuckles bleed inside his gloves, but he didn't stop. In his desperation and fear he flung aside blocks that he'd never have been able to lift before. The others joined him and in a few minutes they'd uncovered a pallid, dusty body. Despite the torture he'd inflicted on his muscles, Querry lifted Reg and carried him clear of the rubble. He sat on his heels and held Reg's face to his chest, then pressed his face to Reg's face. Maybe his morbid vision would prove true after all. "Reggie, please be all right," he said in a weak and cracking voice. He touched the side of Reg's neck and felt a pulse. "Reggie," he said again, shaking the other gently. At last, after an eternity, Reg's eyes fluttered open. "Reggie!" Querry gasped, pressing his lips hard against his partner's forehead, not giving a second thought to the opinions of the others. "Are you all right? Are you hurt at all?"

"My head hurts," he said. "Arm's broken, I think."

"I look," the young woman said. "Mother was—" she struggled to find the word, "—doctor."

She peeled back Reggie's eyelids and examined his wrist. "Broken arm," she confirmed. "But he is all right. Let's get us out of here."

"I couldn't agree more," Reg said, holding his hand out to Querry to help him up. "By the way, what are your names? I didn't get the chance to ask before."

"Mei-Gwai," the woman answered, smiling. Querry felt awkward at not having asked her earlier.

"I'm just Jack," said the freckled man, shaking Reggie's hand vigorously.

The four of them hurried back to the opening in the tower wall.

"How the bloody hell are we supposed to get down?" Jack asked.

Querry had planned to hang by his arms and drop. He realized now that the strategy might be more difficult for his companions. He thought. "Reggie, take off your pants."

"I beg your pardon!"

"Jack, you too."

"What are you on about, mate?" Jack asked.

"Gentlemen," Querry said, "I certainly don't intend to ask this lady to disrobe, and we need to make a rope to lower ourselves down. Now please, don't be shy." He waited until Jack wasn't looking and winked at Reg.

The three men removed their trousers and Querry used his dagger to cut them up the center, making six strips of cloth from the legs. He tied these tightly together. When they lowered them, their rope reached nearly to the ground.

"Ladies first," Jack said, grinning and blushing at Mei. He and Querry held the end of the rope as she climbed down.

"Now Reggie," Querry insisted. "Will you be able to make it with your arm?" he asked him.

Reg nodded and gripped the makeshift rope tightly between his knees and in his good hand. He inched his way down very slowly. When his partner was safely on the ground, Querry said, "Go on, Jack."

"What about you?"

"I'm used to this sort of thing. Go on."

Querry watched him make his way to the ground, and then he dropped his boots, held on to the ledge, and swung his feet over. He dropped and landed softly.

"What now?" Jack asked.

"Hide," Querry said. "Wait until this is over and get away from here. Look out for each other."

"What will you do?" Mei asked.

"I need to find my friend Frolic," Querry said, more for the benefit of Reg and himself.

"Good luck," Jack said, shaking Querry's hand. "And thanks."

"Go on then. I'll see you two again soon." They hurried toward the back end of the ruined cathedral, and Querry turned to Reg, who cradled his wrist in obvious pain. "Reggie, you don't have to come with me if you don't want to. You could say I kidnapped you back at the prison. You could have your life back. I don't want to ruin it for you."

"Did you crack your head?"

"No, I just, I just want you to do what's best for yourself. I don't want to interfere, if you want to raise a family, and all of that."

"Querry love, shut up." Reg stroked the side of Querry's hair and kissed him softly. Then, with a smile in his eyes, he said, "Let's go get our Frolic."

"All right," Querry agreed. They moved around the front of the cathedral and then to the side. Querry saw the magic-siphoning machine standing among the gravestones. When he approached it, he found it not broken or damaged, but just in need of winding. "Where on earth are Frolic and the others?" he wondered aloud. He didn't notice anyone about: not Thimbleroy nor his human or clockwork soldiers. The eerie quiet unnerved Querry. "We need to get out of here," he told Reg.

Before they could retreat, a dozen soldiers and twice as many clockworks emerged from the demolished buildings to surround them. They had no escape in any direction. Querry drew his dagger anyway. The men drew their guns and herded Querry and Reg into the street, smacking their backs with the butts of their rifles if they went too slowly.

"On your knees," one of them commanded, hitting Reg so hard between the shoulders that he pitched forward and fell.

Irate, Querry slashed at the man with his knife. He cut the back of his hand before another soldier grabbed his wrist and removed the weapon. He twisted Querry's arm behind his back and forced him to the ground. "Hands behind your heads," he snarled.

With rifle barrels pressing into their hair, Querry and Reg had no choice but to comply.

Soon the flying disk carrying Thimbleroy and his angels made its obligatory appearance. The soldiers backed away, but kept their weapons trained on the two kneeling men. Querry and Reg looked at one another as it neared the ground. That glance felt so hopeless and final that Querry wanted to cry. Instead he grabbed Reggie's hand, and the sorrow within him converted to anger at what would be stolen.

"You cowardly son of a bitch!" he cried. "Come down from there and face me like a man, if you even know what that means!"

"Oh, I know," said Thimbleroy's tinny, amplified voice. "I have suffered for what I have gained." He held up his disfigured arm. "But it will all be worth it. Angels, make them both into something awful. Make them pray for death for the rest of their days."

Querry braced himself for the magic, but it never came. Thimbleroy couldn't command the clockwork creatures; he wasn't the one meant to do so, despite the sick modifications he'd made to his body. Querry laughed out loud and showed Thimbleroy his fingers. "You charlatan! You know you can't do it! You're not the one."

"Perhaps. But I can do this. Shoot them!" The guards raised their rifles to their shoulders and took aim, but a clear, pure voice halted them.

"Don't do it." Frolic pushed through the ring of armed men and stood before Thimbleroy and his creatures. He spoke not to Thimbleroy or the soldiers assembled around him, but to the clockwork angels and creatures. "Listen to me," he pleaded. Most of the men laughed out loud as he approached the disk. Undaunted, Frolic continued to speak, his open hands lifted toward the angels as if in offering. "I'm the one you're supposed to be listening to. Not him."

The angels didn't move or respond. "Take that thing into custody," Thimbleroy told his men. "Be careful not to damage it. I'd like to dismantle it later and see what we can learn from its interior construction. Perhaps I can incorporate some of its parts into my own mechanical supplements. I'm especially curious to dissect the head and examine its sensory perceptions."

Hearing Thimbleroy talk this way about Frolic enraged Querry. Instinct took over, and he lunged for the aristocrat. He heard a shot, felt a searing pain in his calf, and dropped to the street, unable to stand up again. He snarled with helplessness as the two soldiers secured Frolic's hands behind his back and dragged him off toward the ruins of Thimbleroy Manor. With his speed and strength, Frolic might have escaped, but he didn't bother to resist.

"I have no further use for these two," Thimbleroy said, indicating Reg and Querry with his grotesque claw. "Shoot them in the heads."

"No!" Querry screamed. It couldn't end like this! He tried to get back on his feet as blood gushed from the wound in his leg. He felt cold and shaky. His vision began to dim.

"Querry?" Reg's frightened voice asked. He still believed Querry could save him, but Querry couldn't. He heard a single shot and looked over his shoulder even though he dreaded what he knew he'd see. To his surprise, he saw not Reg, but the soldier nearest him fall, fatally wounded. Three more shots rang out and three more men fell.

"Where is that coming from?" they shouted, darting for cover as Thimbleroy's claw moved among the tower of gears. The angels flung sparkling balls of raw magic into the sky. Some dissipated, one caused the clouds to rain gold dust over a small patch, and another lodged in the branches of a tree and caused the leaves to transform into birds that sang with human voices.

Reg got to Querry and they tried to shield each other's heads with their arms. In their retreat, the soldiers had abandoned Frolic. Reg called out to him, but he just stood staring up at the disk, completely transfixed. The shooters, presumably reinforcements for the resistance, continued their assault and eliminated a few more men. By now the soldiers had collected themselves and fought back, though not very effectively as they couldn't locate their assailants. The clockworks spewed energy with a variety of bizarre results.

Frolic still stared at the angels. Though Querry couldn't hear him over the shouts and shots, he saw clearly the words formed by his lips:

Wake up.

This time the angels responded. All four of them came to stand at the edge of the disk and face Frolic. Their creatures stood behind them, their collective weight tipping the disk almost vertical. Thimbleroy cursed and manipulated the controls hysterically. The fighting lulled momentarily as everyone stopped to watch the miraculous occurrence.

Frolic pulled his hands apart, snapping the manacles that had held them. With calm authority, he said, "Make this stop. Stop taking the magic and make the fighting stop."

The green-robed angel lifted his arm and sent a stream of viridian light toward a rifle one of the soldiers held. It liquefied in the man's hand and dripped to the ground. When it splashed against the cobblestones, little yellow flowers bloomed.

"How?" Thimbleroy growled. "How are you telling them what to do without touching the controls?"

Frolic only smiled serenely and turned to the rest of the men. "Put your weapons down and I'll tell them not to hurt you." The shocked soldiers quickly obeyed. Slowly, the resistance, led by Jean-Andre, emerged from their hiding places and joined the others in the street. The Belvaisian quickly covered Querry and Reg with his long-barreled, ornately engraved pistol. He spared a quick glance at Querry, and the thief nodded once to tell him that they were all right. Then Jean-Andre turned his attention back to their defense. Everyone looked awkwardly at everyone else. No one knew what to do next.

"Come down from there," Frolic told Thimbleroy. "You have no business being there."

"No," the aristocrat said. "I spent my life and my fortune repairing this tower. I opened the way to the Other World so I could have access to its power. This tower is mine! Everything I've done has been to protect our Empire and its traditions! I'll never give it up."

Frolic nodded to the red angel, as if they could communicate without words. The mighty being lifted Thimbleroy by the back of the shirt and flung him down into the street. He landed on his chest and pushed himself up on his remaining elbow.

"What do we do now?" Querry wondered aloud.

"Kill the son of a bitch!" someone shouted. Someone else thrust a gun into Querry's hand. They parted to give him a clear shot.

Querry recalled all that he and his loved ones had suffered at Thimbleroy's hands. He sat up a little straighter, bracing his shoulder against Reg. Thimbleroy deserved to die. Querry raised his arm and aimed, but despite all that he'd been forced to do recently, he hated the idea of taking another life, and he hesitated.

The duchess didn't. Standing behind Reg and Querry, she fired with her pistol and Thimbleroy's head exploded into a red cloud. Afterward she approached the body, nudged it with her toe, and emptied her gun. She continued squeezing the trigger until another woman took her shoulders and led her away.

"Reggie," Querry said weakly, "is it really over?" His leg throbbed, and he'd lost blood, but he would survive it.

"I think it is, love."

Querry let his head relax back against Reg. The clouds above them split and shafts of golden, late-day light gilded the broken pavement. Frolic came over and stood behind Reggie, his hand on Reggie's shoulder. Querry already sensed the magic flowing back into the world, but he wasn't the only one.

Mad laughter drowned the confused conversation in the street. It seemed to rise up from the ground, fall from the sky, to come from everywhere and everything at once. It shook the foundations of the buildings and rumbled below the cobblestones.

"Oh no," Querry breathed, his head shooting up.

The faerie gentleman strode to the center of the crowd like a victorious general after a battle. An aura of palpable power surrounded him, and people scrambled out of his way. Kristof stood a few feet off, his hood up and his eyes on the ground. The faerie raised his arms, threw his head back, and shouted a few words in his language. The people assembled lost any expression in their faces and moved like sleepwalkers toward the clockwork disk.

"What's going on?" Frolic asked. More people arrived from nearby houses and shops, not soldiers but housewives, servants, bakers, and tailors. All of them converged on the tower-top. "Querry, what's he doing?" Frolic asked. "Why is he doing this?"

The hundred or so people began to rip at the beasts and angels, tearing them apart with their bare hands. They pushed past one another, some trampling others, in their fury to dismantle the clockworks. Gears and pieces of metal flew like torn paper. Blood also fell as the crowd fervently pounded and yanked with no regard for their own welfare. Querry saw the face torn away from the yellow angel, revealing the gears beneath. All the while, the faerie gentleman giggled, danced, and twirled around. While Querry hated to see the beautiful work destroyed, he didn't blame the faerie for what he did. It was his nature. He could no more stop himself than the sky could hold back the rain.

Frolic, though, screamed with horror and tried to rush to aid the angels. Reggie caught hold of him and held him back. He fought and thrashed, crying out, begging the people to stop. Reggie faced him and held tight to his wrists. He looked deep into Frolic's eyes and said, "There's nothing you can do."

"No! I have to save them! They didn't do anything wrong! Stop! Please stop!"

"You'd only be killed yourself," Reg said gently. "I'm so sorry, Frolic."

Frolic dropped his head to Reg's chest, sobbing and wailing. Reg wrapped his good arm around Frolic's head and held him tightly until it was all over. The tower, the angels, the animals, everything had been decimated. Nothing larger than a dinner plate remained. The once-glorious clock tower had been reduced to a bent and bloody scrap heap. Afterward, the people turned away from it and went about their business as if nothing unusual had happened. The faerie gentleman also turned away, satisfied. As he passed by Querry, he looked down and said, "Your debt to me is resolved." He went a few more steps before something occurred to him, and he turned back. He knelt down and touched Querry's leg with his graceful finger, healing the wound and dissolving the bullet within. Then, with a smile and wink, both he and Kristof were gone. Querry felt disappointed. He still had a great many questions for his fey companion.

Poor Frolic collapsed to his hands and knees and cried until his voice was gone. He swatted Querry and Reg away when they tried to comfort him. For almost half an hour he remained completely inconsolable. People around them looked for friends and loved ones among the dead and the injured. Alarm bells rang in the distance, and many people hurried away. Jean-Andre knelt and whispered to Querry that he would be in touch. Querry had many questions for him, too, and he tried to grab his sleeve, but the other man slipped from his grasp, winked, and backed away until he disappeared amidst the chaos. Querry thought he and his companions would be wise to do the same. The authorities would come, and someone would be held responsible for the destruction. It would be easier to pin the blame on a couple of fugitives than the Grande Chancellor. "Frolic," Querry urged gently.

The silver-haired clockwork nodded and stood. He walked to the remains of the tower and looked down at the twisted metal for a long time with a blank expression on his face. Querry couldn't imagine what sort of connection Frolic felt with these creatures; he only knew Frolic was hurting, and he couldn't help. Frolic knelt and shifted some of the rubble, digging around until he found what he sought. Then he returned to Querry and Reg with an intricately carved silver feather clutched tightly in his fist. "I'm the last," he said to himself. "They're gone, and I'm all alone."

"Rubbish, and you know it," Reg said, squeezing the back of Frolic's neck and earning a smile from the other. Watching them, Querry smiled too. All of them were hurt and dirty. They'd seen and done things that would haunt them the rest of their days. All of them had suffered losses. *But damn it*, he thought, *here we are.*

EPILOGUE

QUERRY, REG, and Frolic returned to Dink's compound to tend to their wounds. The old machinist had also been injured in the battle and had to rely on his turtle-headed walking stick in earnest for a bit. Dink had become a sort of folk hero to the city for the part he'd played in the battle and the weapons he'd provided. One of the universities had invited the machinist to teach as a guest professor. Dink had declined, vowing to spend the rest of his days researching ways that industry could benefit humankind. After a few weeks, the dead had been buried and repairs to the damaged buildings were well underway.

Querry sat in the kitchen reading the newspaper. Tosser and Toerag prowled along the tabletops, making off with bits of uneaten meat and bread leftover from dinner. Frolic had insisted they go back for the cats, and Querry had happily agreed. The three men had spent a delightful afternoon in Reg's old house. Smiling at the memory, Querry turned his attention back to the paper. The authorities had covered up the truth behind the fight, blamed it on a malfunction in the construction of the tower. Nobody would ever know what Querry and the others had saved them from. Despite her condition, the duchess resumed her former seat in the house and continued to fight for the rights of her people. She'd desired to run for Grande Chancellor but had been forbidden, as a woman, to declare candidacy. She remained a strong voice for the foreigners and middle-class. Even so, her proposal to limit the hours workers could toil in the factories fell rejected, as did her bid to loosen the restrictions on magical practice and allow some of the banished wizards to return. Querry wondered what Kristof would say. He'd gone back to Neroche a few times in search of the wizard and the faerie gentleman. Part of him still wondered over the jobs to steal old boots, what the gentleman had really been trying to do. Though he wouldn't admit it aloud, part of Querry missed the fey a little. Unlike the rest of the city, the faerie quarter had healed itself almost overnight, but despite his searching, Querry had been unable to locate any sign of his former employer. Deep down, Querry knew he'd meet the gentleman again along his travels. The human citizens of the city would have to learn to live alongside the fey now. Querry wondered how it would all go.

Not that it would affect him much. He'd be leaving with Reg and Frolic in the morning. He smiled. The other two men had hinted at their desire for some time together, time they wouldn't have to share. Querry understood. He'd been craving some exclusive time with Reg himself, and with Frolic. Their relationship had ventured into strange and uncharted territory; they would need to draw the map as they went. For a long time Querry sat staring at his paper, not really seeing the smudged words and pictures as he thought about everything they would give up, and what would lie ahead for them. Wondering how he'd make a living led him to wonder what had become of Jean-Andre. The man hadn't kept his promise to keep in touch. Querry didn't suppose it mattered; he had no intention of leaving Reg and Frolic behind, not for all the riches in the world.

Had they really changed anything? One madman was dead, but the technology to construct soldiers from clockwork existed, and it wouldn't go away. That knowledge would spread and develop in ways Querry couldn't even imagine. With Dink's pilfered prototype, someone would perfect and expand air travel. Worst of all, the ability to siphon and harness magic by non-magic users had been discovered. A dangerous door had been opened. Jean-Andre had told Querry the world would change, and the thief didn't doubt it would happen fast and imperfectly. He reached down and stroked Toerag's soft back, feeling insignificant, one of a million insignificant men in a world that neither needed nor cared about him.

Before long Querry's companions joined him, smiling and satisfied. "All right, Querry?" Reg asked.

The thief shrugged. "It's strange. After everything that's happened, after wanting to get away from here all of my life, I'm going to miss this place."

Reg nodded knowingly. "We can't stay. You're still a criminal, and it will only be a matter of time before somebody else comes after Frolic. Curiosity or the lust for power will compel them."

"Let's take a last walk around the city," Frolic suggested. "I'd like to see everything again."

"That's a fine idea," Querry said, standing. He took each of their hands in his and the three of them headed for the lift. After tomorrow, he didn't know where life and fate would lead them. He didn't even know how they'd live. He only knew he would protect these men with his life, and that they would protect him. They would manage somehow, somewhere, because they needed and loved each other.

Tonight, though, the city beyond the scrap yard smelled of spring flowers and new leaves. A rosy, round moon hung just above the buildings, and a gentle breeze ruffled Querry's hair. Reg's and Frolic's hands felt warm against his, and Querry realized that for the first time, he had nothing to fight against. He was safe and comfortable, and his stomach was full. The people he cared about would be all right. He looked over at Reg with his shirtsleeves rolled up, something Reg would never have done in public before, then at Frolic, with his fascinated smile at everything and his marvelous eyes sparkling in the moonlight. Querry had everything he'd ever wanted, and he let himself be content at last.

AUGUST (GUS) LI is a creator of fantasy worlds. When not writing, he enjoys drawing, illustration, costuming and cosplay, and making things in general. He lives near Philadelphia with two cats and too many ball-jointed dolls. He loves to travel and is trying to see as much of the world as possible. Other hobbies include reading (of course), tattoos, and playing video games.

For more info, visit Books by Eon and Gus:
http://www.booksbyeonandgus.com

EON DE BEAUMONT is a versatile author, craftsmen, and raconteur. He has written a number of short stories, novellas, and novels, both solo and with his long-time writing partner and best friend, Augusta Li. Eon is an accomplished playwright and actor under an alternate identity. Above all Eon loves storytelling in all its myriad forms and sometimes has trouble sleeping for the abundance of ideas in his brain. Eon is alternately a mask maker, seamstress, doll maker, and amateur cook, as well. His passions include makeup, shoes, comics, movies, and the pursuit of an ever-higher gamer score. He's currently working on a number of projects in various states of completion including a manga, a pirate story, a thriller/horror script, and a young adult novel. Eon welcomes and encourages feedback and questions from his readers at mascaraboy13@ hotmail.com, or through his Facebook or Gus and Eon's website: http://www.yaoimagic.com, and above all he hopes that his readers find enjoyment in his work.

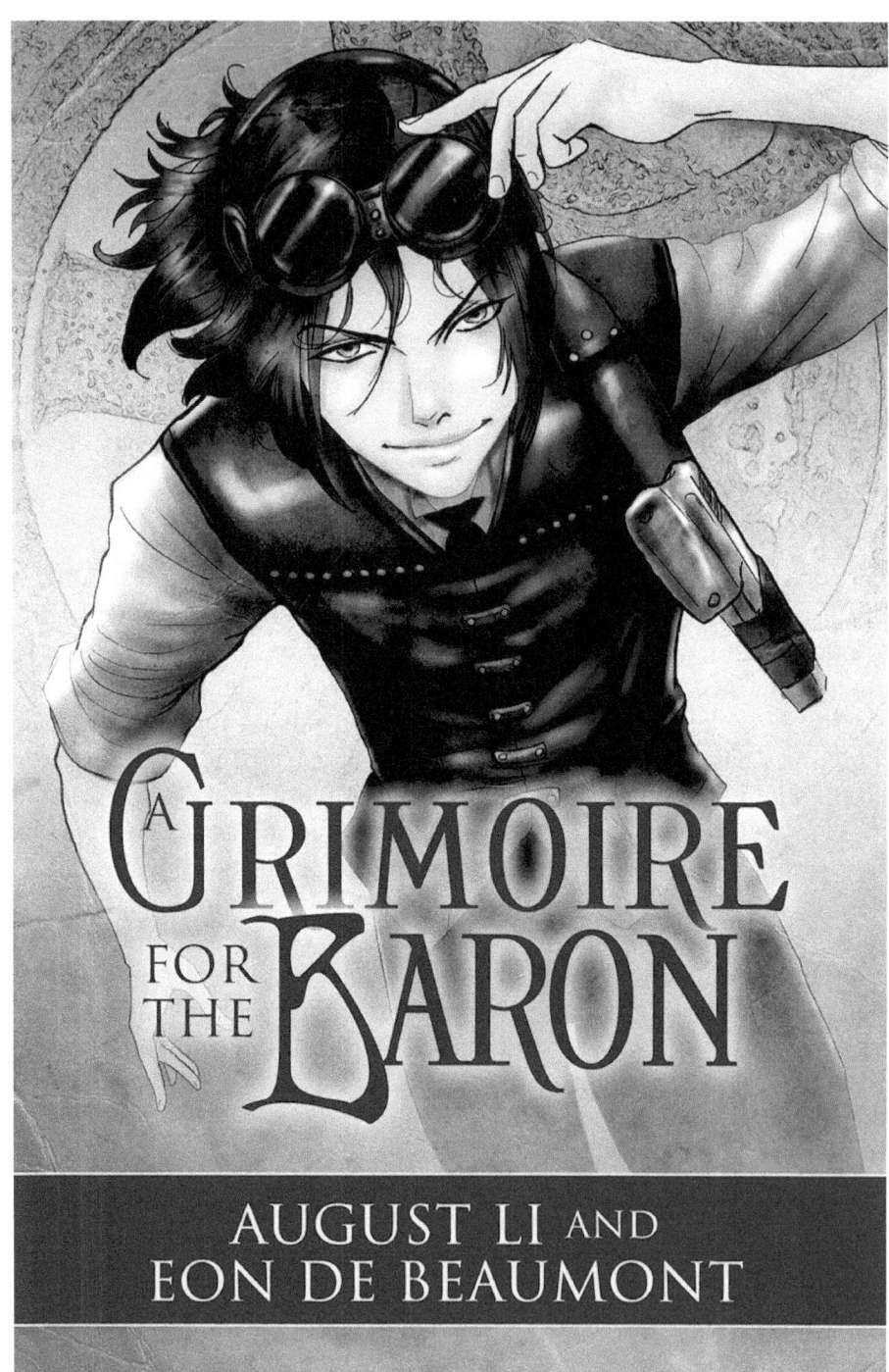

A GRIMOIRE
FOR THE BARON

AUGUST LI AND
EON DE BEAUMONT

http://www.dreamspinnerpress.com

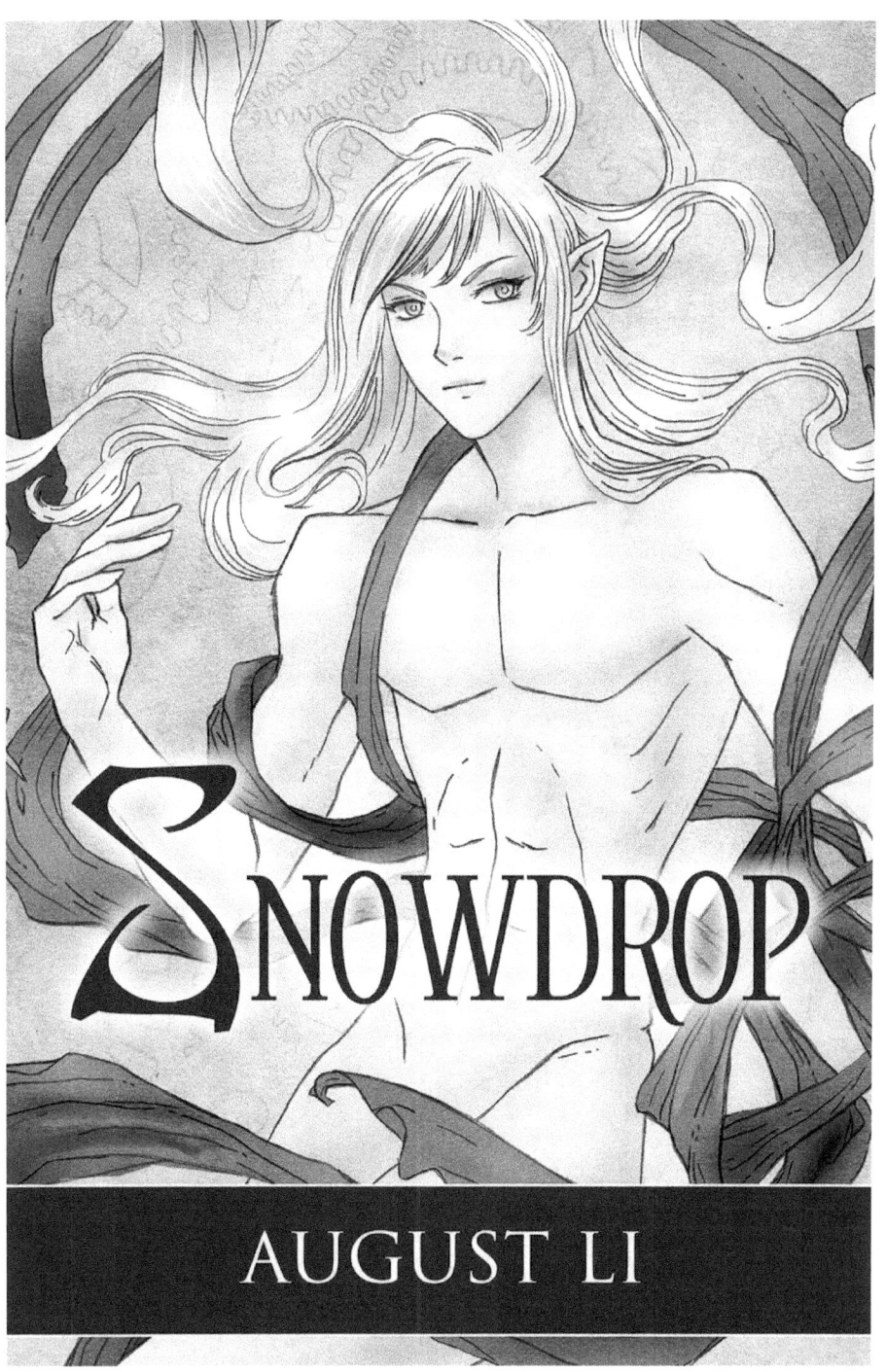

SNOWDROP

AUGUST LI

http://www.dreamspinnerpress.com

Coal TO DIAMONDS

AUGUST LI

http://www.dreamspinnerpress.com

Wine
AND
Roses

Other Paths: Book One
A TALE OF THE
BLESSED EPOCH
AUGUST LI

http://www.dreamspinnerpress.com

WAYWARD GRACE

EON DE BEAUMONT

http://www.dreamspinnerpress.com

EON DE BEAUMONT

RUM &
GINGER

http://www.dreamspinnerpress.com

ON
TINSEL
Wings

AUGUST LI

http://www.dreamspinnerpress.com

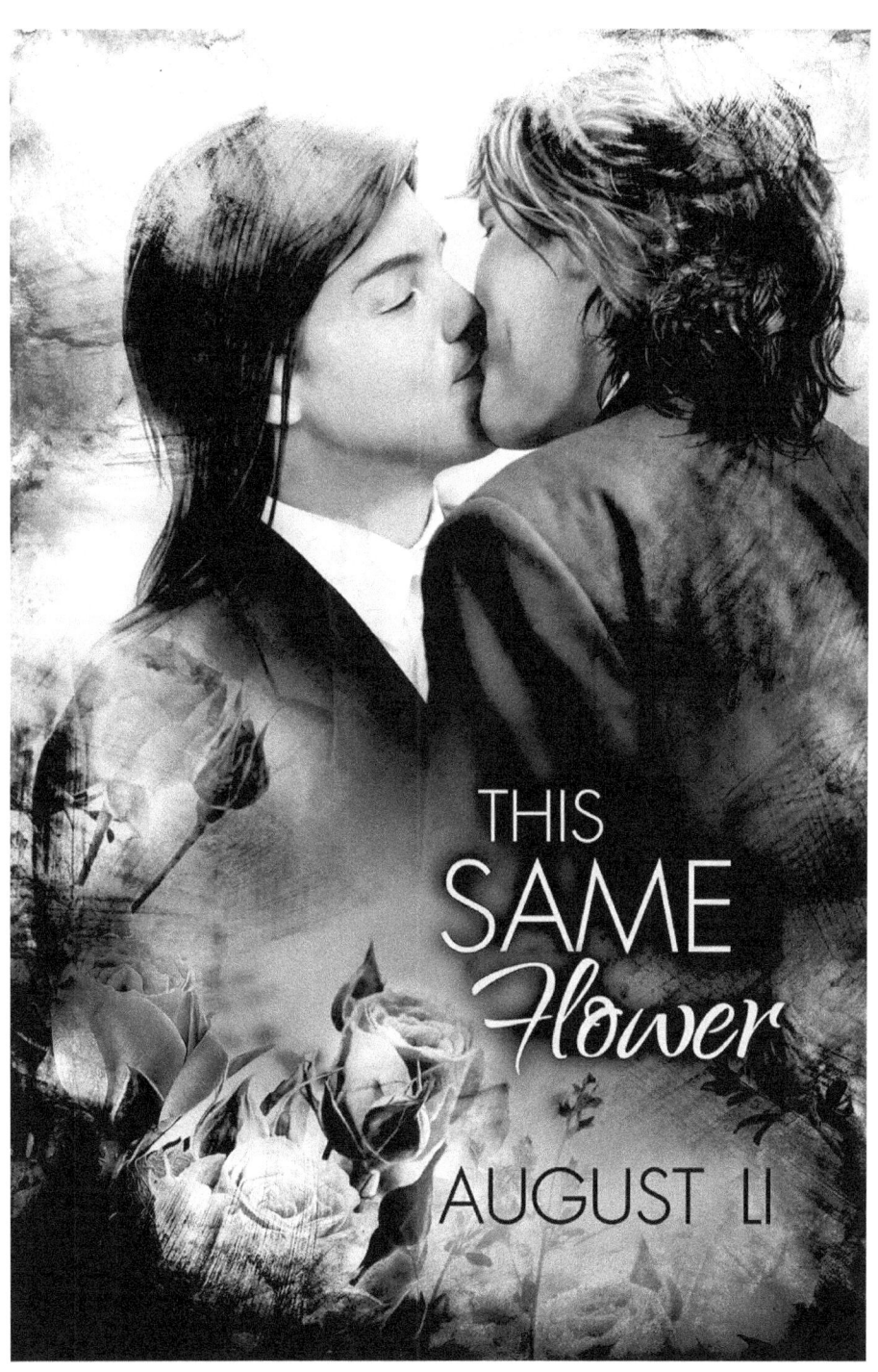

THIS SAME Flower

AUGUST LI

http://www.dreamspinnerpress.com

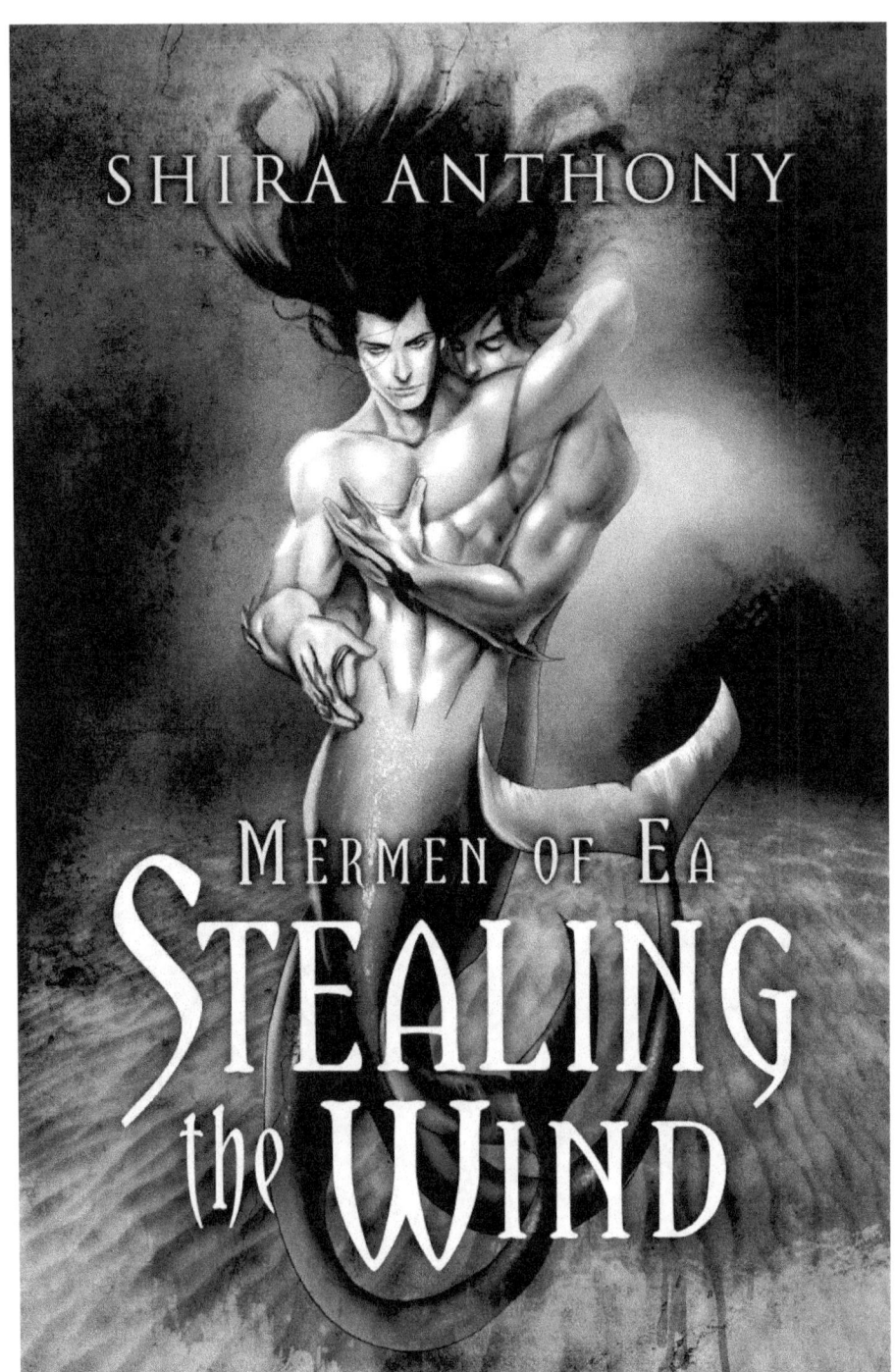

SHIRA ANTHONY

MERMEN OF EA
STEALING
the WIND

http://www.dreamspinnerpress.com

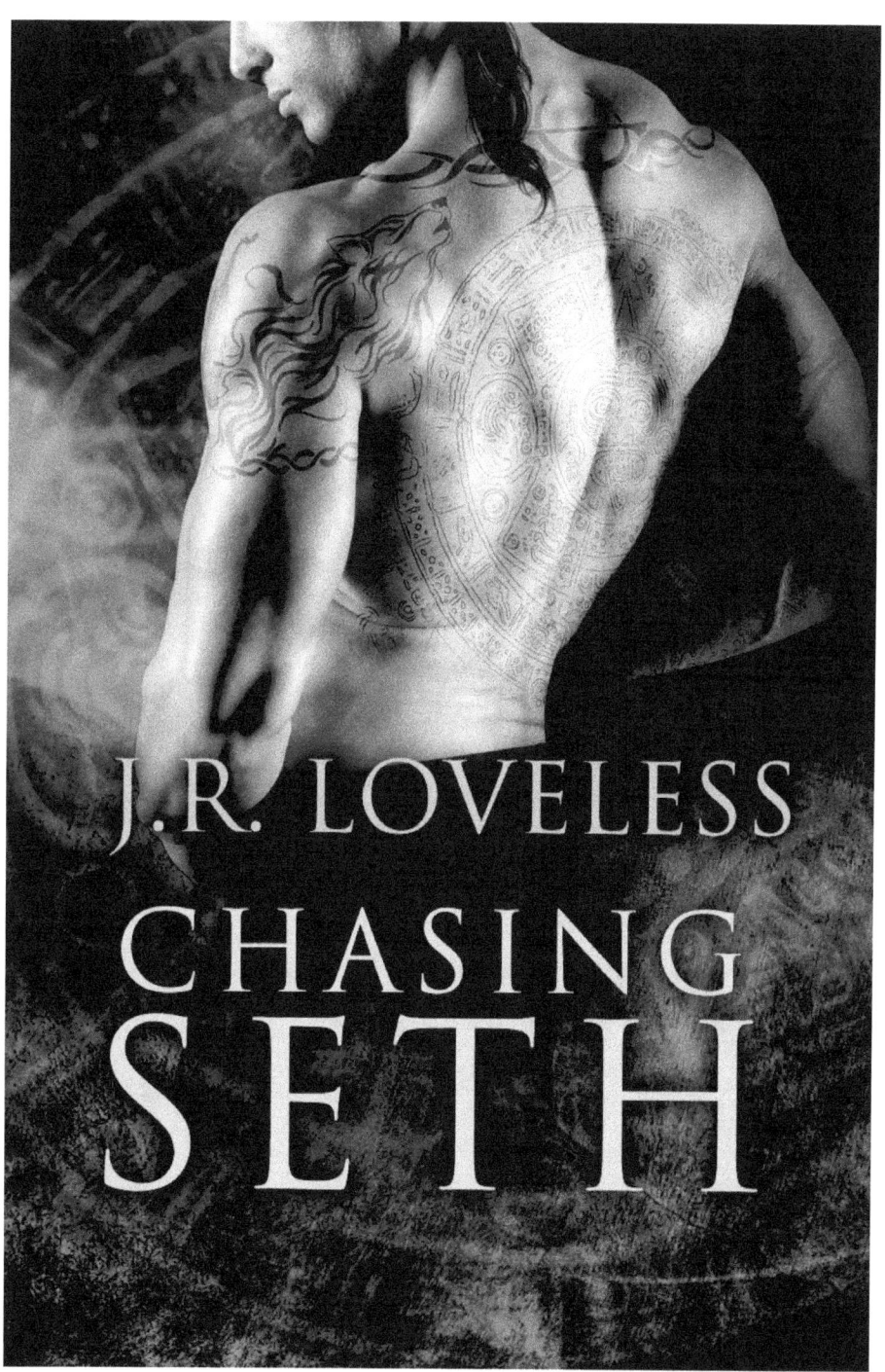

J.R. LOVELESS

CHASING
SETH

http://www.dreamspinnerpress.com

JoAnne Soper-Cook

The Eye of Heaven

http://www.dreamspinnerpress.com

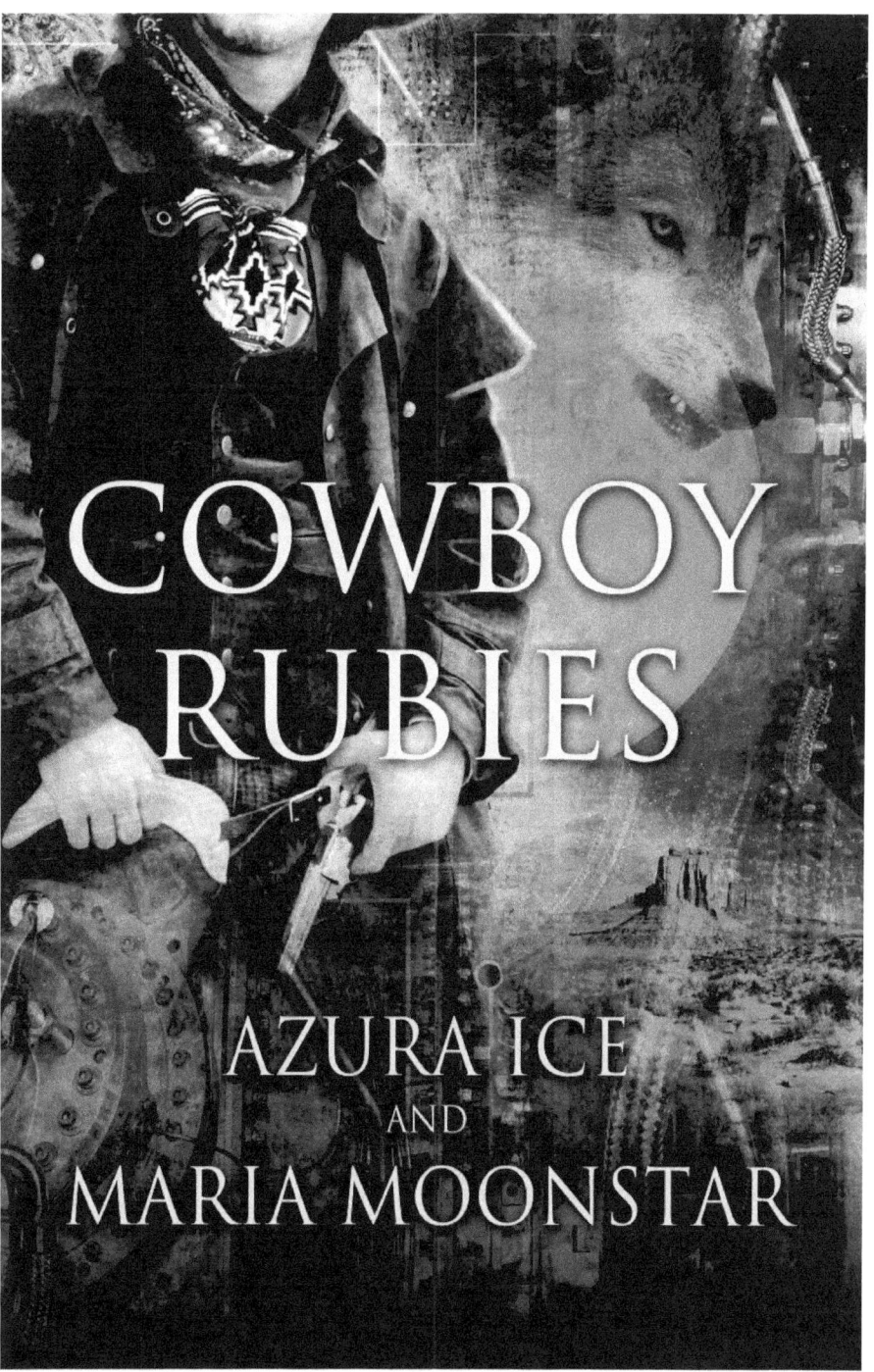

COWBOY
RUBIES

AZURA ICE
AND
MARIA MOONSTAR

http://www.dreamspinnerpress.com

http://www.dreamspinnerpress.com

They've fought to be together,
now they have to learn to live
with one another

Our Sacred
Balance

Marguerite
Labbe

Triquetra Trilogy

http://www.dreamspinnerpress.com

http://www.dreamspinnerpress.com

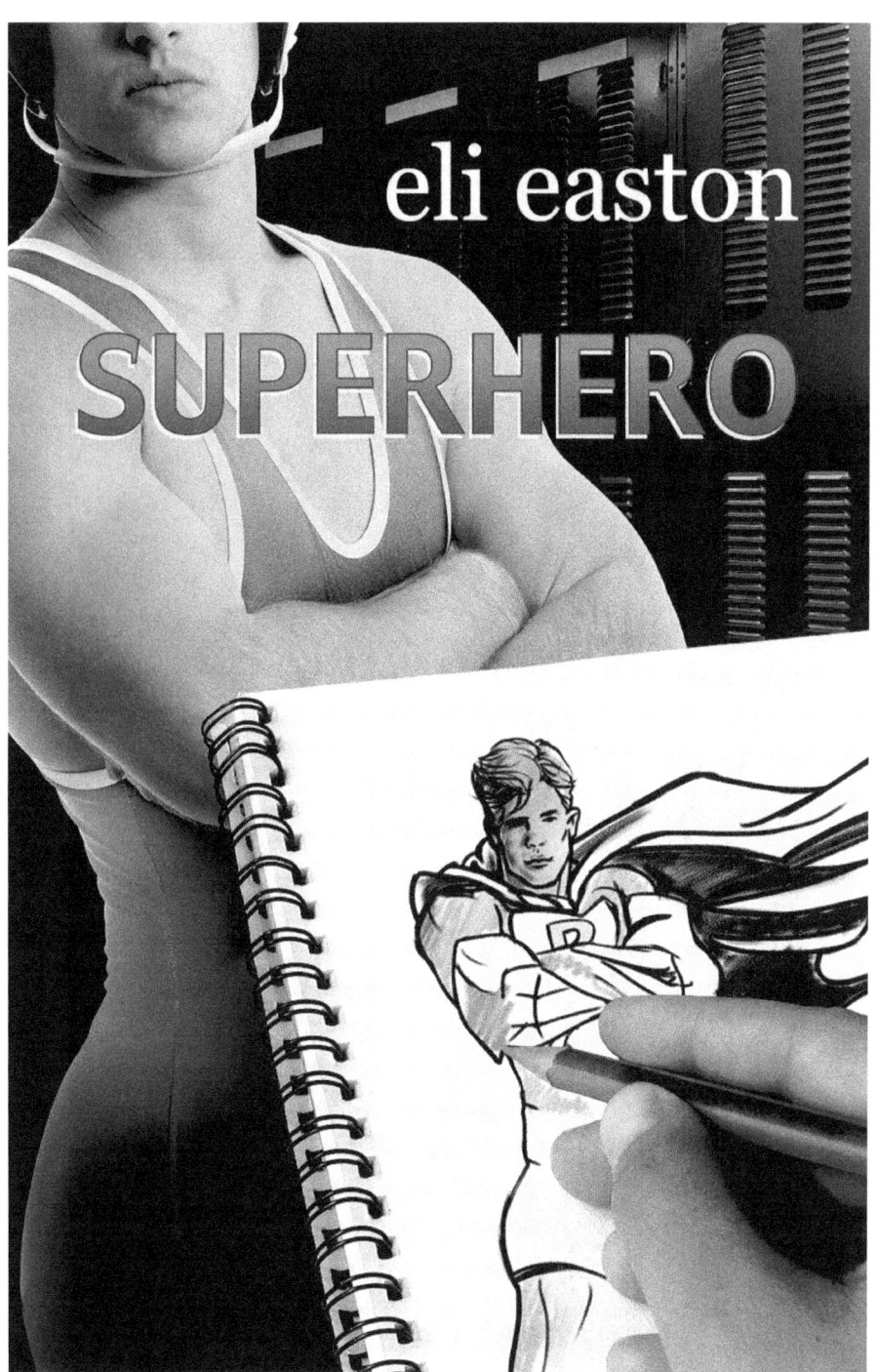

eli easton

SUPERHERO

http://www.dreamspinnerpress.com

www.ingramcontent.com/pod-product-compliance
Lightning Source LLC
Chambersburg PA
CBHW070047030726
47506CB00002B/389